Mobile Suit Gundam SEED

3

Art by Masatsugu Iwase

Original Story by
Hajime Yatate and Yoshiyuki Tomino

TRANSLATED AND ADAPTED BY
David Ury

LETTERED BY
Foltz Design

DEL REY
BOOKS • NEW YORK

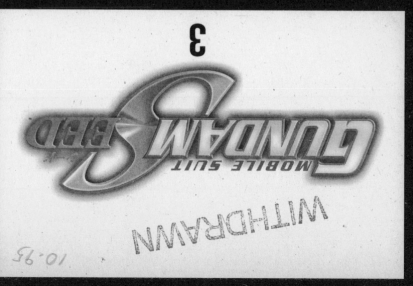

A Del Rey® Book
Published by The Random House Publishing Group

Copyright © 2004 by Hajime Yatate, Yoshiyuki Tomino, and Masatsugu Iwase
All rights reserved.
Copyright © by Sotsu Agency, Sunrise, MBS
First published in Japan in 2003 by Kodansha Ltd., Tokyo.
This publication rights arranged through Kodansha Ltd.

All rights reserved under International and Pan-American Copyright Convention.
Published in the United States by Del Rey Books, an imprint of The Random House
Publishing Group, of Random House, Inc., New York, and simultaneously in
Canada by Random House of Canada Limited, Toronto.

Del Rey is a registered trademark and the Del Rey colophon is a trademark of
Random House, Inc.

www.delreymanga.com

Library of Congress Control Number: 2004049397

ISBN 0-345-47230-6

Text Design—Foltz Design

Manufactured in the United States of America

First Edition: December 2004

1 2 3 4 5 6 7 8 9

Contents

Honorifics Explained

Throughout the Del Rey Manga books, you will find Japanese honorifics left intact in the translations. For those not familiar with how the Japanese use honorifics, and, more important, how they differ from American honorifics, we present this brief overview.

Politeness has always been a critical facet of Japanese culture. Ever since the feudal era, when Japan was a highly stratified society, use of honorifics—which can be defined as polite speech that indicates relationship or status—has played an essential role in the Japanese language. When addressing someone in Japanese, an honorific usually takes the form of a suffix attached to one's name (e.g. "Asuna-san"), as a title at the end of one's name, or in place of the name itself (e.g. "Negi-sensei" or simply "Sensei!").

Honorifics can be expressions of respect or endearment. In the context of manga and anime, honorifics give insight into the nature of the relationship between characters. Many translations into English leave out these important honorifics, and therefore distort the feel of the original Japanese. Because Japanese honorifics contain nuances that English honorifics lack, it is our policy at Del Rey not to translate them. Here, instead, is a guide to some of the honorifics you may encounter in Del Rey Manga.

-*san:*   This is the most common honorific and is equivalent to Mr., Miss, Ms., Mrs., etc. It is the all-purpose honorific and can be used in any situation where politeness is required.

-*sama:* This is one level higher than -*san.* It is used to confer great respect.

-*dono:* This comes from the word *tono,* which means *lord.* It is an even higher level than -*sama* and confers utmost respect.

-*kun:*   This suffix is used at the end of boys' names to express familiarity or endearment. It is also sometimes used by men among friends, or when addressing someone younger or of a lower station.

-chan: This is used to express endearment, mostly toward girls. It is also used for little boys, pets, and between lovers. It gives a sense of childish cuteness.

Bozu: This is an informal way to refer to a boy, similar to the English terms "kid" or "squirt."

Sempai: This title suggests that the addressee is one's senior in a group or organization. It is most often used in a school setting, where underclassmen refer to their upperclassmen as *sempai*. It can also be used in the workplace, such as when a newer employee addresses an employee who has seniority in the company.

Kohai: This is the opposite of *-sempai*, and is used toward underclassmen in school or newcomers in the workplace. It connotes that the addressee is of a lower station.

Sensei: Literally meaning "one who has come before," this title is used for teachers, doctors, or masters of any profession or art.

-[blank]: This is usually forgotten on these lists, but it's perhaps the most significant difference between Japanese and English. The lack of honorific means that the speaker has permission to address the person in a very intimate way. Usually, only family, spouses, or very close friends have this kind of license. Known as *yobisute*, it can be gratifying when someone who has earned the intimacy starts to call one by one's name without an honorific. But when that intimacy hasn't been earned, it can also be insulting.

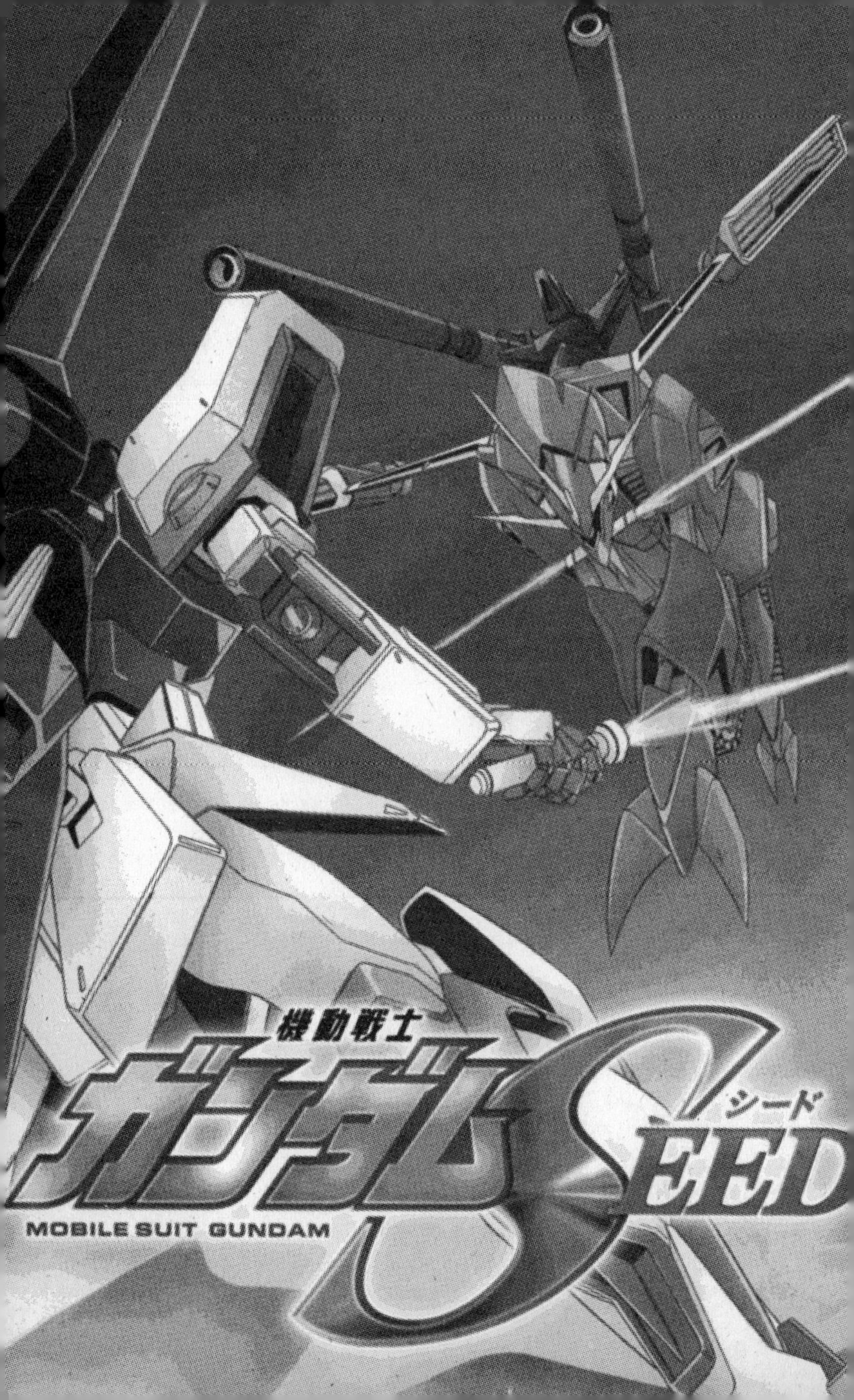
機動戦士
ガンダム
シード
SEED
MOBILE SUIT GUNDAM

THE STORY SO FAR

AFTER EXPERIENCING ENGINE TROUBLE THE ARCHANGEL IS HURLED INTO THE PERILOUS DEBRIS BELT. THERE THE CREW FINDS THE RUINS OF JUNIUS SEVEN, WHERE THE "BLOODY VALENTINE" TOOK PLACE. WHILE GATHERING MATERIALS KIRA FINDS AN ESCAPE POD. ATHRUN'S FIANCÉE LACUS, THE DAUGHTER OF ONE OF PLANT'S CHAIRMEN, IS ABOARD THE POD. A TRUCE IS ARRANGED WITH THE CREUSET UNIT IN EXCHANGE FOR HANDING OVER LACUS. ATHRUN ATTEMPTS TO PERSUADE KIRA TO COME TO PLANT, BUT KIRA REFUSES, SAYING THAT HE MUST PROTECT HIS FRIENDS. KIRA AND ATHRUN'S FRIENDSHIP IS EFFECTIVELY OVER. THE ARCHANGEL JOINS UP WITH THE EARTH ALLIANCE FORCES 8TH FLEET AND IS ORDERED TO LAND IN ALASKA. ZAFT ATTEMPTS TO STOP THE 8TH FLEET AND A BITTER BATTLE FOLLOWS. MEANWHILE, STRIKE IS CAUGHT IN THE EARTH'S GRAVITATIONAL FIELD AND PULLED INTO THE EARTH'S ATMOSPHERE ALONE. THE ARCHANGEL SHIFTS ITS DIRECTION IN ORDER TO SAVE KIRA AND LANDS IN THE AFRICAN DESERT. IN THE DESERT THEY MEET THE LOCAL RESISTANCE. THEY LEARN THAT CAGALLI, WHO THEY MET IN HELIOPOLIS, IS FIGHTING FOR THE RESISTANCE. THE ARCHANGEL CREW TEAMS UP WITH THE RESISTANCE TO FIGHT AGAINST THE ARMY OF ZAFT GENERAL WALTFELD "THE DESERT TIGER" WHO RULES OVER AFRICA. WHEN KIRA LANDS IN THE DESERT TO GATHER SUPPLIES HE COINCIDENTALLY SAVES THE LIFE OF THE "DESERT TIGER". KIRA WONDERS IF THE PECULIAR GENERAL COULD REALLY BE HIS ENEMY. THE NEXT TIME THEY MEET IS ON THE BATTLEFIELD.

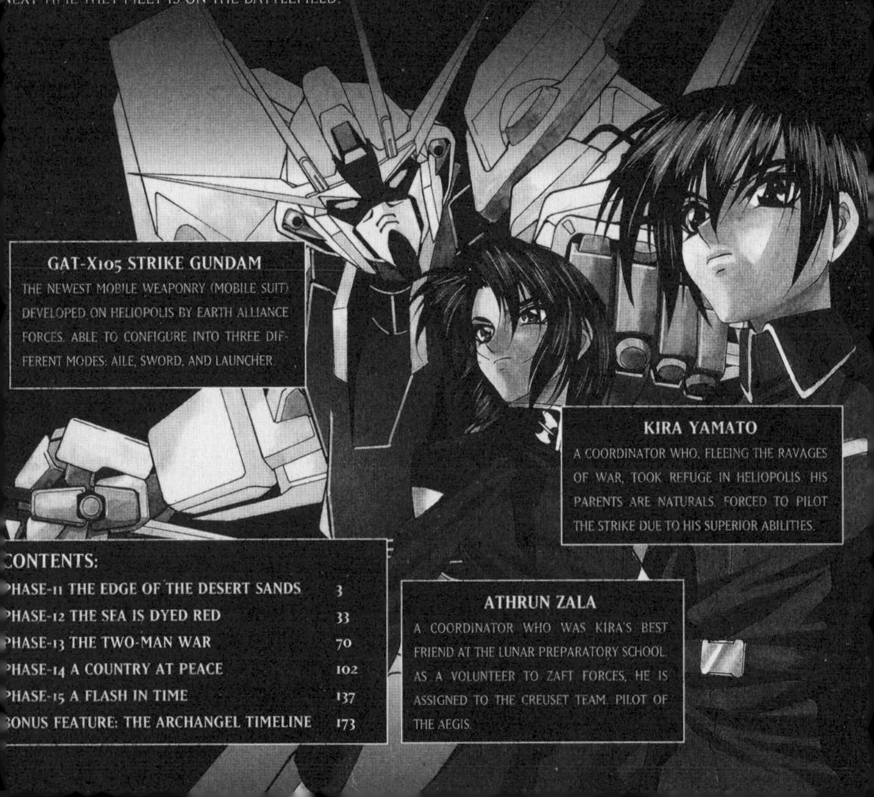

GAT-X105 STRIKE GUNDAM

THE NEWEST MOBILE WEAPONRY (MOBILE SUIT) DEVELOPED ON HELIOPOLIS BY EARTH ALLIANCE FORCES. ABLE TO CONFIGURE INTO THREE DIFFERENT MODES: AILE, SWORD, AND LAUNCHER.

KIRA YAMATO

A COORDINATOR WHO, FLEEING THE RAVAGES OF WAR, TOOK REFUGE IN HELIOPOLIS. HIS PARENTS ARE NATURALS. FORCED TO PILOT THE STRIKE DUE TO HIS SUPERIOR ABILITIES.

CONTENTS:

ATHRUN ZALA

A COORDINATOR WHO WAS KIRA'S BEST FRIEND AT THE LUNAR PREPARATORY SCHOOL. AS A VOLUNTEER TO ZAFT FORCES, HE IS ASSIGNED TO THE CREUSET TEAM. PILOT OF THE AEGIS.

PHASE-11: THE EDGE OF THE DESERT SANDS

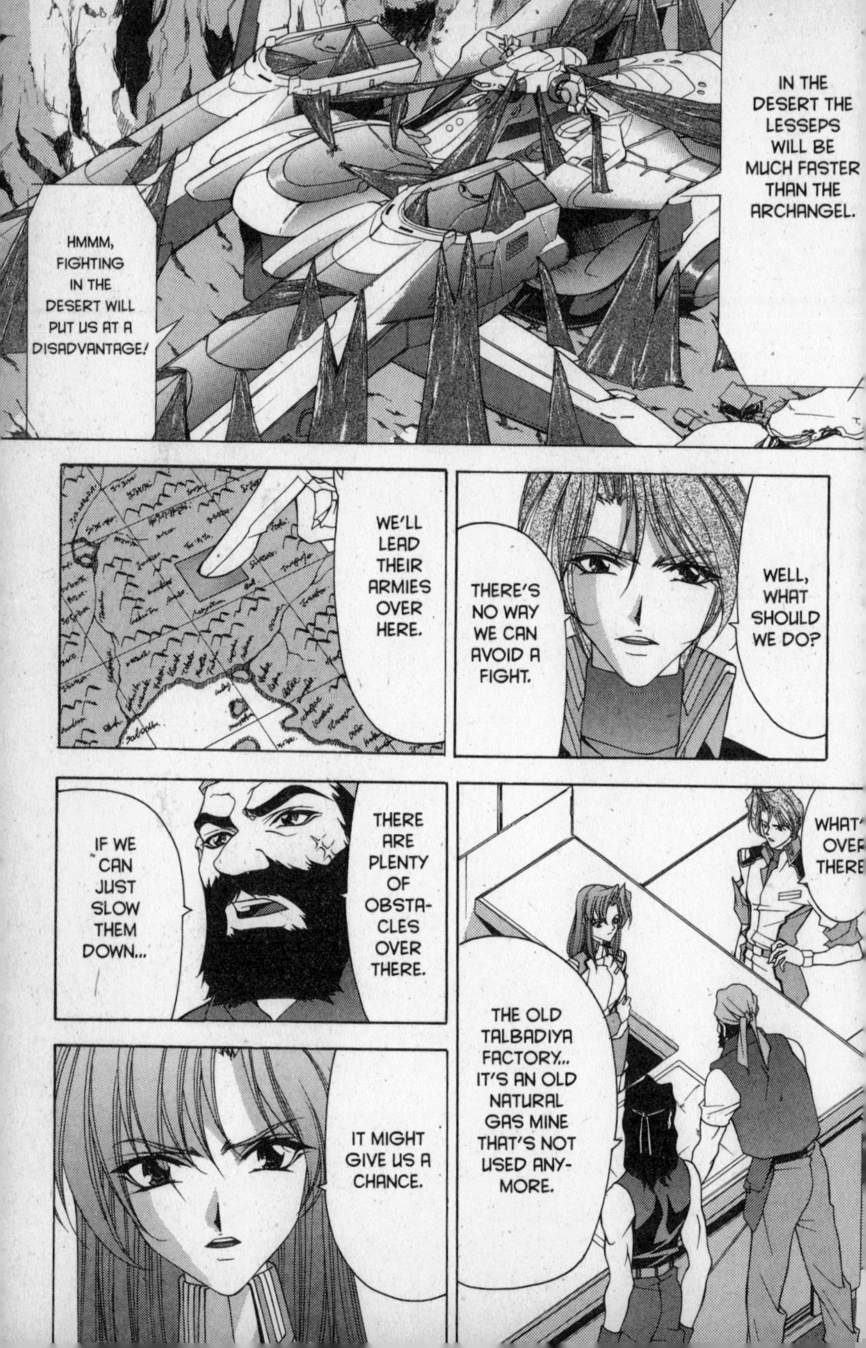
IN THE DESERT THE LESSEPS WILL BE MUCH FASTER THAN THE ARCHANGEL.
HMMM, FIGHTING IN THE DESERT WILL PUT US AT A DISADVANTAGE!
WELL, WHAT SHOULD WE DO?
THERE'S NO WAY WE CAN AVOID A FIGHT.
WE'LL LEAD THEIR ARMIES OVER HERE.
WHAT' OVER THERE
THE OLD TALBADIYA FACTORY... IT'S AN OLD NATURAL GAS MINE THAT'S NOT USED ANY-MORE.
THERE ARE PLENTY OF OBSTA-CLES OVER THERE.
IF WE CAN JUST SLOW THEM DOWN...
IT MIGHT GIVE US A CHANCE.

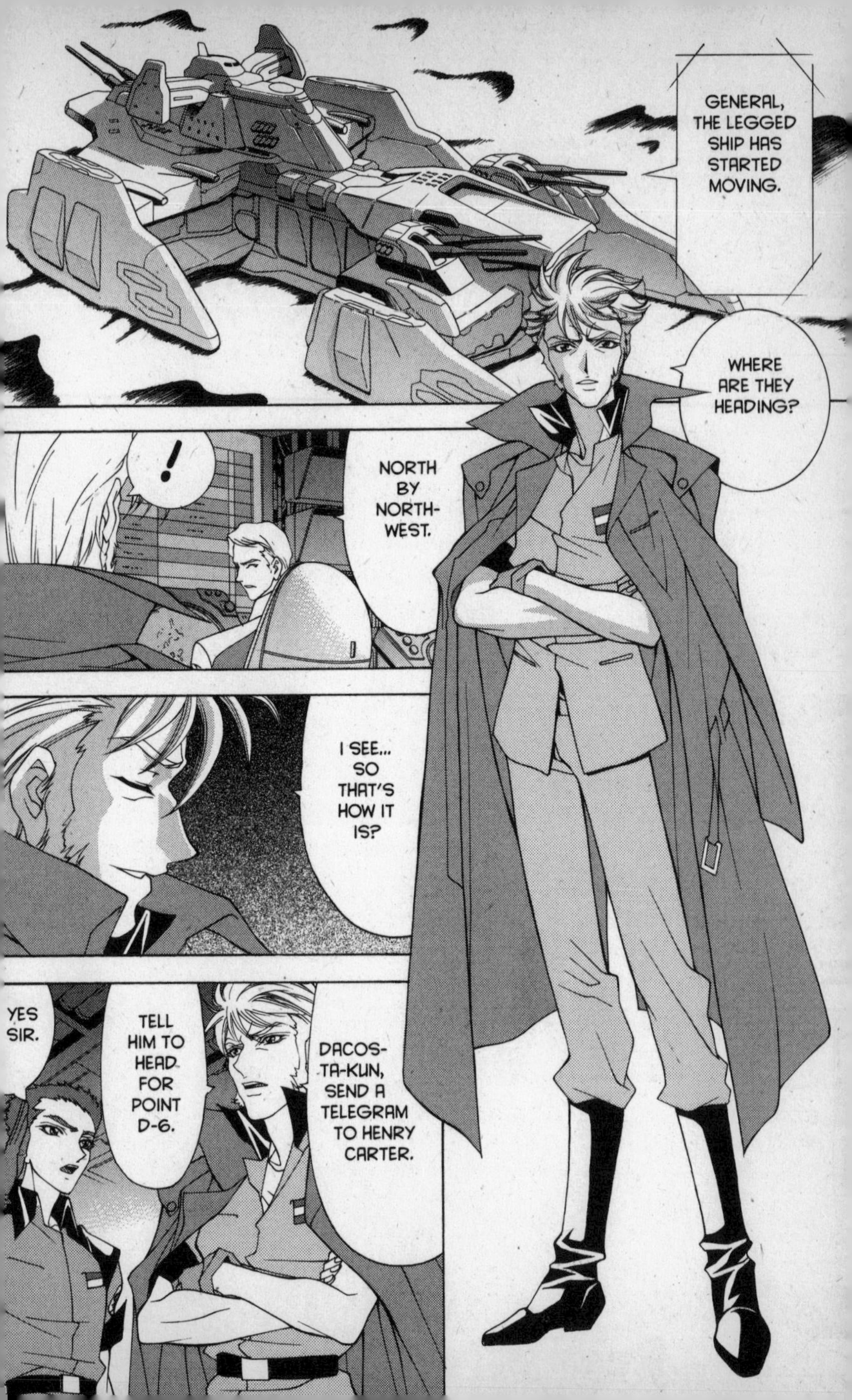
GENERAL, THE LEGGED SHIP HAS STARTED MOVING.
WHERE ARE THEY HEADING?
!
NORTH BY NORTH-WEST.
I SEE... SO THAT'S HOW IT IS?
DACOS-TA-KUN, SEND A TELEGRAM TO HENRY CARTER.
TELL HIM TO HEAD FOR POINT D-6.
YES SIR.

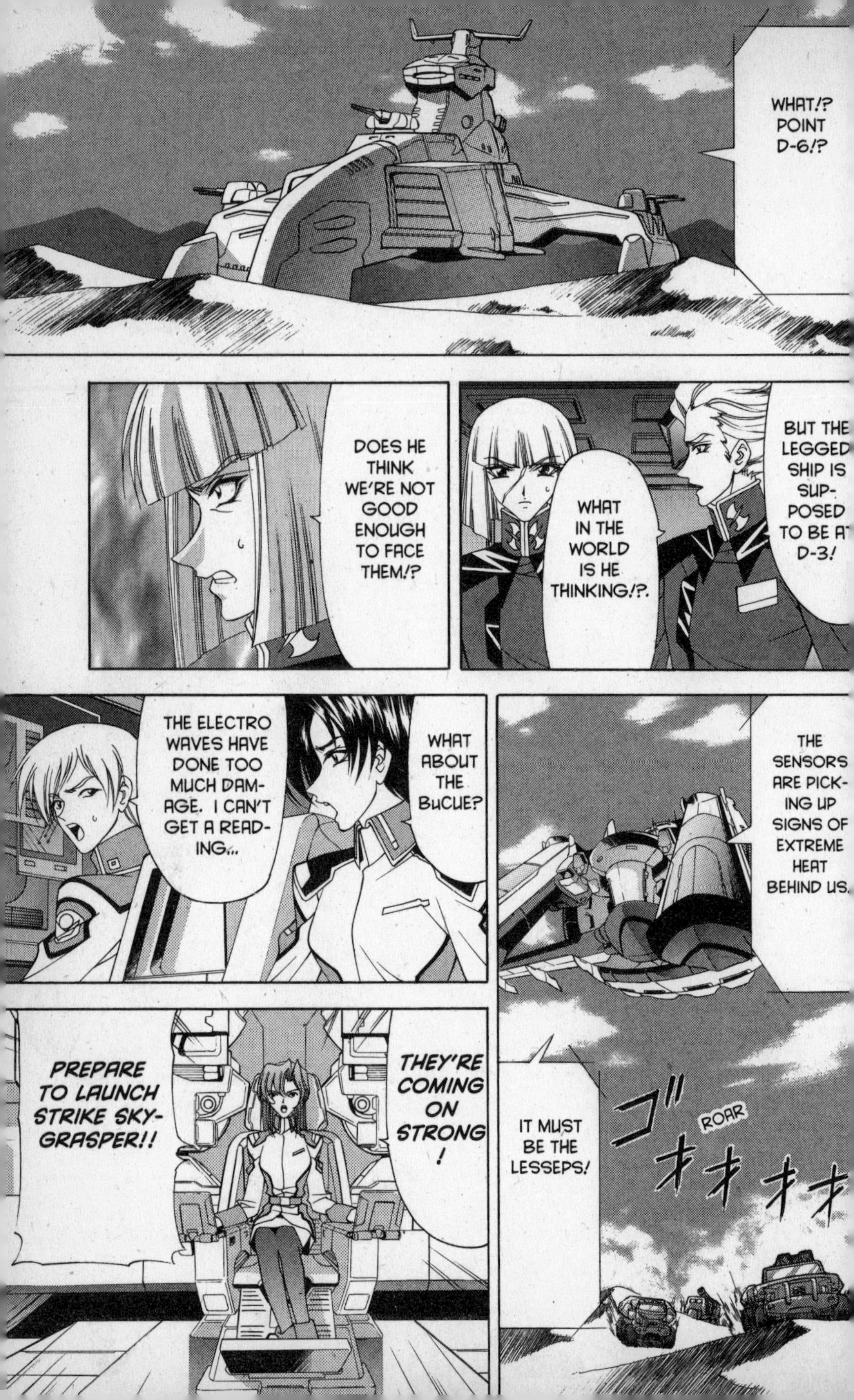
WHAT!? POINT D-6!?
BUT THE LEGGED SHIP IS SUP-POSED TO BE AT D-3!
WHAT IN THE WORLD IS HE THINKING!?.
DOES HE THINK WE'RE NOT GOOD ENOUGH TO FACE THEM!?
THE SENSORS ARE PICK-ING UP SIGNS OF EXTREME HEAT BEHIND US.
IT MUST BE THE LESSEPS!
ROAR
WHAT ABOUT THE BuCUE?
THE ELECTRO WAVES HAVE DONE TOO MUCH DAM-AGE. I CAN'T GET A READ-ING...
THEY'RE COMING ON STRONG!
PREPARE TO LAUNCH STRIKE SKY-GRASPER!!

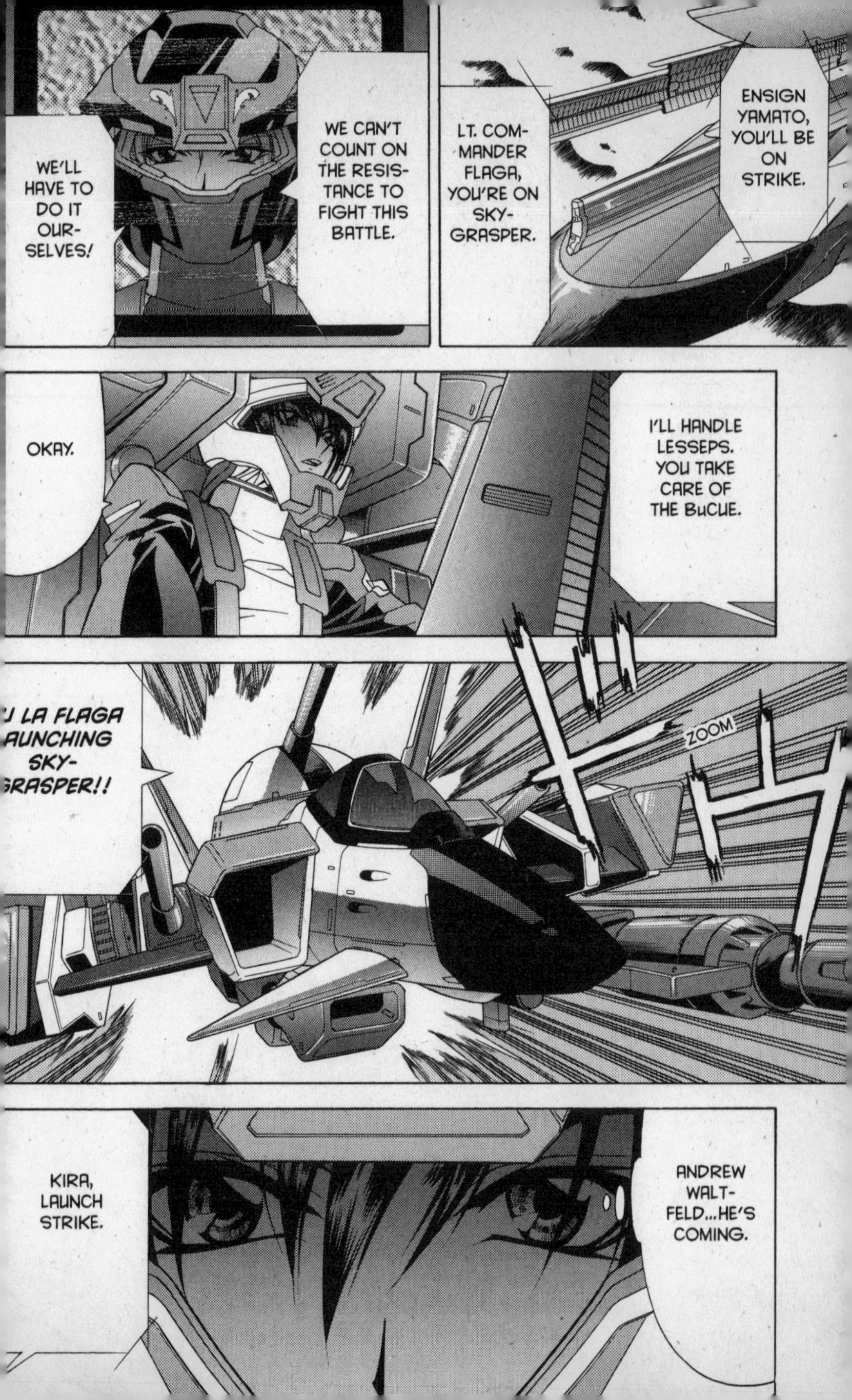
ENSIGN YAMATO, YOU'LL BE ON STRIKE.
LT. COM-MANDER FLAGA, YOU'RE ON SKY-GRASPER.
WE CAN'T COUNT ON THE RESIS-TANCE TO FIGHT THIS BATTLE.
WE'LL HAVE TO DO IT OUR-SELVES!
I'LL HANDLE LESSEPS. YOU TAKE CARE OF THE BuCUE.
OKAY.
ZOOM
U LA FLAGA AUNCHING SKY-RASPER!!
ANDREW WALT-FELD...HE'S COMING.
KIRA, LAUNCH STRIKE.

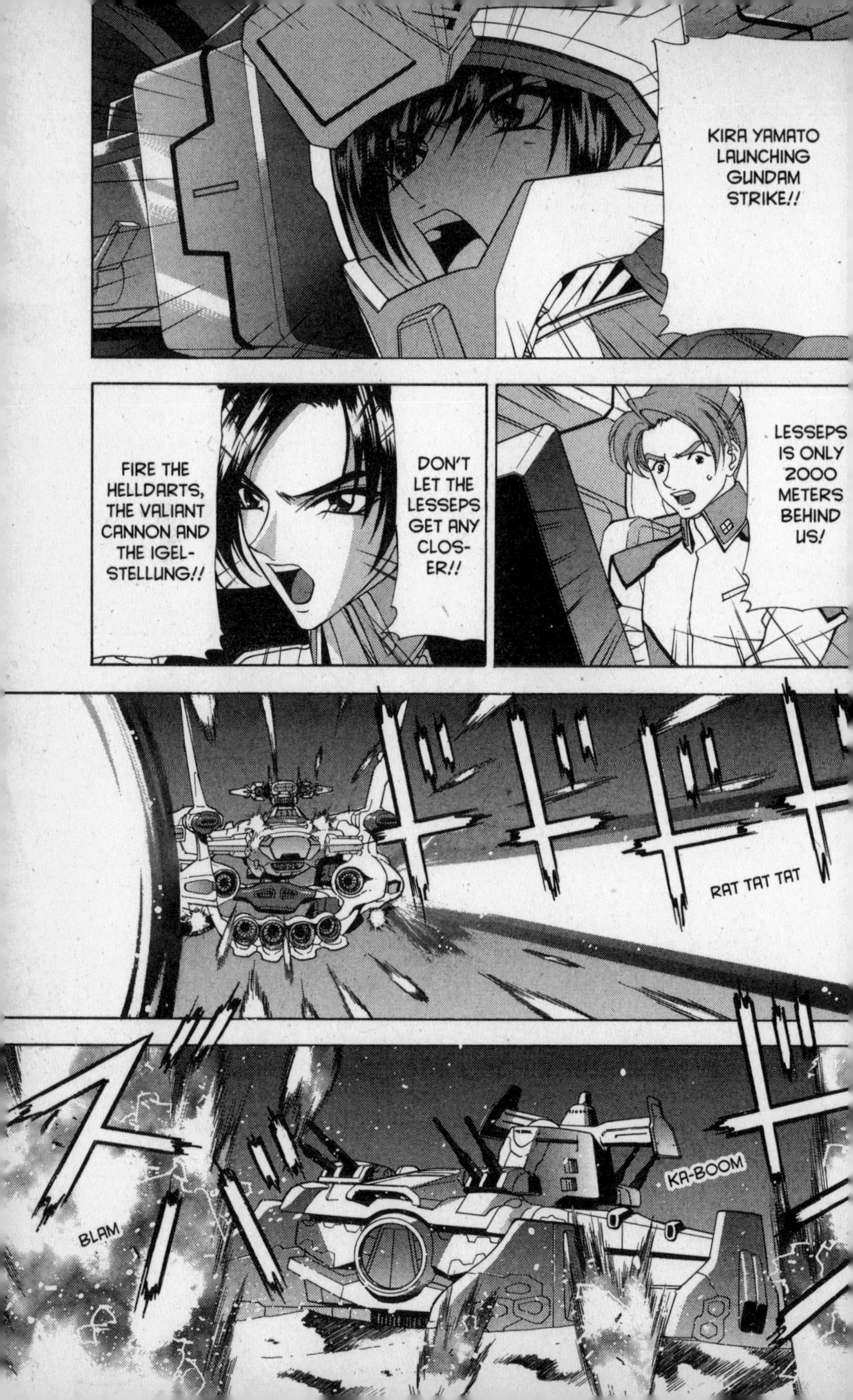
KIRA YAMATO LAUNCHING GUNDAM STRIKE!!
LESSEPS IS ONLY 2000 METERS BEHIND US!
DON'T LET THE LESSEPS GET ANY CLOS-ER!!
FIRE THE HELLDARTS, THE VALIANT CANNON AND THE IGEL-STELLUNG!!
RAT TAT TAT
KA-BOOM
BLAM

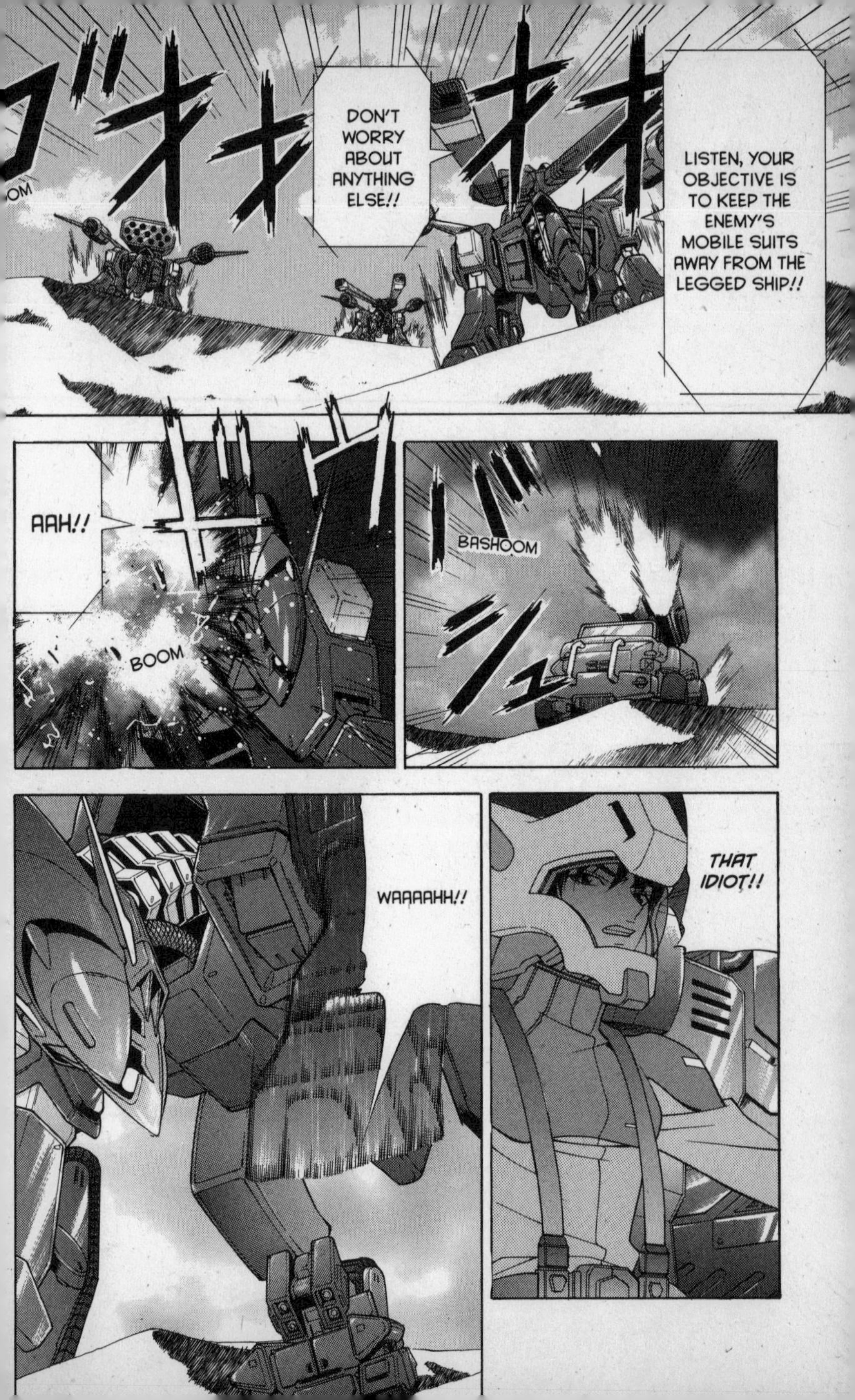
LISTEN, YOUR OBJECTIVE IS TO KEEP THE ENEMY'S MOBILE SUITS AWAY FROM THE LEGGED SHIP!!
DON'T WORRY ABOUT ANYTHING ELSE!!
OOM
BASHOOM
AAH!!
BOOM
THAT IDIOT!!
WAAAAHH!!

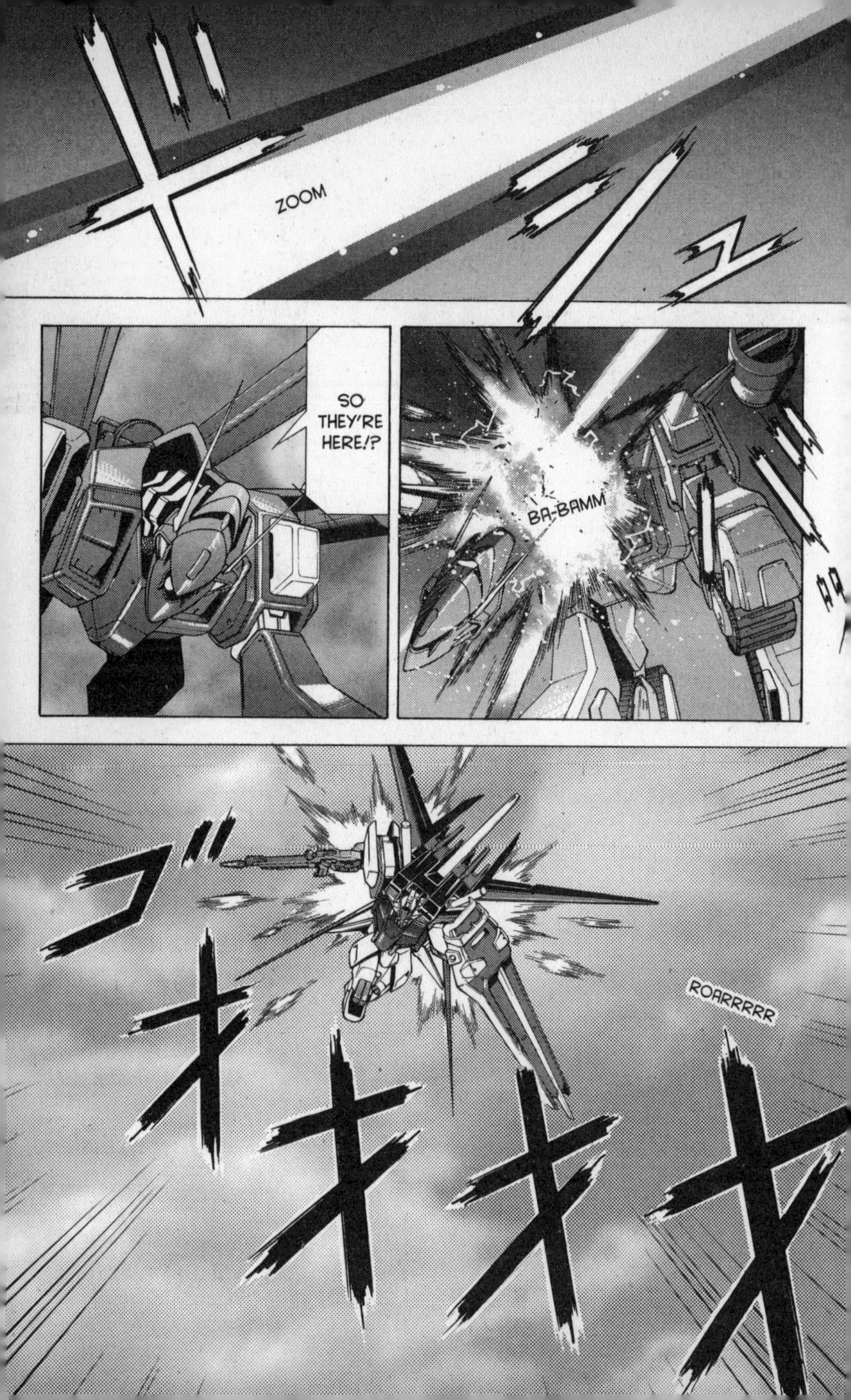
ZOOM
BA-BAMM
SO THEY'RE HERE!?
ROARRRRR

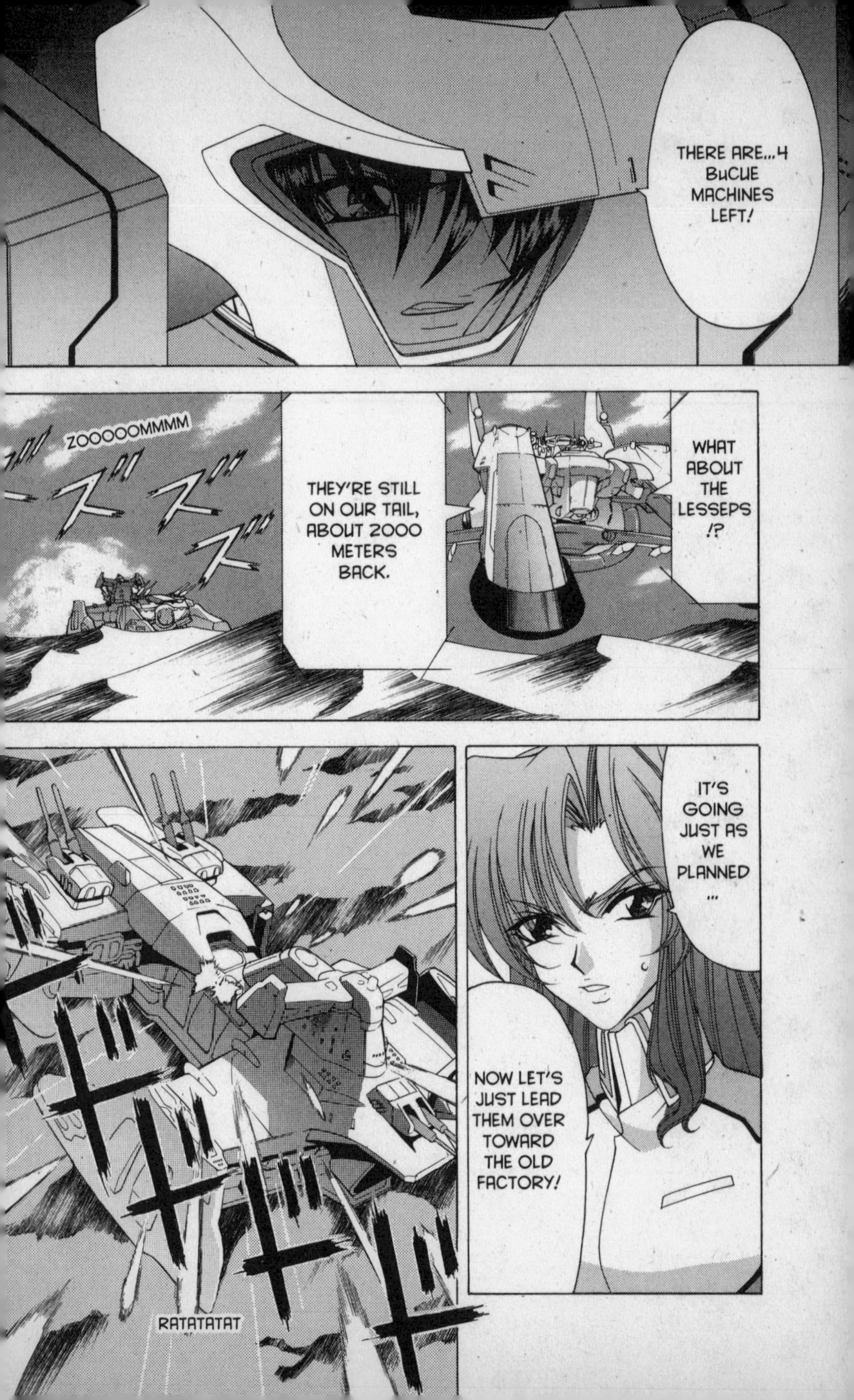
THERE ARE...4 BuCUE MACHINES LEFT!
WHAT ABOUT THE LESSEPS !?
THEY'RE STILL ON OUR TAIL, ABOUT 2000 METERS BACK.
ZOOOOOMMMM
IT'S GOING JUST AS WE PLANNED ...
NOW LET'S JUST LEAD THEM OVER TOWARD THE OLD FACTORY!
RATATATAT

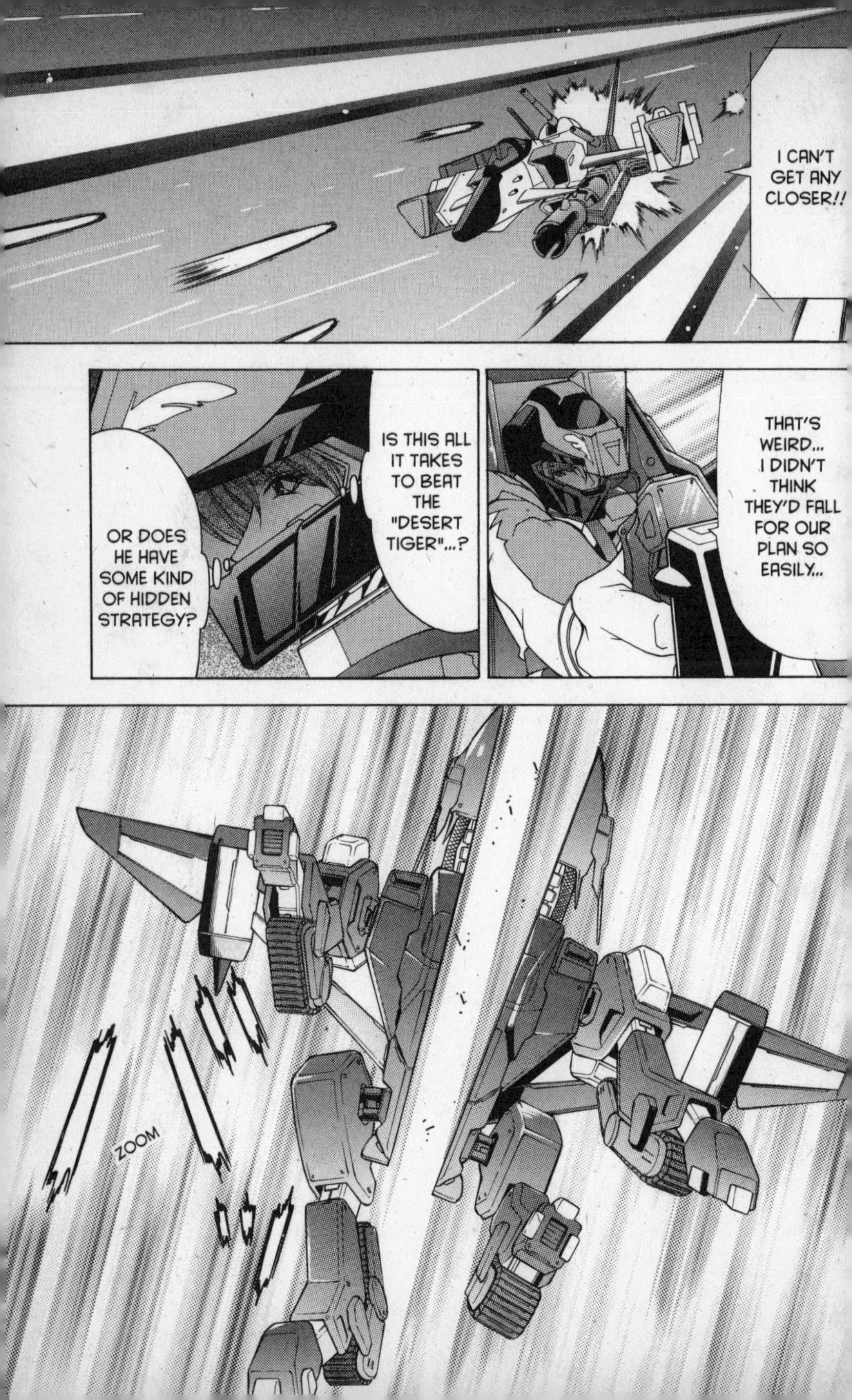
I CAN'T GET ANY CLOSER!!
THAT'S WEIRD... I DIDN'T THINK THEY'D FALL FOR OUR PLAN SO EASILY...
IS THIS ALL IT TAKES TO BEAT THE "DESERT TIGER"...?
OR DOES HE HAVE SOME KIND OF HIDDEN STRATEGY?
ZOOM

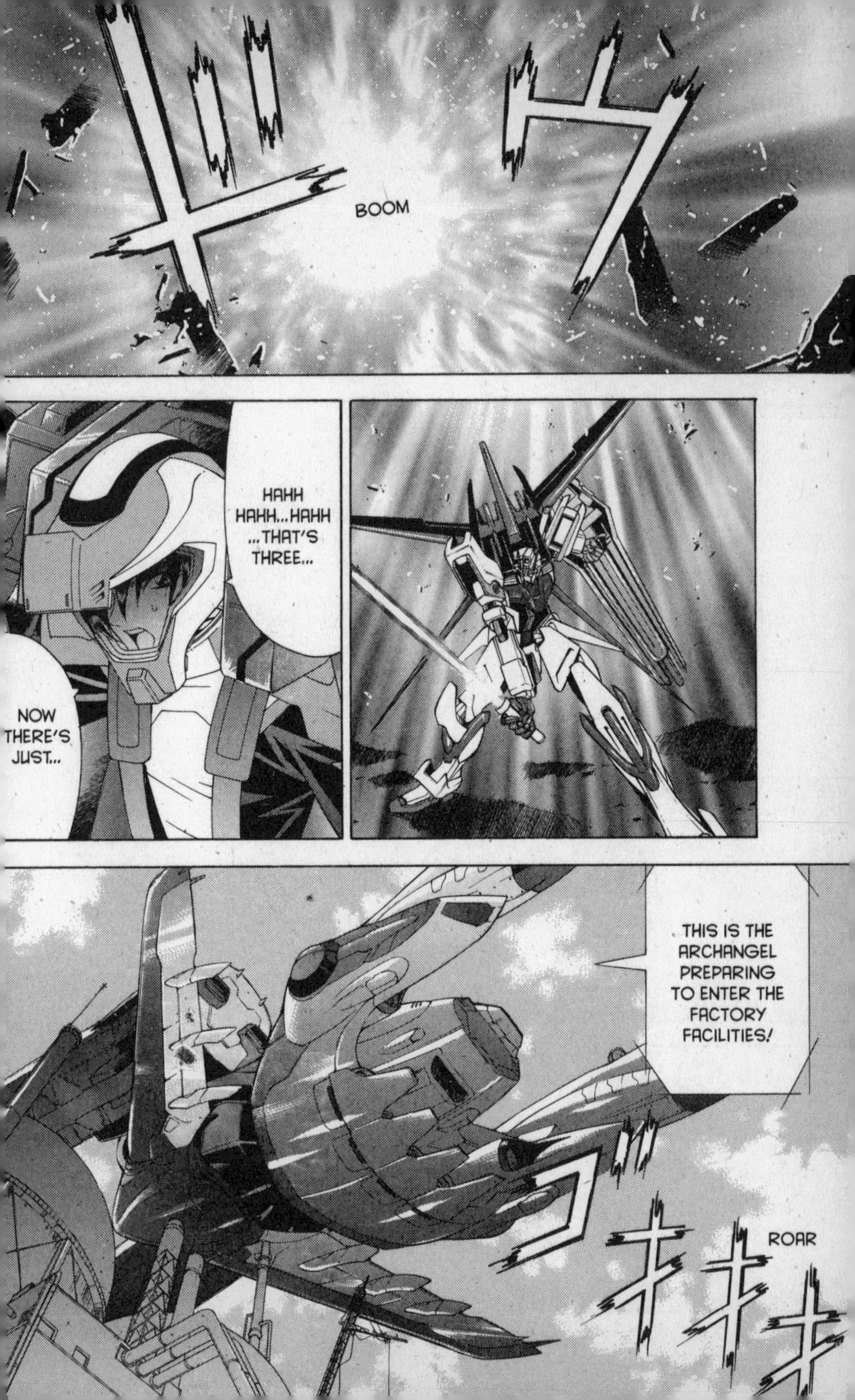
BOOM
HAHH HAHH...HAHH ...THAT'S THREE...
NOW THERE'S JUST...
THIS IS THE ARCHANGEL PREPARING TO ENTER THE FACTORY FACILITIES!
ROAR

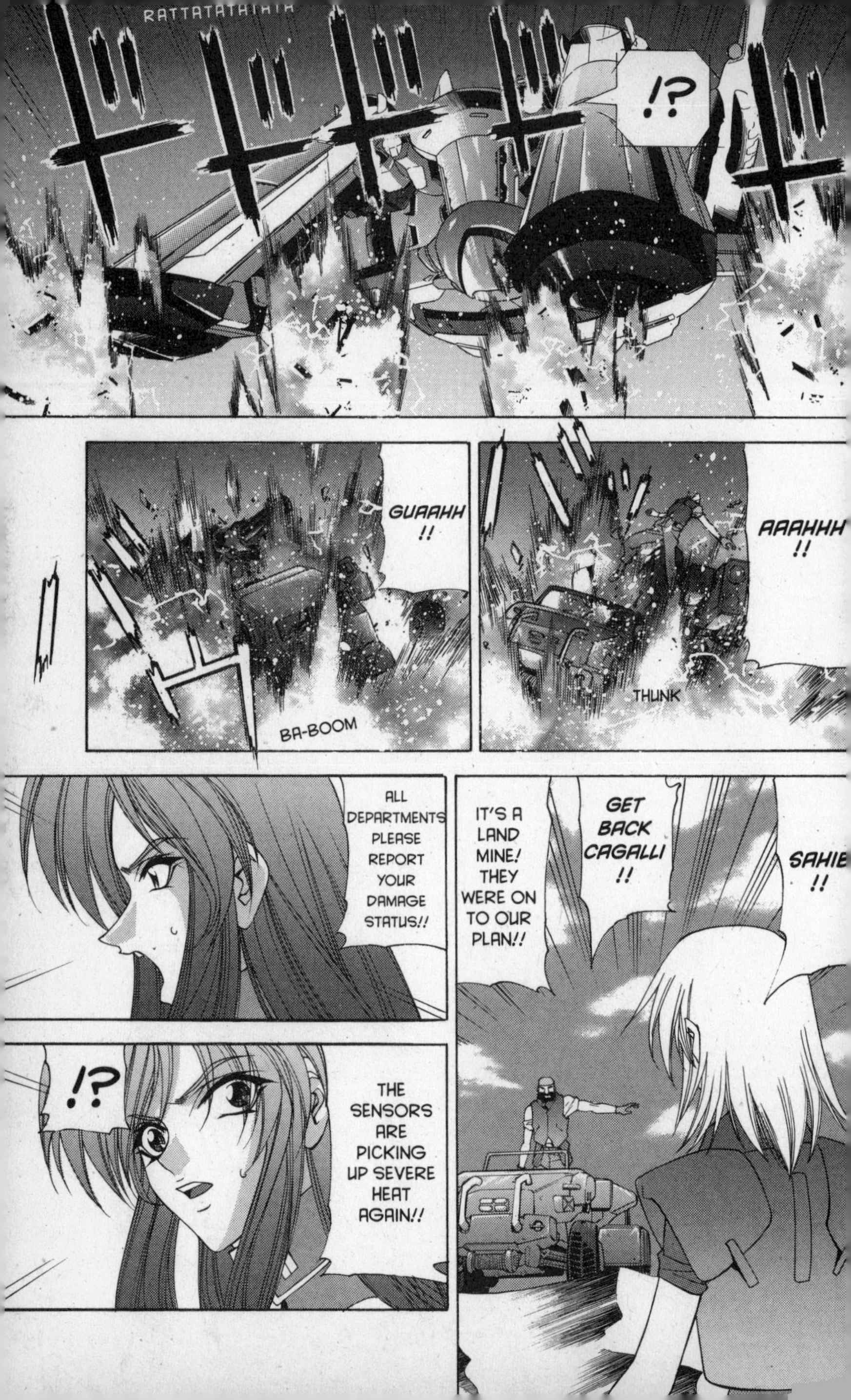
RATTATATATATA
!?
AAAHHH !!
THUNK
GUAAHH !!
BA-BOOM
SAHIB !!
GET BACK CAGALLI !!
IT'S A LAND MINE! THEY WERE ON TO OUR PLAN!!
ALL DEPARTMENTS PLEASE REPORT YOUR DAMAGE STATUS!!
THE SENSORS ARE PICKING UP SEVERE HEAT AGAIN!!
!?

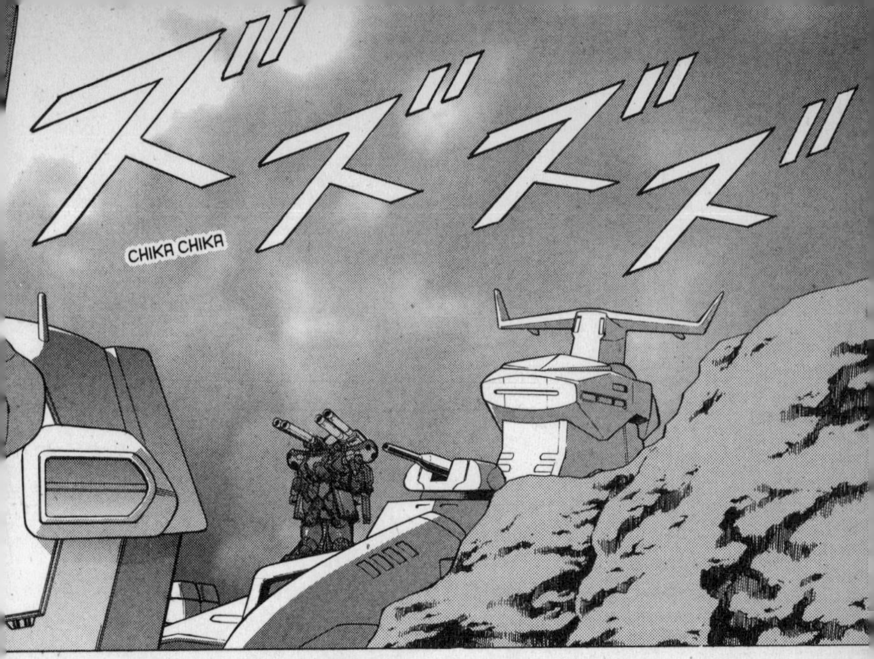
ズズズズ
CHIKA CHIKA
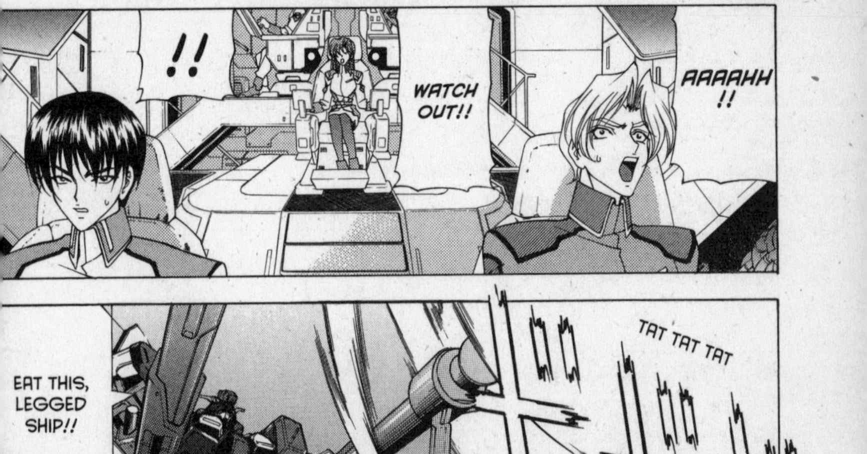
AAAAHH!!
WATCH OUT!!
!!
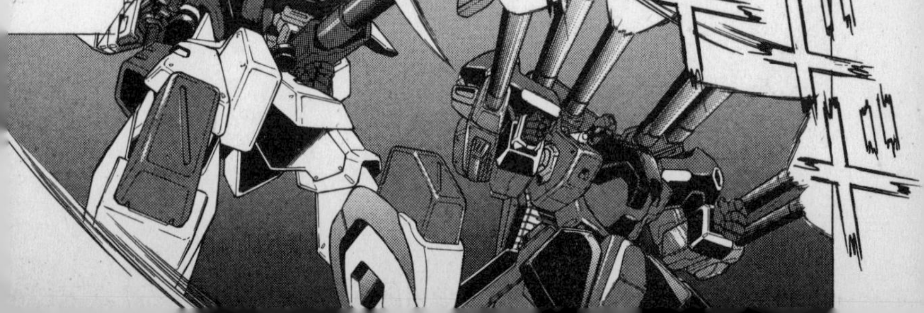
TAT TAT TAT
EAT THIS, LEGGED SHIP!!

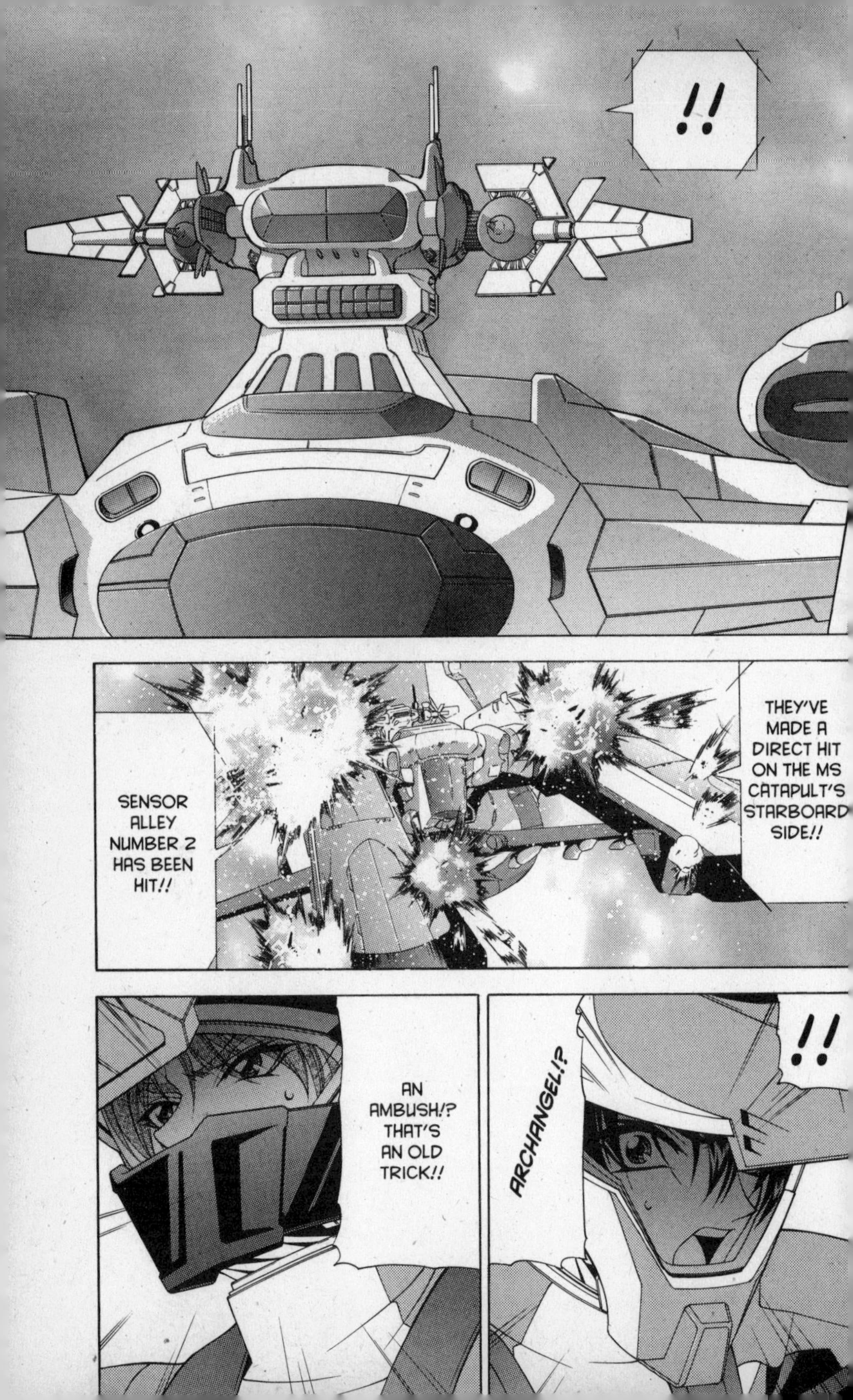
!!
THEY'VE MADE A DIRECT HIT ON THE MS CATAPULT'S STARBOARD SIDE!!
SENSOR ALLEY NUMBER 2 HAS BEEN HIT!!
!!
ARCHANGEL!?
AN AMBUSH!? THAT'S AN OLD TRICK!!

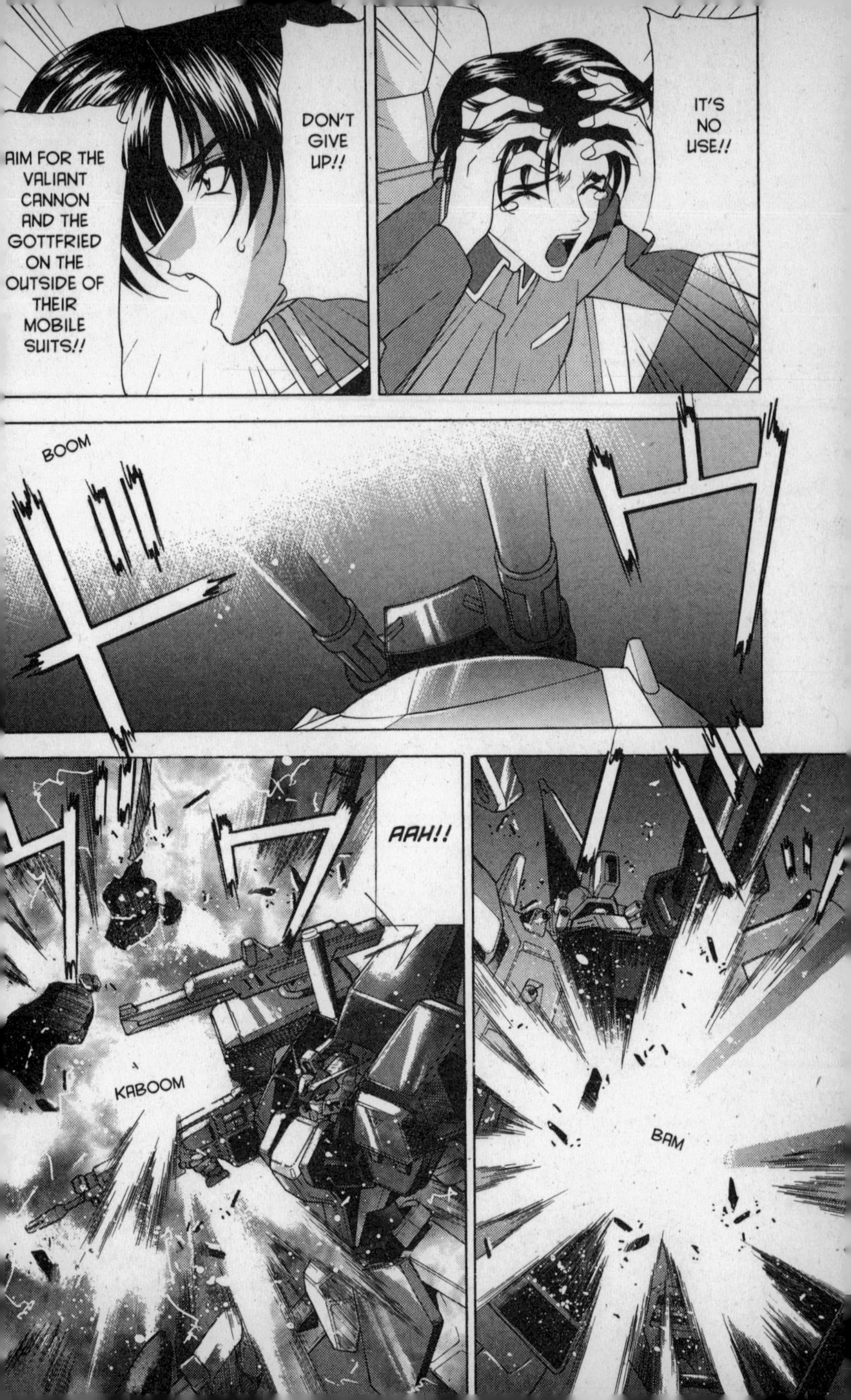
IT'S NO USE!!
DON'T GIVE UP!!
AIM FOR THE VALIANT CANNON AND THE GOTTFRIED ON THE OUTSIDE OF THEIR MOBILE SUITS!!
BOOM
BAM
AAH!!
KABOOM

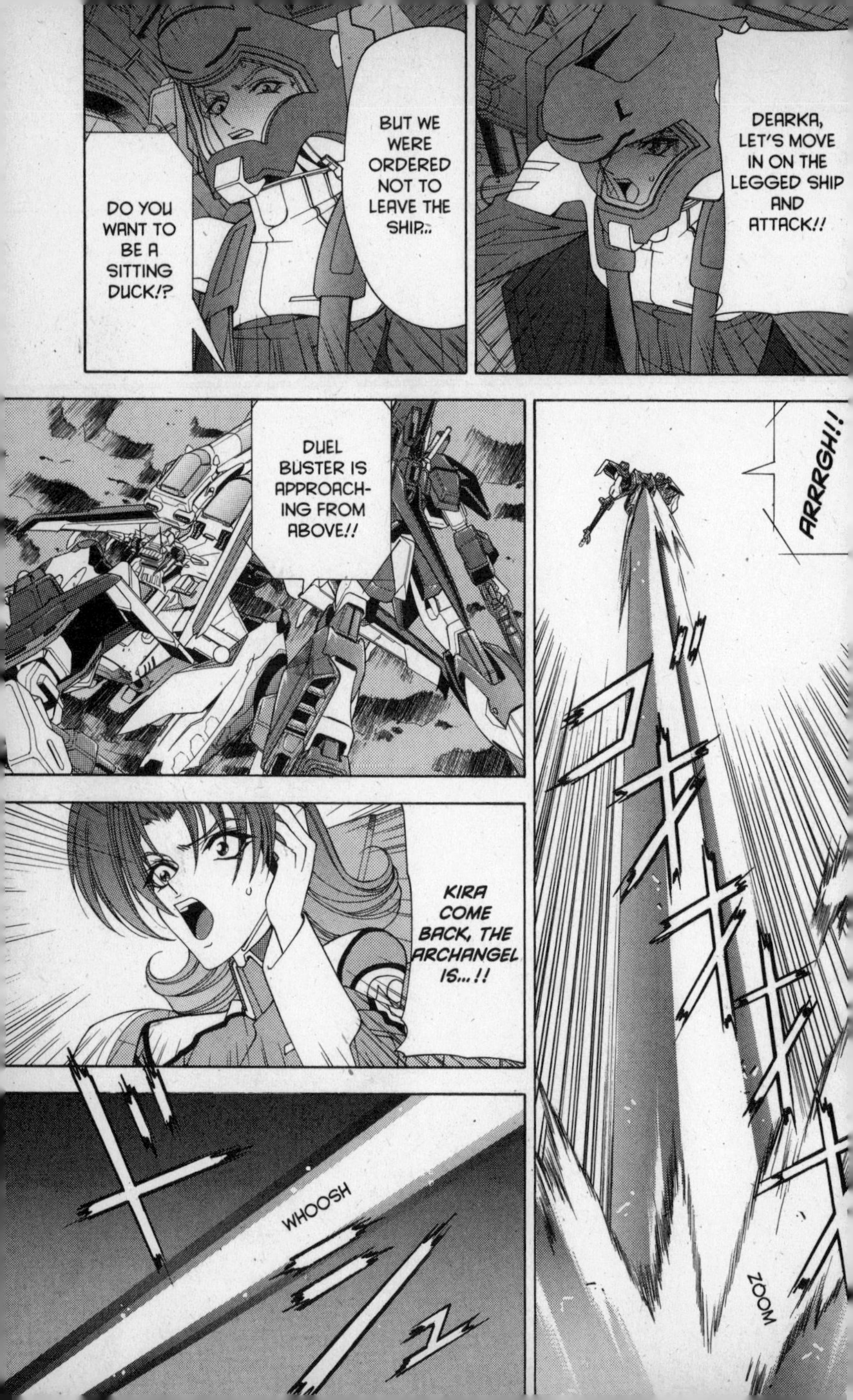
DEARKA, LET'S MOVE IN ON THE LEGGED SHIP AND ATTACK!!
BUT WE WERE ORDERED NOT TO LEAVE THE SHIP...
DO YOU WANT TO BE A SITTING DUCK!?
ARRRGH!!
ZOOM
DUEL BUSTER IS APPROACH-ING FROM ABOVE!!
KIRA COME BACK, THE ARCHANGEL IS...!!
WHOOSH

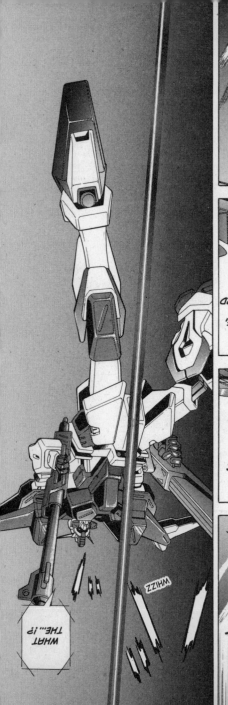

WHAT THE...!?

ZZIHM

STOMP

STRIKE, YOU BASTARD!!

DEARKA!!

BOOM

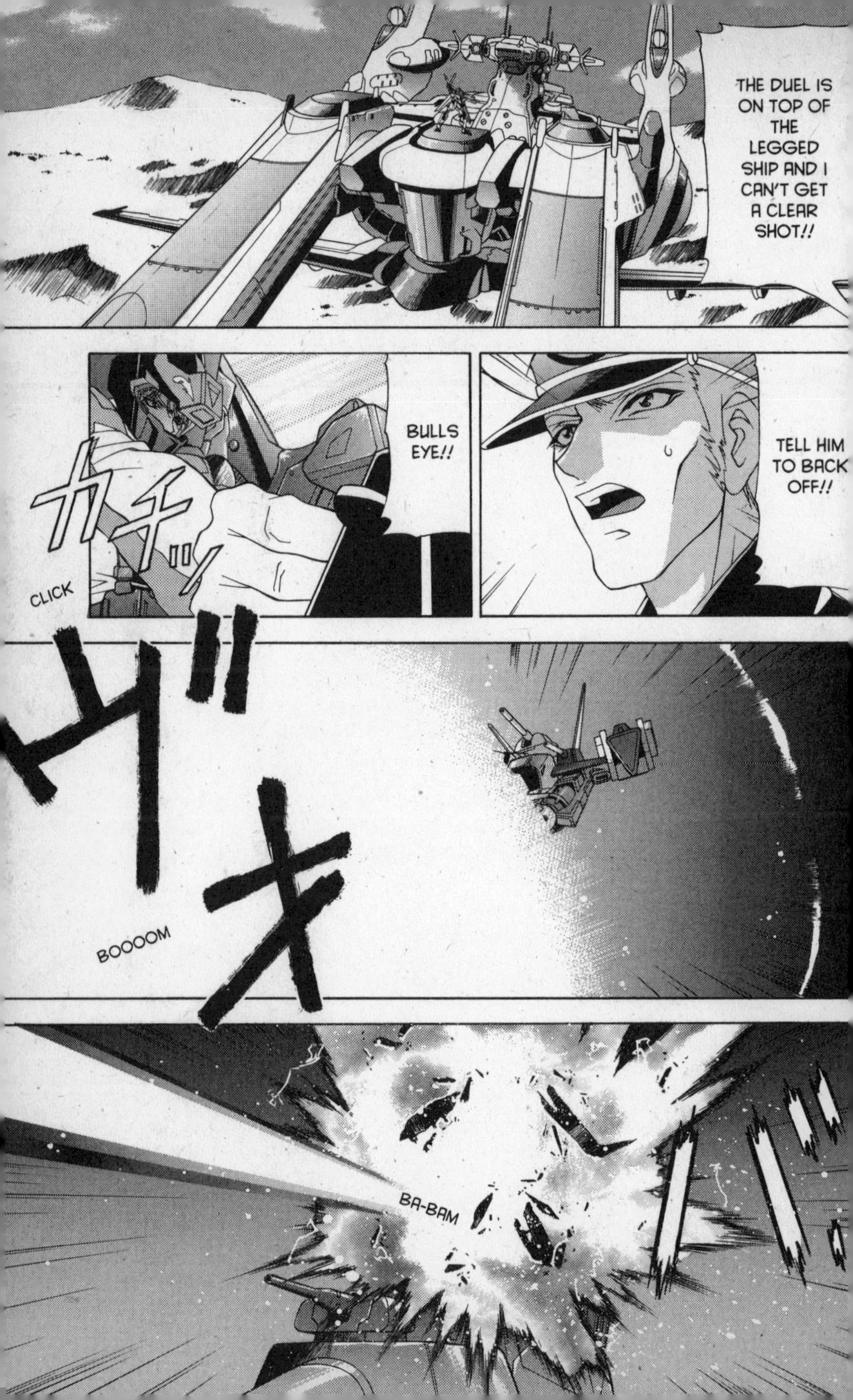
THE DUEL IS ON TOP OF THE LEGGED SHIP AND I CAN'T GET A CLEAR SHOT!!
TELL HIM TO BACK OFF!!
BULLS EYE!!
カチッ
CLICK
ドゴォ
BOOOOM
BA-BAM

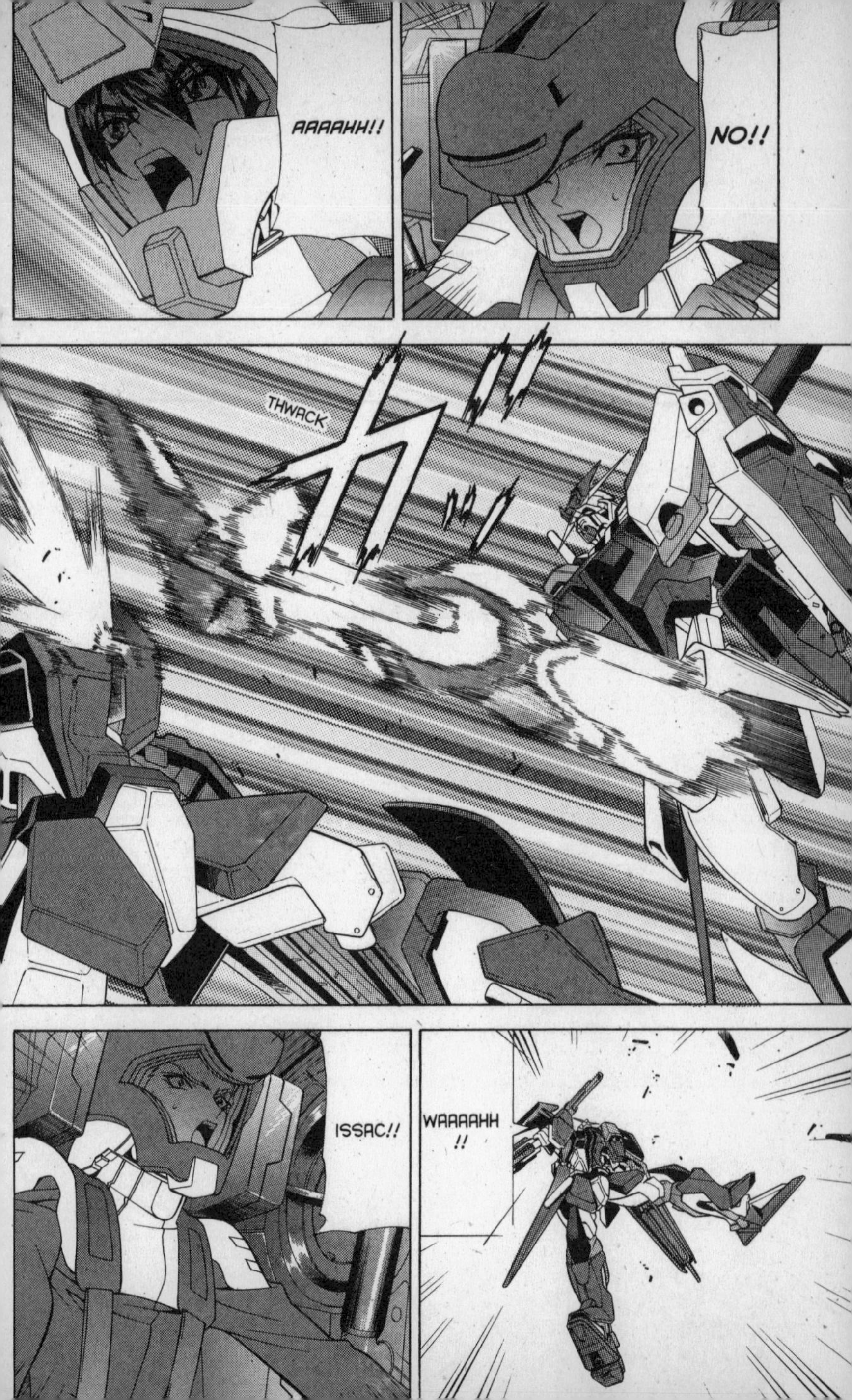
NO!!
AAAAHH!!
THWACK
WAAAAHH
!!
ISSAC!!

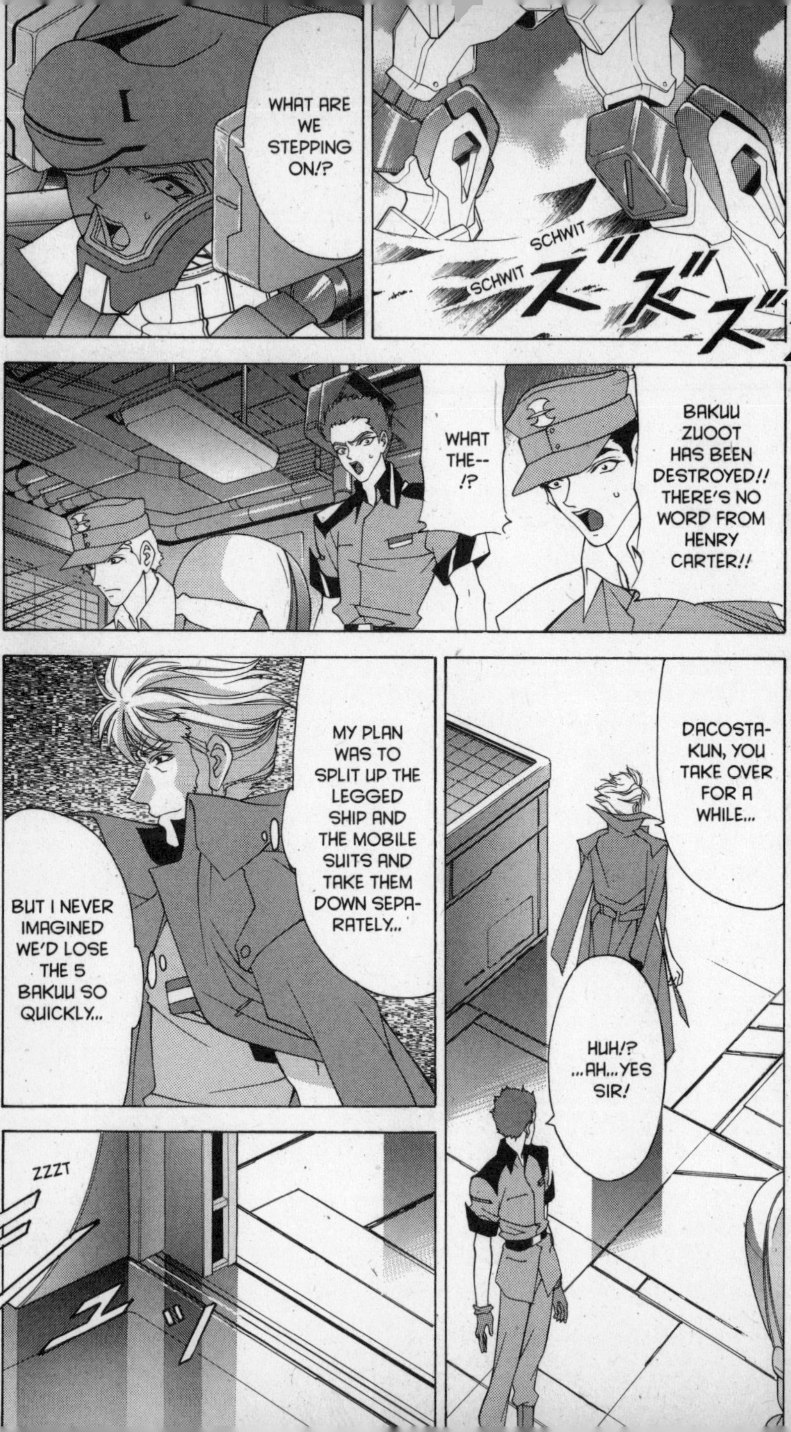
SCHWIT
SCHWIT
WHAT ARE WE STEPPING ON!?
BAKUU ZUOOT HAS BEEN DESTROYED!! THERE'S NO WORD FROM HENRY CARTER!!
WHAT THE-- !?
DACOSTA-KUN, YOU TAKE OVER FOR A WHILE...
HUH!? ...AH...YES SIR!
MY PLAN WAS TO SPLIT UP THE LEGGED SHIP AND THE MOBILE SUITS AND TAKE THEM DOWN SEPA-RATELY...
BUT I NEVER IMAGINED WE'D LOSE THE 5 BAKUU SO QUICKLY...
ZZZT

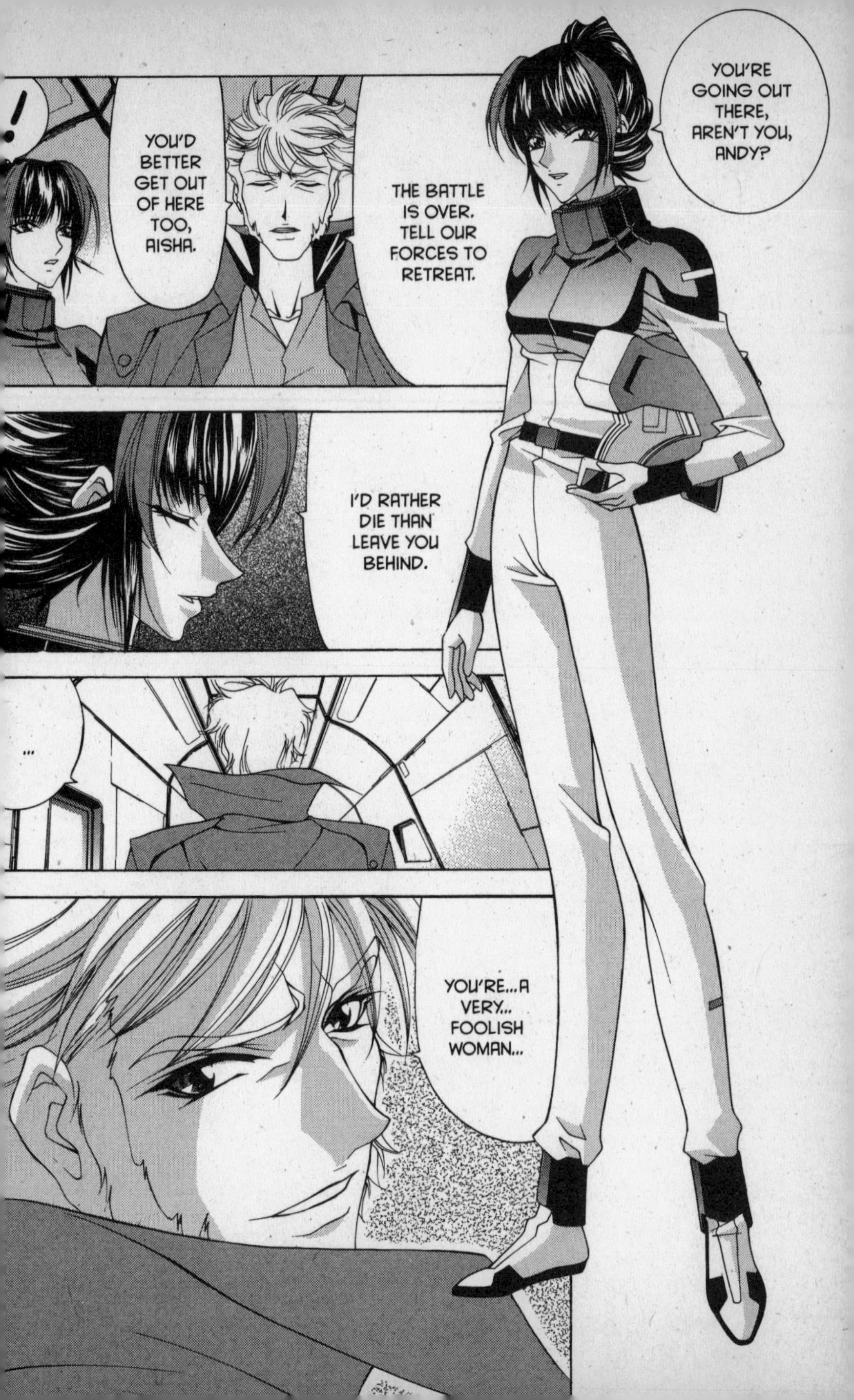
YOU'RE GOING OUT THERE, AREN'T YOU, ANDY?
THE BATTLE IS OVER. TELL OUR FORCES TO RETREAT.
YOU'D BETTER GET OUT OF HERE TOO, AISHA.
!
I'D RATHER DIE THAN LEAVE YOU BEHIND.
...
YOU'RE...A VERY... FOOLISH WOMAN...

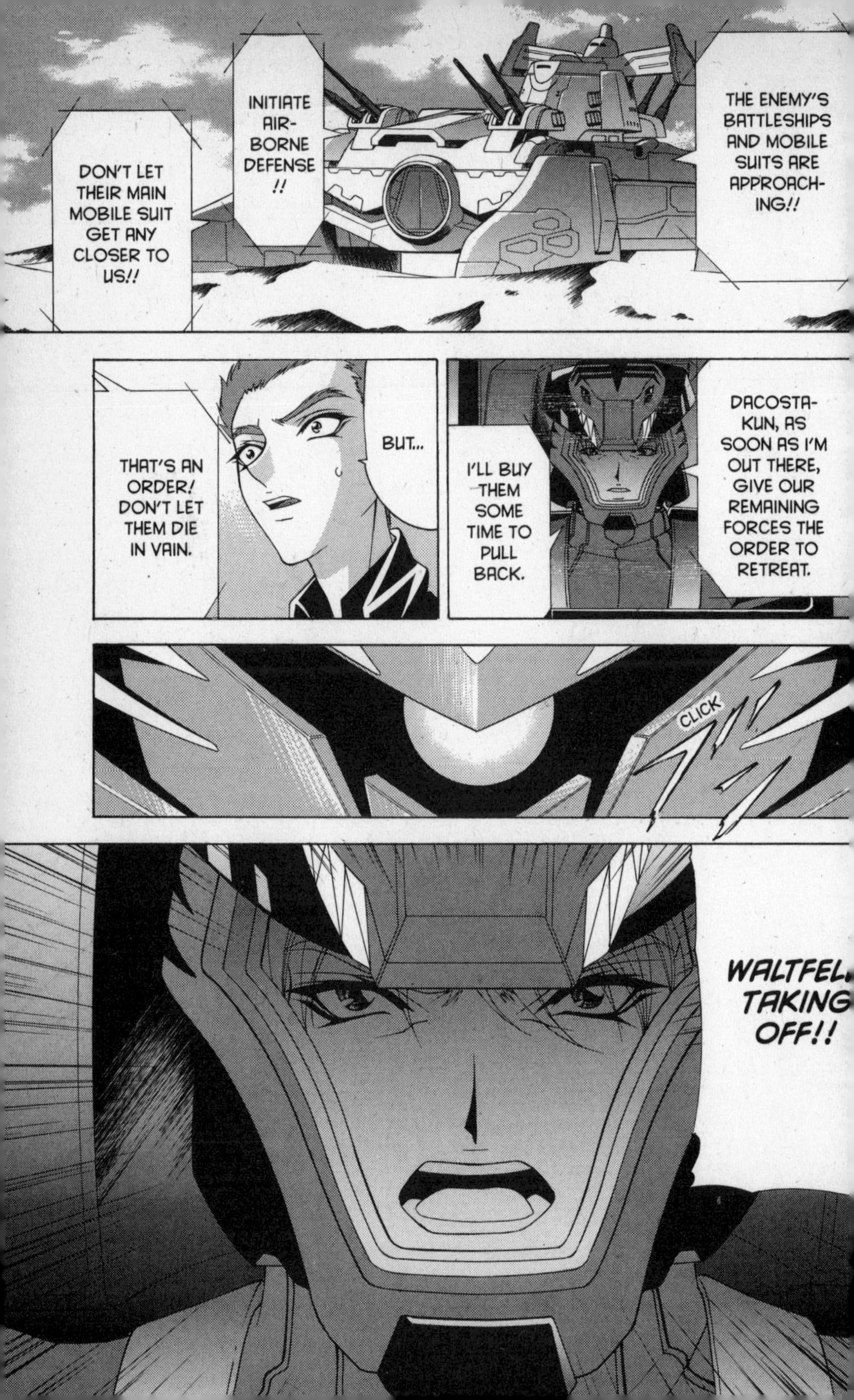
THE ENEMY'S BATTLESHIPS AND MOBILE SUITS ARE APPROACH-ING!!
INITIATE AIR-BORNE DEFENSE!!
DON'T LET THEIR MAIN MOBILE SUIT GET ANY CLOSER TO US!!
DACOSTA-KUN, AS SOON AS I'M OUT THERE, GIVE OUR REMAINING FORCES THE ORDER TO RETREAT.
I'LL BUY THEM SOME TIME TO PULL BACK.
BUT...
THAT'S AN ORDER! DON'T LET THEM DIE IN VAIN.
CLICK
WALTFEL, TAKING OFF!!

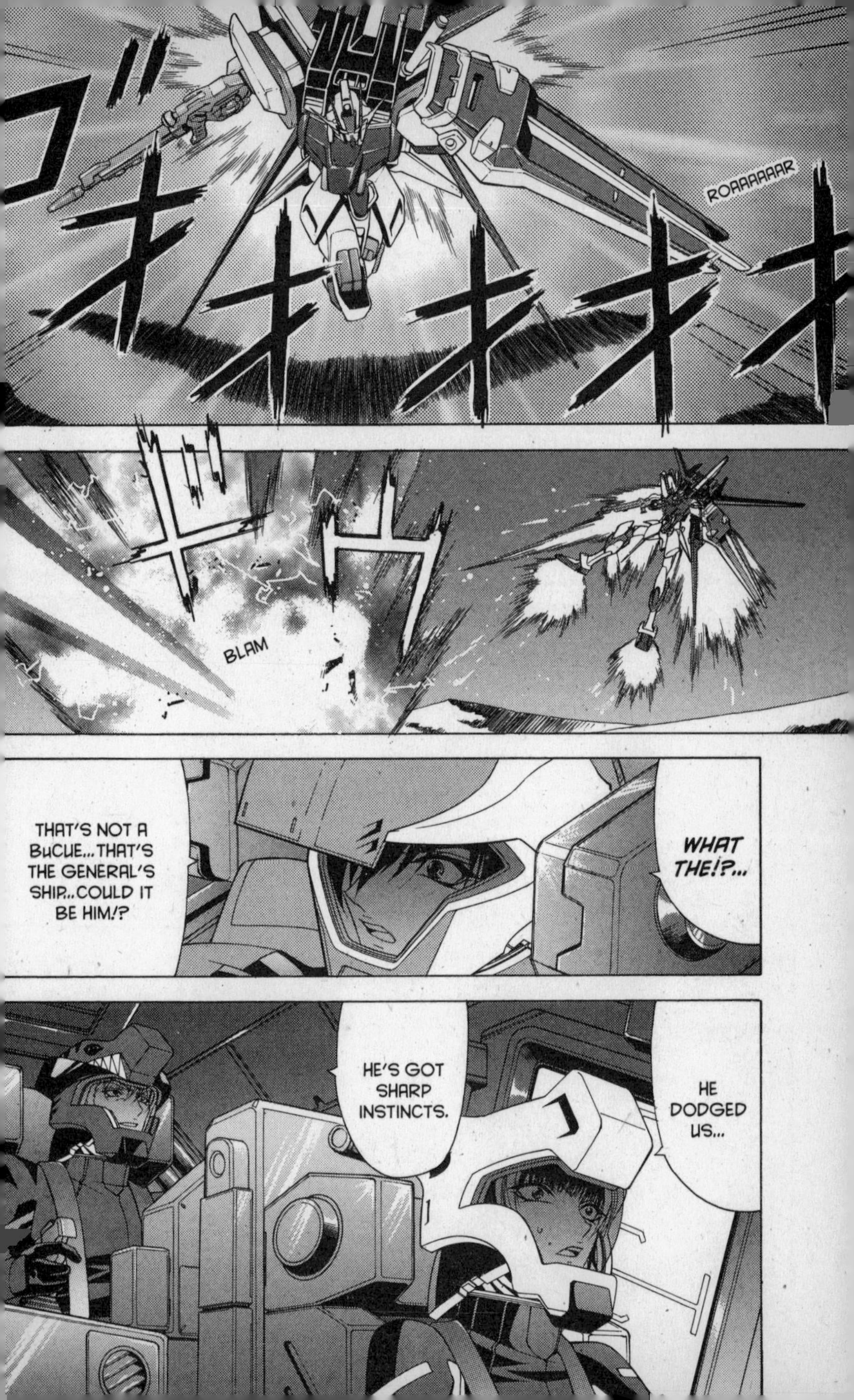
ROARRRRRR
BLAM
WHAT THE!?...
THAT'S NOT A BuCUE...THAT'S THE GENERAL'S SHIP...COULD IT BE HIM!?
HE DODGED US...
HE'S GOT SHARP INSTINCTS.

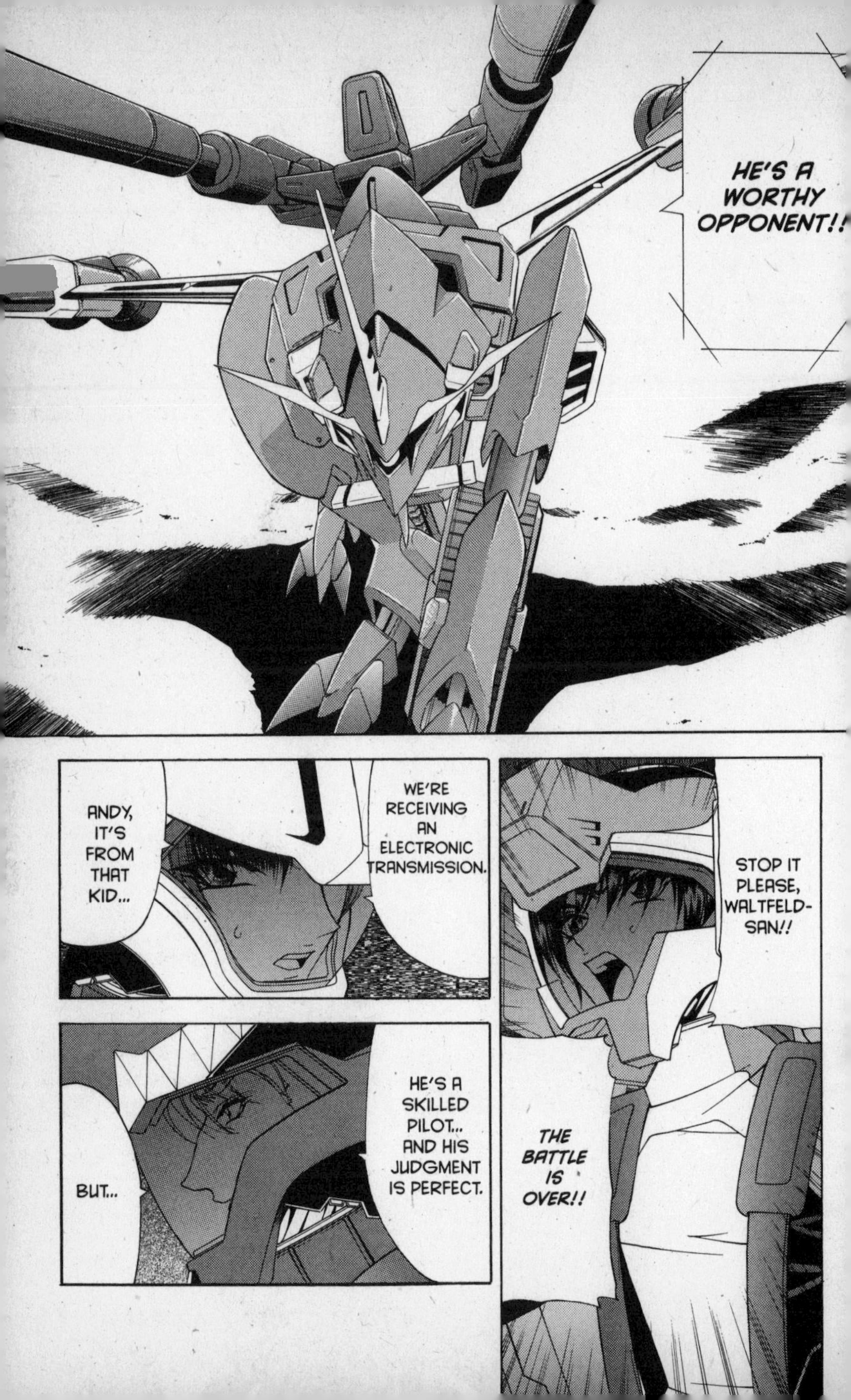
HE'S A WORTHY OPPONENT!!
STOP IT PLEASE, WALTFELD-SAN!!
THE BATTLE IS OVER!!
WE'RE RECEIVING AN ELECTRONIC TRANSMISSION.
ANDY, IT'S FROM THAT KID...
HE'S A SKILLED PILOT... AND HIS JUDGMENT IS PERFECT.
BUT...

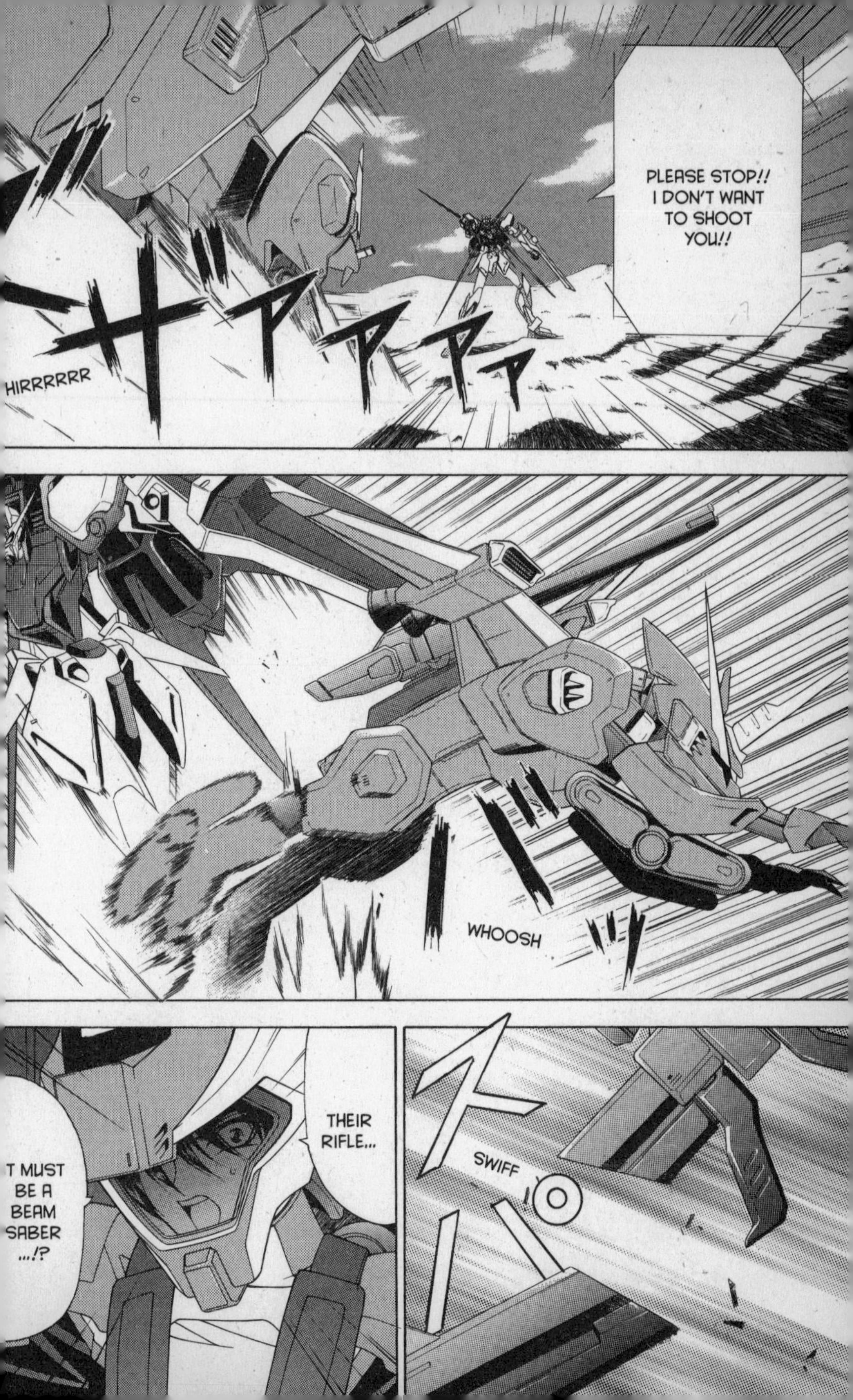
PLEASE STOP!! I DON'T WANT TO SHOOT YOU!!
HIRRRRRR
WHOOSH
SWIFF
THEIR RIFLE...
T MUST BE A BEAM SABER ...!?

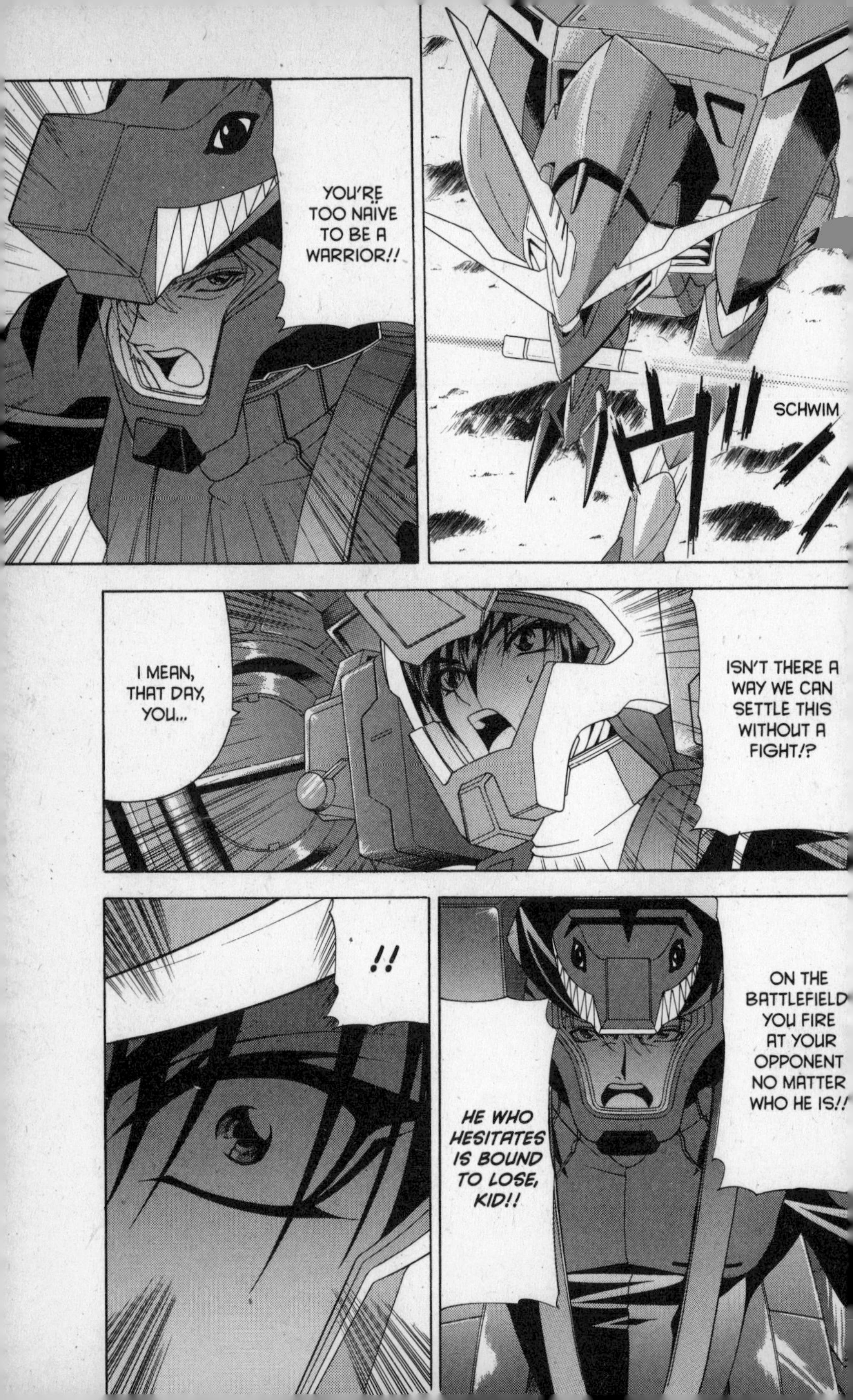
SCHWIM
YOU'RE TOO NAÏVE TO BE A WARRIOR!!
ISN'T THERE A WAY WE CAN SETTLE THIS WITHOUT A FIGHT!?
I MEAN, THAT DAY, YOU...
ON THE BATTLEFIELD YOU FIRE AT YOUR OPPONENT NO MATTER WHO HE IS!!
HE WHO HESITATES IS BOUND TO LOSE, KID!!
!!

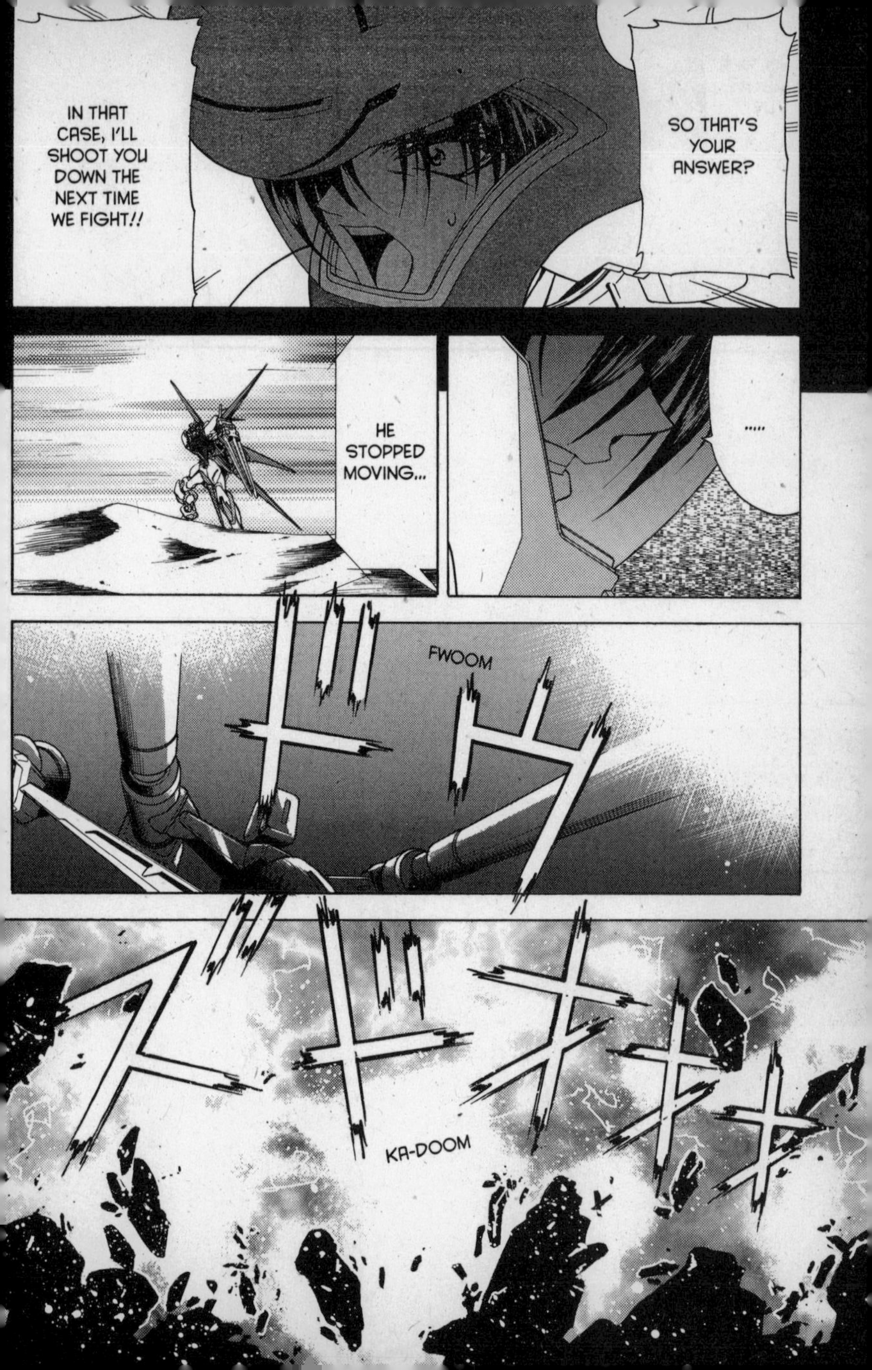
SO THAT'S YOUR ANSWER?
IN THAT CASE, I'LL SHOOT YOU DOWN THE NEXT TIME WE FIGHT!!
.....
HE STOPPED MOVING...
FWOOM
KA-DOOM

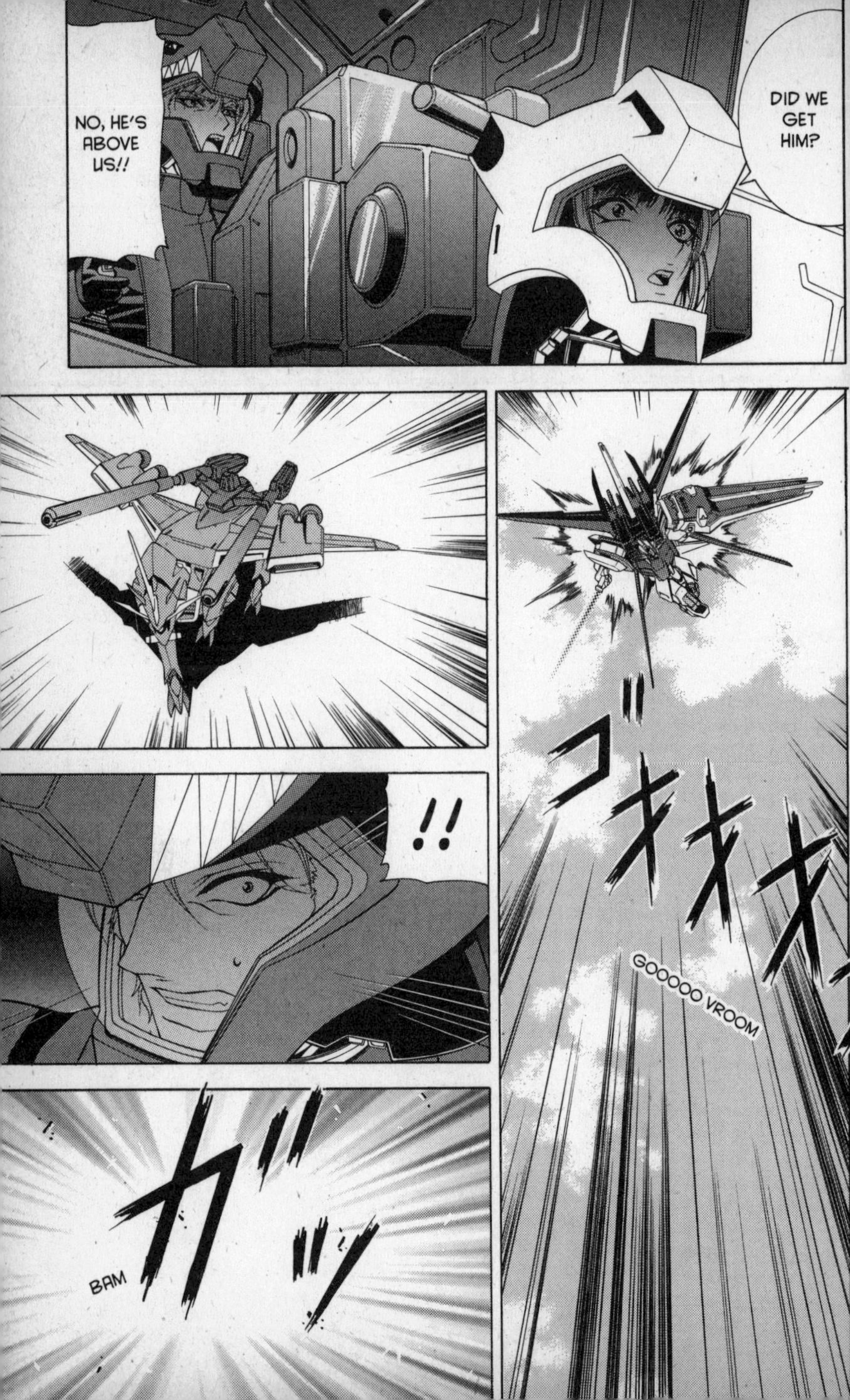
DID WE GET HIM?
NO, HE'S ABOVE US!!
ゴォォォ
GOOOOO VROOM
!!
ガッ
BAM

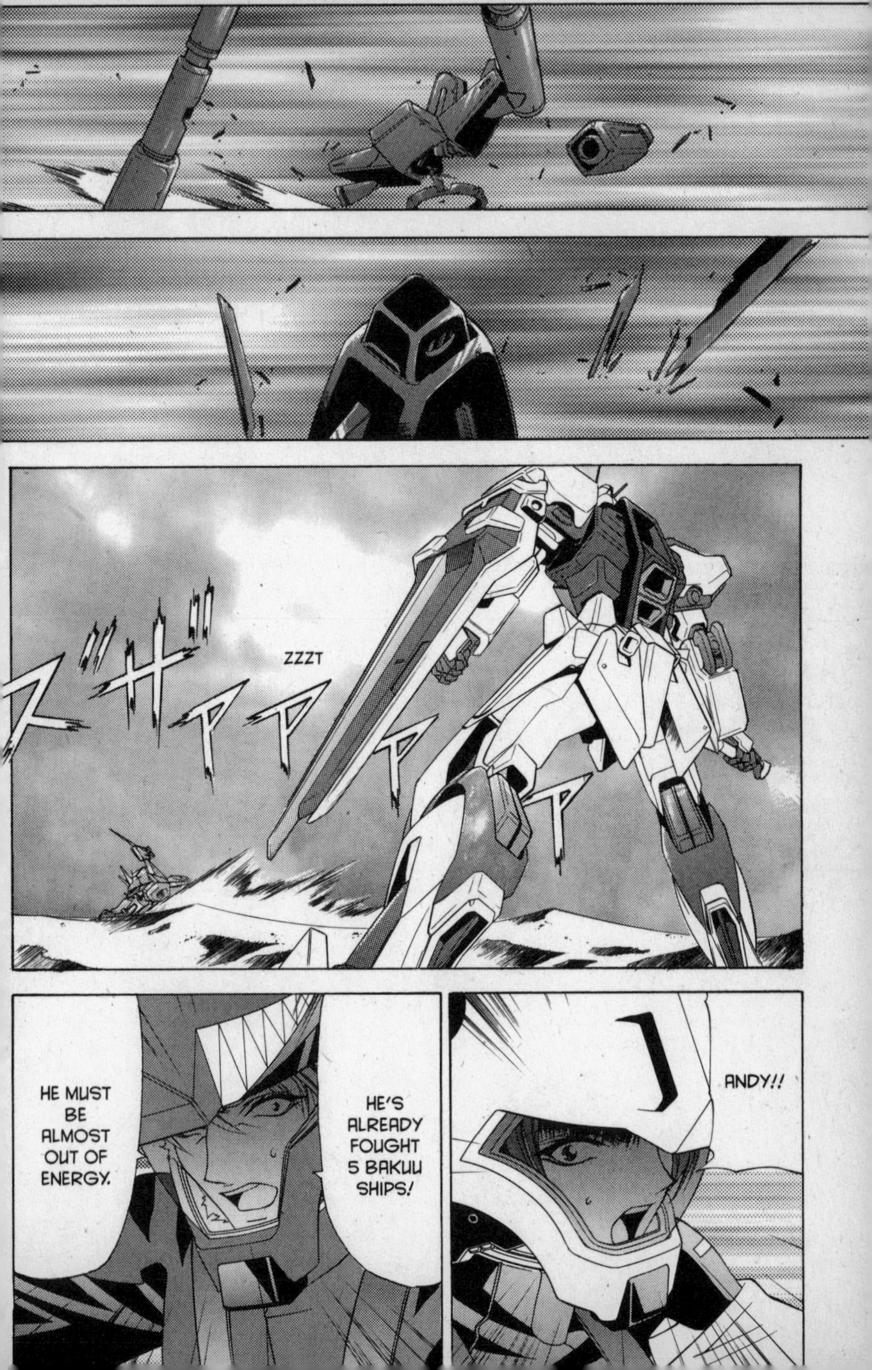
ZZZT
ANDY!!
HE'S ALREADY FOUGHT 5 BAKUU SHIPS!
HE MUST BE ALMOST OUT OF ENERGY.

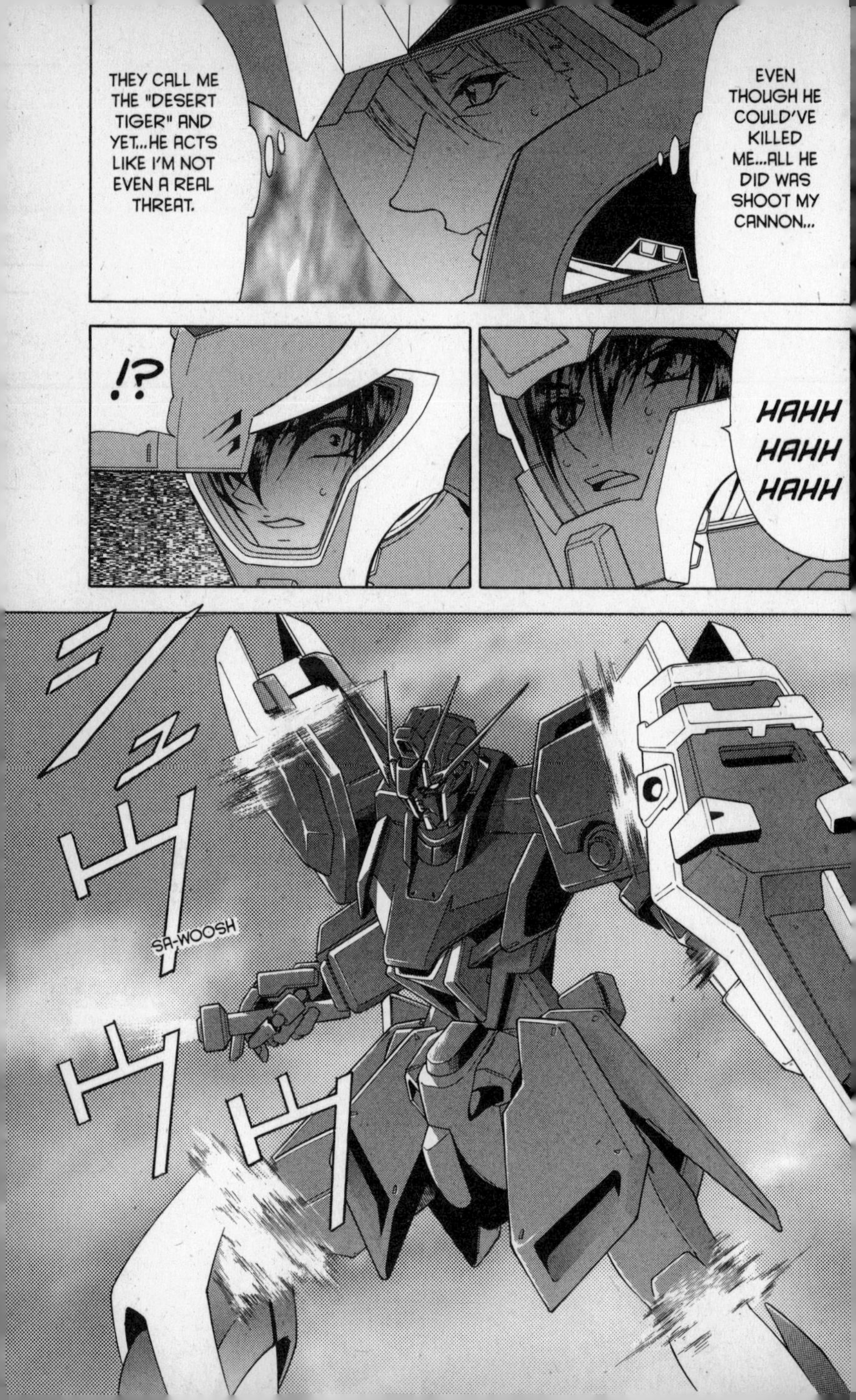
EVEN THOUGH HE COULD'VE KILLED ME...ALL HE DID WAS SHOOT MY CANNON...
THEY CALL ME THE "DESERT TIGER" AND YET...HE ACTS LIKE I'M NOT EVEN A REAL THREAT.
HAHH HAHH HAHH
!?
SA-WOOSH

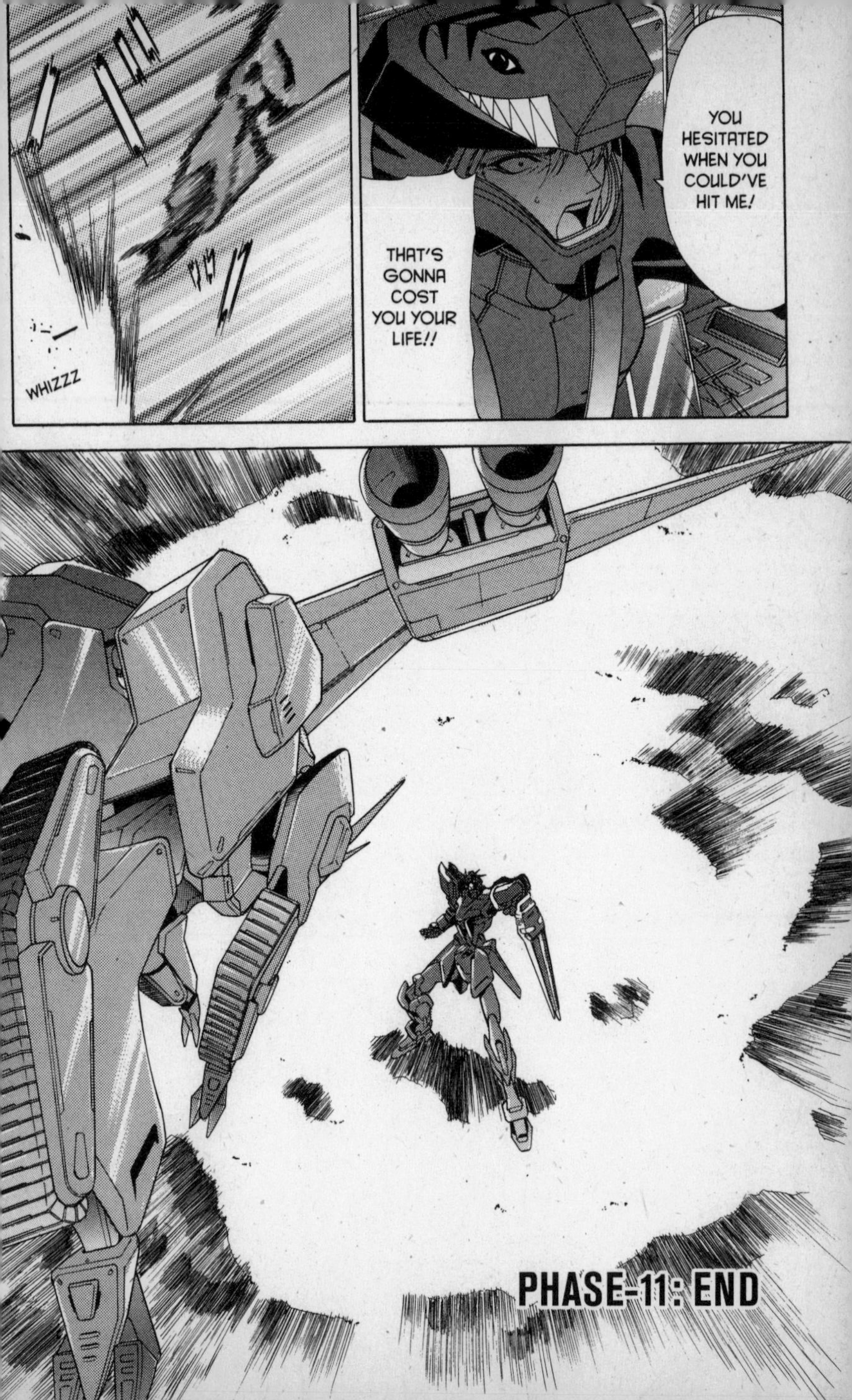
YOU HESITATED WHEN YOU COULD'VE HIT ME!
THAT'S GONNA COST YOU YOUR LIFE!!
WHIZZZ
PHASE-11: END

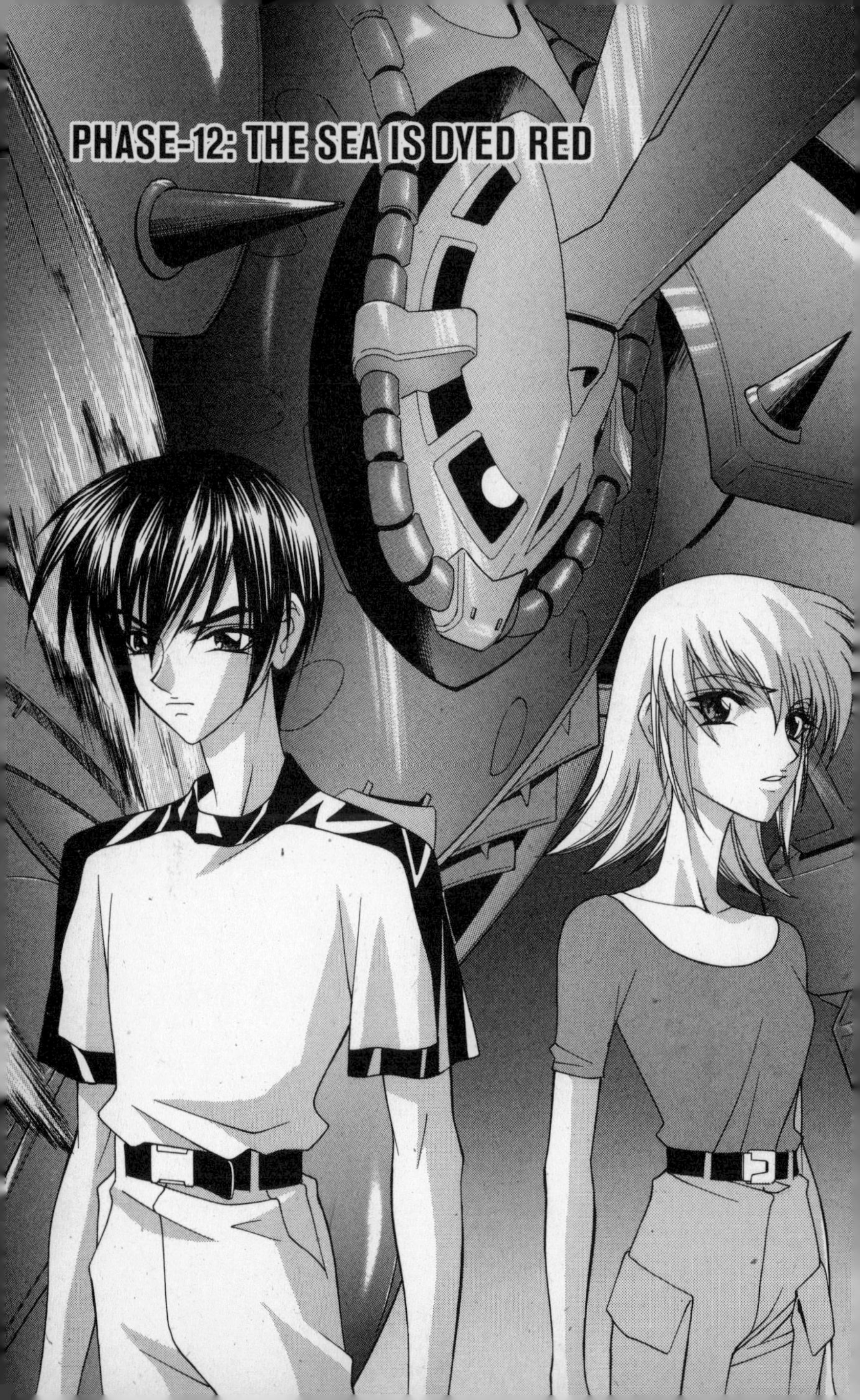
PHASE-12: THE SEA IS DYED RED

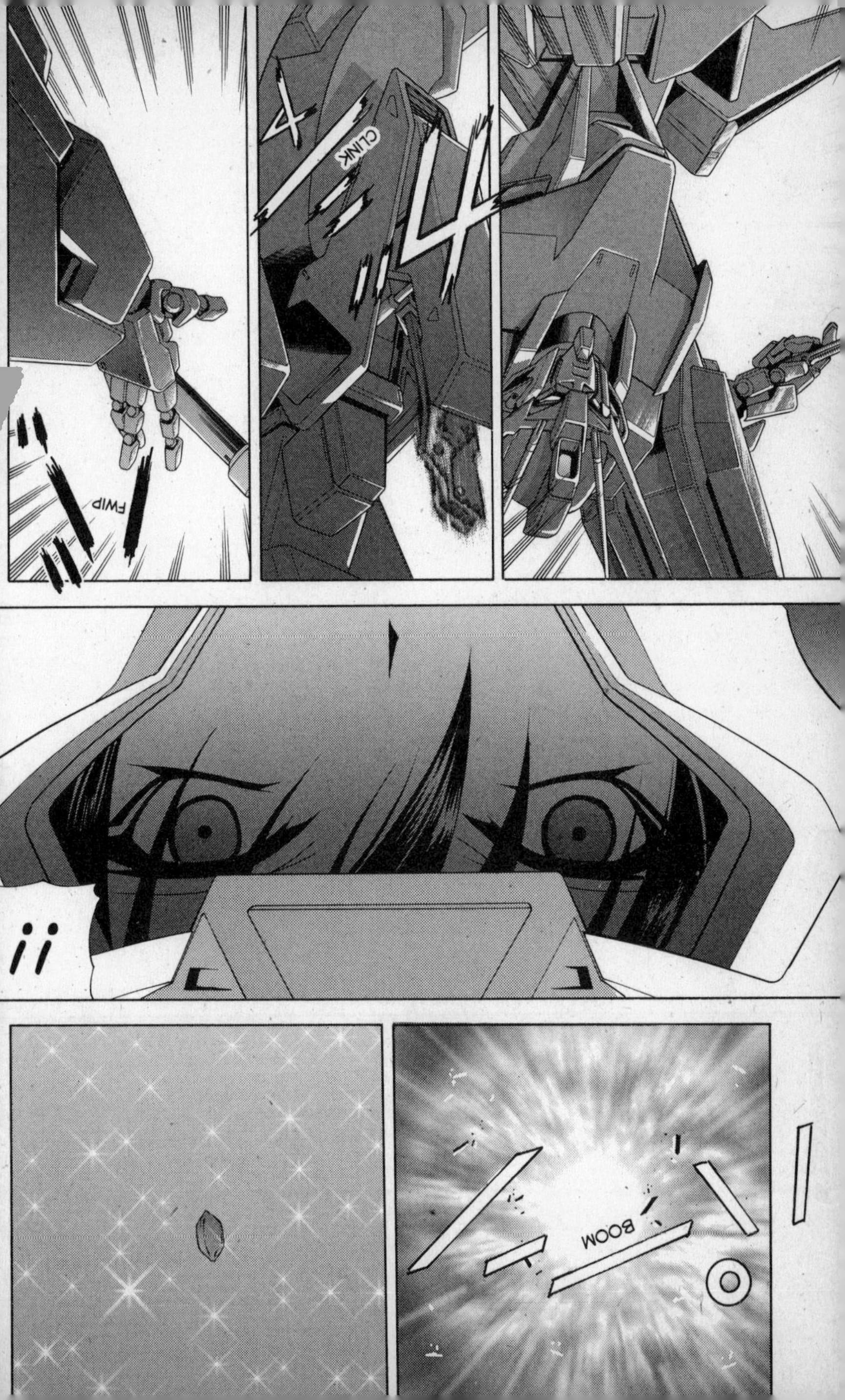
CLINK
FWIP
BOOM

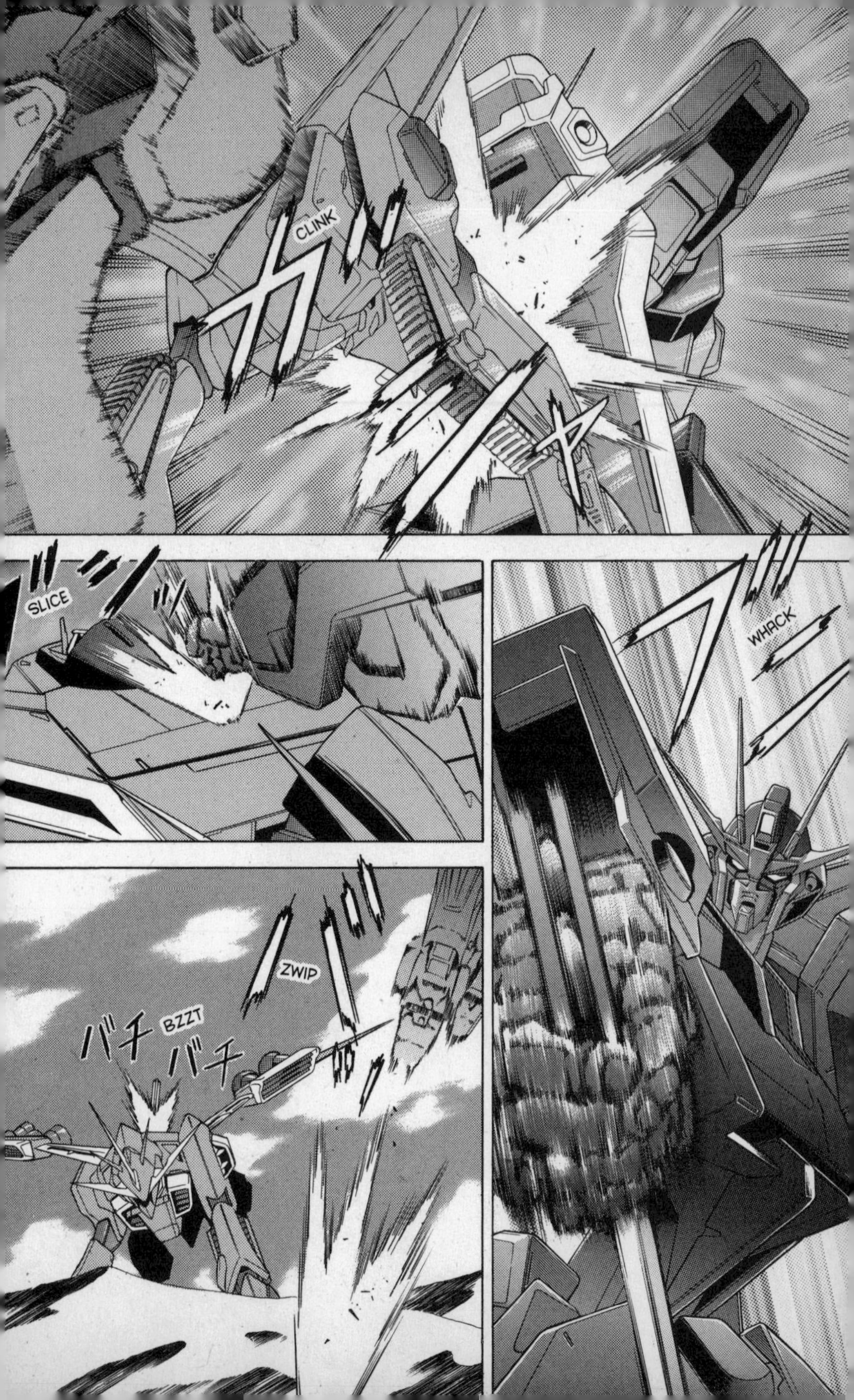
CLINK
WHACK
SLICE
ZWIP
バチ BZZT バチ

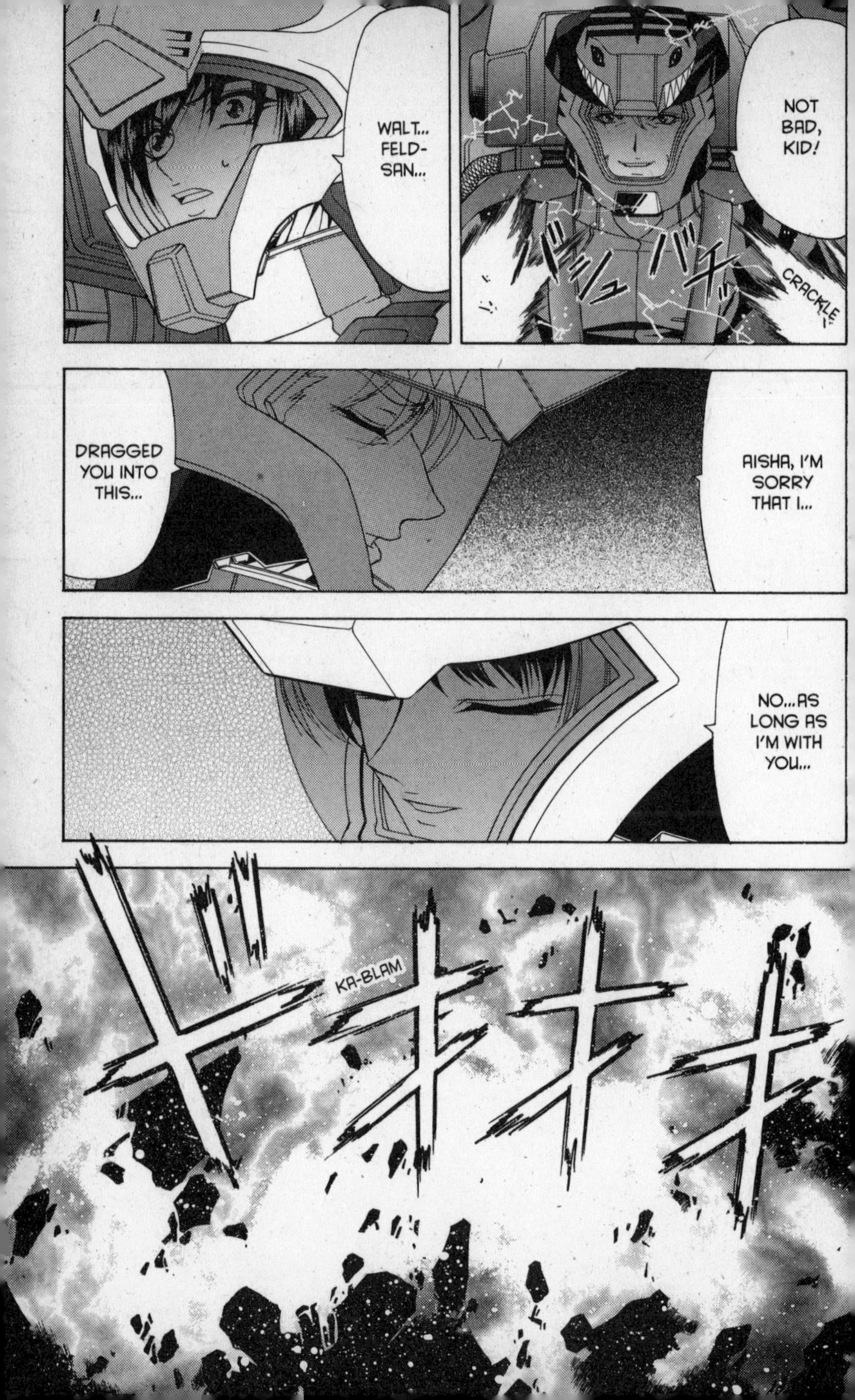
NOT BAD, KID!
CRACKLE
WALT... FELD-SAN...
AISHA, I'M SORRY THAT I...
DRAGGED YOU INTO THIS...
NO...AS LONG AS I'M WITH YOU...
KA-BLAM

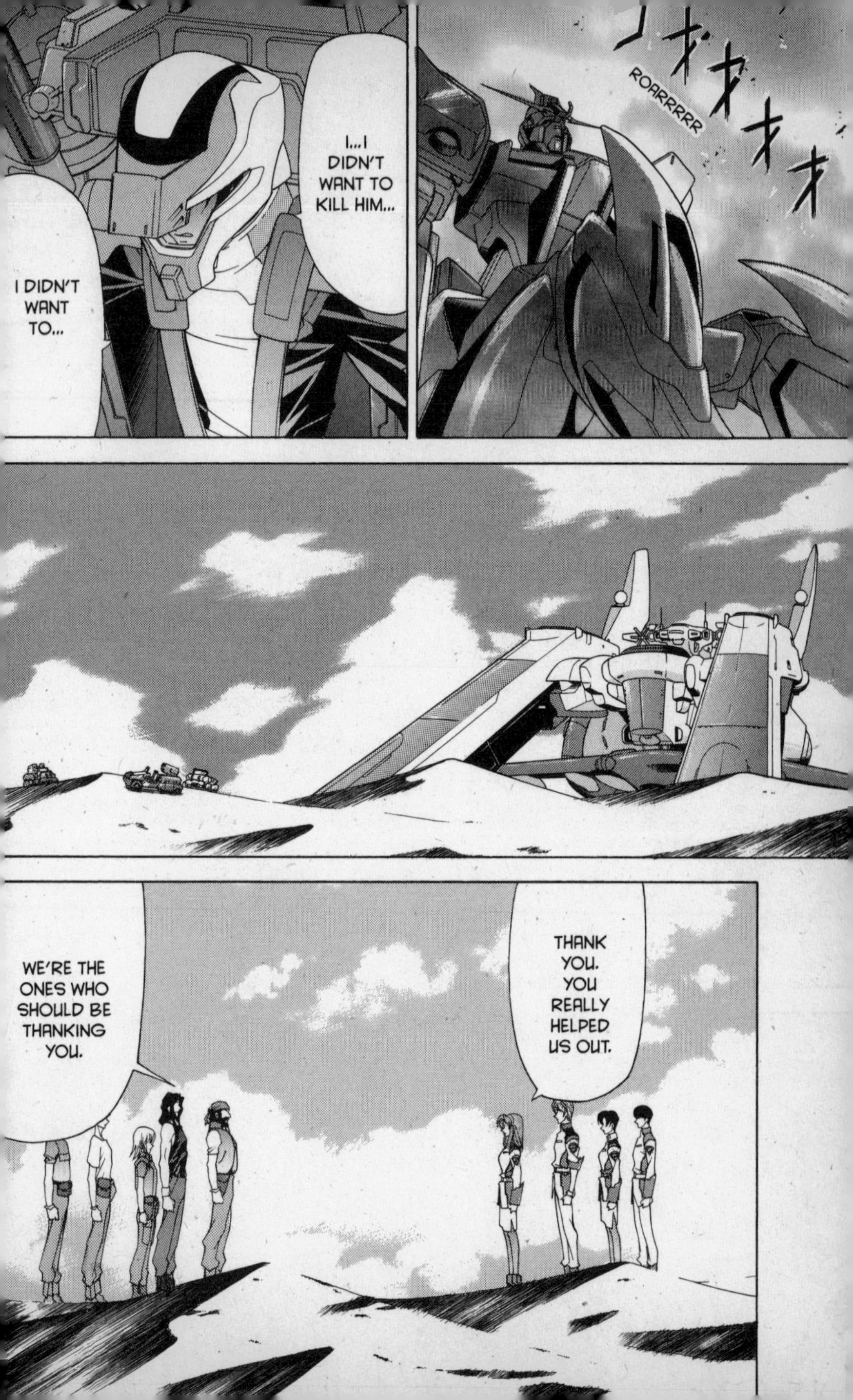
ROARRRRR
I...I DIDN'T WANT TO KILL HIM...
I DIDN'T WANT TO...
THANK YOU. YOU REALLY HELPED US OUT.
WE'RE THE ONES WHO SHOULD BE THANKING YOU.

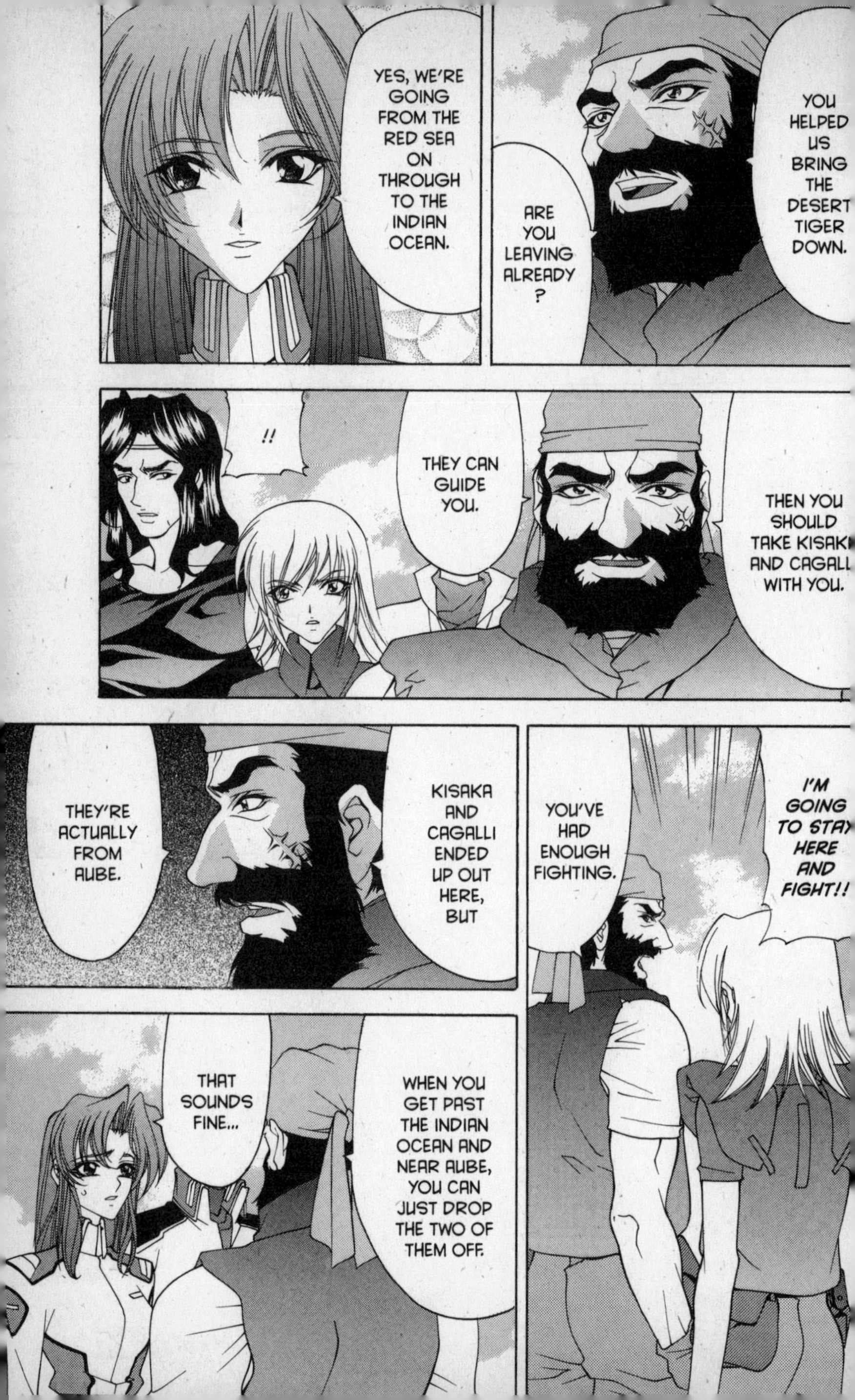
YOU HELPED US BRING THE DESERT TIGER DOWN.
ARE YOU LEAVING ALREADY ?
YES, WE'RE GOING FROM THE RED SEA ON THROUGH TO THE INDIAN OCEAN.
THEN YOU SHOULD TAKE KISAKI AND CAGALLI WITH YOU.
THEY CAN GUIDE YOU.
!!
I'M GOING TO STAY HERE AND FIGHT!!
YOU'VE HAD ENOUGH FIGHTING.
KISAKA AND CAGALLI ENDED UP OUT HERE, BUT
THEY'RE ACTUALLY FROM AUBE.
WHEN YOU GET PAST THE INDIAN OCEAN AND NEAR AUBE, YOU CAN JUST DROP THE TWO OF THEM OFF.
THAT SOUNDS FINE...

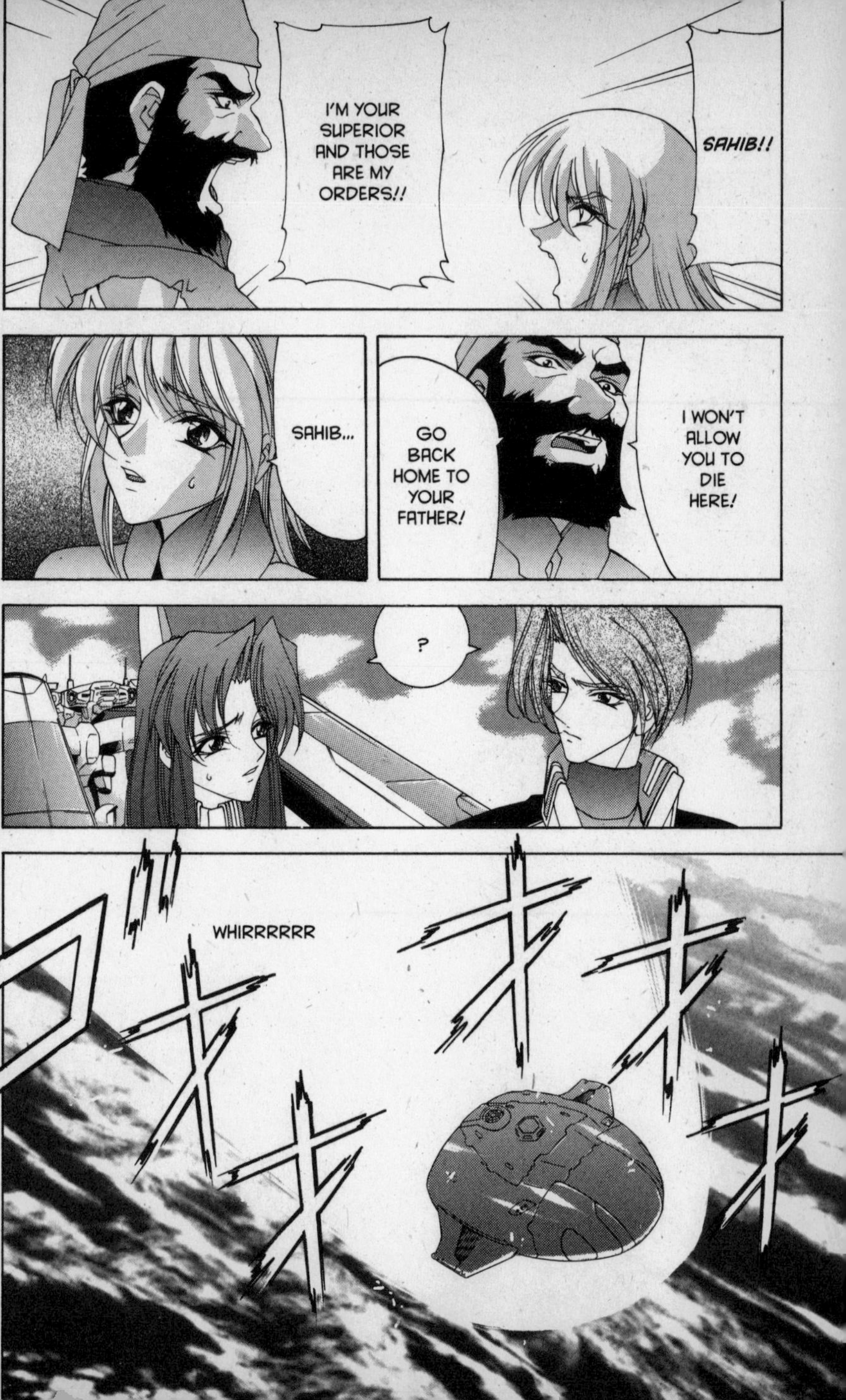
SAHIB!!
I'M YOUR SUPERIOR AND THOSE ARE MY ORDERS!!
I WON'T ALLOW YOU TO DIE HERE!
GO BACK HOME TO YOUR FATHER!
SAHIB...
?
WHIRRRRRR

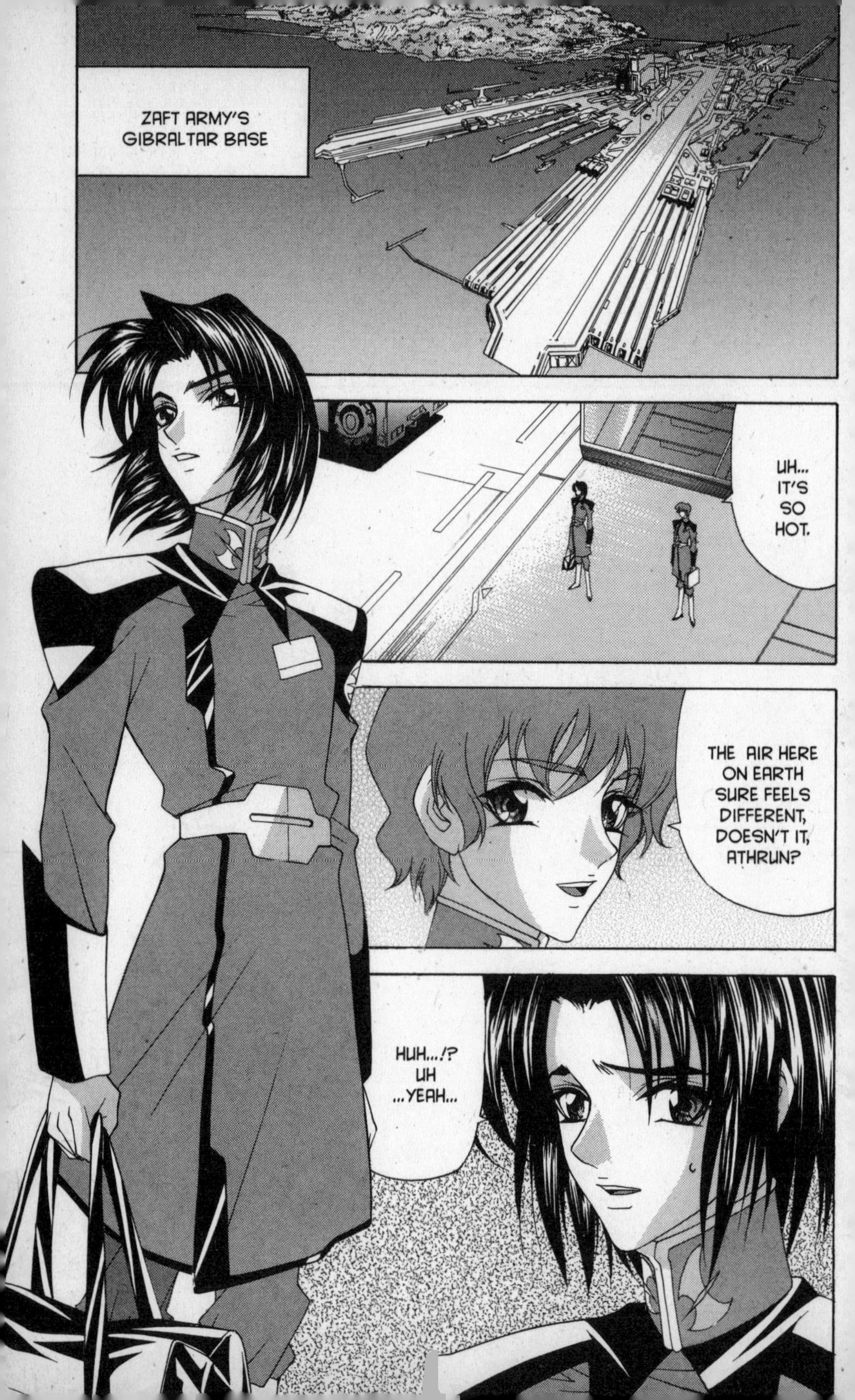
ZAFT ARMY'S GIBRALTAR BASE
UH... IT'S SO HOT.
THE AIR HERE ON EARTH SURE FEELS DIFFERENT, DOESN'T IT, ATHRUN?
HUH...!? UH ...YEAH...

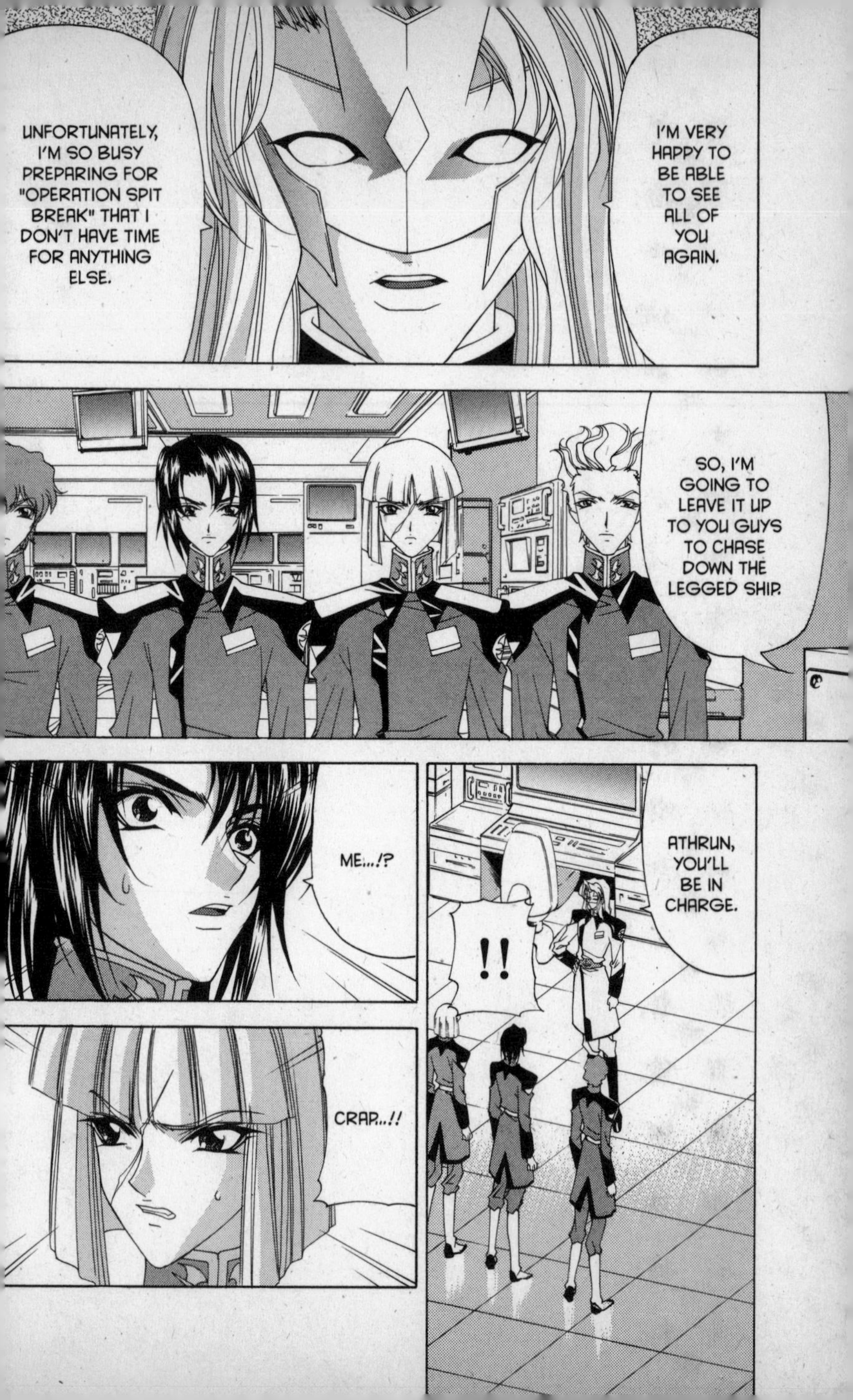
I'M VERY HAPPY TO BE ABLE TO SEE ALL OF YOU AGAIN.
UNFORTUNATELY, I'M SO BUSY PREPARING FOR "OPERATION SPIT BREAK" THAT I DON'T HAVE TIME FOR ANYTHING ELSE.
SO, I'M GOING TO LEAVE IT UP TO YOU GUYS TO CHASE DOWN THE LEGGED SHIP.
ATHRUN, YOU'LL BE IN CHARGE.
!!
ME...!?
CRAP...!!

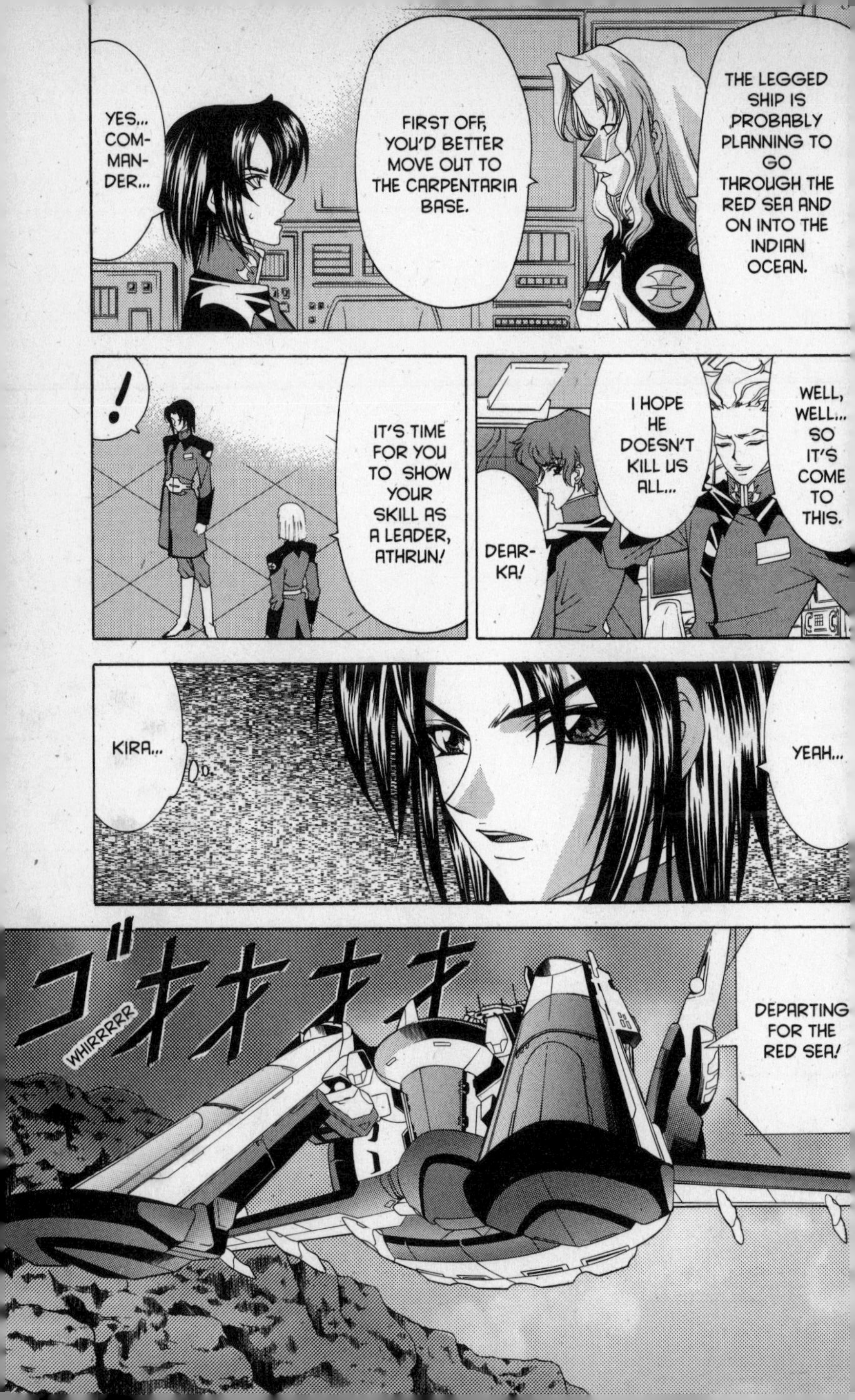
THE LEGGED SHIP IS PROBABLY PLANNING TO GO THROUGH THE RED SEA AND ON INTO THE INDIAN OCEAN.
FIRST OFF, YOU'D BETTER MOVE OUT TO THE CARPENTARIA BASE.
YES... COM-MAN-DER...
WELL, WELL... SO IT'S COME TO THIS.
I HOPE HE DOESN'T KILL US ALL...
DEAR-KA!
IT'S TIME FOR YOU TO SHOW YOUR SKILL AS A LEADER, ATHRUN!
!
YEAH...
KIRA...
DEPARTING FOR THE RED SEA!
ゴオオオ
WHIRRRRR

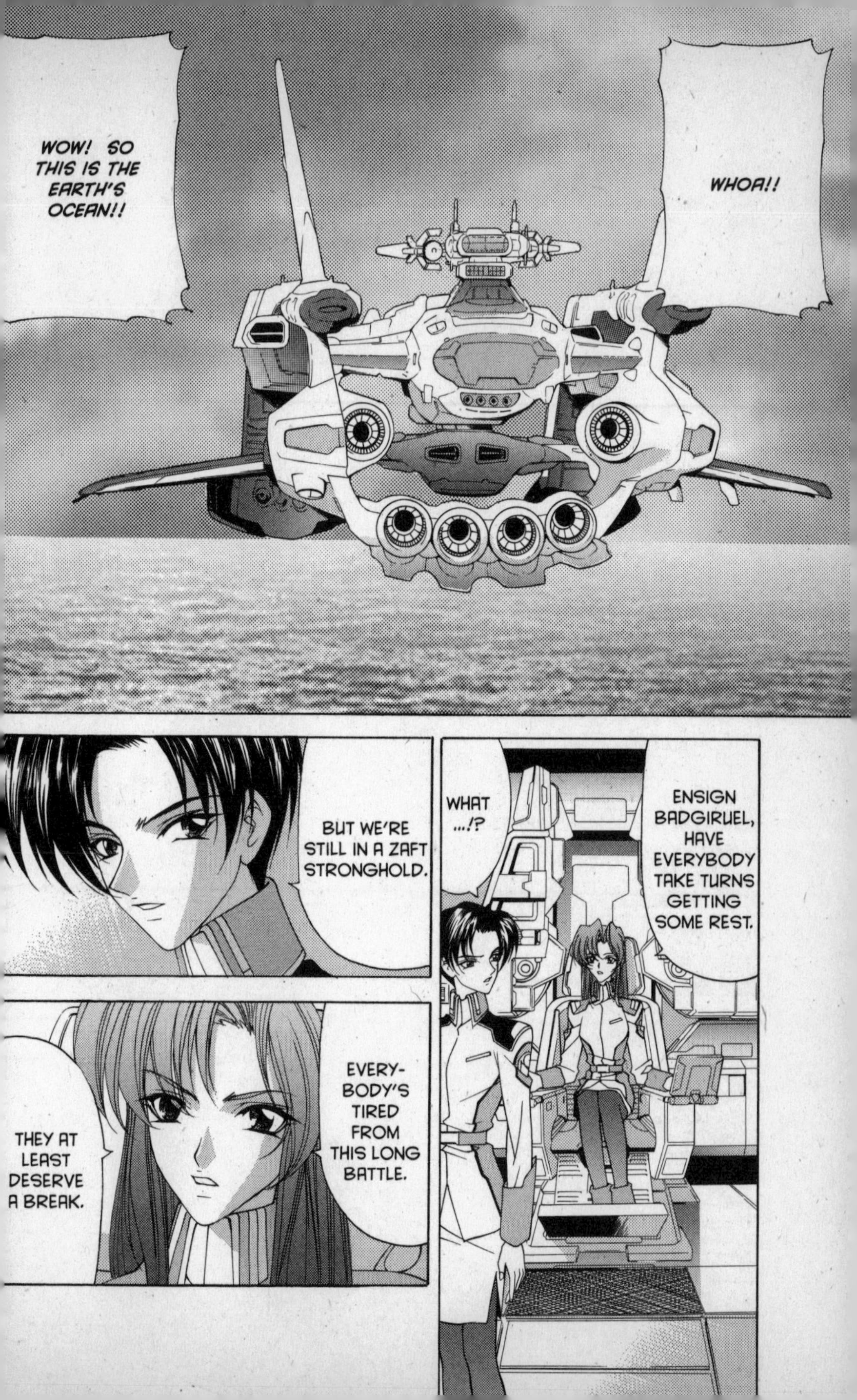
WHOA!!
WOW! SO THIS IS THE EARTH'S OCEAN!!
ENSIGN BADGIRUEL, HAVE EVERYBODY TAKE TURNS GETTING SOME REST.
WHAT ...!?
BUT WE'RE STILL IN A ZAFT STRONGHOLD.
EVERY-BODY'S TIRED FROM THIS LONG BATTLE.
THEY AT LEAST DESERVE A BREAK.

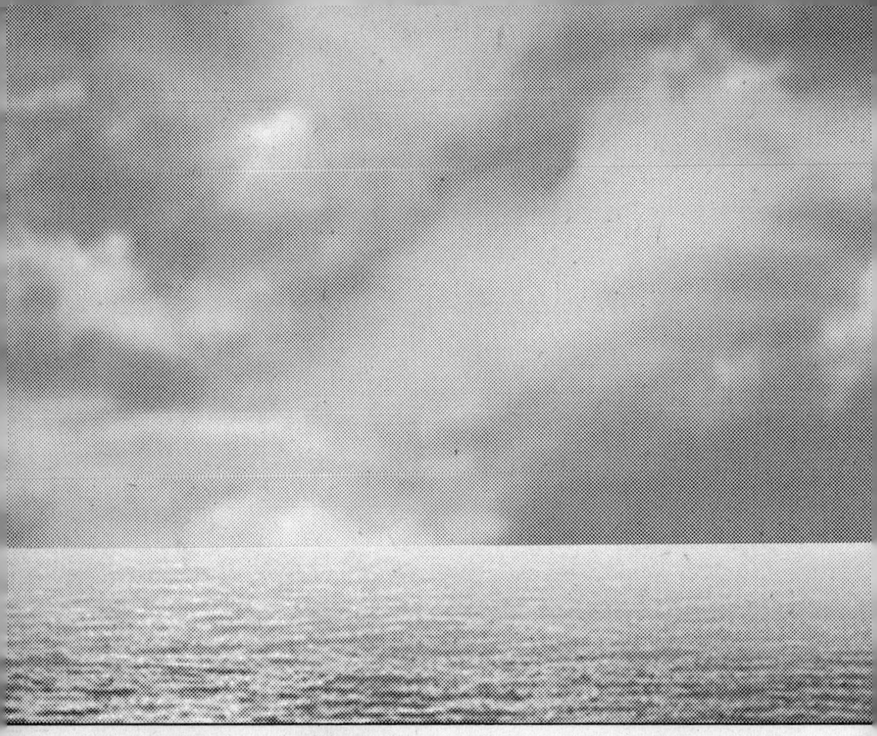

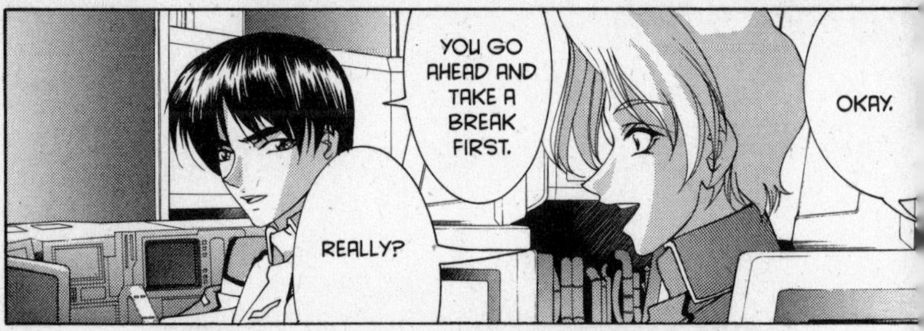
OKAY.
YOU GO AHEAD AND TAKE A BREAK FIRST.
REALLY?

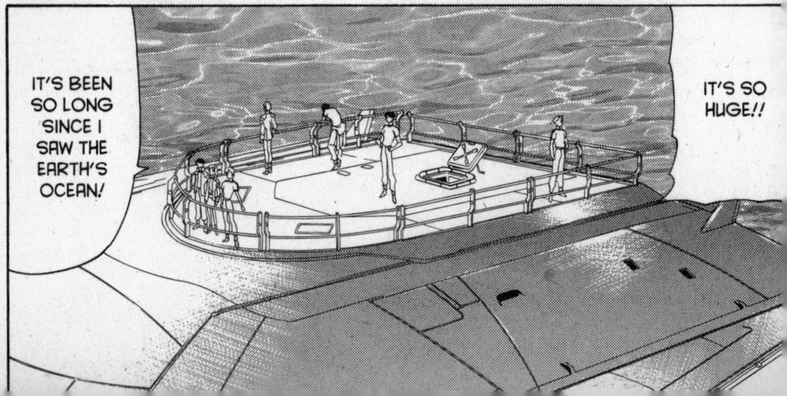
IT'S SO HUGE!!
IT'S BEEN SO LONG SINCE I SAW THE EARTH'S OCEAN!

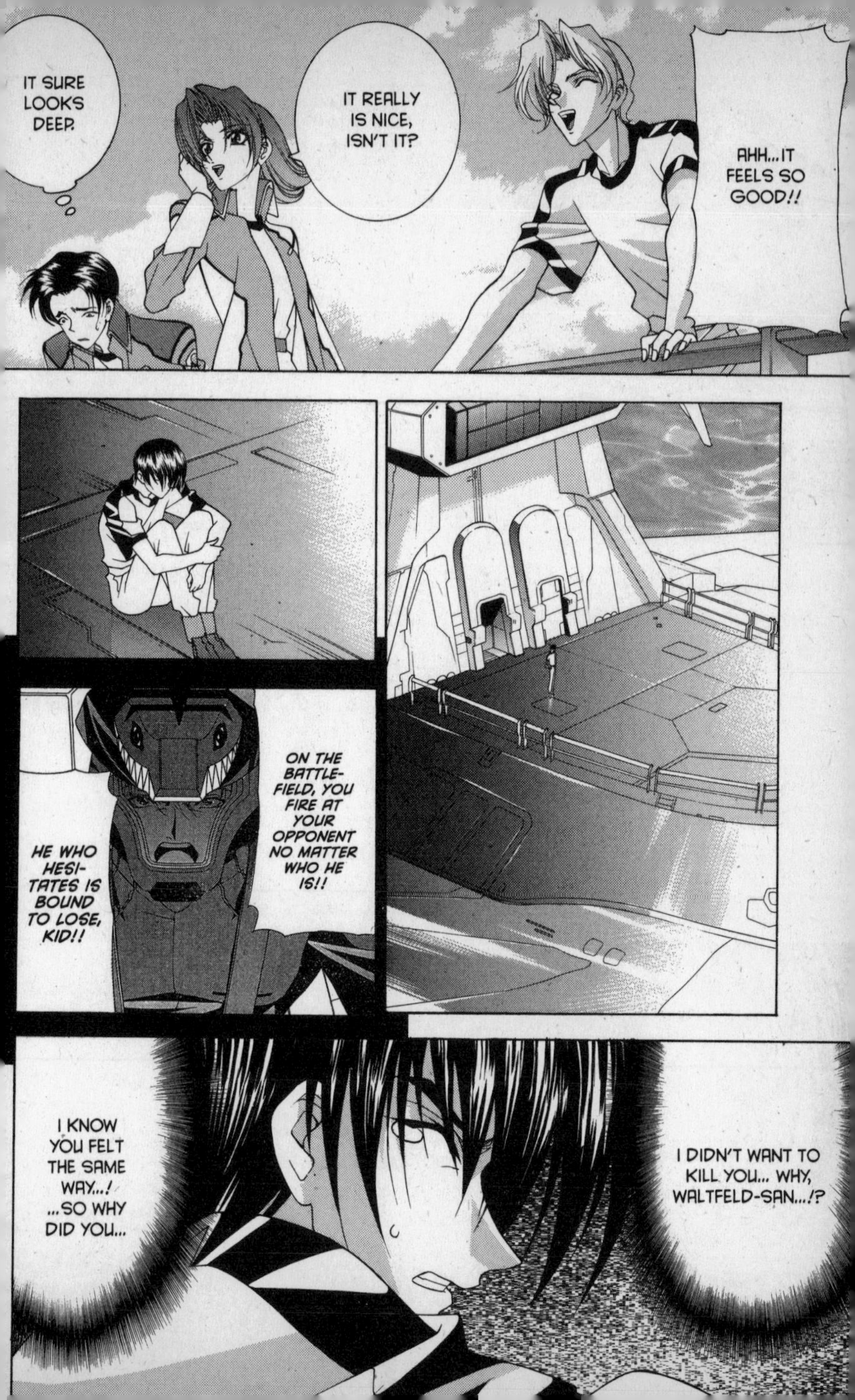
AHH...IT FEELS SO GOOD!!
IT REALLY IS NICE, ISN'T IT?
IT SURE LOOKS DEEP.
ON THE BATTLE-FIELD, YOU FIRE AT YOUR OPPONENT NO MATTER WHO HE IS!!
HE WHO HESI-TATES IS BOUND TO LOSE, KID!!
I DIDN'T WANT TO KILL YOU... WHY, WALTFELD-SAN...!?
I KNOW YOU FELT THE SAME WAY...! ...SO WHY DID YOU...

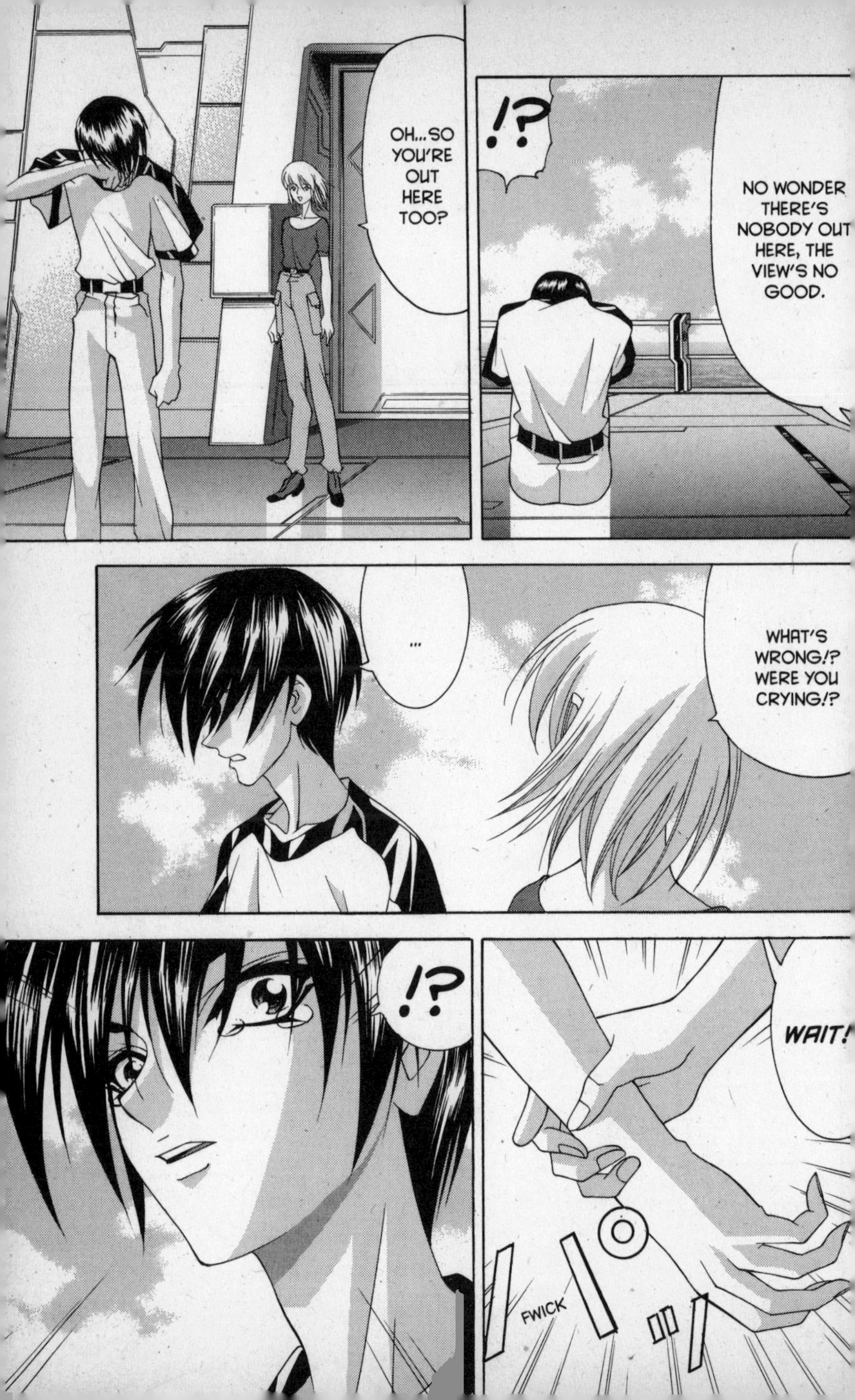
NO WONDER THERE'S NOBODY OUT HERE, THE VIEW'S NO GOOD.
!?
OH...SO YOU'RE OUT HERE TOO?
WHAT'S WRONG!? WERE YOU CRYING!?
...
WAIT!
FWICK
!?

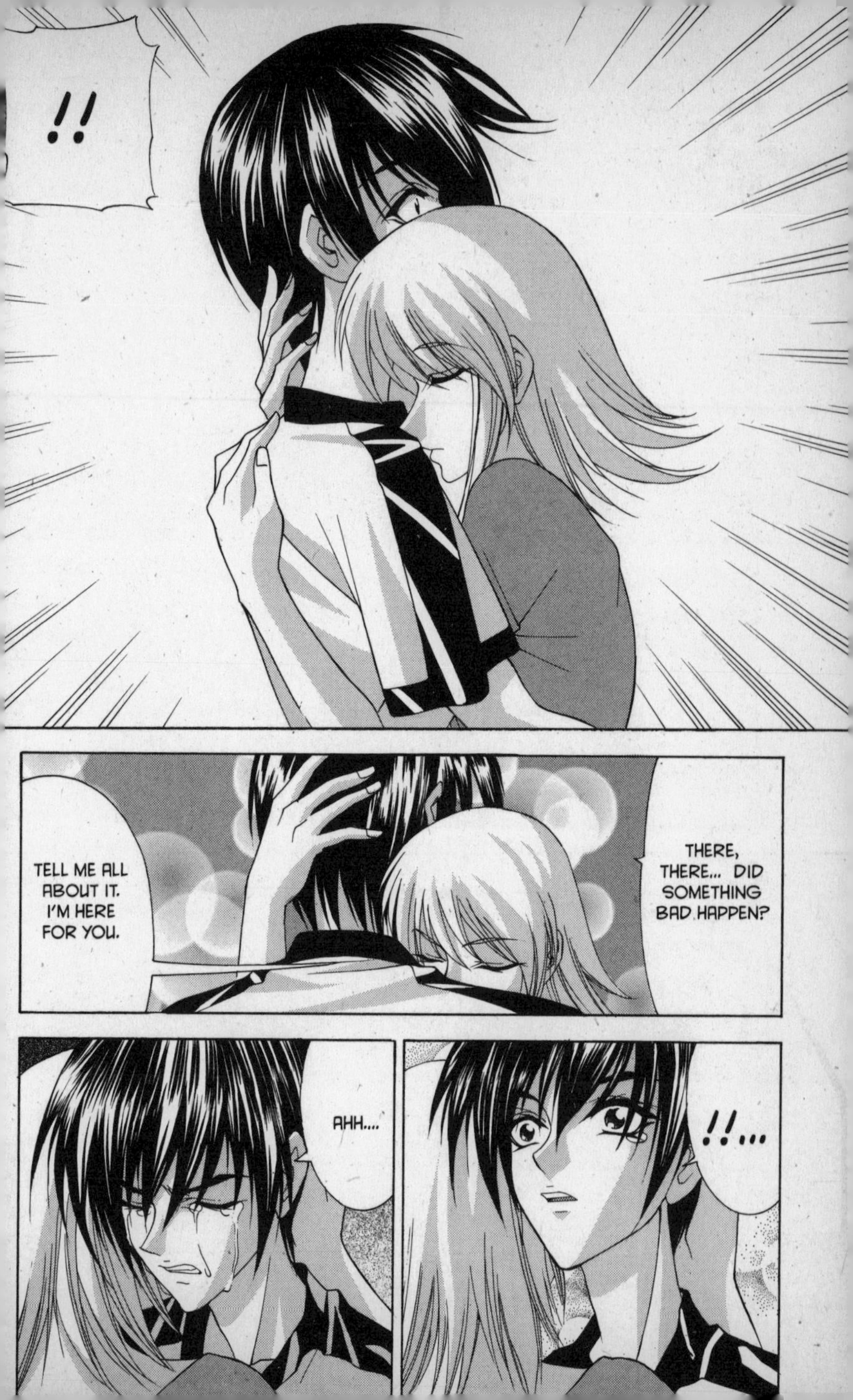
!!
THERE, THERE... DID SOMETHING BAD HAPPEN?
TELL ME ALL ABOUT IT. I'M HERE FOR YOU.
!!...
AHH....

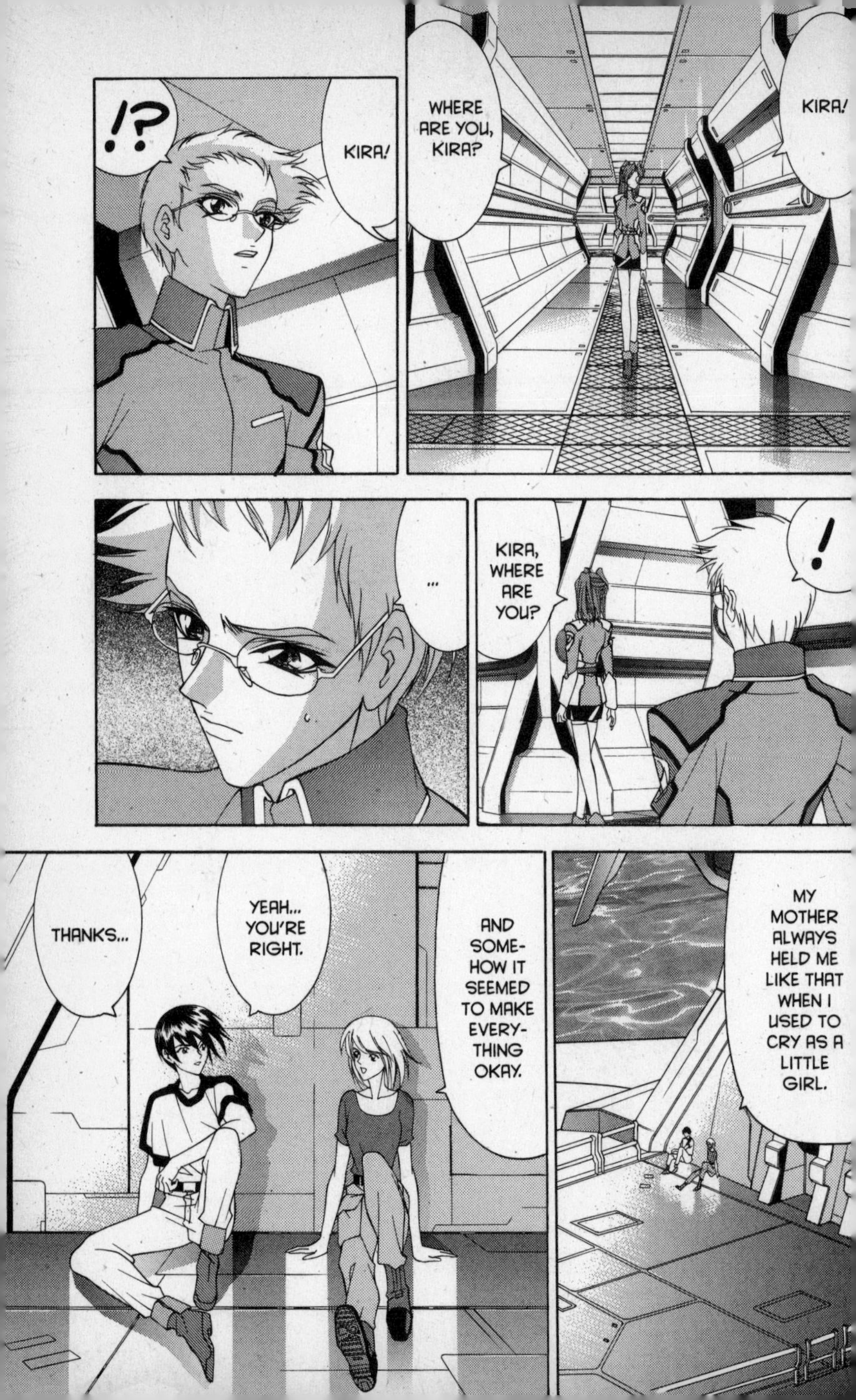
KIRA!
WHERE ARE YOU, KIRA?
KIRA!
!?
!
KIRA, WHERE ARE YOU?
...
MY MOTHER ALWAYS HELD ME LIKE THAT WHEN I USED TO CRY AS A LITTLE GIRL.
AND SOME-HOW IT SEEMED TO MAKE EVERY-THING OKAY.
YEAH... YOU'RE RIGHT.
THANKS...

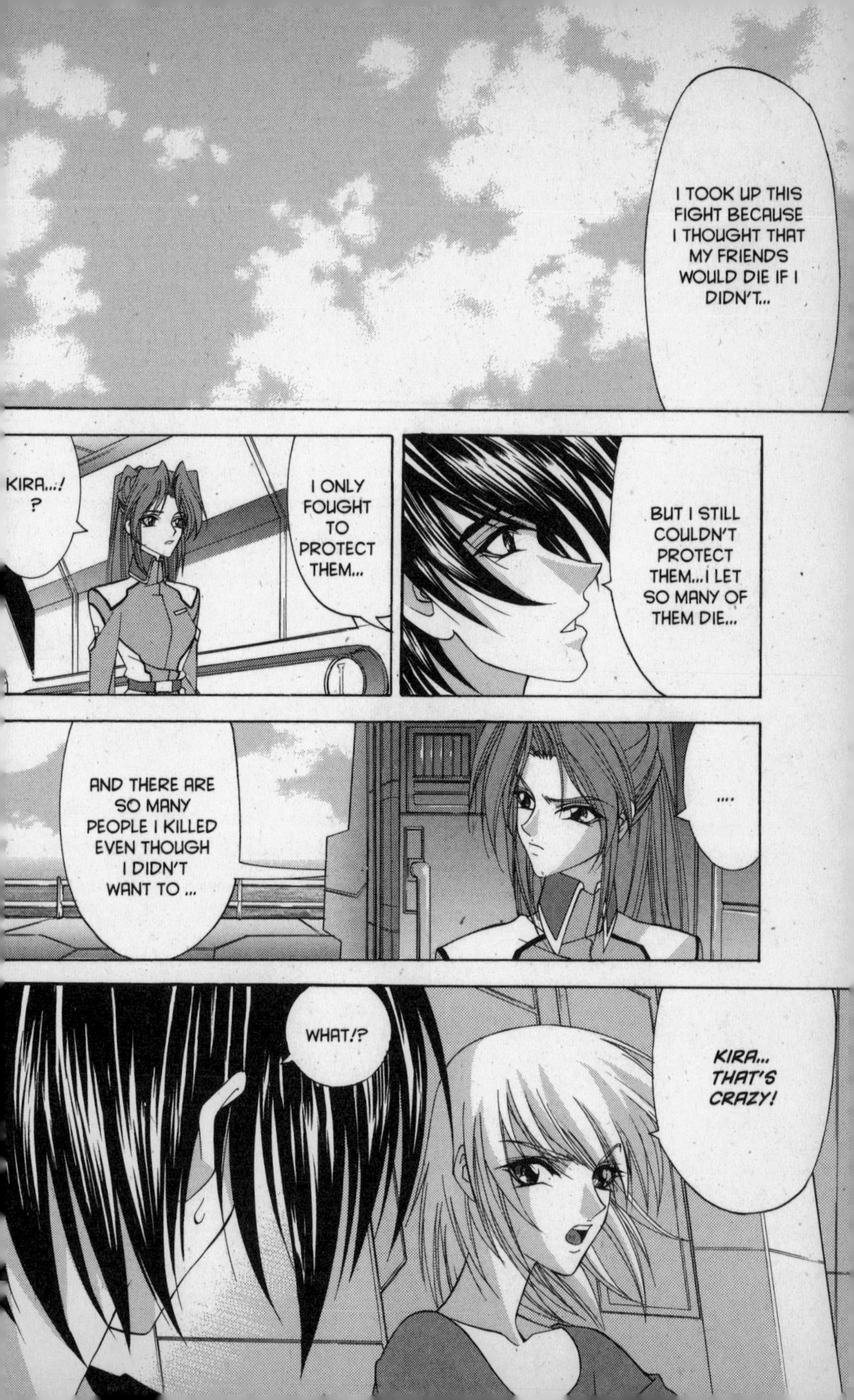
I TOOK UP THIS FIGHT BECAUSE I THOUGHT THAT MY FRIENDS WOULD DIE IF I DIDN'T...
BUT I STILL COULDN'T PROTECT THEM...I LET SO MANY OF THEM DIE...
I ONLY FOUGHT TO PROTECT THEM...
KIRA...!?
....
AND THERE ARE SO MANY PEOPLE I KILLED EVEN THOUGH I DIDN'T WANT TO ...
KIRA... THAT'S CRAZY!
WHAT!?

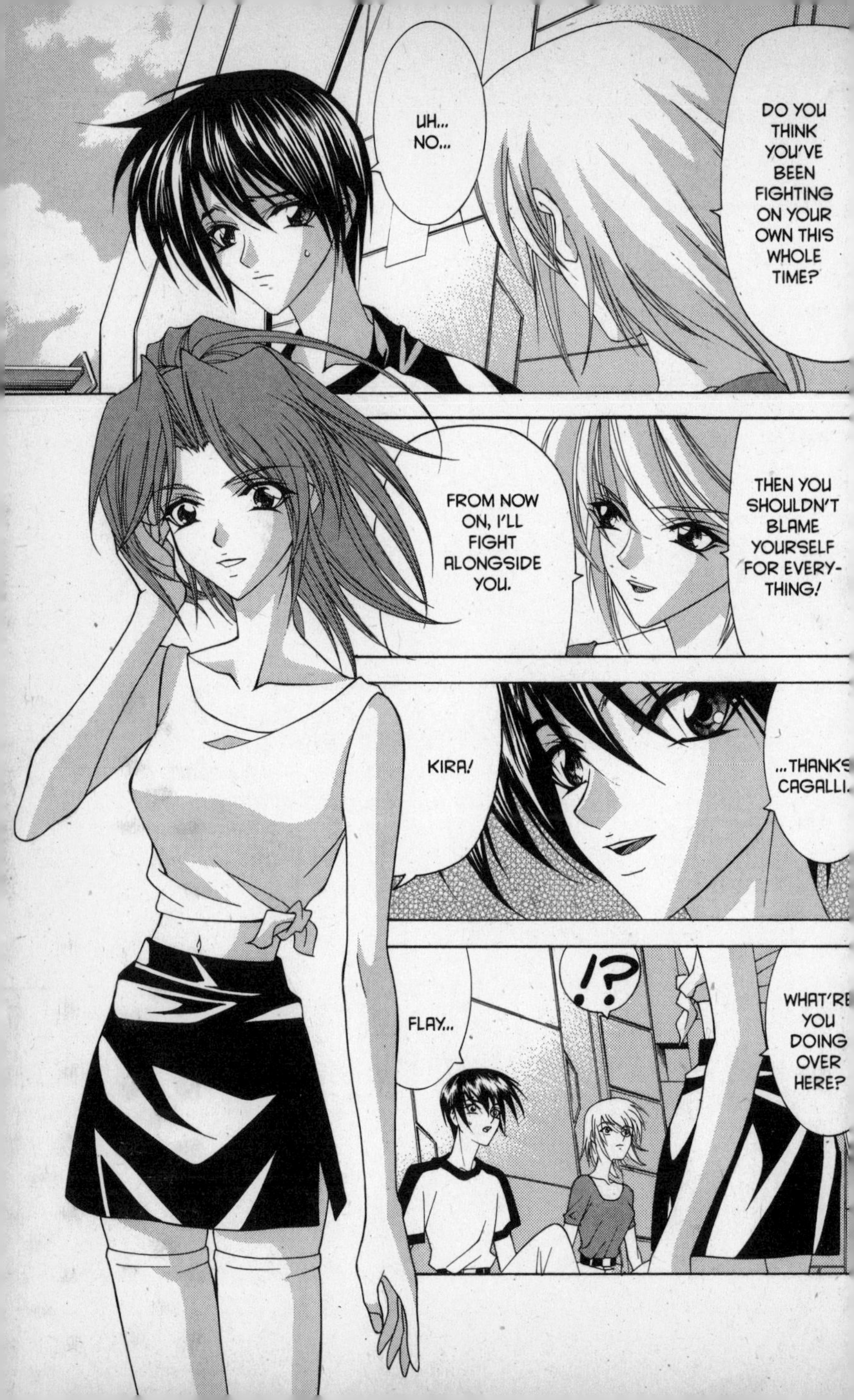
DO YOU THINK YOU'VE BEEN FIGHTING ON YOUR OWN THIS WHOLE TIME?
UH... NO...
THEN YOU SHOULDN'T BLAME YOURSELF FOR EVERY-THING!
FROM NOW ON, I'LL FIGHT ALONGSIDE YOU.
...THANKS CAGALLI.
KIRA!
WHAT'RE YOU DOING OVER HERE?
!?
FLAY...

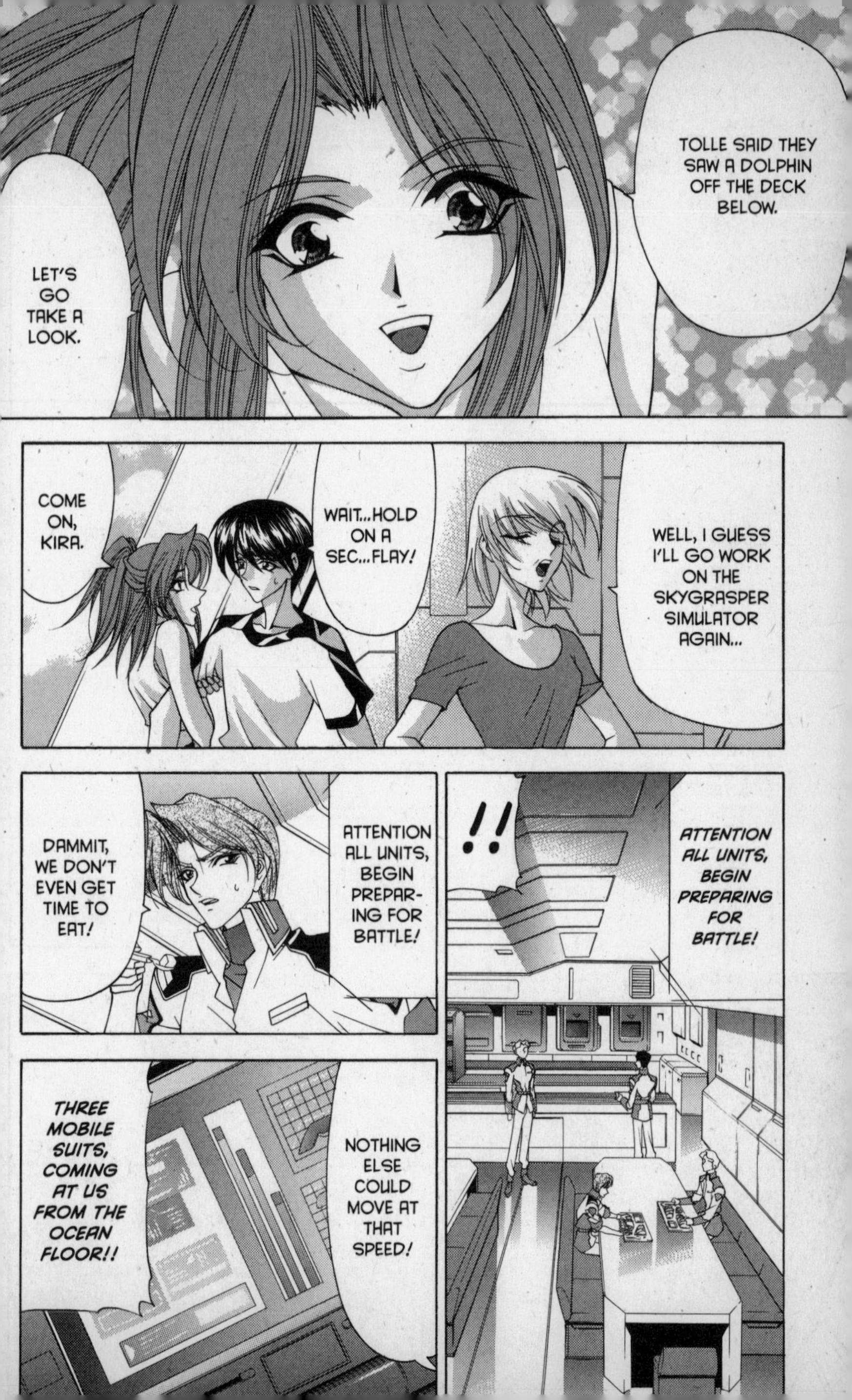
TOLLE SAID THEY SAW A DOLPHIN OFF THE DECK BELOW.
LET'S GO TAKE A LOOK.
WELL, I GUESS I'LL GO WORK ON THE SKYGRASPER SIMULATOR AGAIN...
WAIT...HOLD ON A SEC...FLAY!
COME ON, KIRA.
ATTENTION ALL UNITS, BEGIN PREPARING FOR BATTLE!
!!
ATTENTION ALL UNITS, BEGIN PREPAR-ING FOR BATTLE!
DAMMIT, WE DON'T EVEN GET TIME TO EAT!
NOTHING ELSE COULD MOVE AT THAT SPEED!
THREE MOBILE SUITS, COMING AT US FROM THE OCEAN FLOOR!!

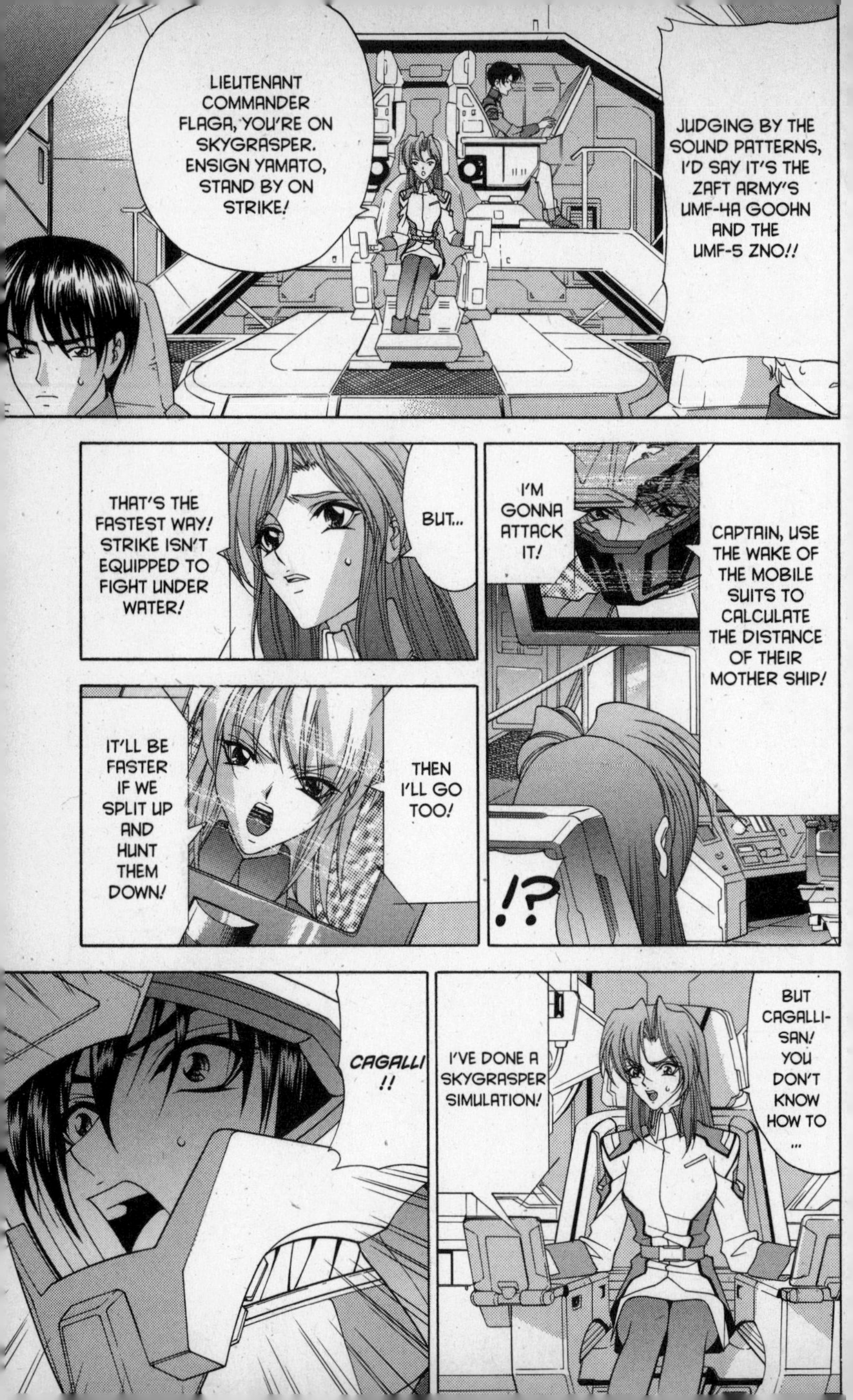
JUDGING BY THE SOUND PATTERNS, I'D SAY IT'S THE ZAFT ARMY'S UMF-4A GOOHN AND THE UMF-5 ZNO!!
LIEUTENANT COMMANDER FLAGA, YOU'RE ON SKYGRASPER. ENSIGN YAMATO, STAND BY ON STRIKE!
CAPTAIN, USE THE WAKE OF THE MOBILE SUITS TO CALCULATE THE DISTANCE OF THEIR MOTHER SHIP!
I'M GONNA ATTACK IT!
!?
BUT...
THAT'S THE FASTEST WAY! STRIKE ISN'T EQUIPPED TO FIGHT UNDER WATER!
THEN I'LL GO TOO!
IT'LL BE FASTER IF WE SPLIT UP AND HUNT THEM DOWN!
BUT CAGALLI-SAN! YOU DON'T KNOW HOW TO ...
I'VE DONE A SKYGRASPER SIMULATION!
CAGALLI !!

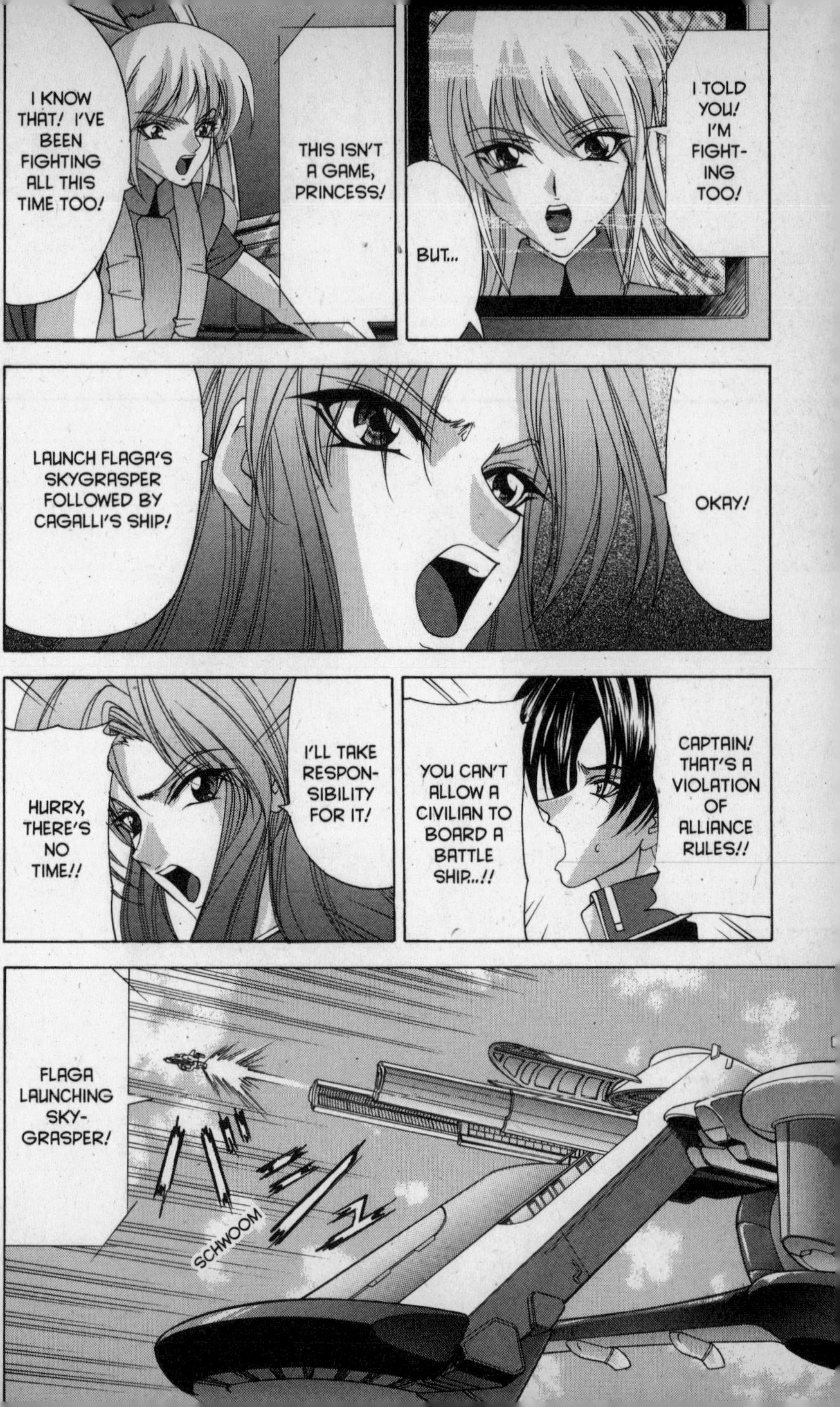
I TOLD YOU! I'M FIGHT-ING TOO!
BUT...
THIS ISN'T A GAME, PRINCESS!
I KNOW THAT! I'VE BEEN FIGHTING ALL THIS TIME TOO!
OKAY!
LAUNCH FLAGA'S SKYGRASPER FOLLOWED BY CAGALLI'S SHIP!
CAPTAIN! THAT'S A VIOLATION OF ALLIANCE RULES!!
YOU CAN'T ALLOW A CIVILIAN TO BOARD A BATTLE SHIP...!!
I'LL TAKE RESPON-SIBILITY FOR IT!
HURRY, THERE'S NO TIME!!
FLAGA LAUNCHING SKY-GRASPER!
SCHWOOM

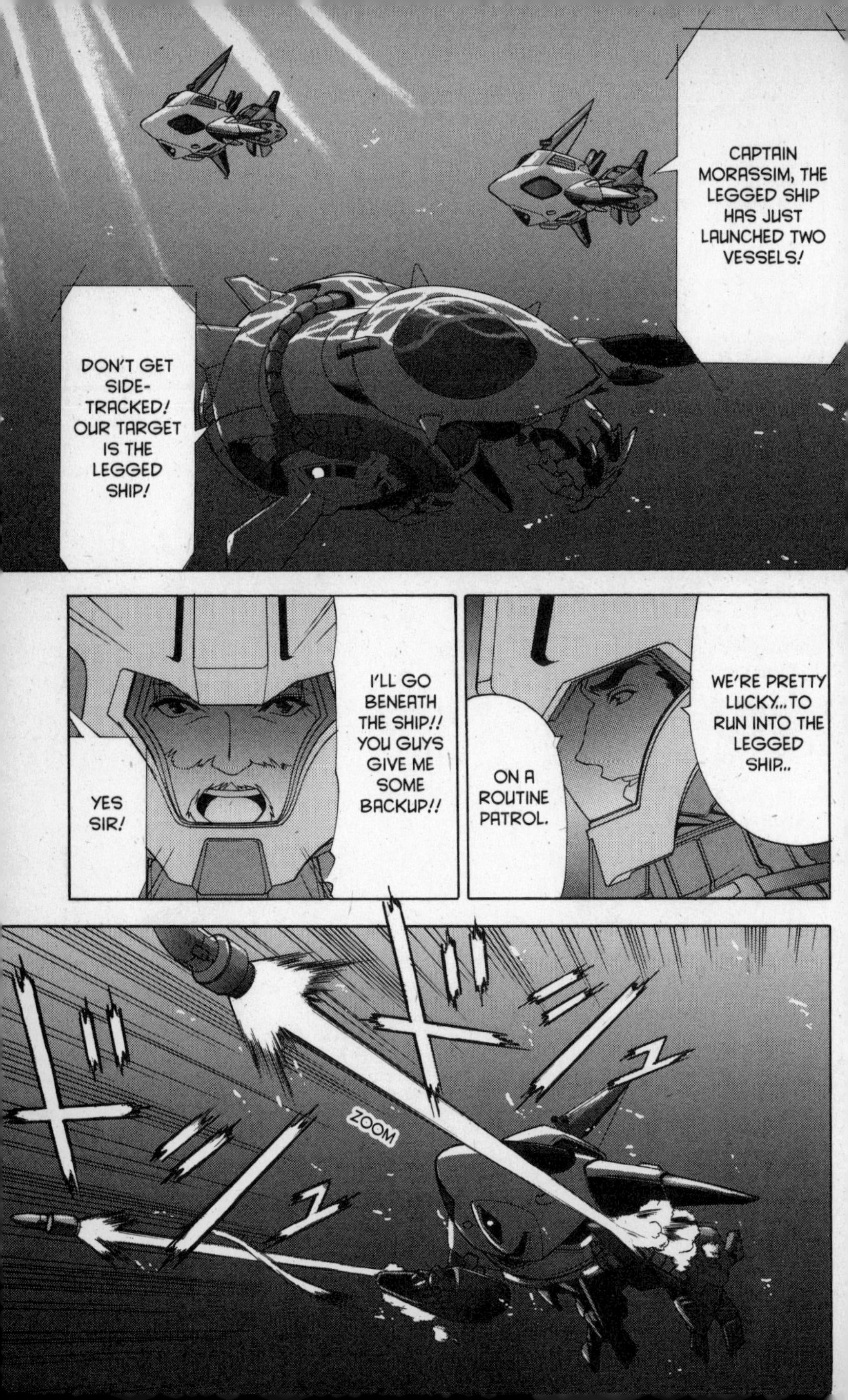
CAPTAIN MORASSIM, THE LEGGED SHIP HAS JUST LAUNCHED TWO VESSELS!
DON'T GET SIDE-TRACKED! OUR TARGET IS THE LEGGED SHIP!
WE'RE PRETTY LUCKY...TO RUN INTO THE LEGGED SHIP...
ON A ROUTINE PATROL.
I'LL GO BENEATH THE SHIP!! YOU GUYS GIVE ME SOME BACKUP!!
YES SIR!
ZOOM

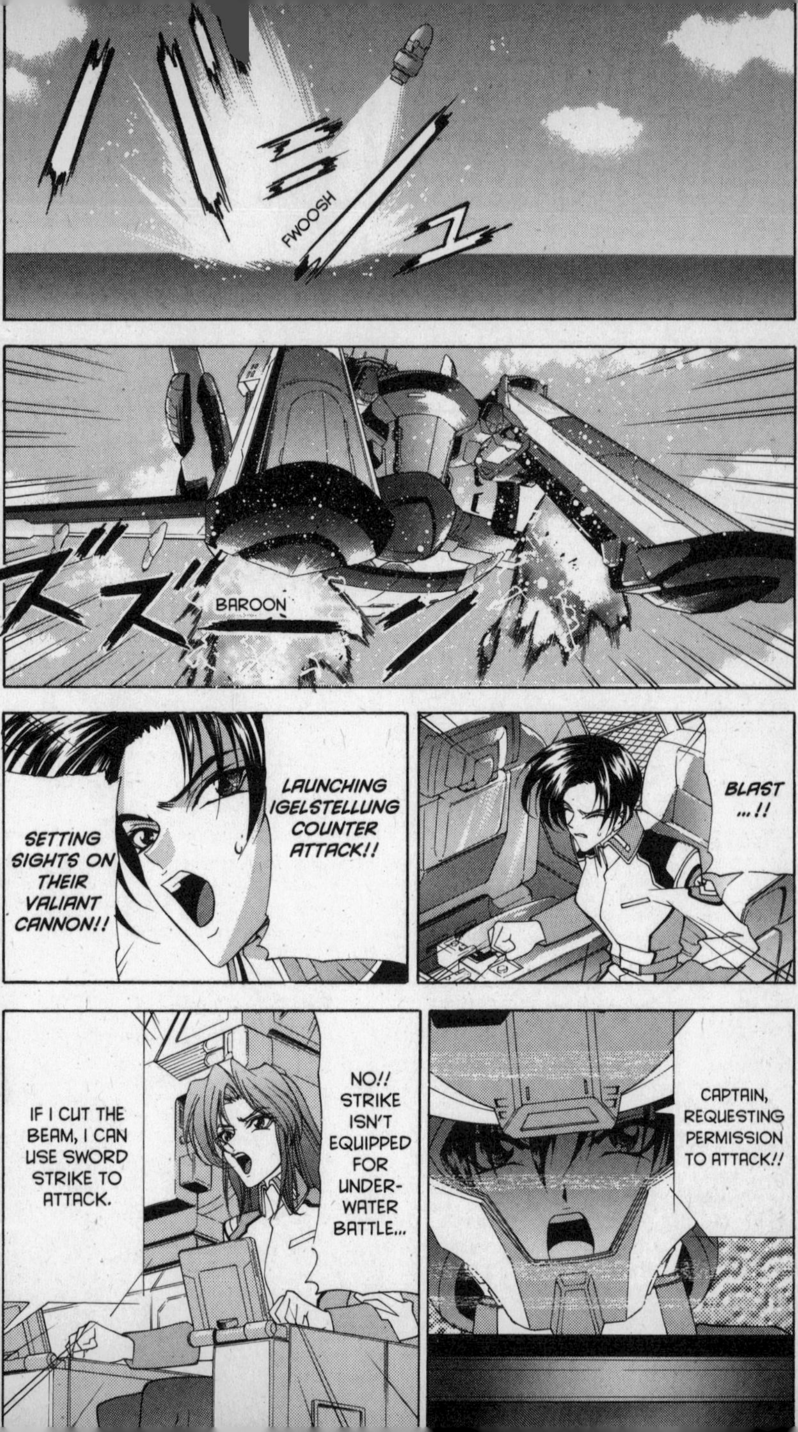
FWOOSH
BAROON
BLAST ...!!
LAUNCHING IGELSTELLUNG COUNTER ATTACK!!
SETTING SIGHTS ON THEIR VALIANT CANNON!!
CAPTAIN, REQUESTING PERMISSION TO ATTACK!!
NO!! STRIKE ISN'T EQUIPPED FOR UNDER-WATER BATTLE...
IF I CUT THE BEAM, I CAN USE SWORD STRIKE TO ATTACK.

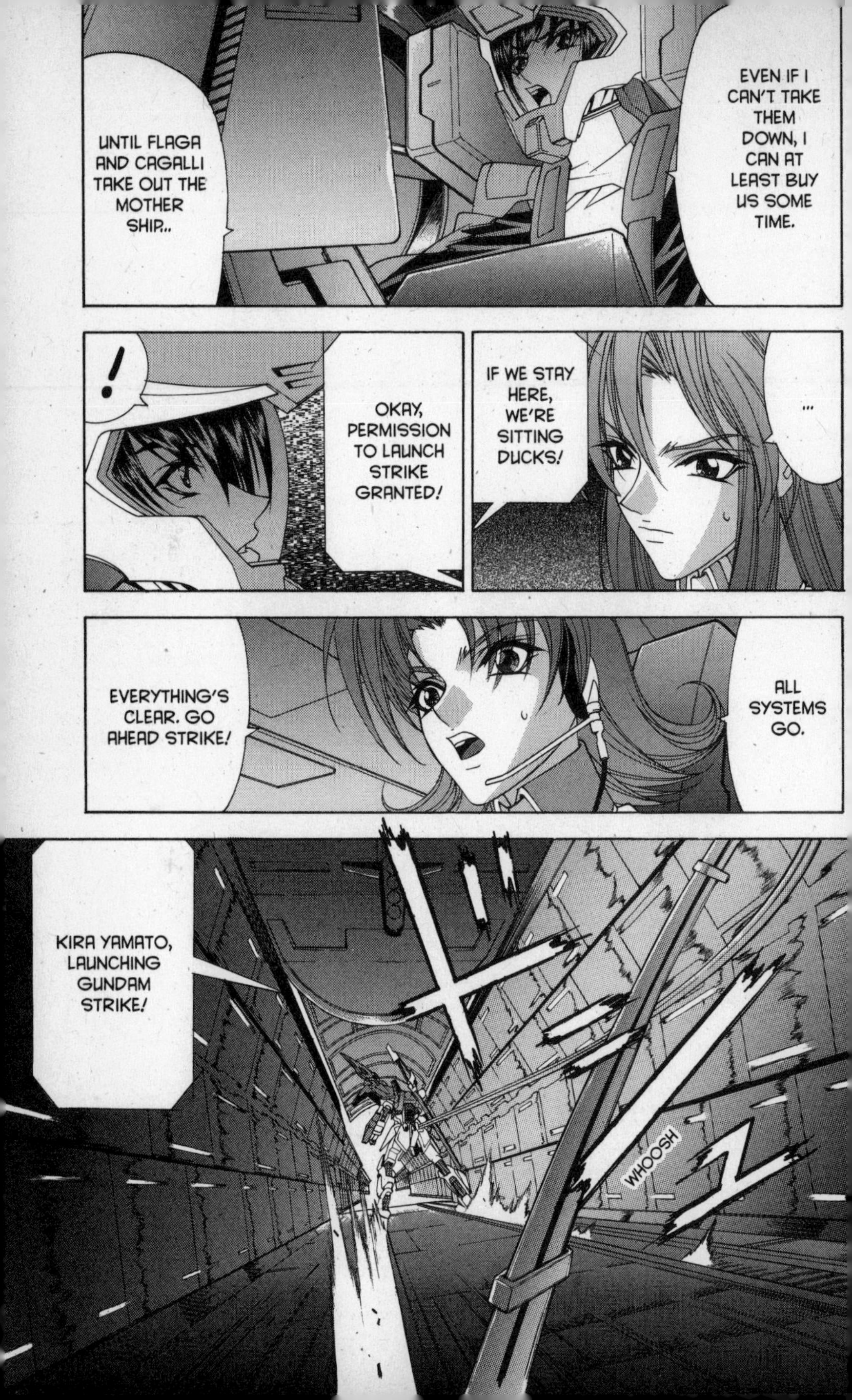
EVEN IF I CAN'T TAKE THEM DOWN, I CAN AT LEAST BUY US SOME TIME.
UNTIL FLAGA AND CAGALLI TAKE OUT THE MOTHER SHIP...
...
IF WE STAY HERE, WE'RE SITTING DUCKS!
OKAY, PERMISSION TO LAUNCH STRIKE GRANTED!
!
ALL SYSTEMS GO.
EVERYTHING'S CLEAR. GO AHEAD STRIKE!
WHOOSH
KIRA YAMATO, LAUNCHING GUNDAM STRIKE!

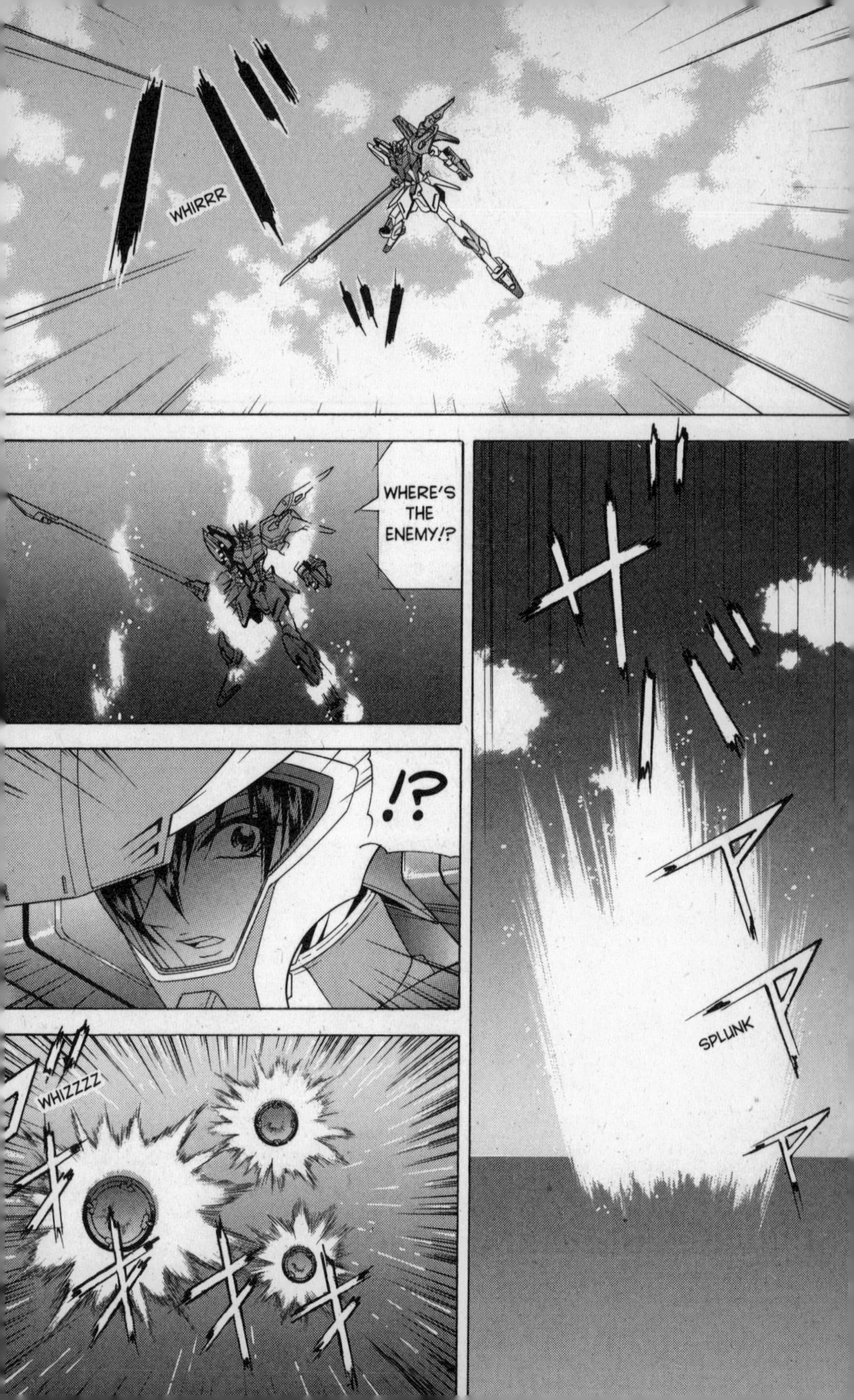
WHIRRR
SPLUNK
WHERE'S THE ENEMY!?
!?
WHIZZZZ

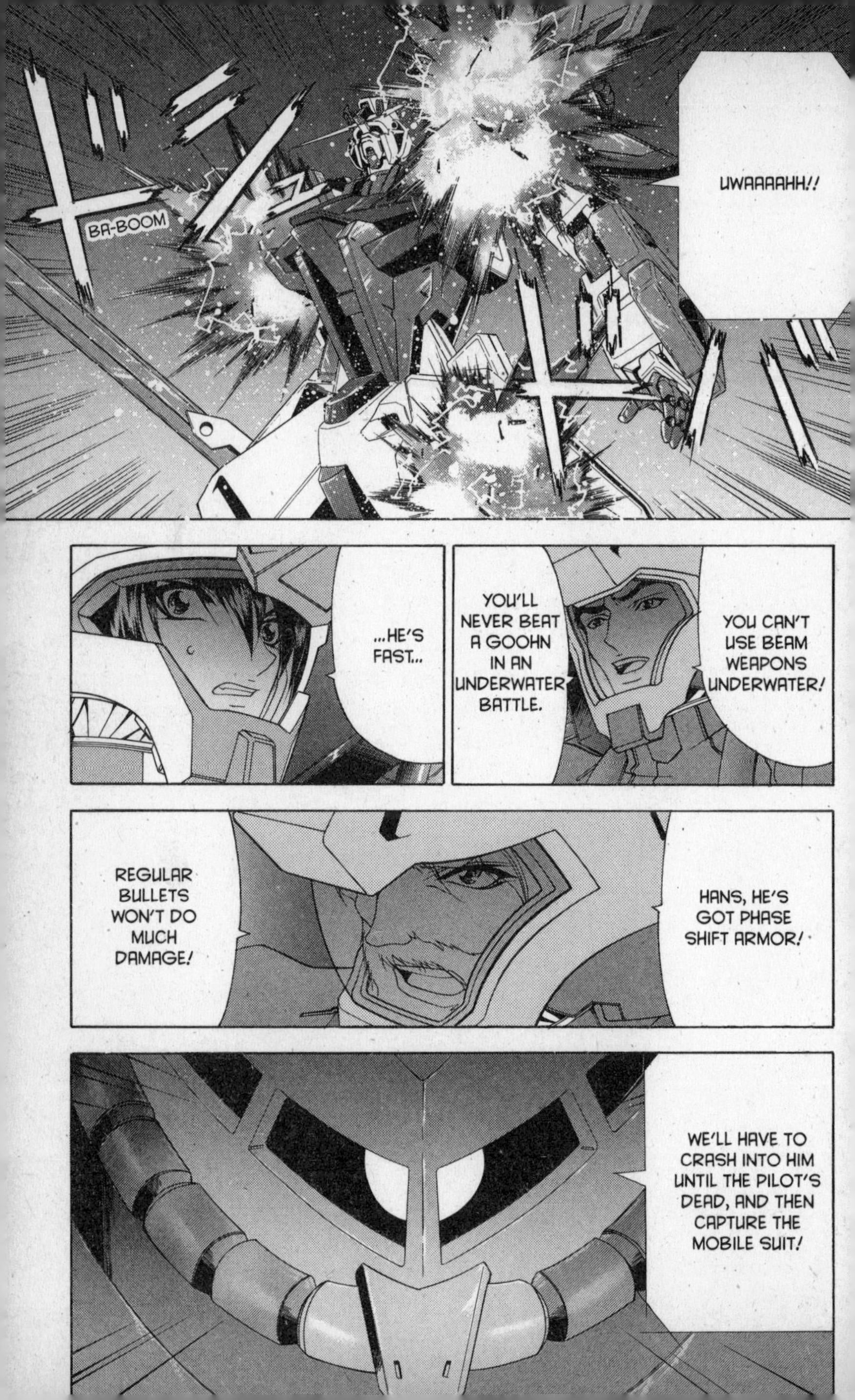
UWAAAAHH!!
BA-BOOM
YOU CAN'T USE BEAM WEAPONS UNDERWATER!
YOU'LL NEVER BEAT A GOOHN IN AN UNDERWATER BATTLE.
...HE'S FAST...
HANS, HE'S GOT PHASE SHIFT ARMOR!
REGULAR BULLETS WON'T DO MUCH DAMAGE!
WE'LL HAVE TO CRASH INTO HIM UNTIL THE PILOT'S DEAD, AND THEN CAPTURE THE MOBILE SUIT!

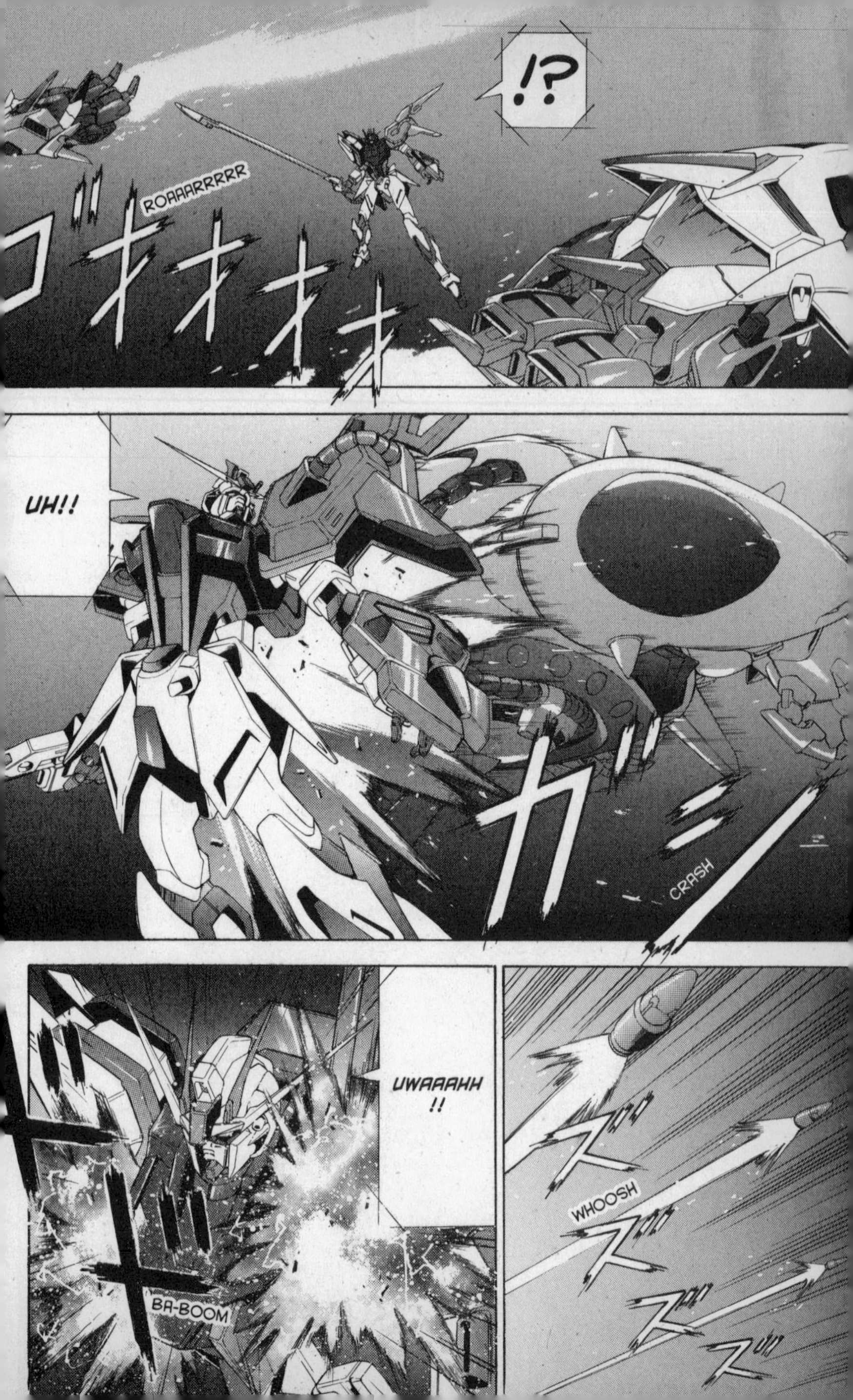
!?
ROAAARRRR
UH!!
CRASH
WHOOSH
UWAAAHH !!
BA-BOOM

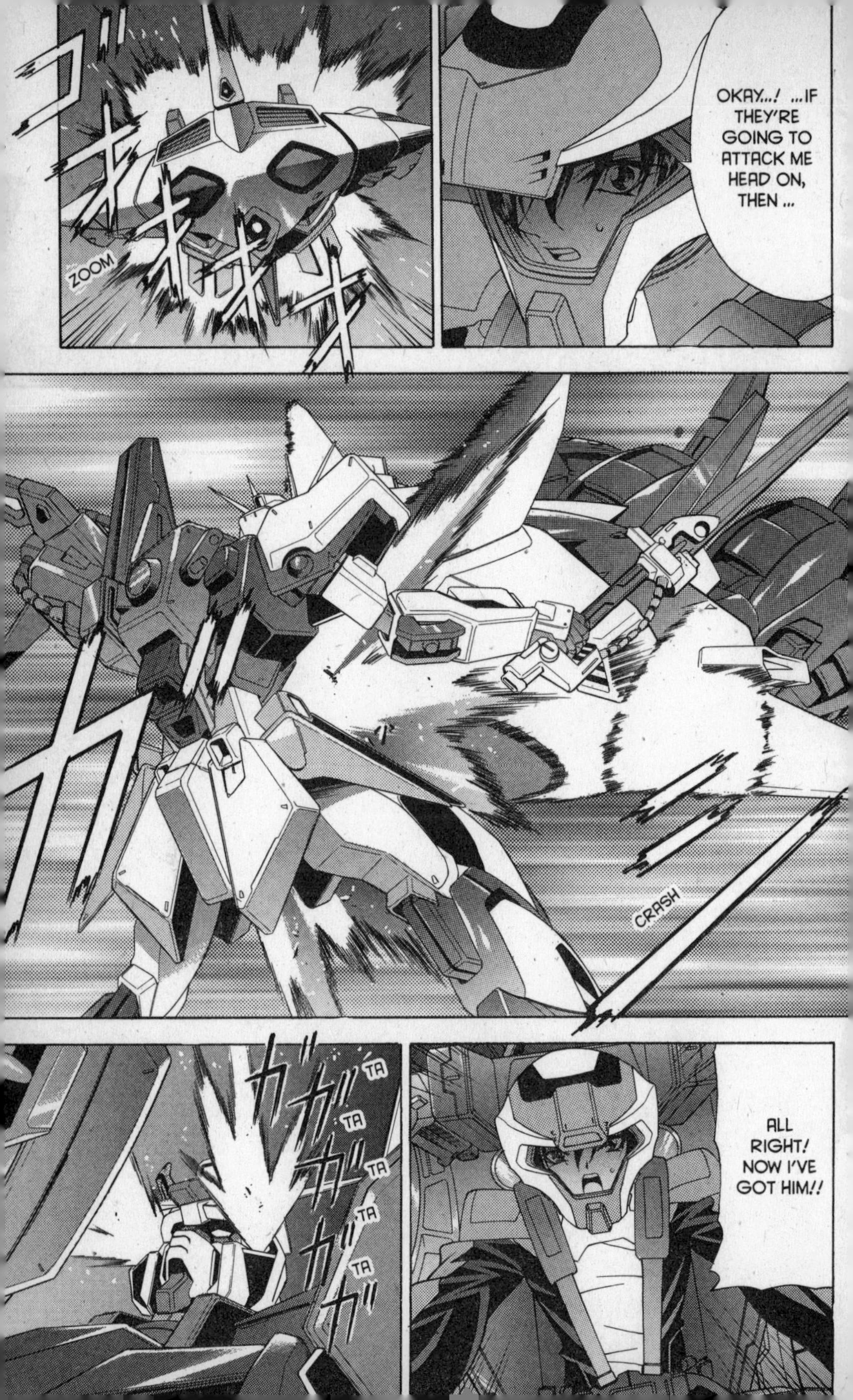
OKAY...! ...IF THEY'RE GOING TO ATTACK ME HEAD ON, THEN ...
ZOOM
CRASH
ALL RIGHT! NOW I'VE GOT HIM!!
TA
TA
TA
TA
TA

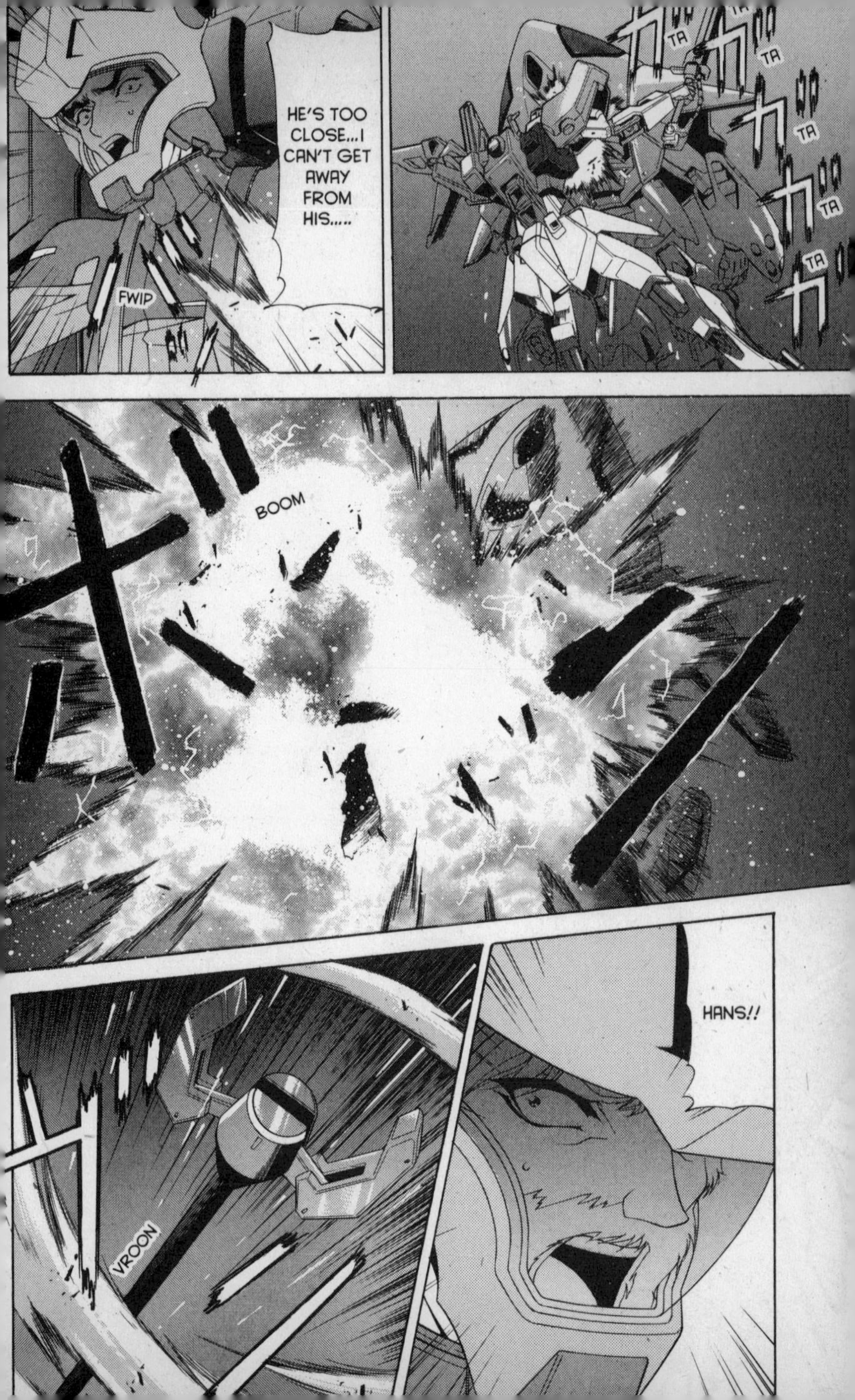
TA
TA
TA
TA
TA
HE'S TOO CLOSE...I CAN'T GET AWAY FROM HIS.....
FWIP
BOOM
HANS!!
VROON

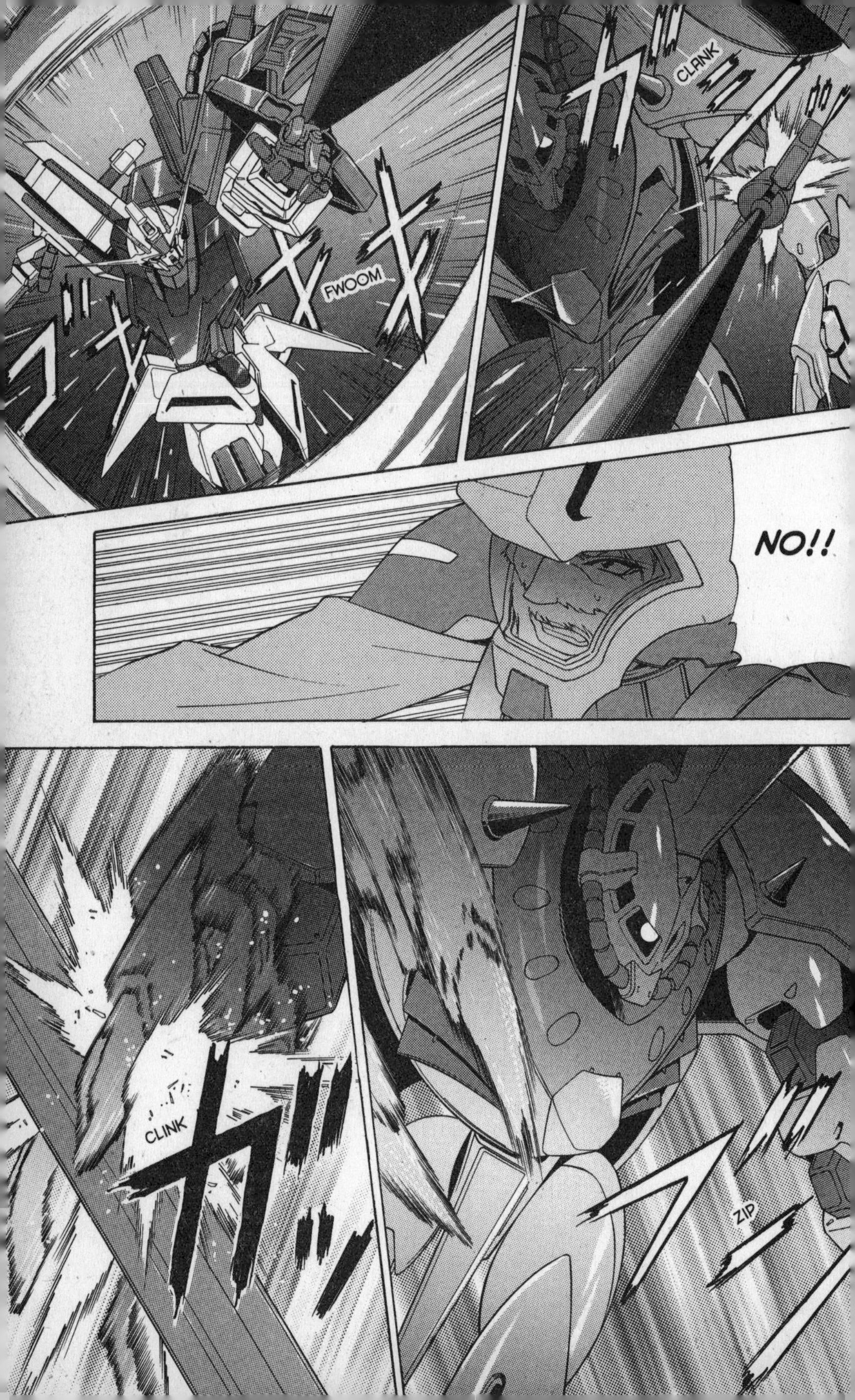
CLANK
FWOOM
NO!!
ZIP
CLINK

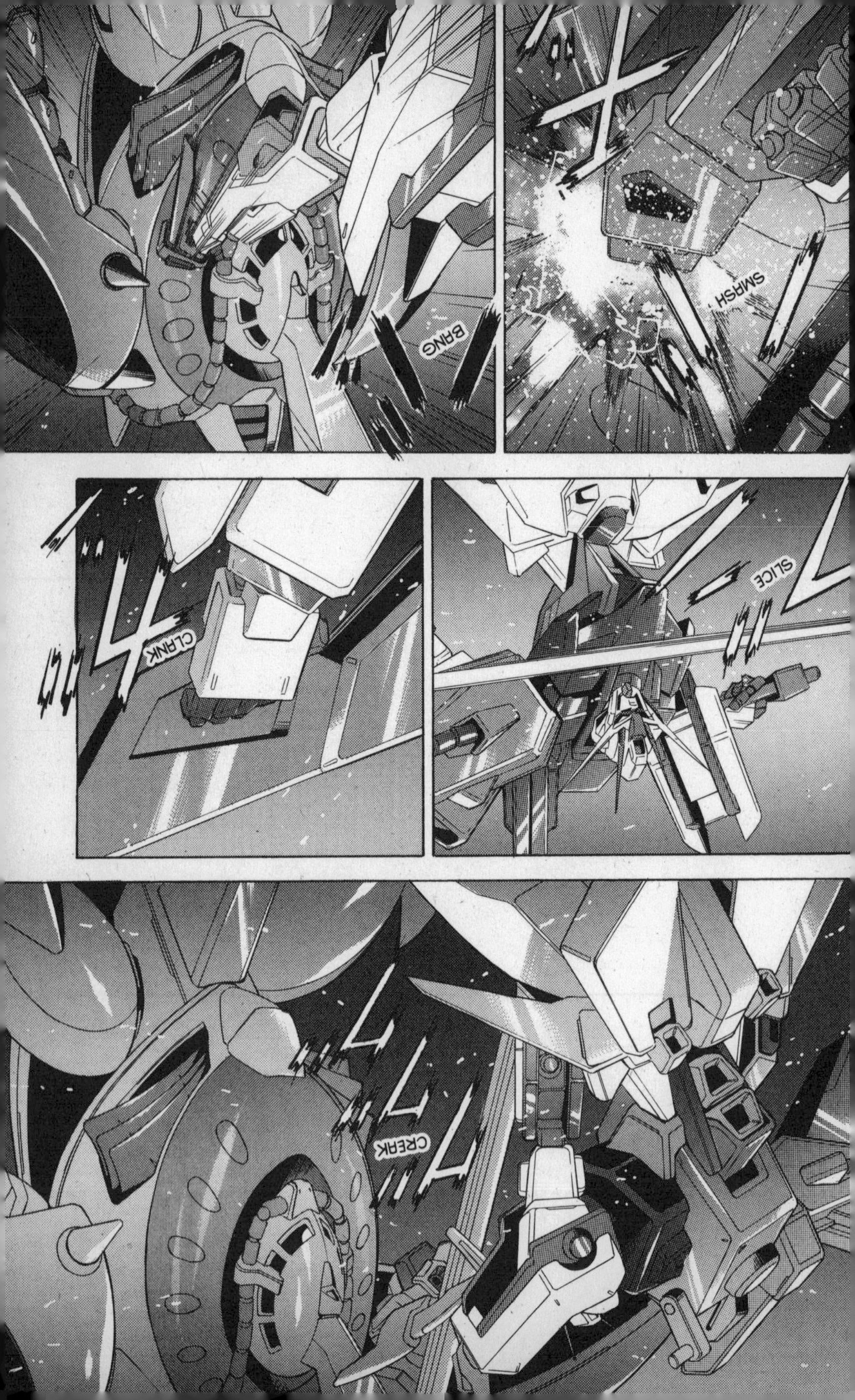
SMASH
BANG
SLICE
CLANK
CREAK

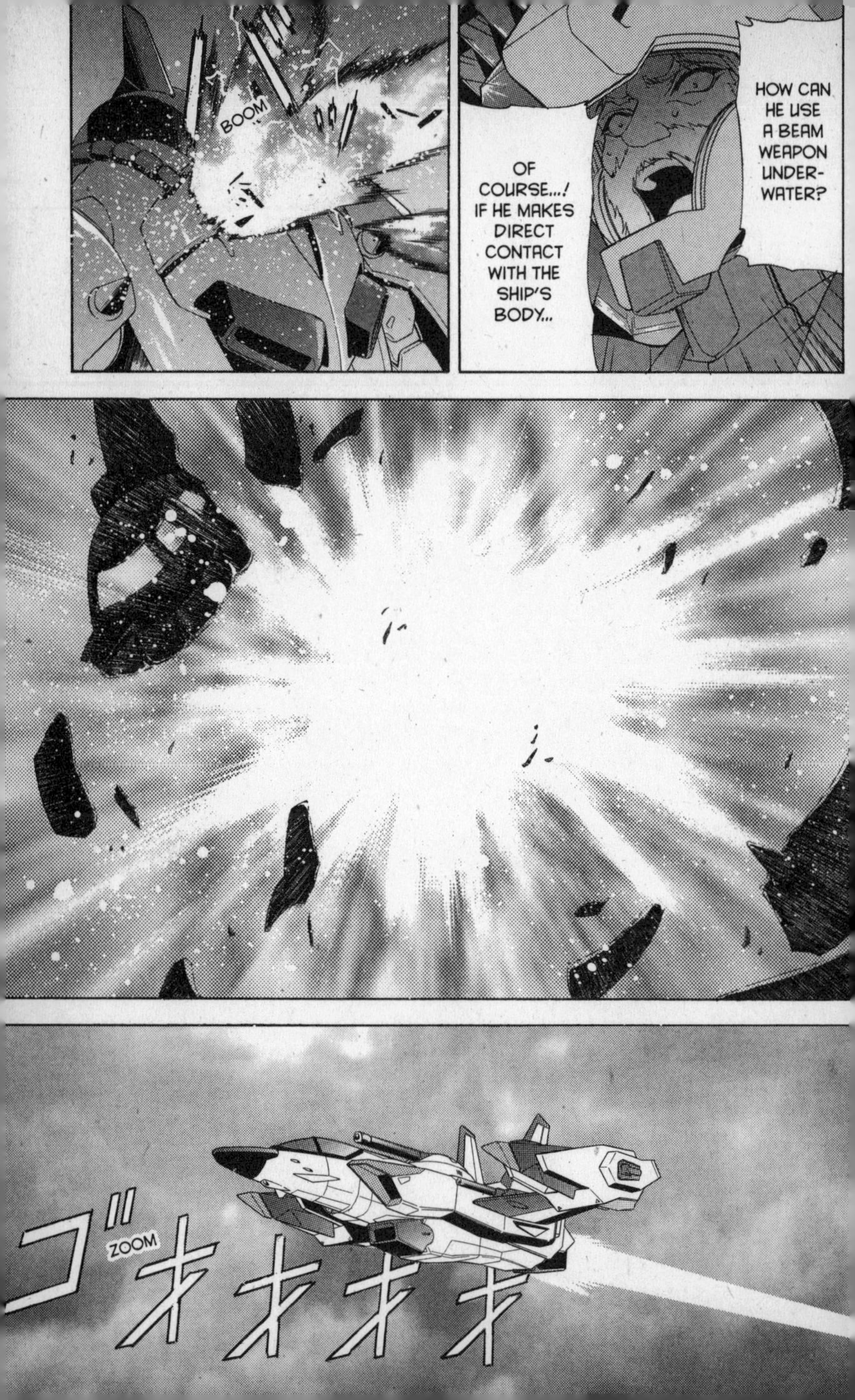
HOW CAN HE USE A BEAM WEAPON UNDER-WATER?
OF COURSE...! IF HE MAKES DIRECT CONTACT WITH THE SHIP'S BODY...
BOOM
ゴオオオオ
ZOOM

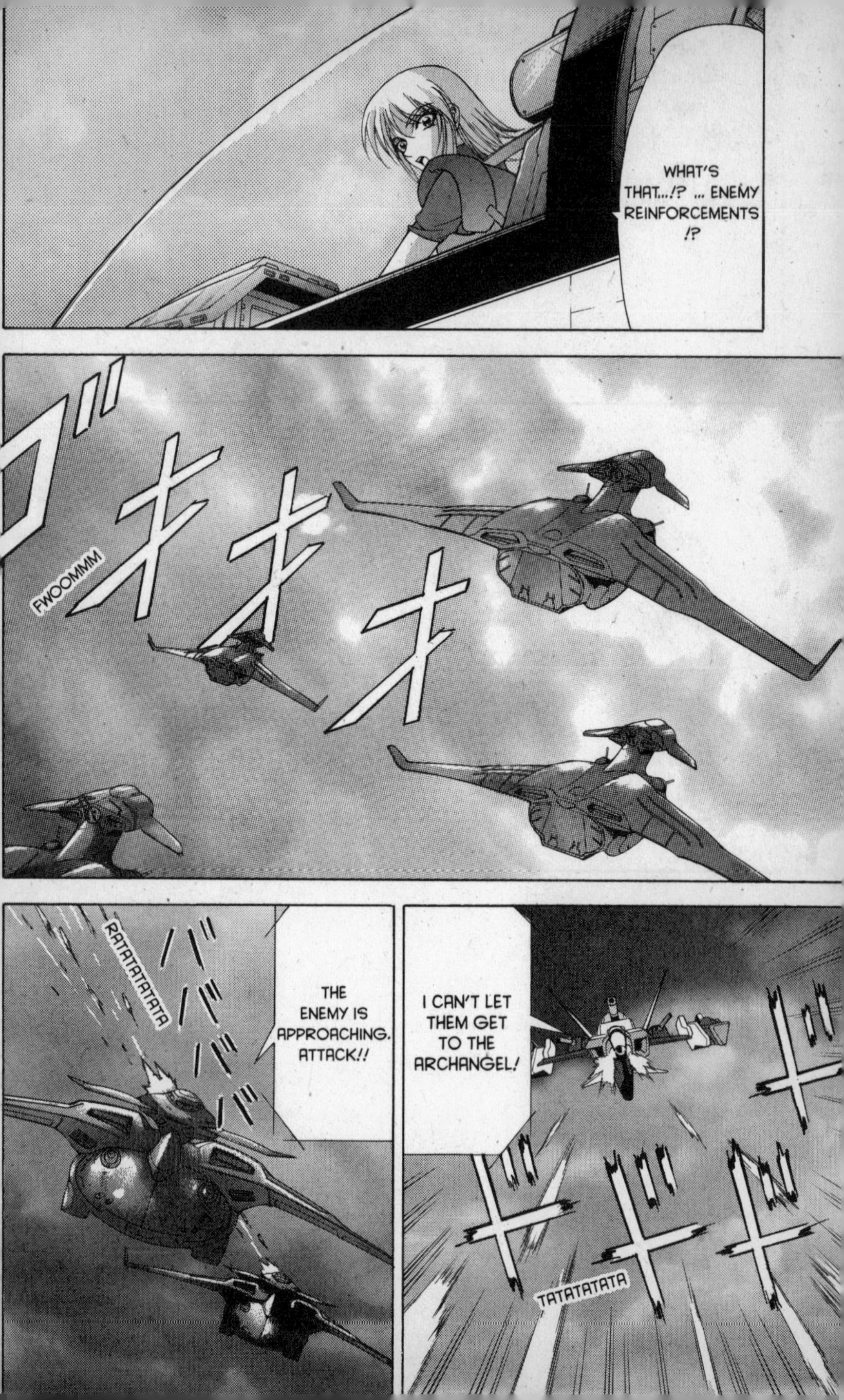
WHAT'S THAT...!? ... ENEMY REINFORCEMENTS !?
FWOOMMM
I CAN'T LET THEM GET TO THE ARCHANGEL!
TATATATATA
THE ENEMY IS APPROACHING. ATTACK!!
RATATATATATA

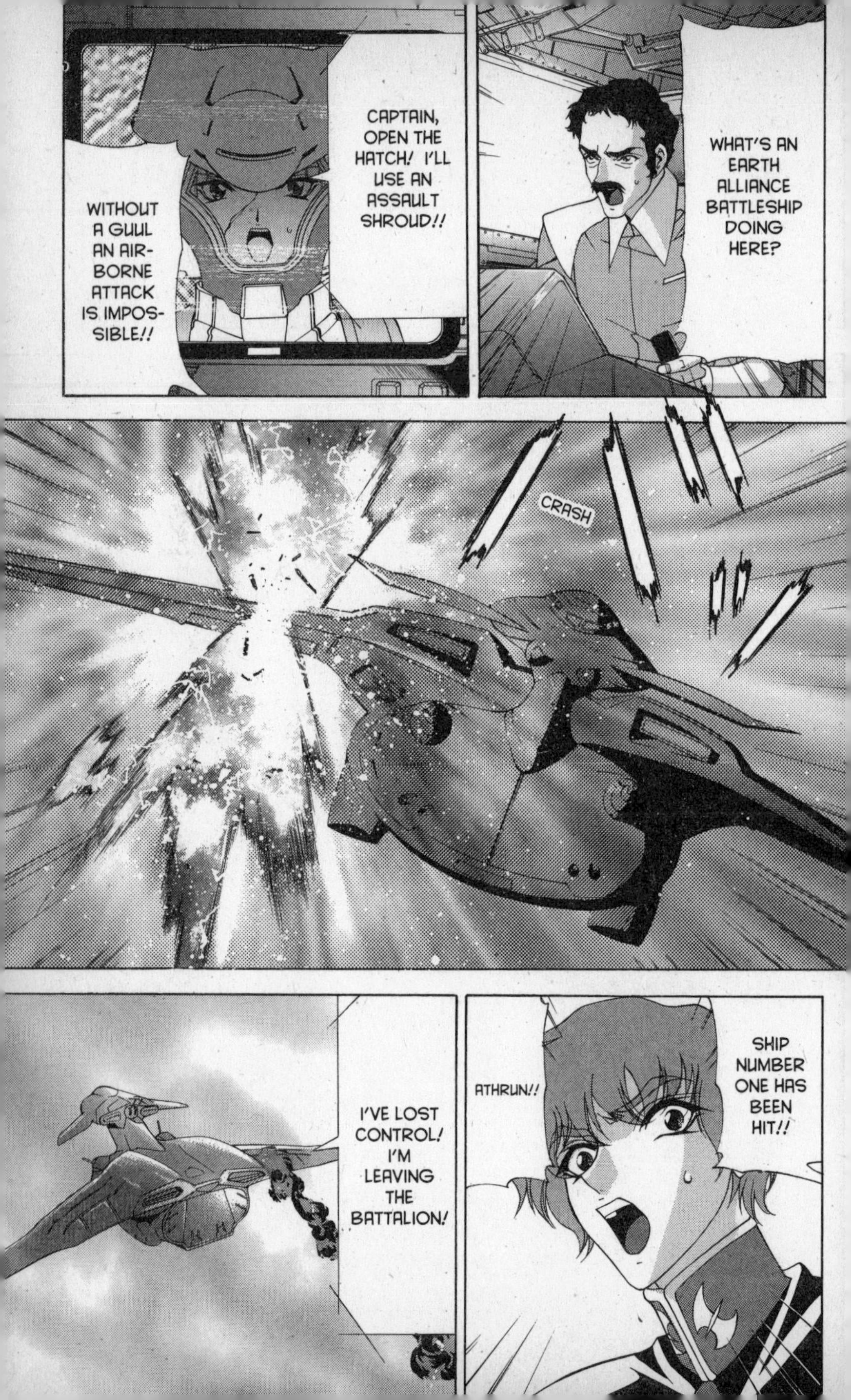
WHAT'S AN EARTH ALLIANCE BATTLESHIP DOING HERE?
CAPTAIN, OPEN THE HATCH! I'LL USE AN ASSAULT SHROUD!!
WITHOUT A GUUL AN AIR-BORNE ATTACK IS IMPOS-SIBLE!!
CRASH
SHIP NUMBER ONE HAS BEEN HIT!!
ATHRUN!!
I'VE LOST CONTROL! I'M LEAVING THE BATTALION!

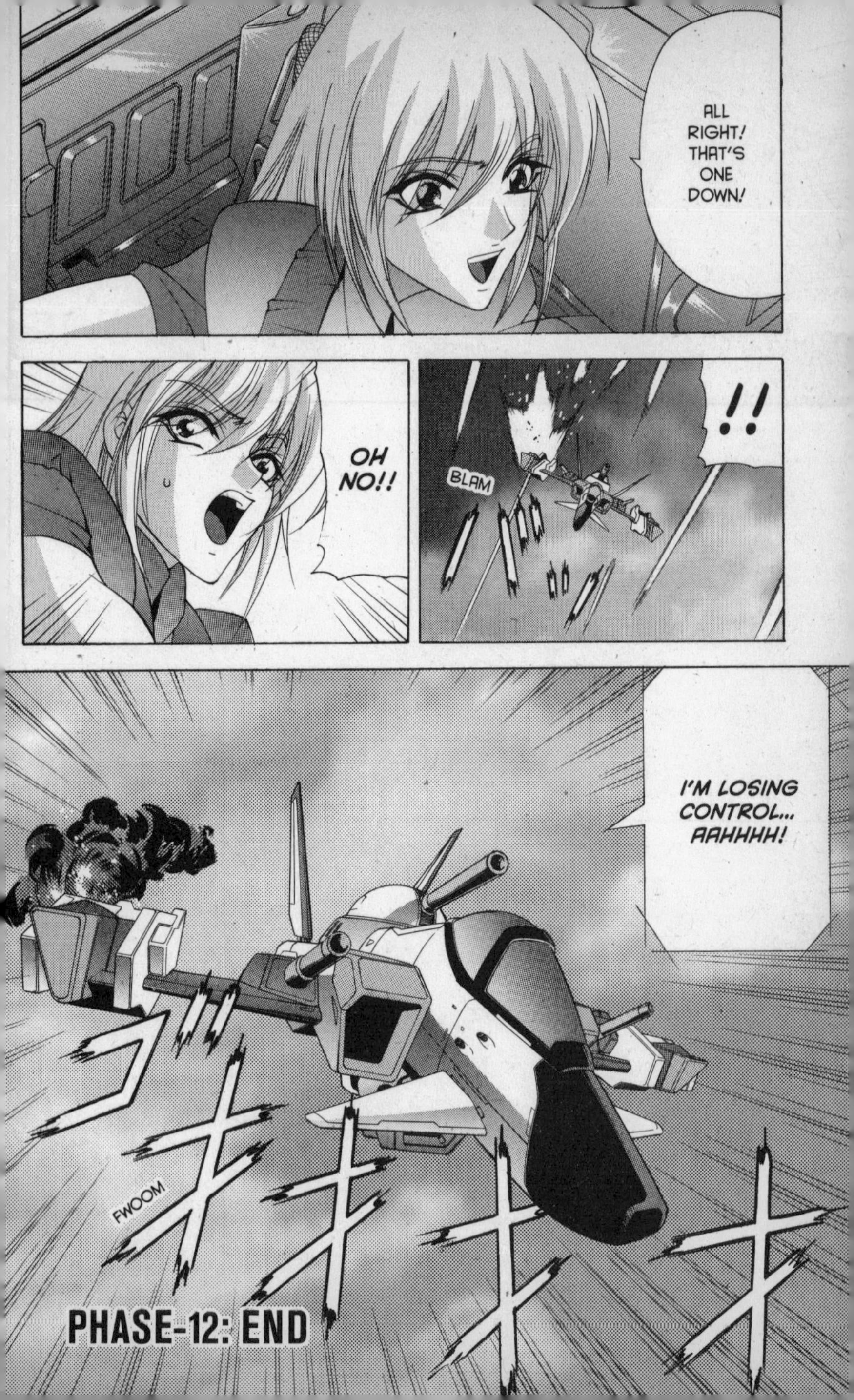
ALL RIGHT! THAT'S ONE DOWN!
!!
BLAM
OH NO!!
I'M LOSING CONTROL... AAHHHH!
FWOOM
PHASE-12: END

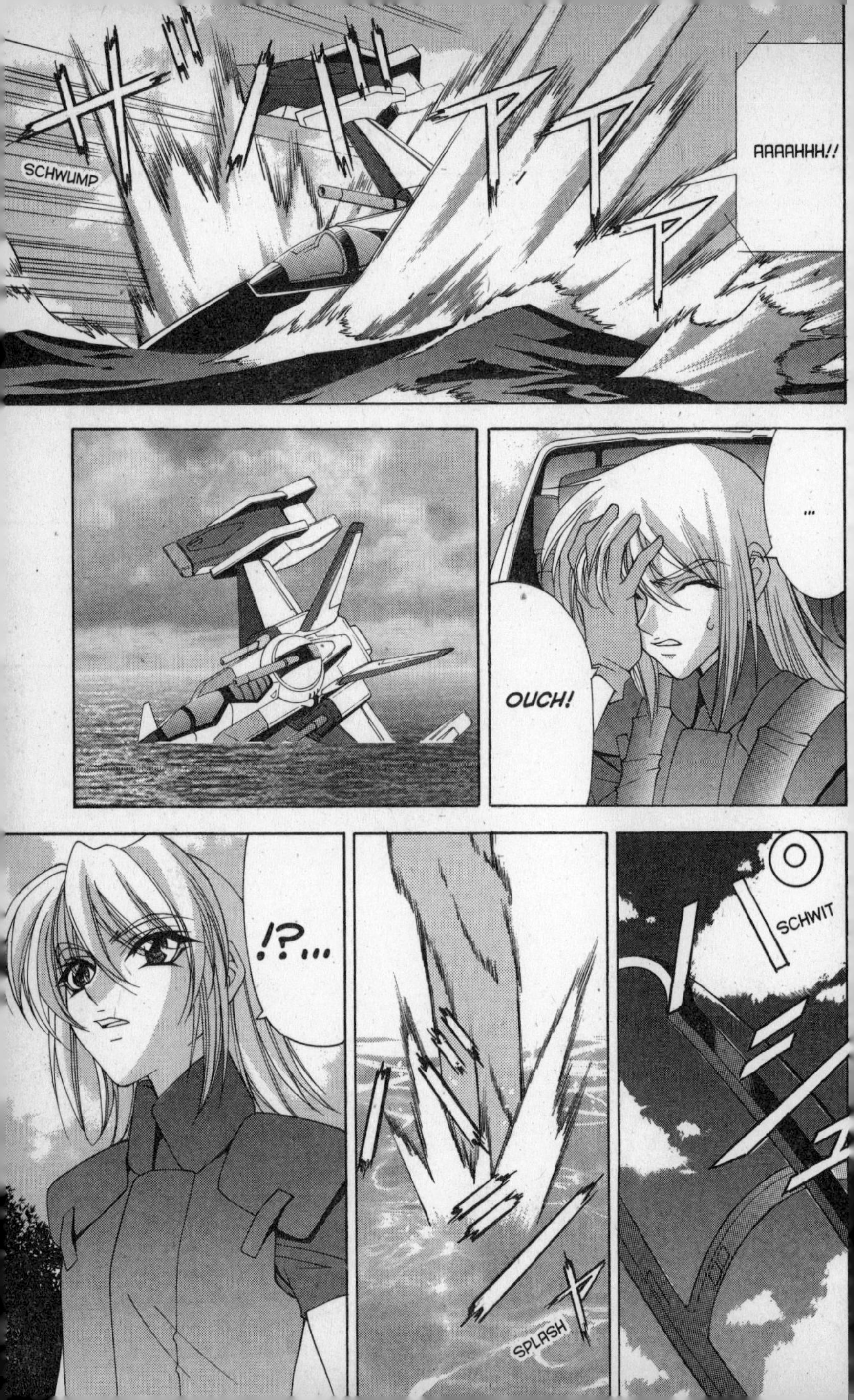
AAAAHHH!!
SCHWUMP
...
OUCH!
SCHWIT
SPLASH
!?...

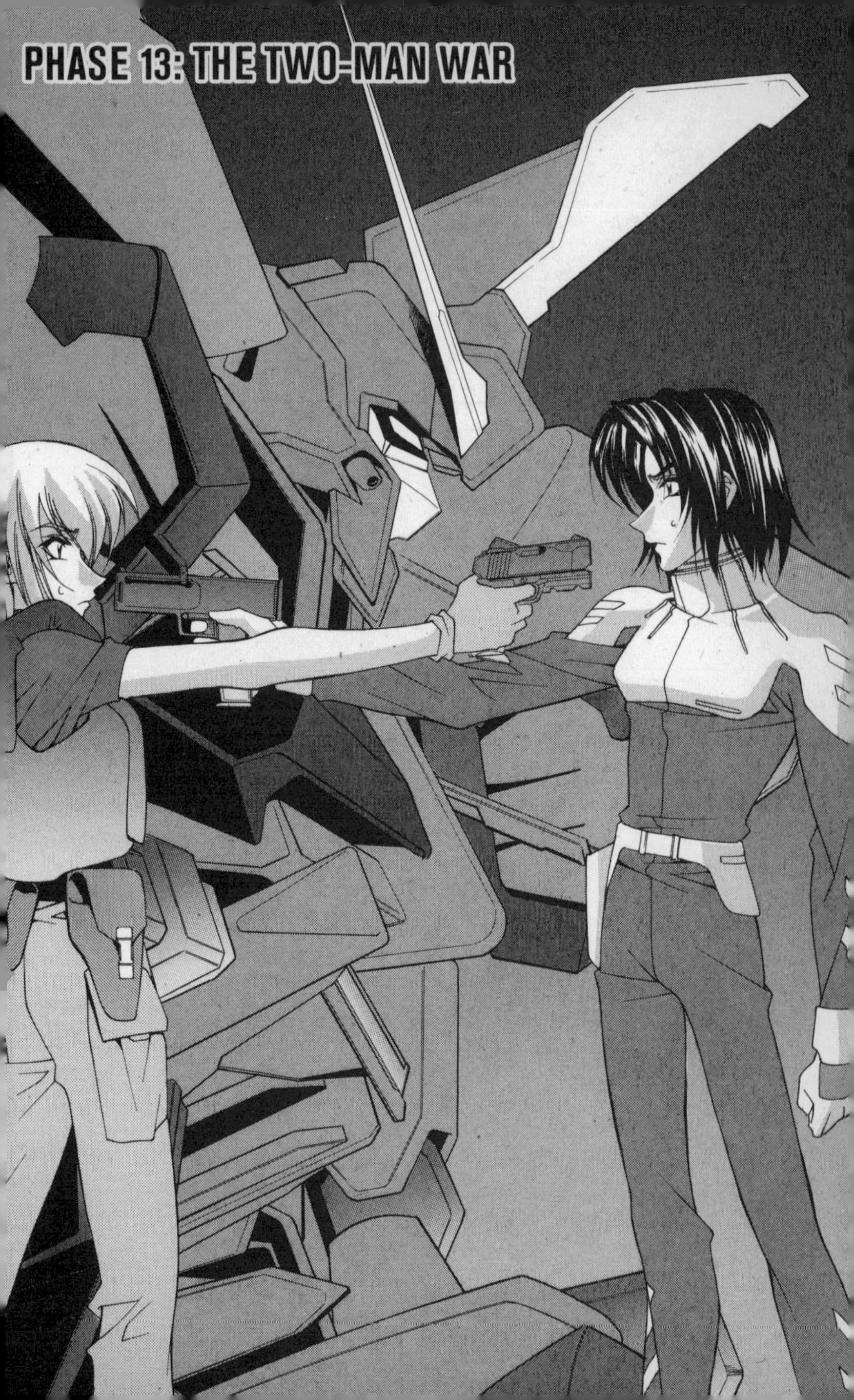
PHASE 13: THE TWO-MAN WAR

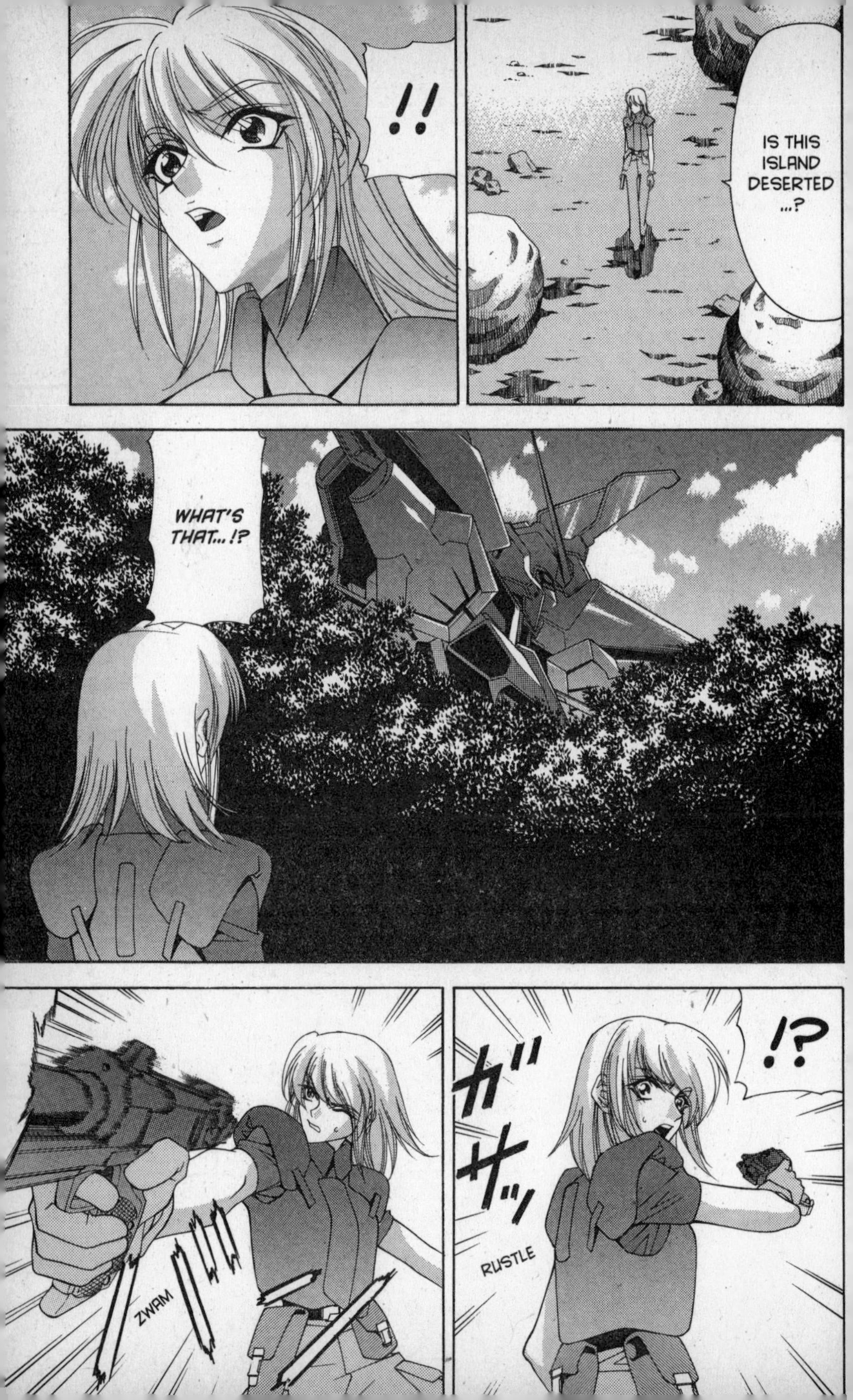
IS THIS ISLAND DESERTED ...?
!!
WHAT'S THAT... !?
!?
ガサッ
RUSTLE
ZWAM

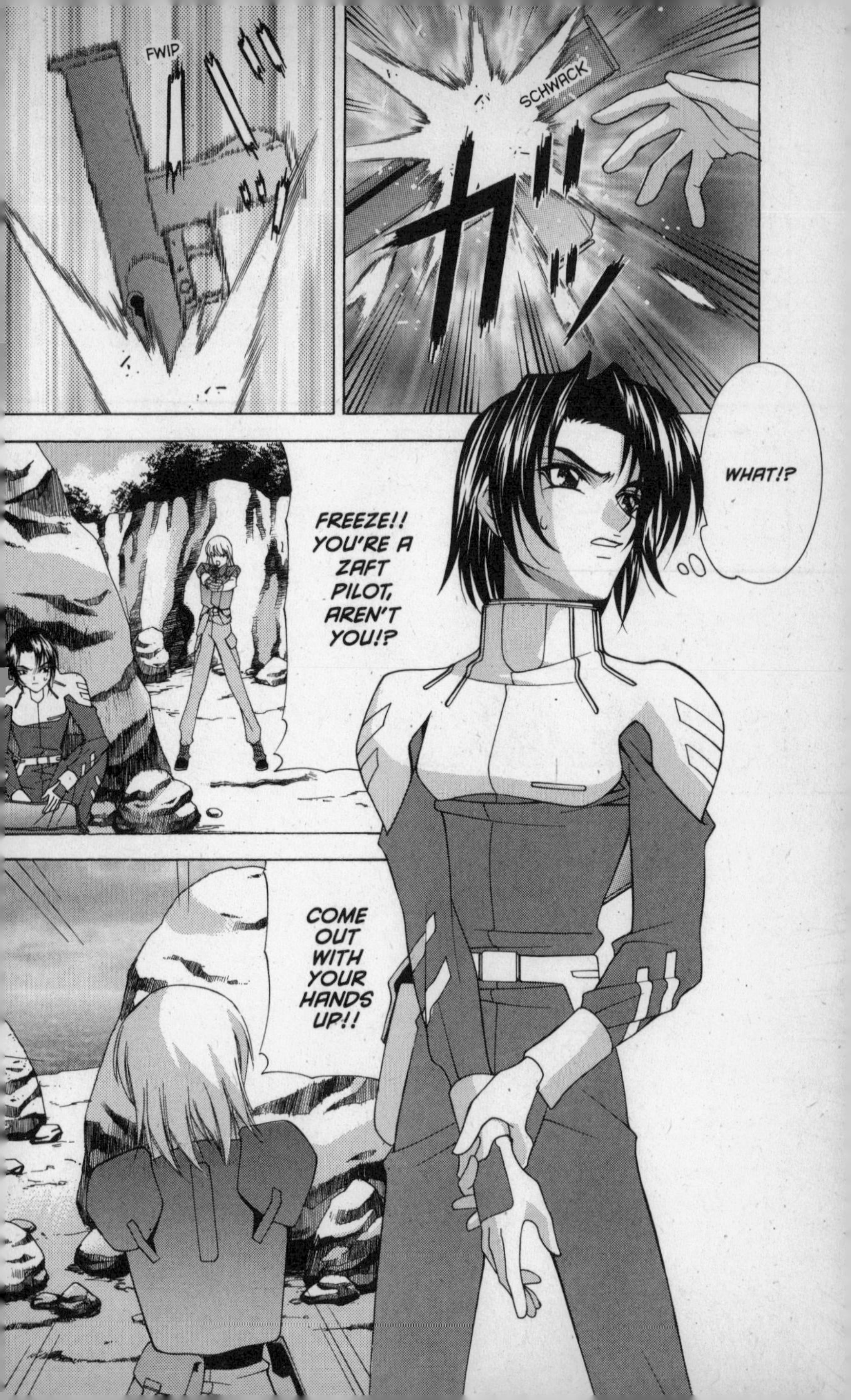
SCHWACK
FWIP
WHAT!?
FREEZE!! YOU'RE A ZAFT PILOT, AREN'T YOU!?
COME OUT WITH YOUR HANDS UP!!

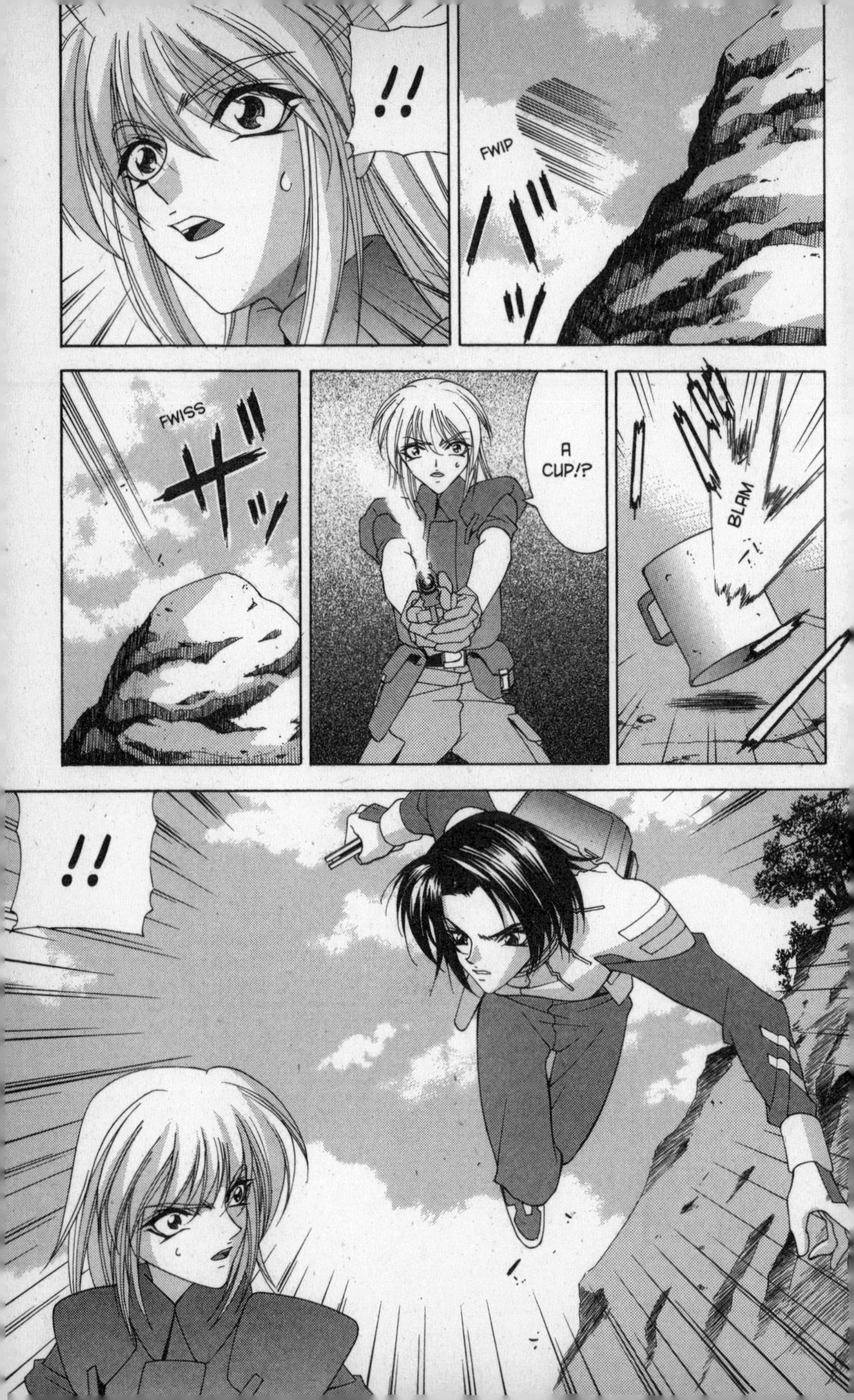
FWIP
!!
BLAM
A CUP!?
FWISS
!!

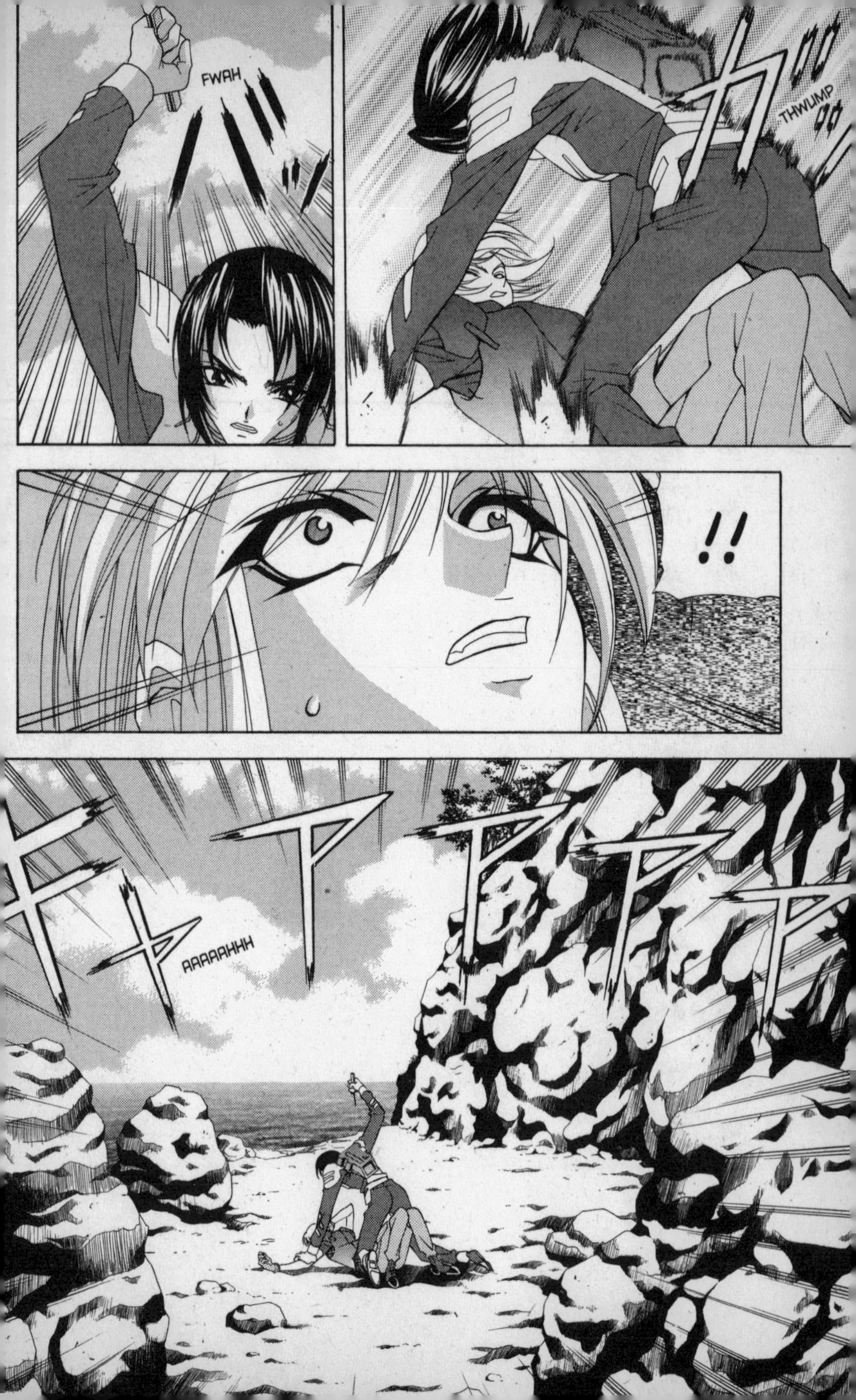
THWUMP
FWAH
!!
AAAAAHHH

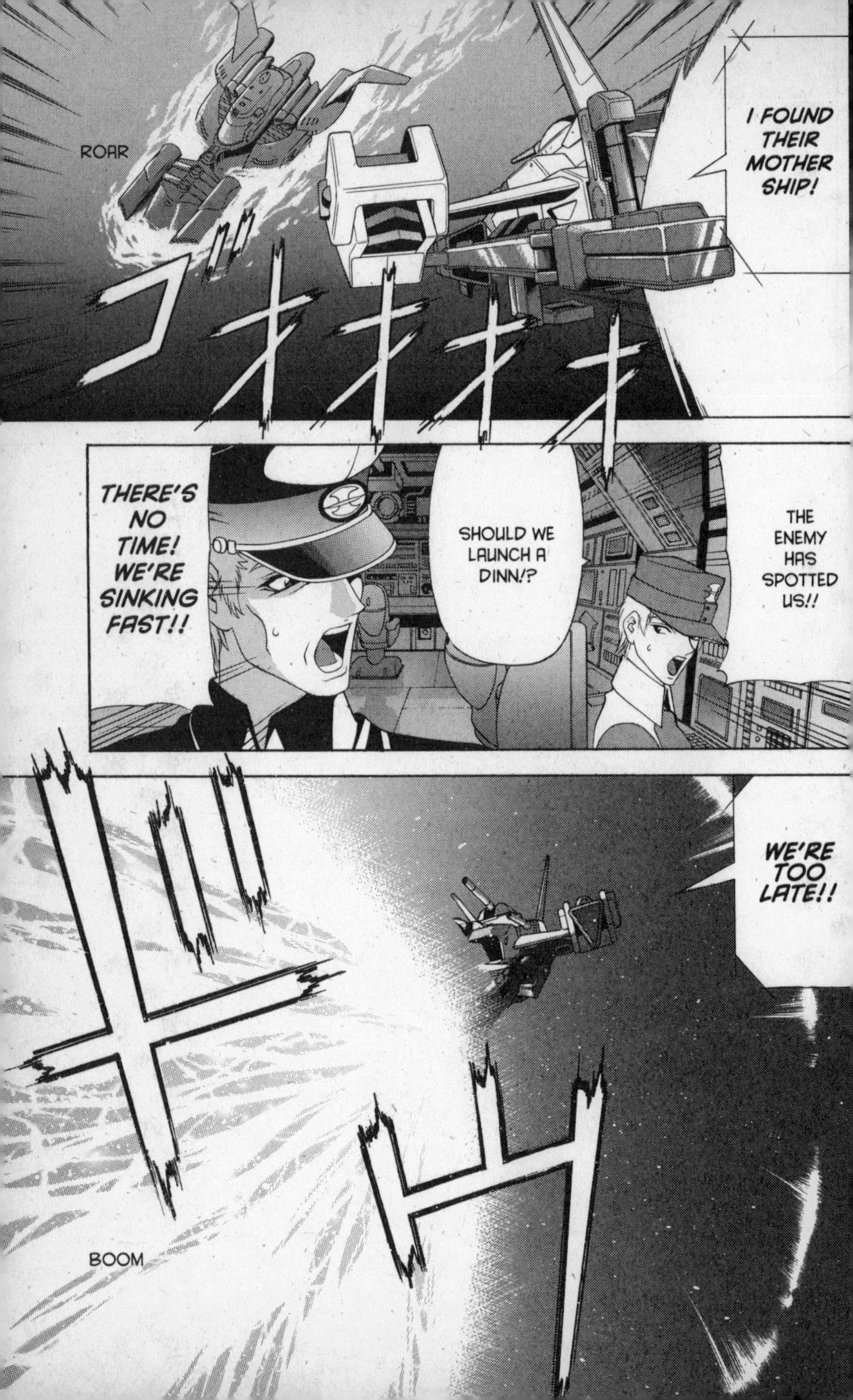
I FOUND THEIR MOTHER SHIP!
ROAR
THE ENEMY HAS SPOTTED US!!
SHOULD WE LAUNCH A DINN!?
THERE'S NO TIME! WE'RE SINKING FAST!!
WE'RE TOO LATE!!
BOOM

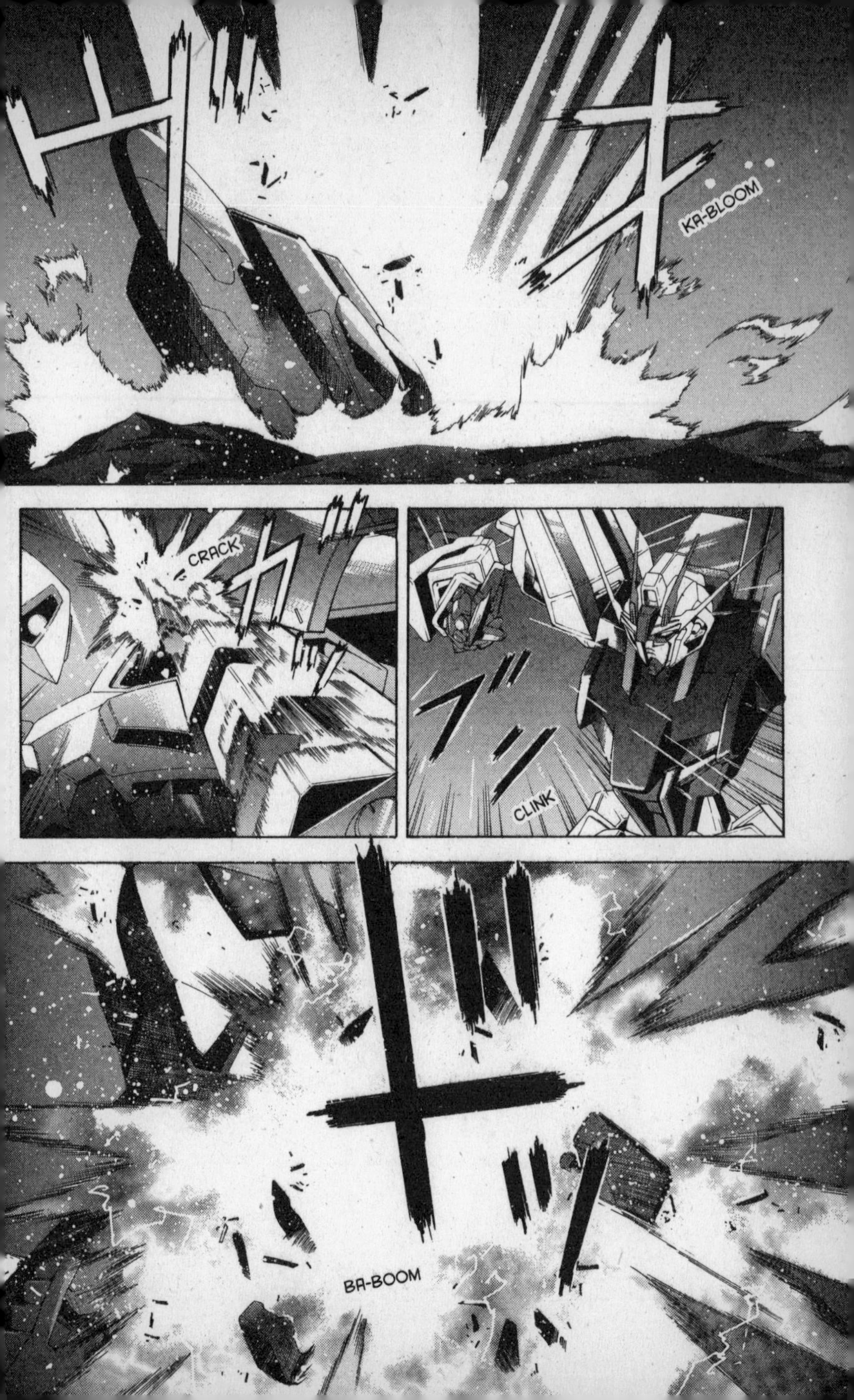
KA-BLOOM
CLINK
CRACK
BA-BOOM

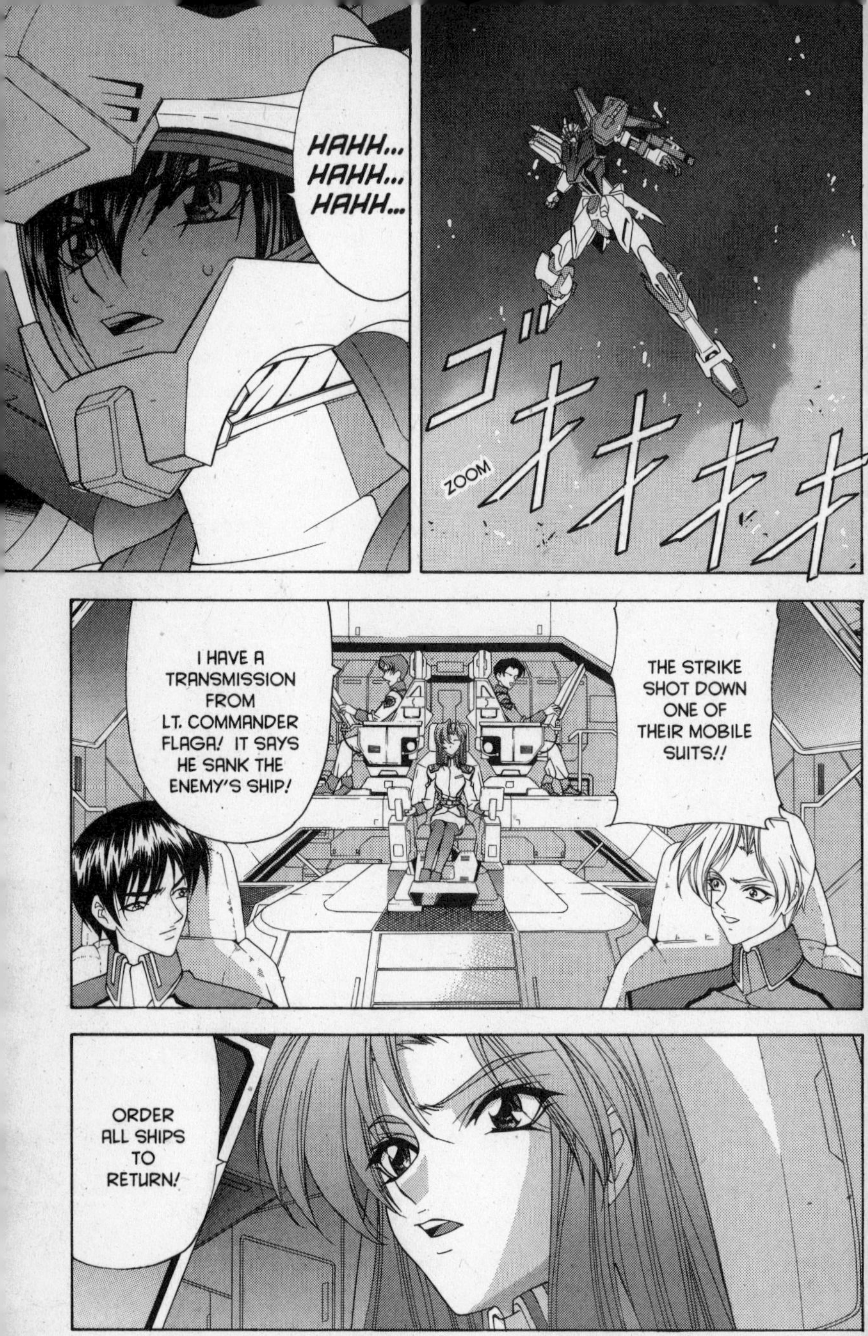
ゴォォォォ
ZOOM
HAHH... HAHH... HAHH...
THE STRIKE SHOT DOWN ONE OF THEIR MOBILE SUITS!!
I HAVE A TRANSMISSION FROM LT. COMMANDER FLAGA! IT SAYS HE SANK THE ENEMY'S SHIP!
ORDER ALL SHIPS TO RETURN!

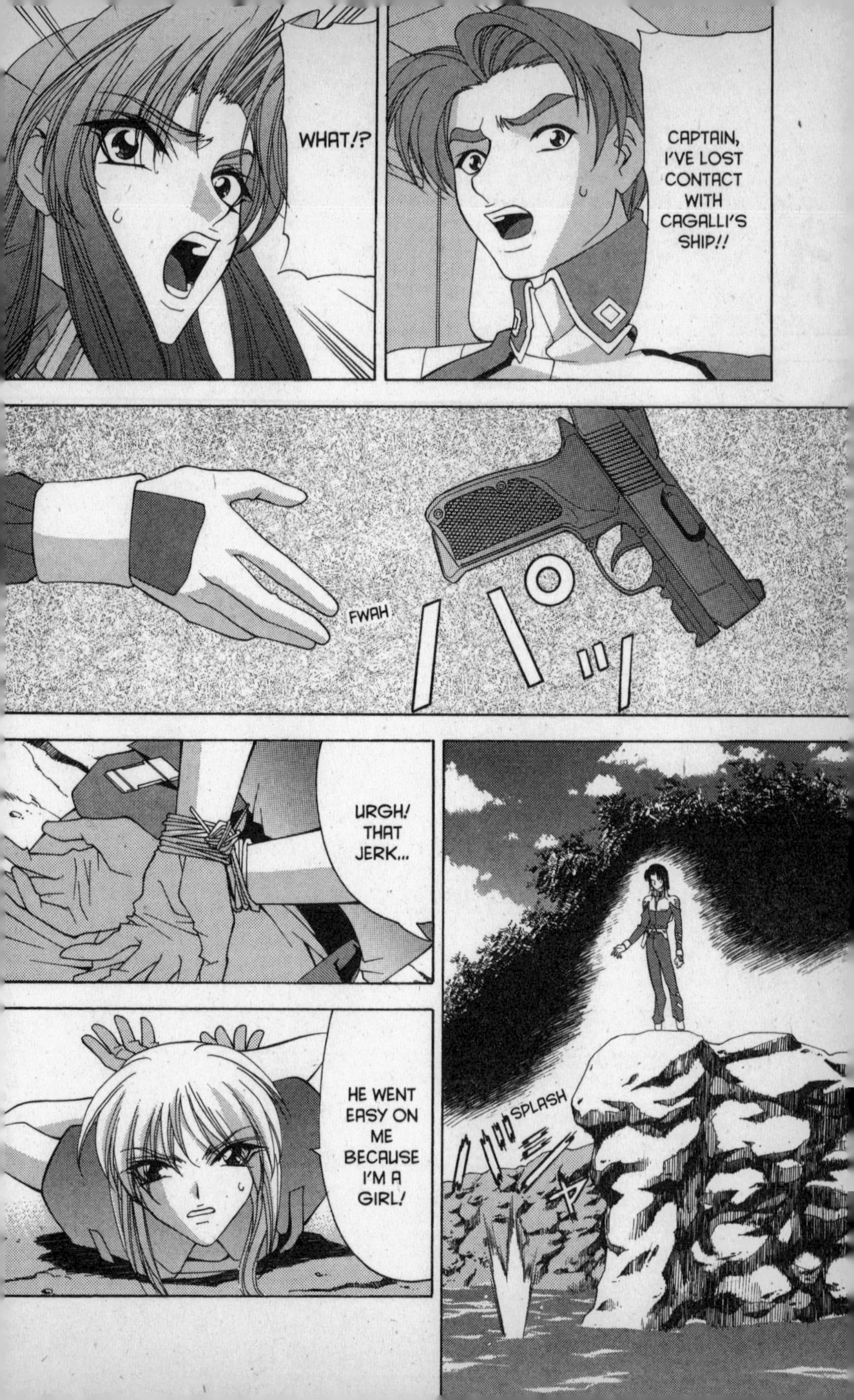
CAPTAIN, I'VE LOST CONTACT WITH CAGALLI'S SHIP!!
WHAT!?
FWAH
SPLASH
URGH! THAT JERK...
HE WENT EASY ON ME BECAUSE I'M A GIRL!

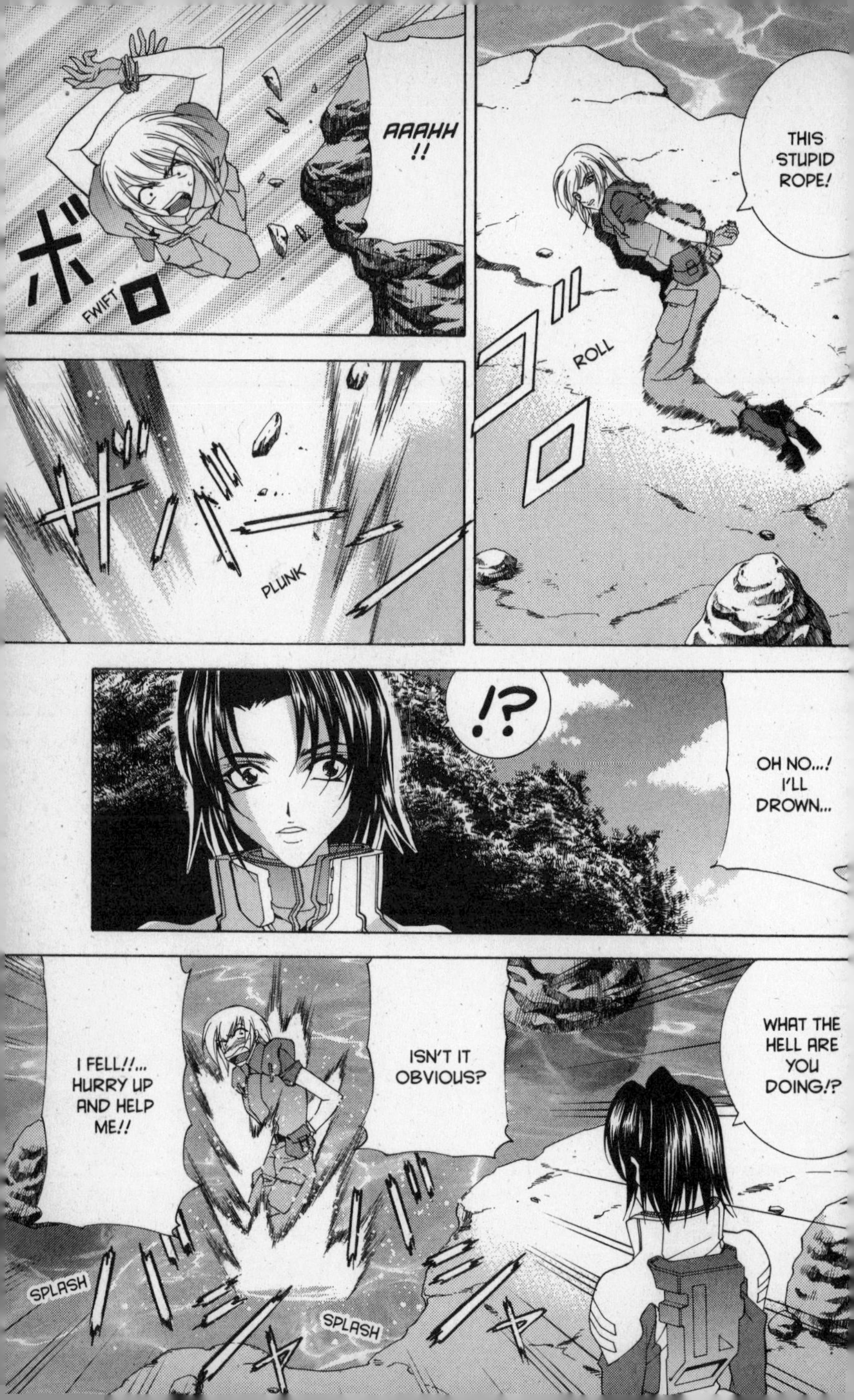
THIS STUPID ROPE!
ゴロ
ROLL
AAAHH !!
ボロ
FWIFT
PLUNK
!?
OH NO...! I'LL DROWN...
WHAT THE HELL ARE YOU DOING!?
ISN'T IT OBVIOUS?
I FELL!!... HURRY UP AND HELP ME!!
SPLASH
SPLASH

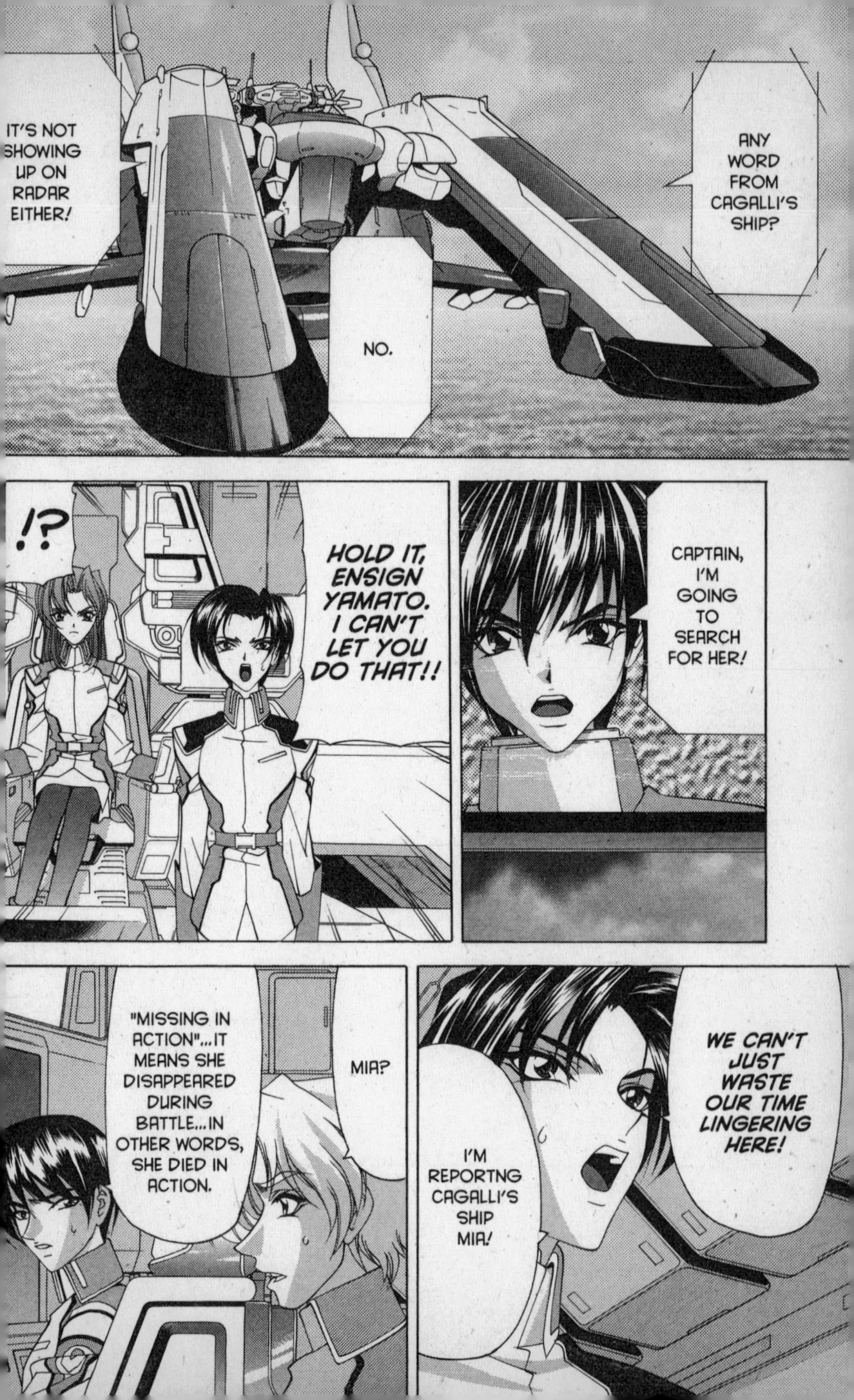
ANY WORD FROM CAGALLI'S SHIP?
NO.
IT'S NOT SHOWING UP ON RADAR EITHER!
CAPTAIN, I'M GOING TO SEARCH FOR HER!
HOLD IT, ENSIGN YAMATO. I CAN'T LET YOU DO THAT!!
!?
WE CAN'T JUST WASTE OUR TIME LINGERING HERE!
I'M REPORTNG CAGALLI'S SHIP MIA!
MIA?
"MISSING IN ACTION"...IT MEANS SHE DISAPPEARED DURING BATTLE...IN OTHER WORDS, SHE DIED IN ACTION.

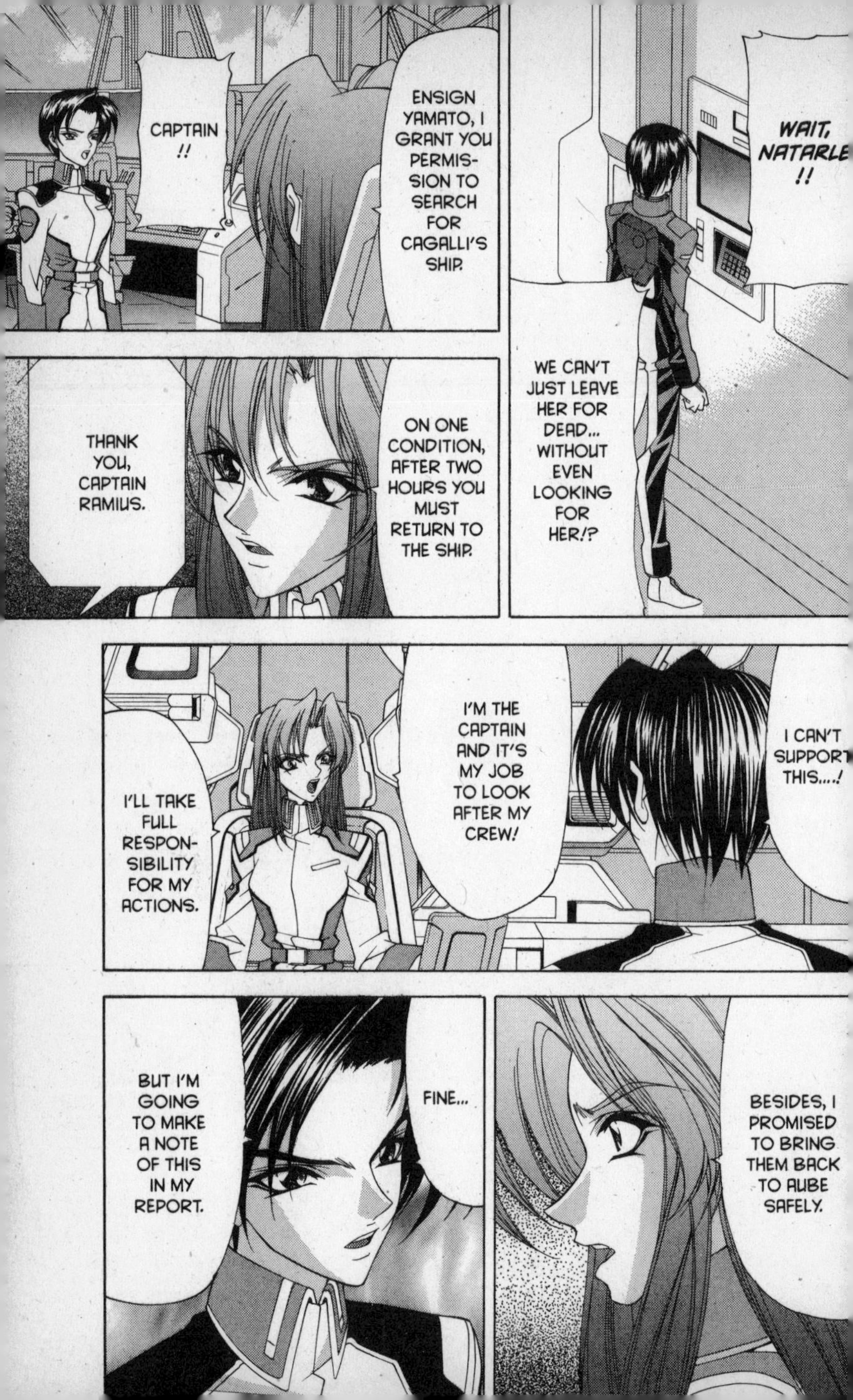
WAIT, NATARLE !!
WE CAN'T JUST LEAVE HER FOR DEAD... WITHOUT EVEN LOOKING FOR HER!?
ENSIGN YAMATO, I GRANT YOU PERMISSION TO SEARCH FOR CAGALLI'S SHIP.
CAPTAIN !!
ON ONE CONDITION, AFTER TWO HOURS YOU MUST RETURN TO THE SHIP.
THANK YOU, CAPTAIN RAMIUS.
I CAN'T SUPPORT THIS....!
I'M THE CAPTAIN AND IT'S MY JOB TO LOOK AFTER MY CREW!
I'LL TAKE FULL RESPONSIBILITY FOR MY ACTIONS.
BESIDES, I PROMISED TO BRING THEM BACK TO AUBE SAFELY.
FINE...
BUT I'M GOING TO MAKE A NOTE OF THIS IN MY REPORT.

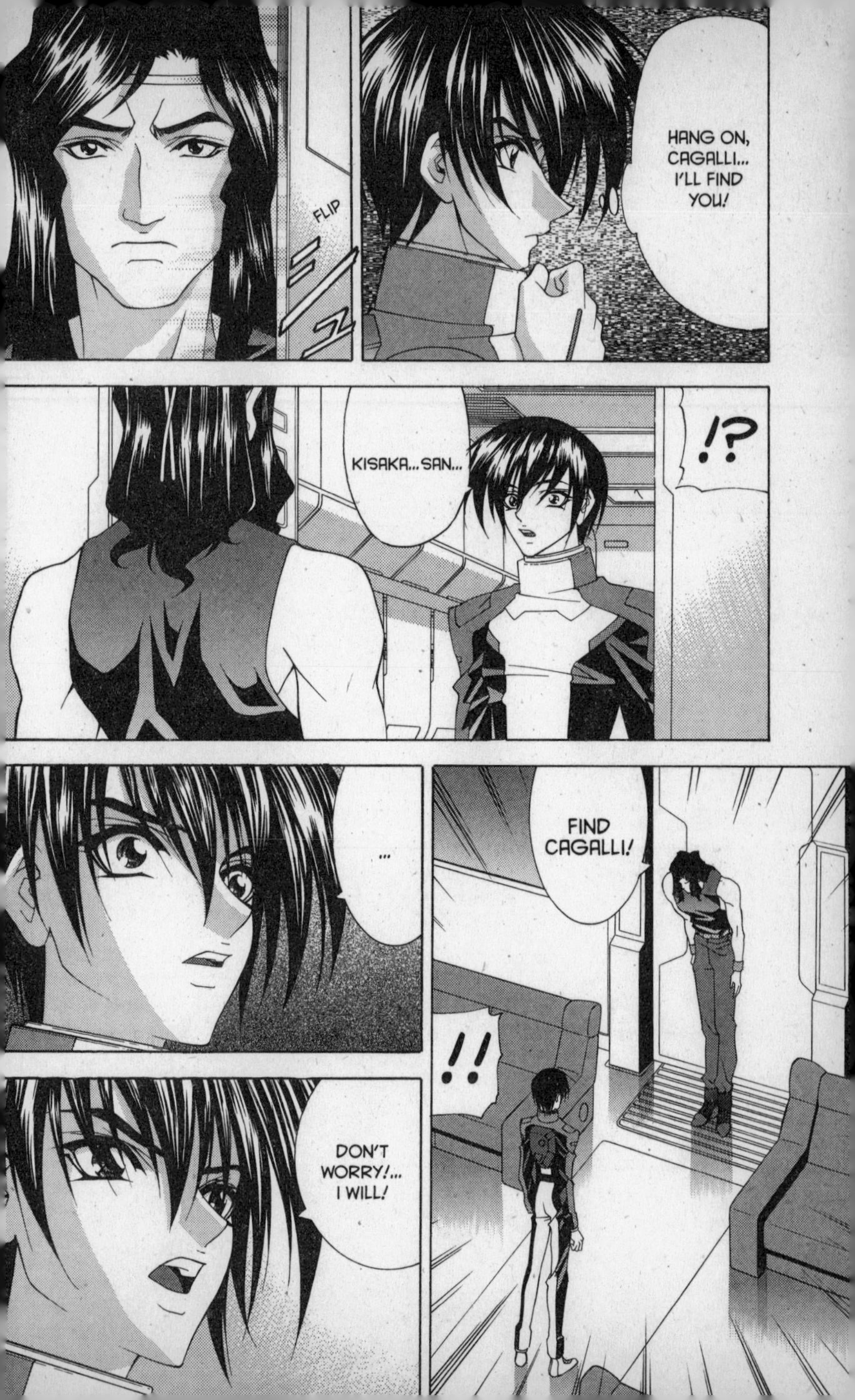
HANG ON, CAGALLI... I'LL FIND YOU!
FLIP
!?
KISAKA...SAN...
FIND CAGALLI!
!!
...
DON'T WORRY!... I WILL!

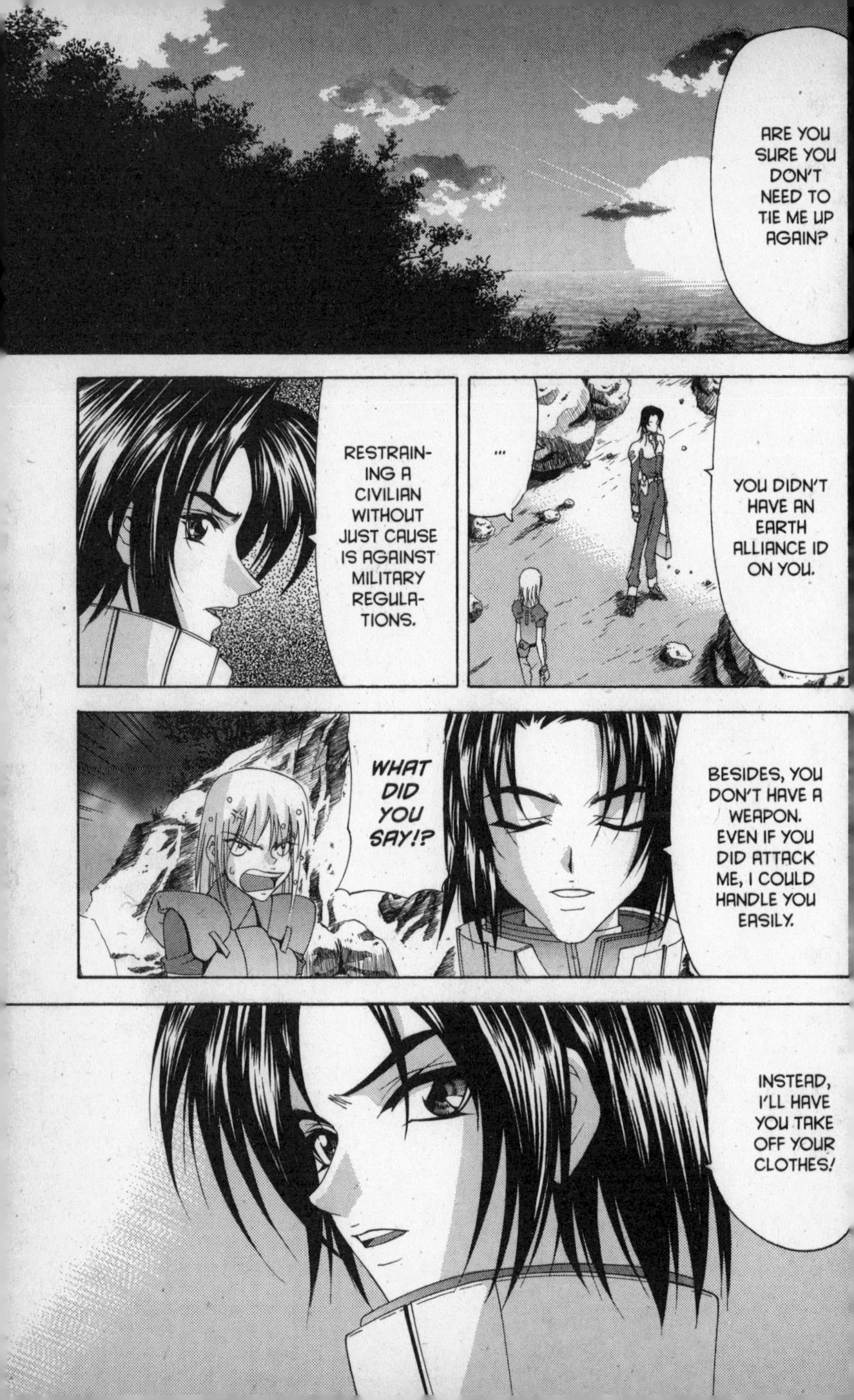
ARE YOU SURE YOU DON'T NEED TO TIE ME UP AGAIN?
YOU DIDN'T HAVE AN EARTH ALLIANCE ID ON YOU.
...
RESTRAIN-ING A CIVILIAN WITHOUT JUST CAUSE IS AGAINST MILITARY REGULA-TIONS.
BESIDES, YOU DON'T HAVE A WEAPON. EVEN IF YOU DID ATTACK ME, I COULD HANDLE YOU EASILY.
WHAT DID YOU SAY!?
INSTEAD, I'LL HAVE YOU TAKE OFF YOUR CLOTHES!

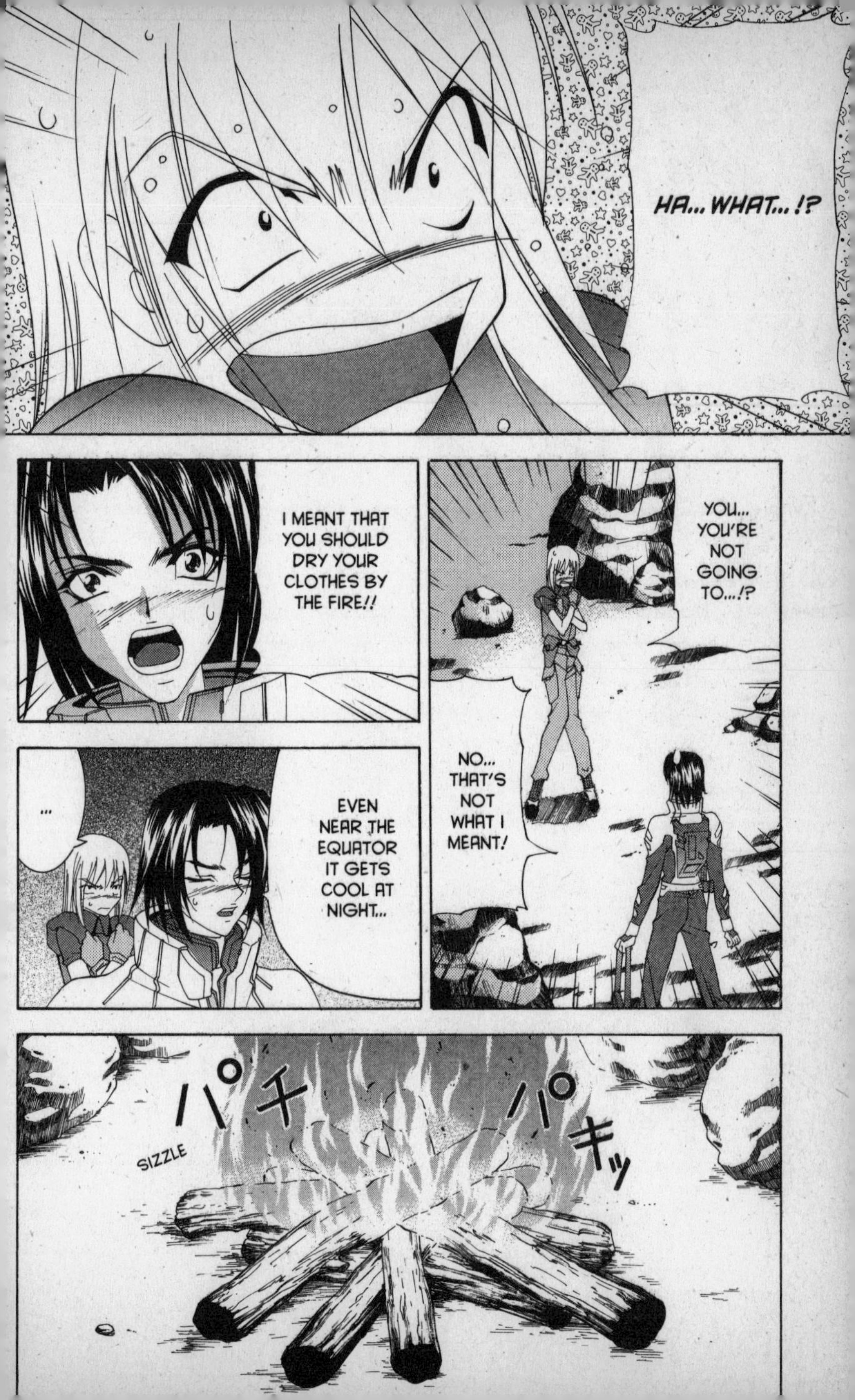
HA... WHAT... !?
YOU... YOU'RE NOT GOING TO...!?
NO... THAT'S NOT WHAT I MEANT!
I MEANT THAT YOU SHOULD DRY YOUR CLOTHES BY THE FIRE!!
...
EVEN NEAR THE EQUATOR IT GETS COOL AT NIGHT...
パチ
パキッ
SIZZLE

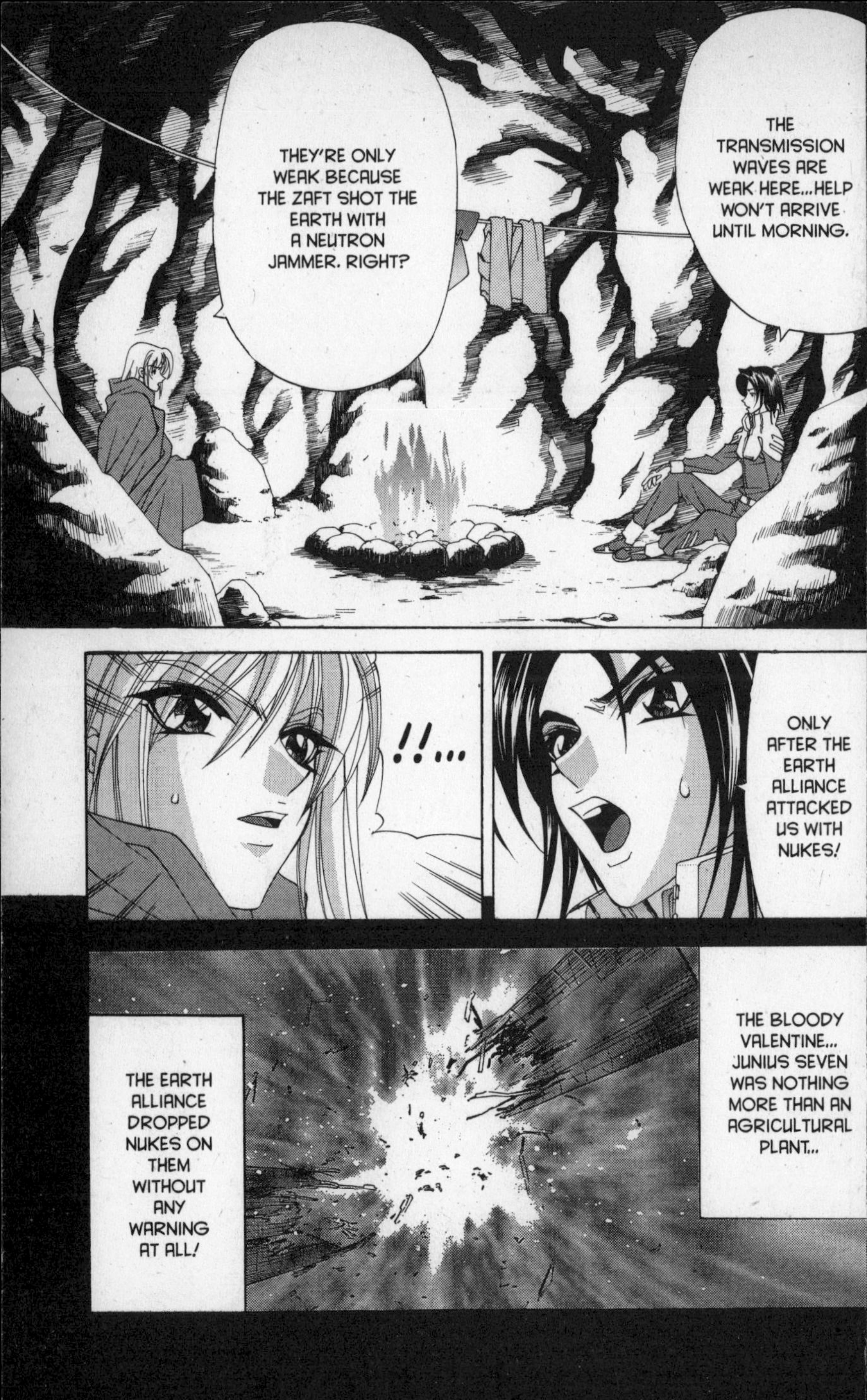
THE TRANSMISSION WAVES ARE WEAK HERE...HELP WON'T ARRIVE UNTIL MORNING.
THEY'RE ONLY WEAK BECAUSE THE ZAFT SHOT THE EARTH WITH A NEUTRON JAMMER. RIGHT?
ONLY AFTER THE EARTH ALLIANCE ATTACKED US WITH NUKES!
!!...
THE BLOODY VALENTINE... JUNIUS SEVEN WAS NOTHING MORE THAN AN AGRICULTURAL PLANT...
THE EARTH ALLIANCE DROPPED NUKES ON THEM WITHOUT ANY WARNING AT ALL!

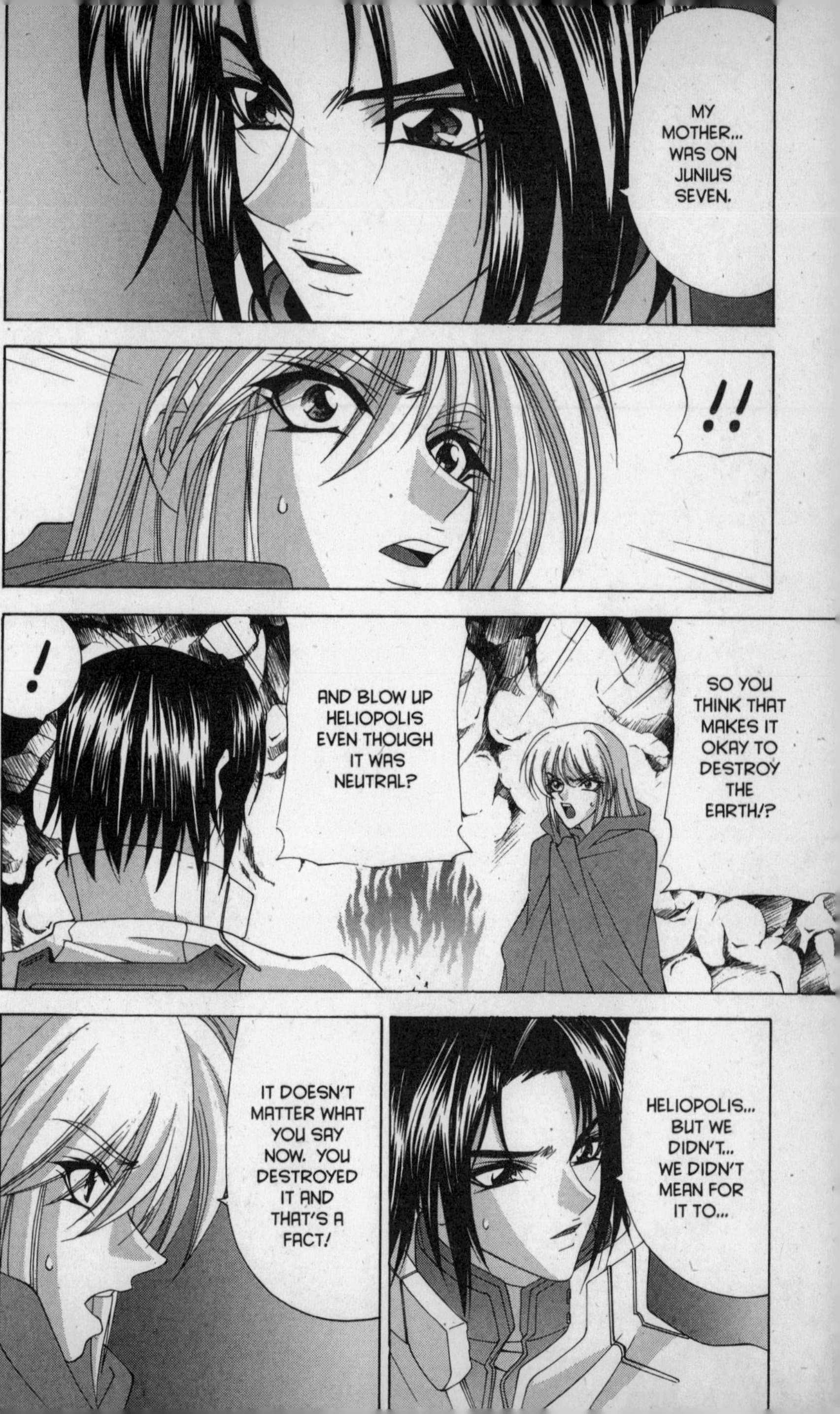
MY MOTHER... WAS ON JUNIUS SEVEN.
!!
SO YOU THINK THAT MAKES IT OKAY TO DESTROY THE EARTH!?
AND BLOW UP HELIOPOLIS EVEN THOUGH IT WAS NEUTRAL?
!
HELIOPOLIS... BUT WE DIDN'T... WE DIDN'T MEAN FOR IT TO...
IT DOESN'T MATTER WHAT YOU SAY NOW. YOU DESTROYED IT AND THAT'S A FACT!

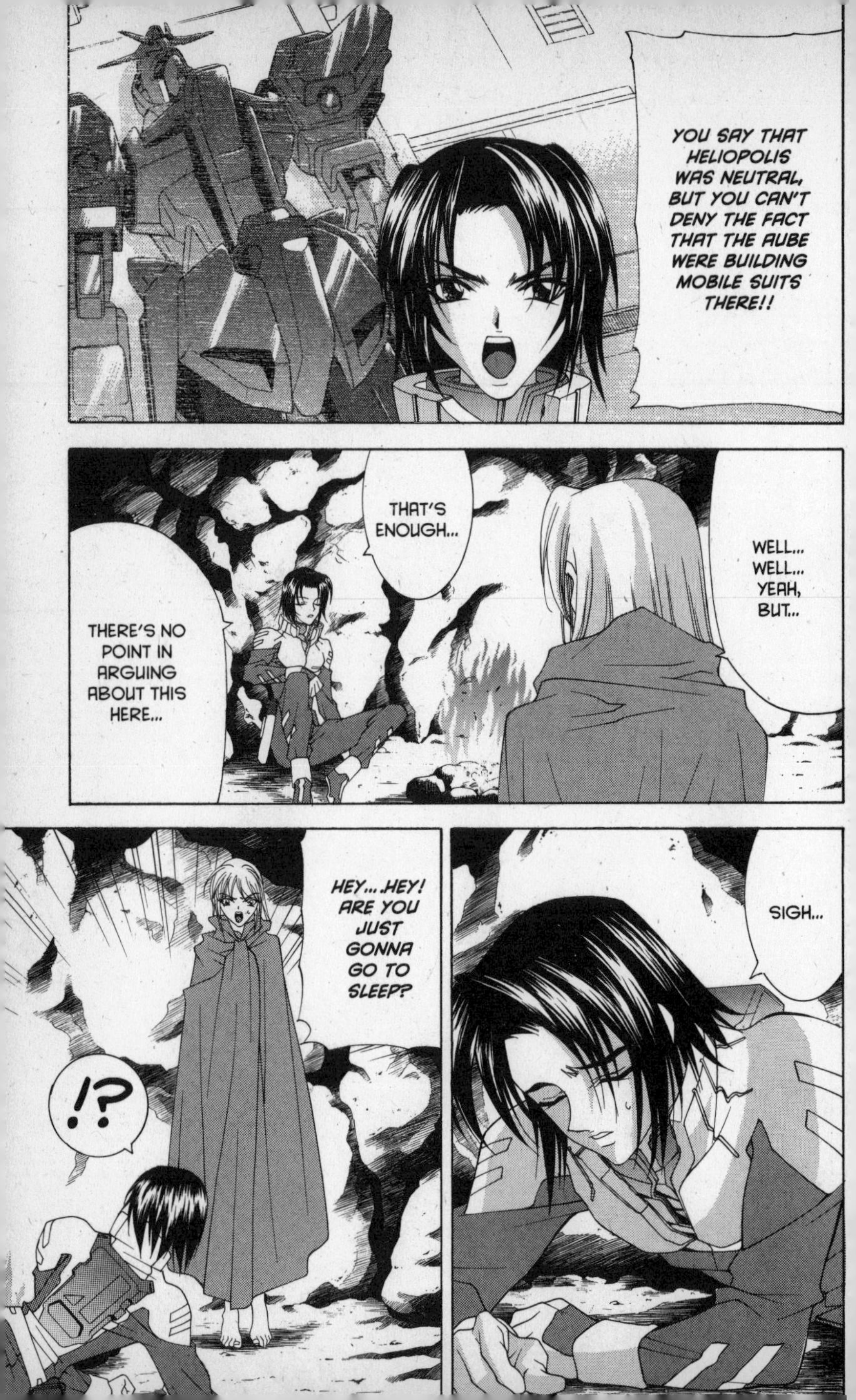
YOU SAY THAT HELIOPOLIS WAS NEUTRAL, BUT YOU CAN'T DENY THE FACT THAT THE AUBE WERE BUILDING MOBILE SUITS THERE!!
WELL... WELL... YEAH, BUT...
THAT'S ENOUGH...
THERE'S NO POINT IN ARGUING ABOUT THIS HERE...
SIGH...
HEY... HEY! ARE YOU JUST GONNA GO TO SLEEP?
!?

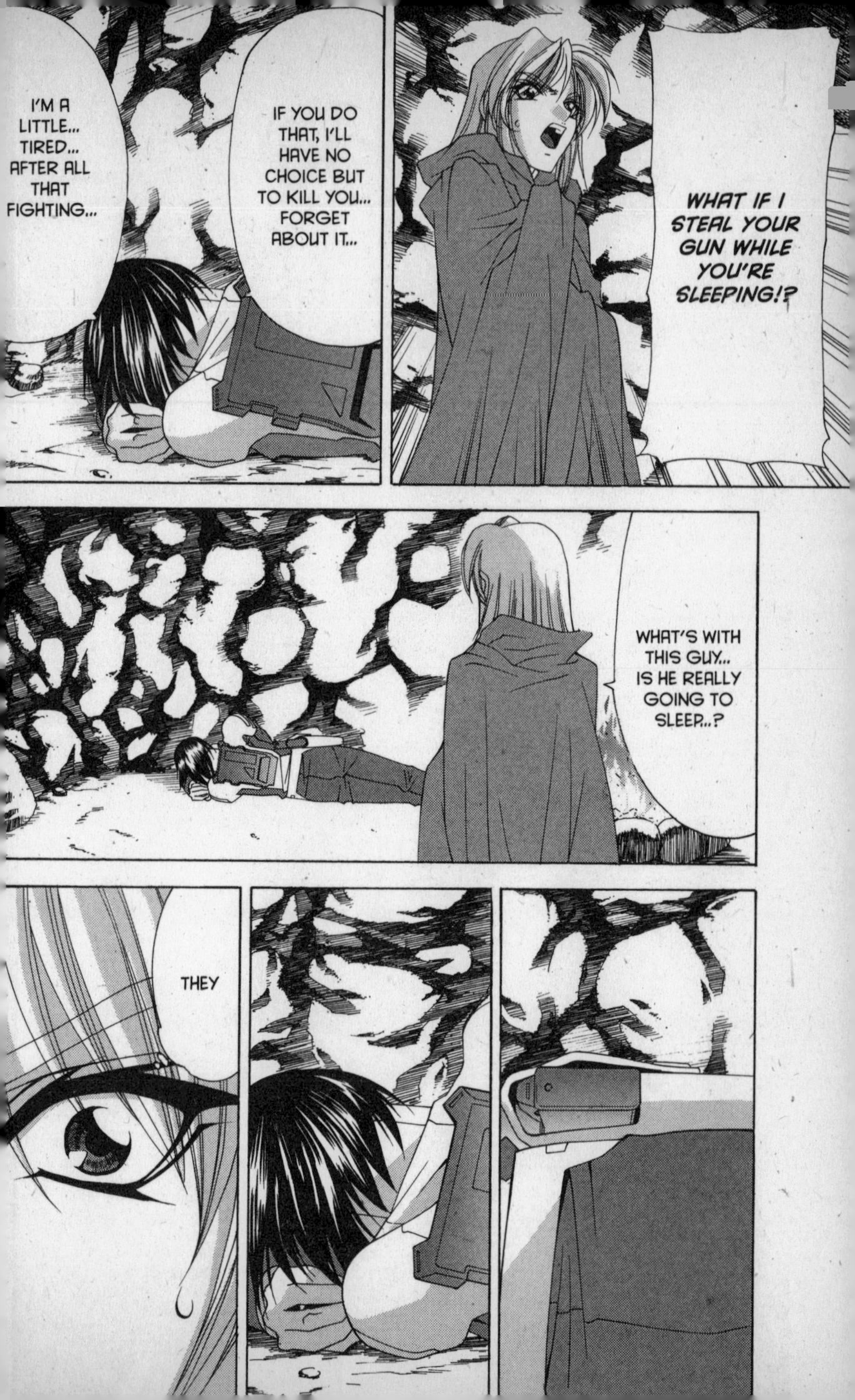
WHAT IF I STEAL YOUR GUN WHILE YOU'RE SLEEPING!?
I'M A LITTLE... TIRED... AFTER ALL THAT FIGHTING...
IF YOU DO THAT, I'LL HAVE NO CHOICE BUT TO KILL YOU... FORGET ABOUT IT...
WHAT'S WITH THIS GUY... IS HE REALLY GOING TO SLEEP...?
THEY

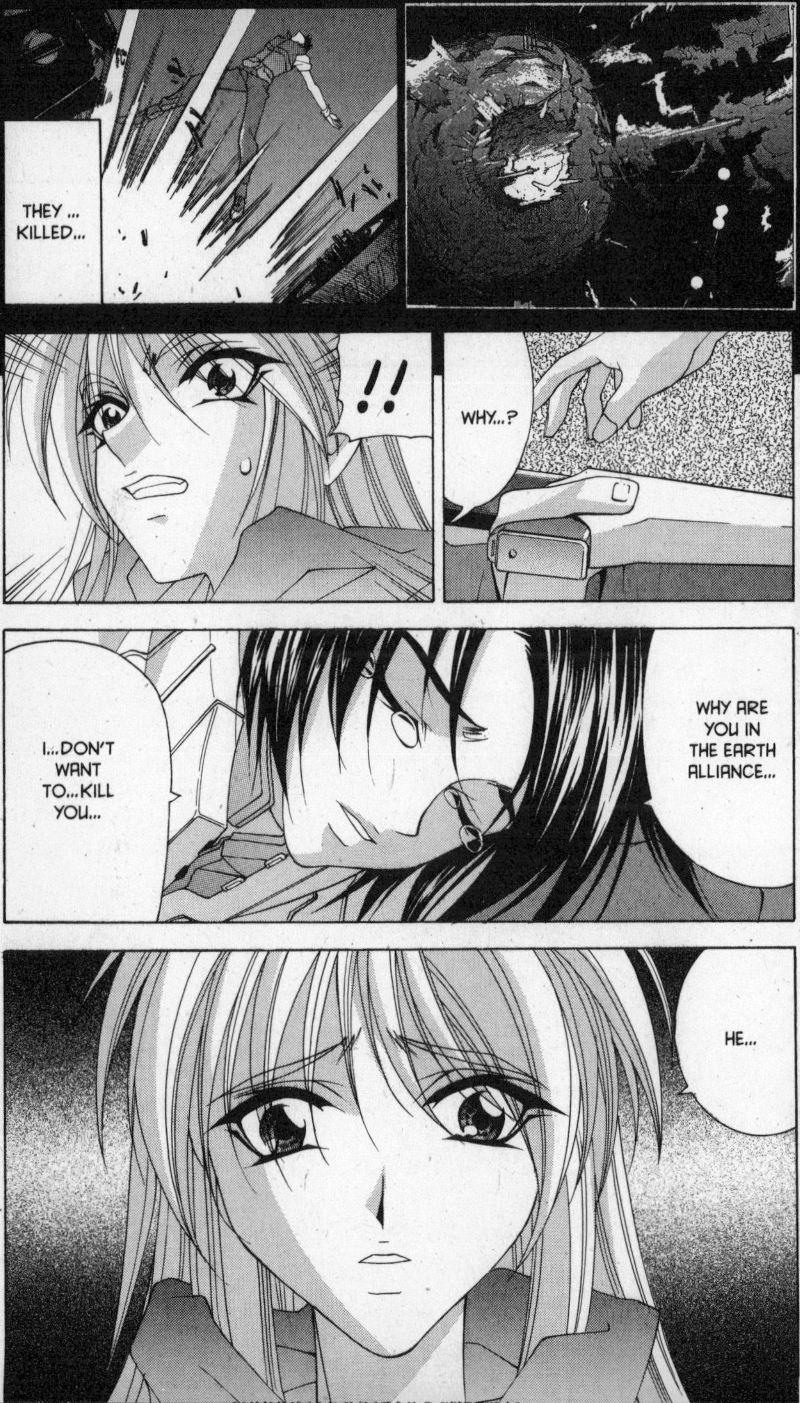
THEY ... KILLED...
WHY...?
!!
WHY ARE YOU IN THE EARTH ALLIANCE...
I...DON'T WANT TO...KILL YOU...
HE...

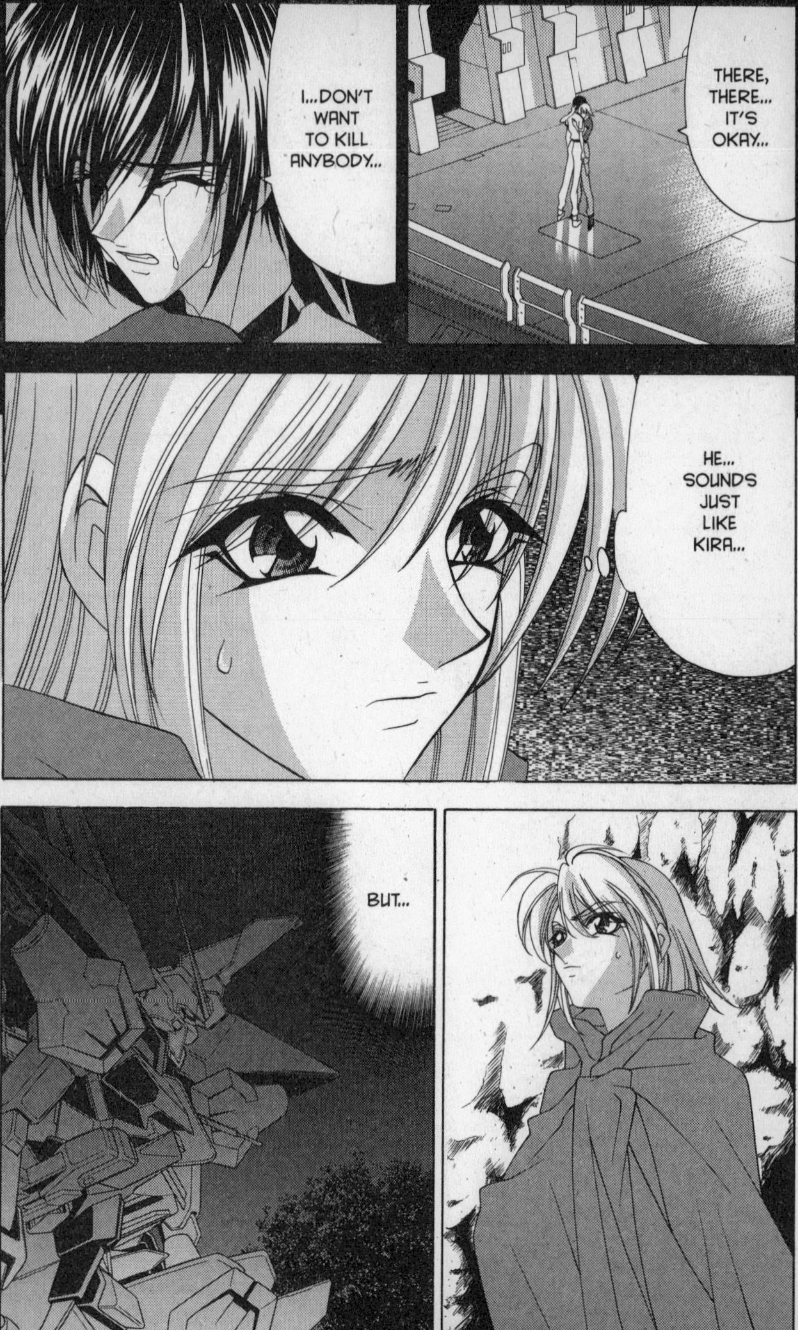
THERE, THERE... IT'S OKAY...
I...DON'T WANT TO KILL ANYBODY...
HE... SOUNDS JUST LIKE KIRA...
BUT...

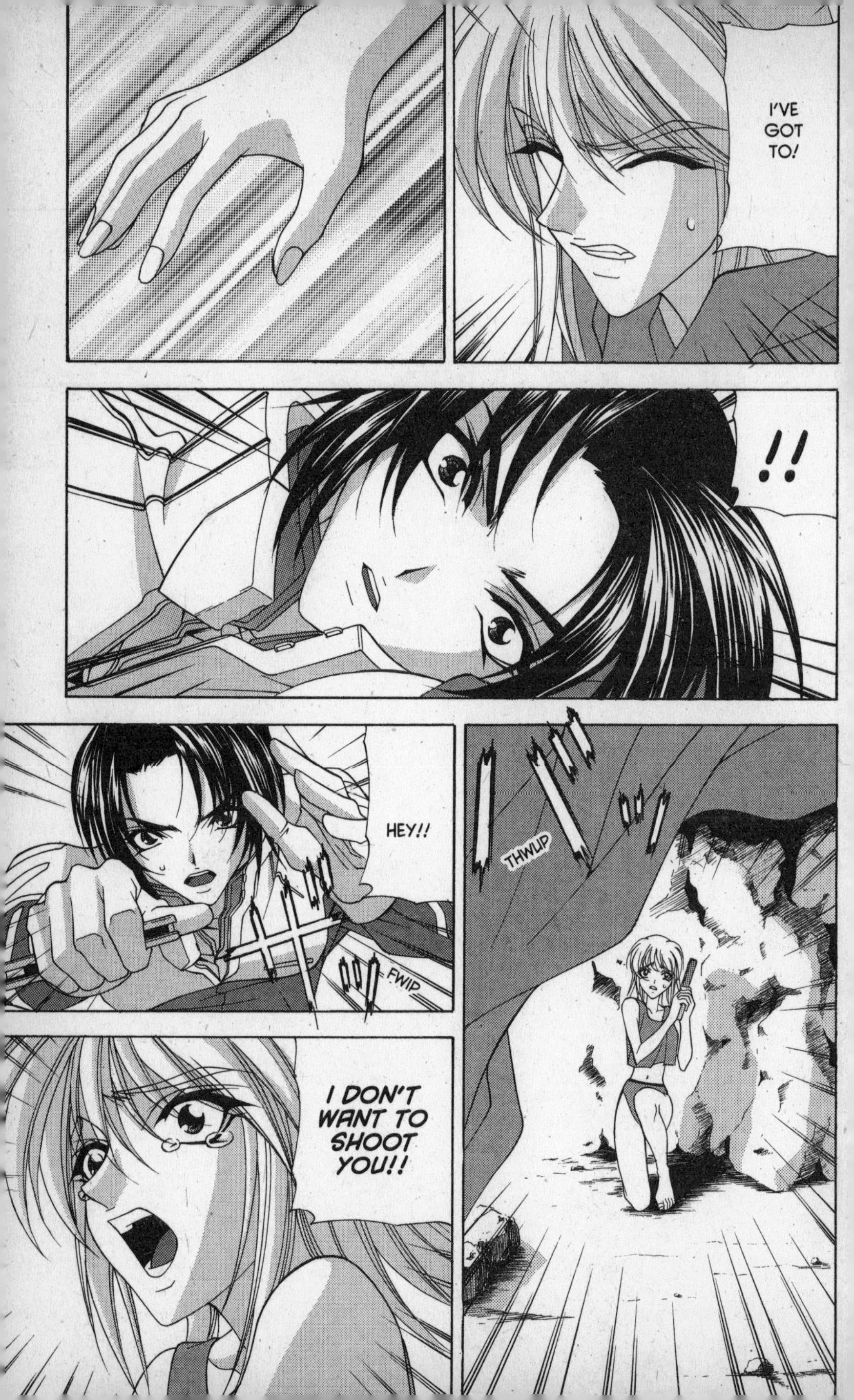
I'VE GOT TO!
!!
THWUP
HEY!!
FWIP
I DON'T WANT TO SHOOT YOU!!

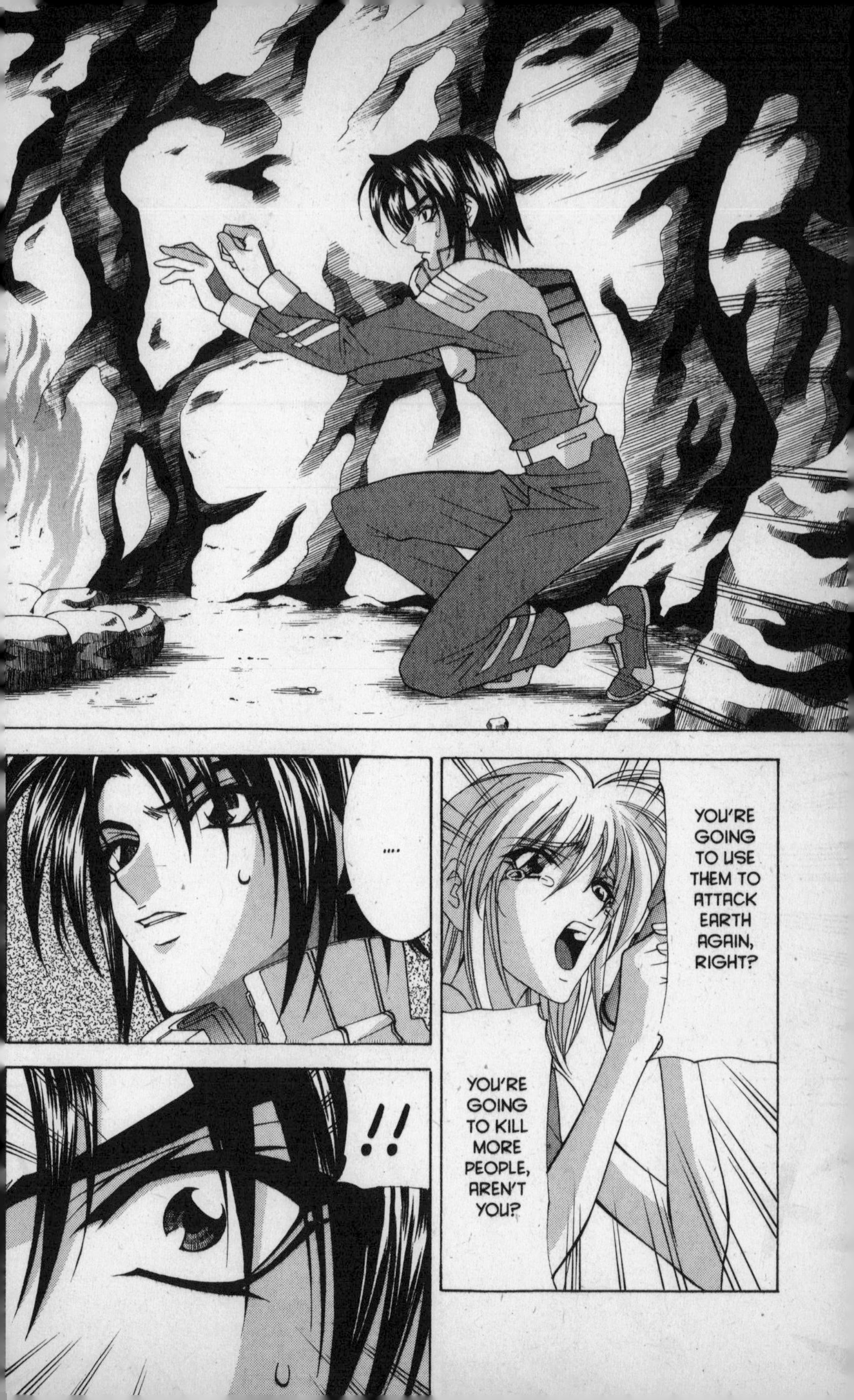
YOU'RE GOING TO USE THEM TO ATTACK EARTH AGAIN, RIGHT?
YOU'RE GOING TO KILL MORE PEOPLE, AREN'T YOU?
....
!!

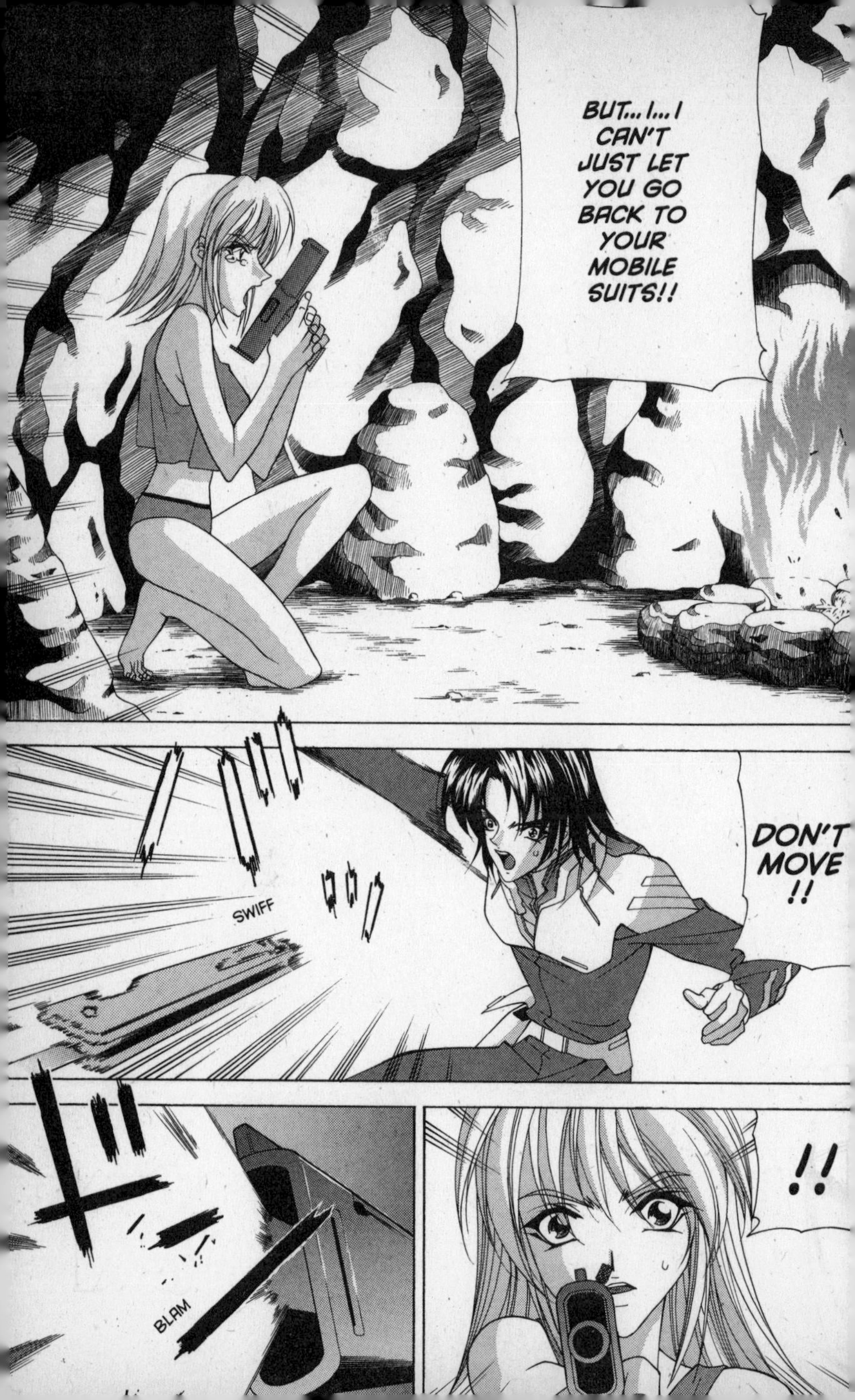
BUT... I... I CAN'T JUST LET YOU GO BACK TO YOUR MOBILE SUITS!!
DON'T MOVE !!
SWIFF
!!
BLAM

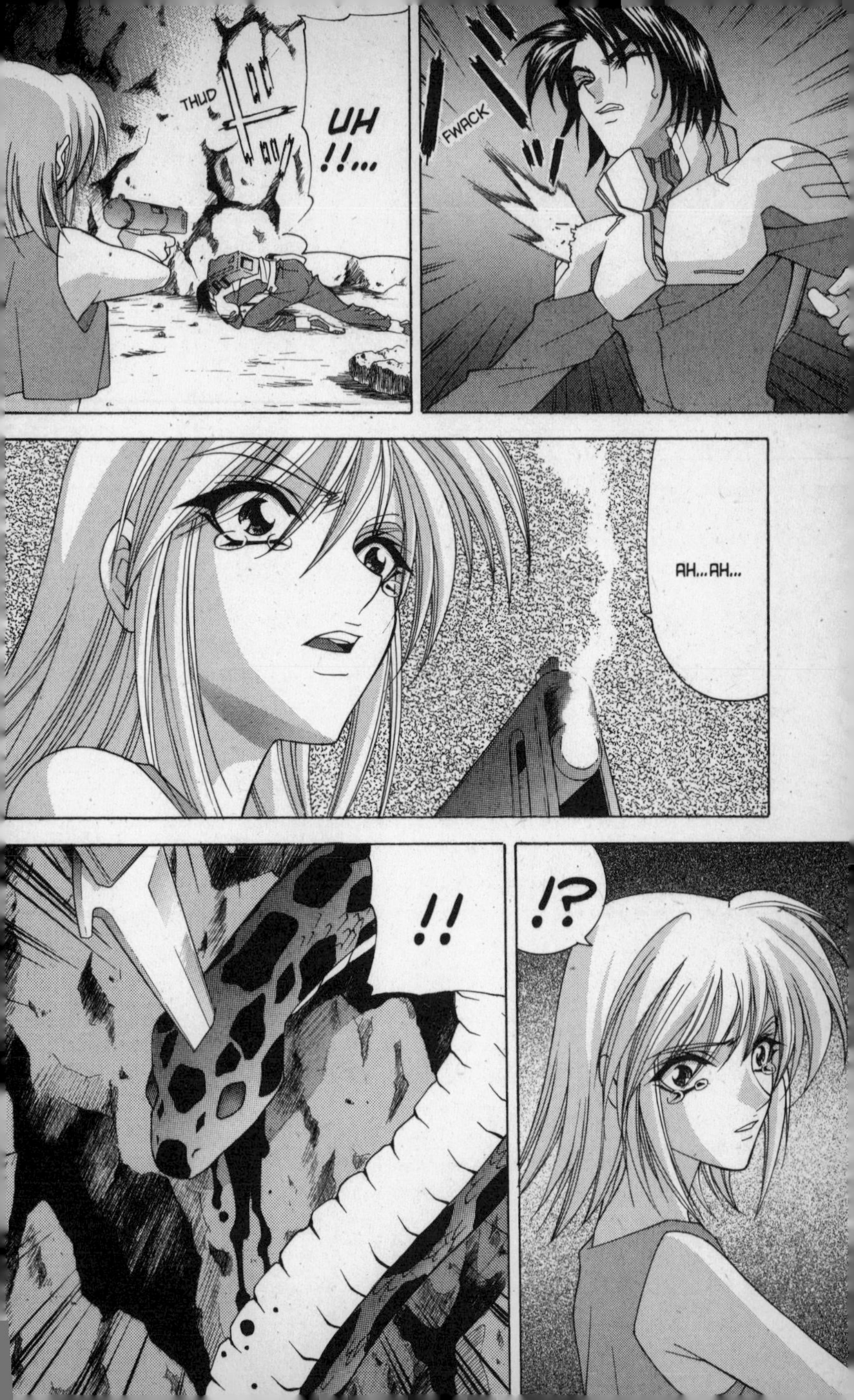
FWACK
THUD
UH !!...
AH...AH...
!?
!!

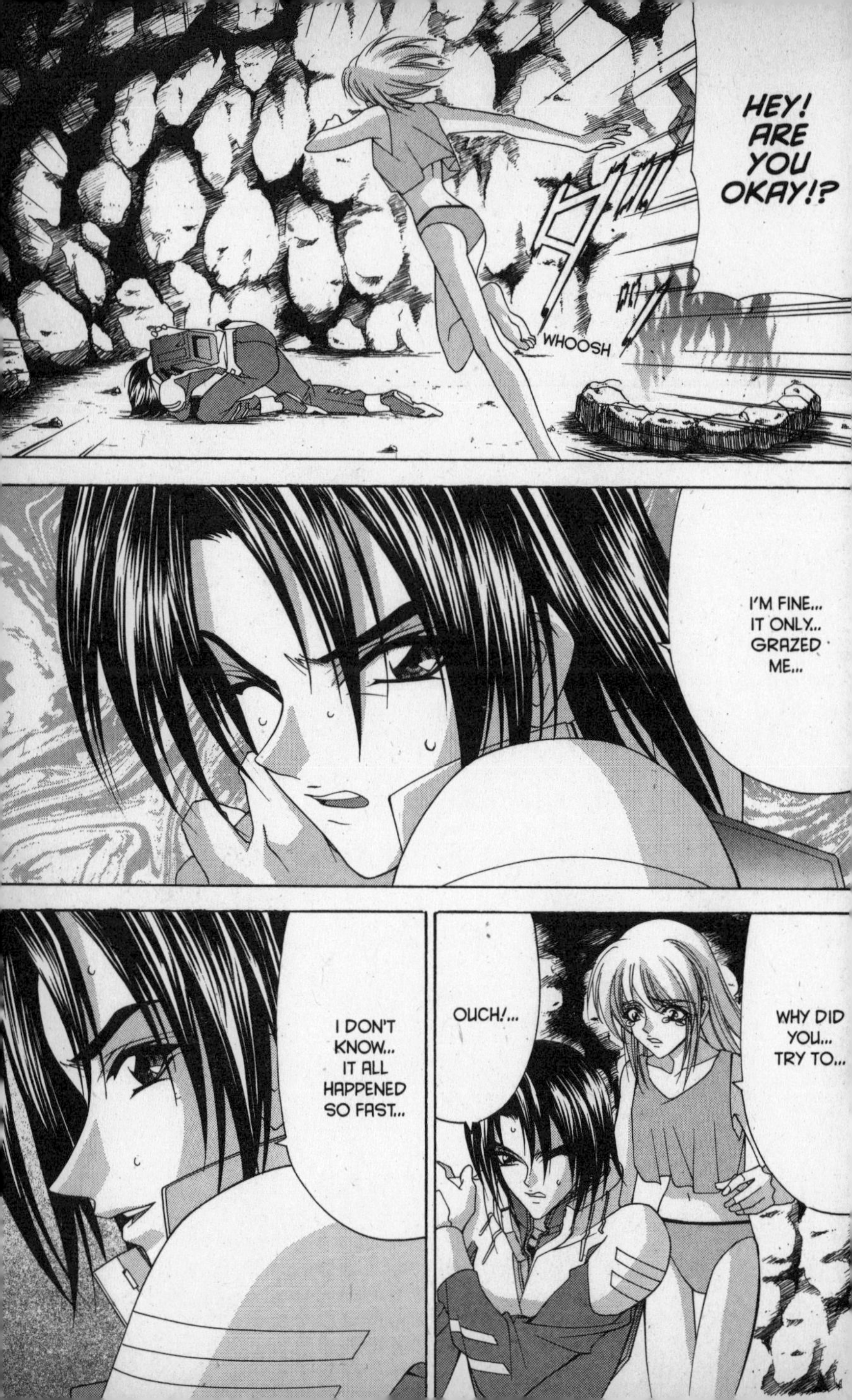
HEY! ARE YOU OKAY!?
WHOOSH
I'M FINE... IT ONLY... GRAZED ME...
WHY DID YOU... TRY TO...
OUCH!...
I DON'T KNOW... IT ALL HAPPENED SO FAST...

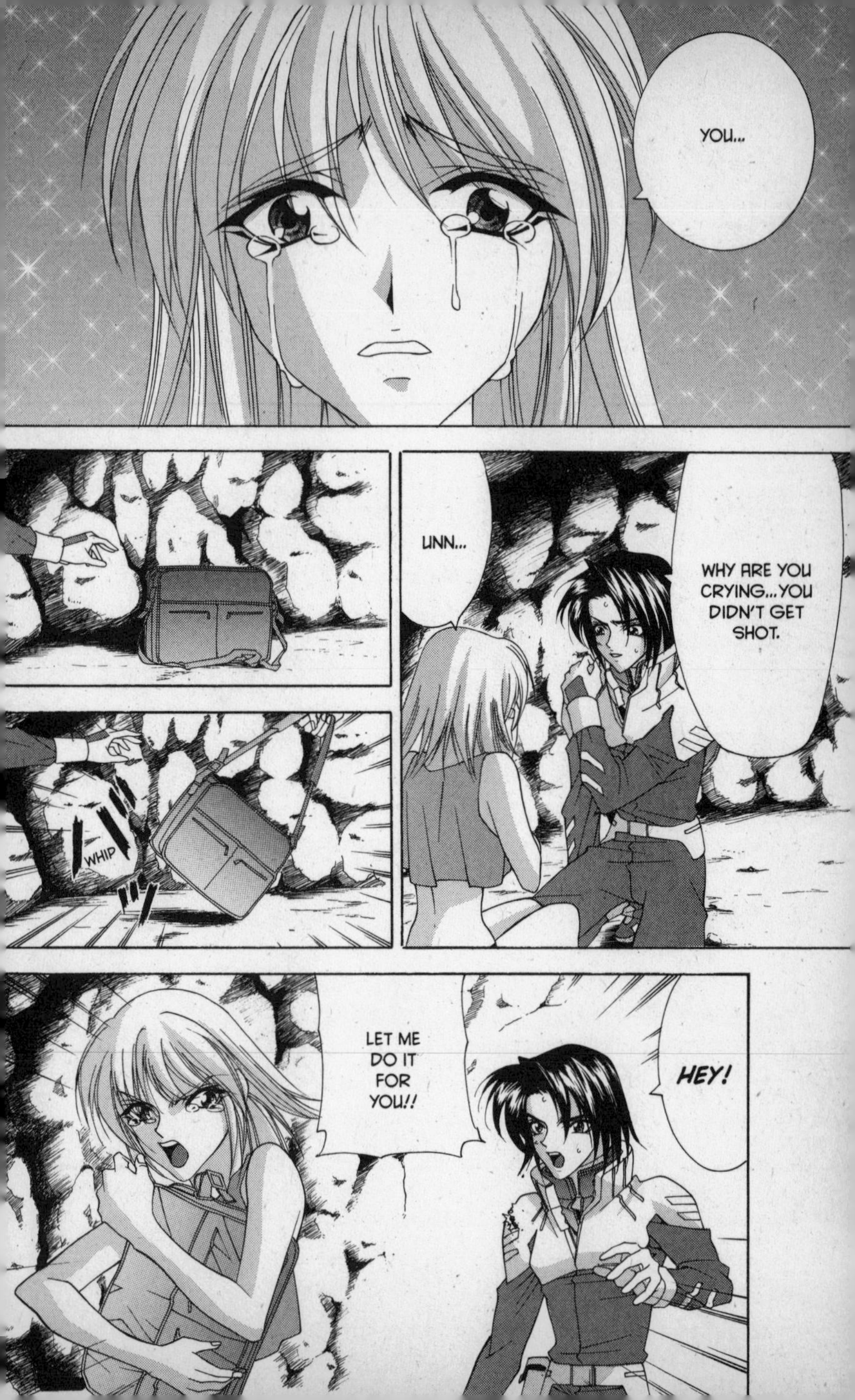
YOU...
WHY ARE YOU CRYING...YOU DIDN'T GET SHOT.
UNN...
WHIP
HEY!
LET ME DO IT FOR YOU!!

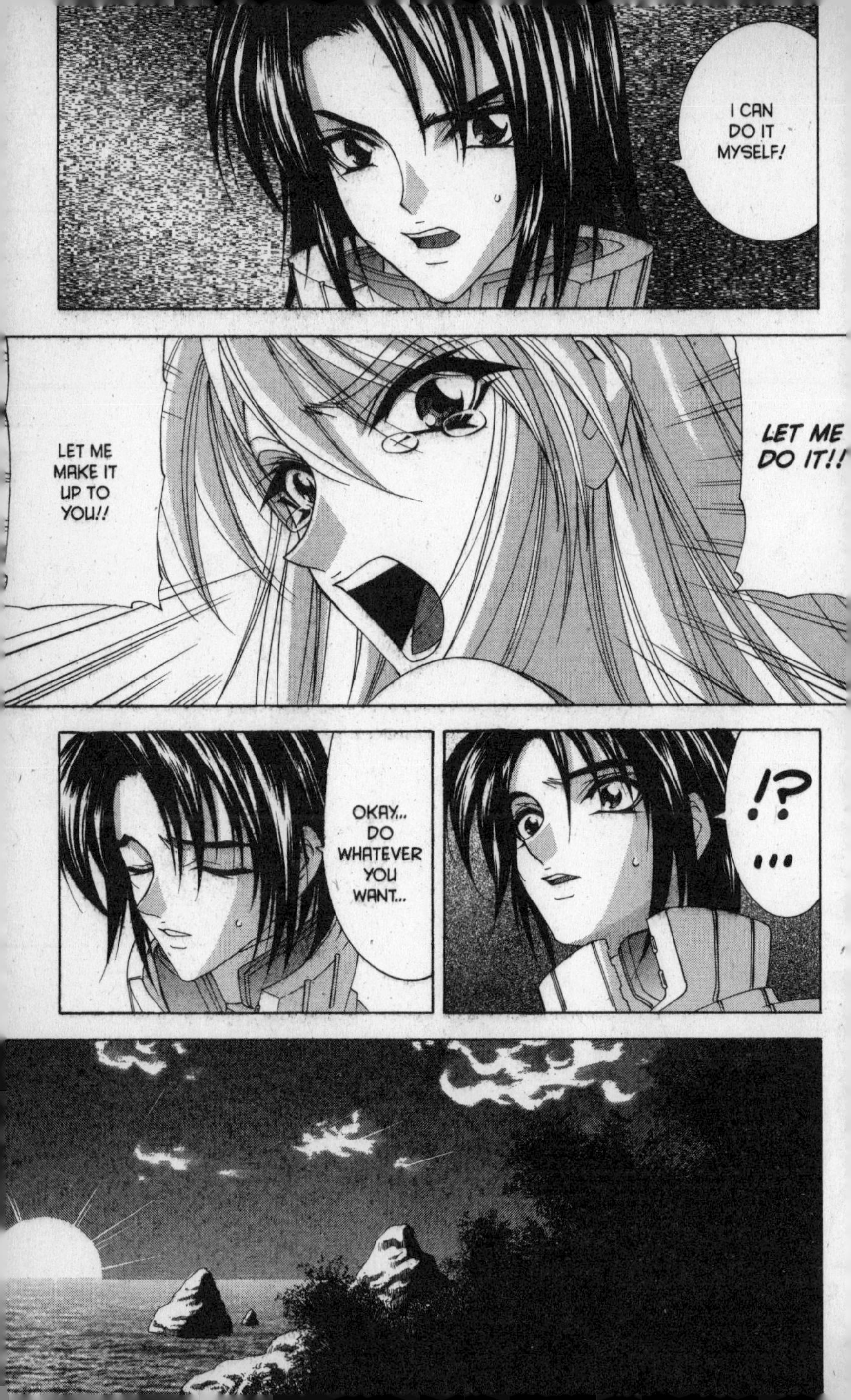
I CAN DO IT MYSELF!
LET ME DO IT!!
LET ME MAKE IT UP TO YOU!!
!? ...
OKAY... DO WHATEVER YOU WANT...

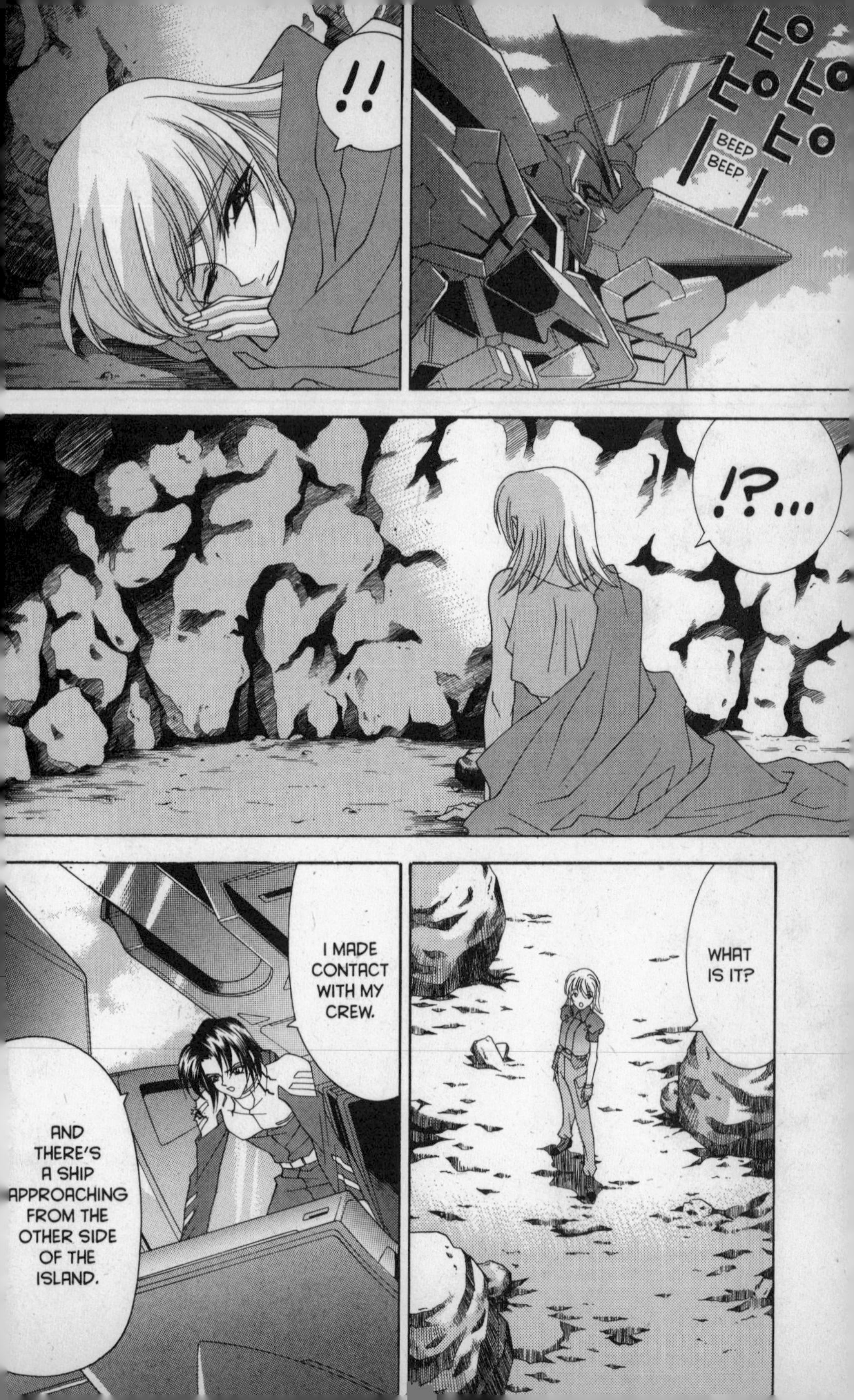
BEEP BEEP
!!
!?...
WHAT IS IT?
I MADE CONTACT WITH MY CREW.
AND THERE'S A SHIP APPROACHING FROM THE OTHER SIDE OF THE ISLAND.

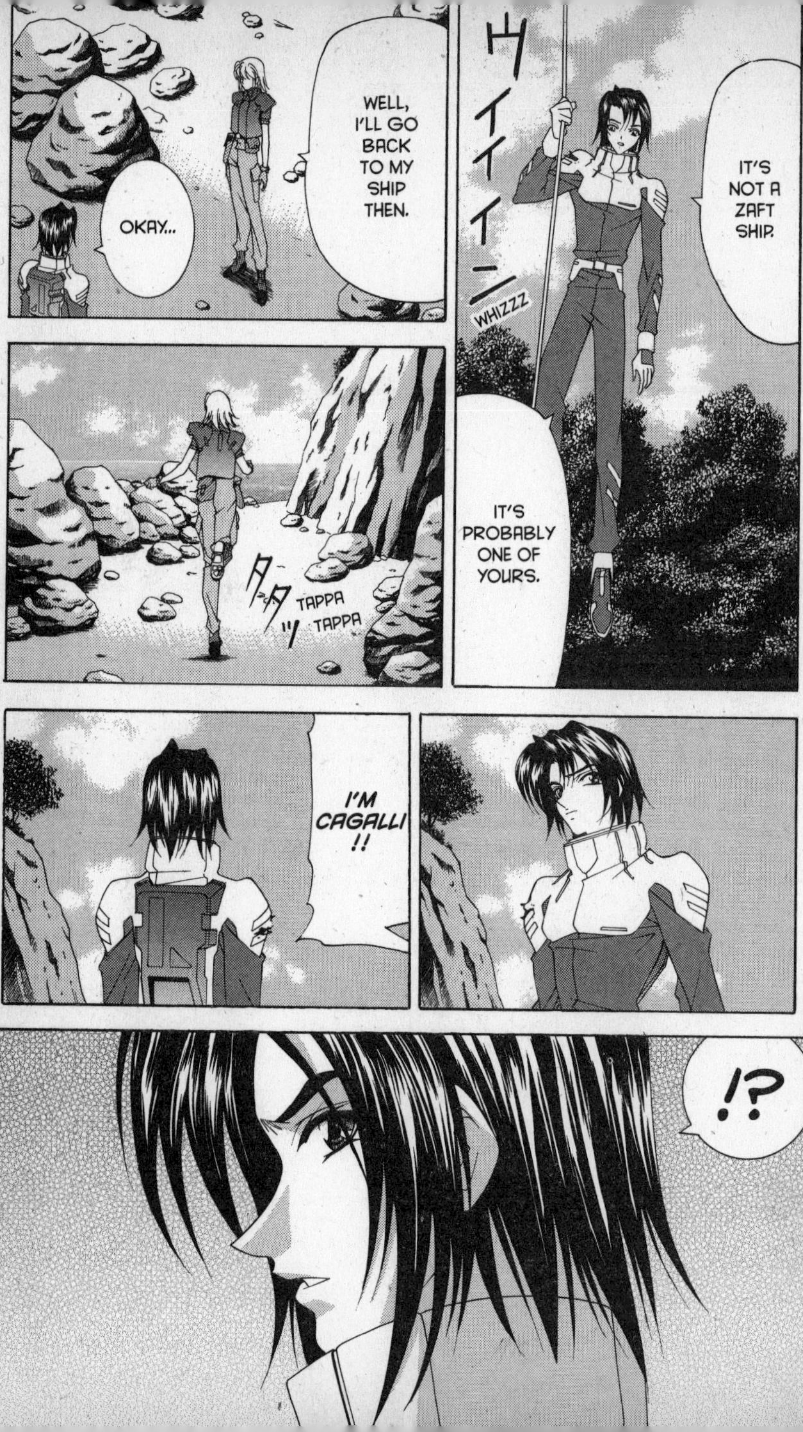
IT'S NOT A ZAFT SHIP.
WHIZZZ
IT'S PROBABLY ONE OF YOURS.
WELL, I'LL GO BACK TO MY SHIP THEN.
OKAY...
TAPPA TAPPA
I'M CAGALLI !!
!?

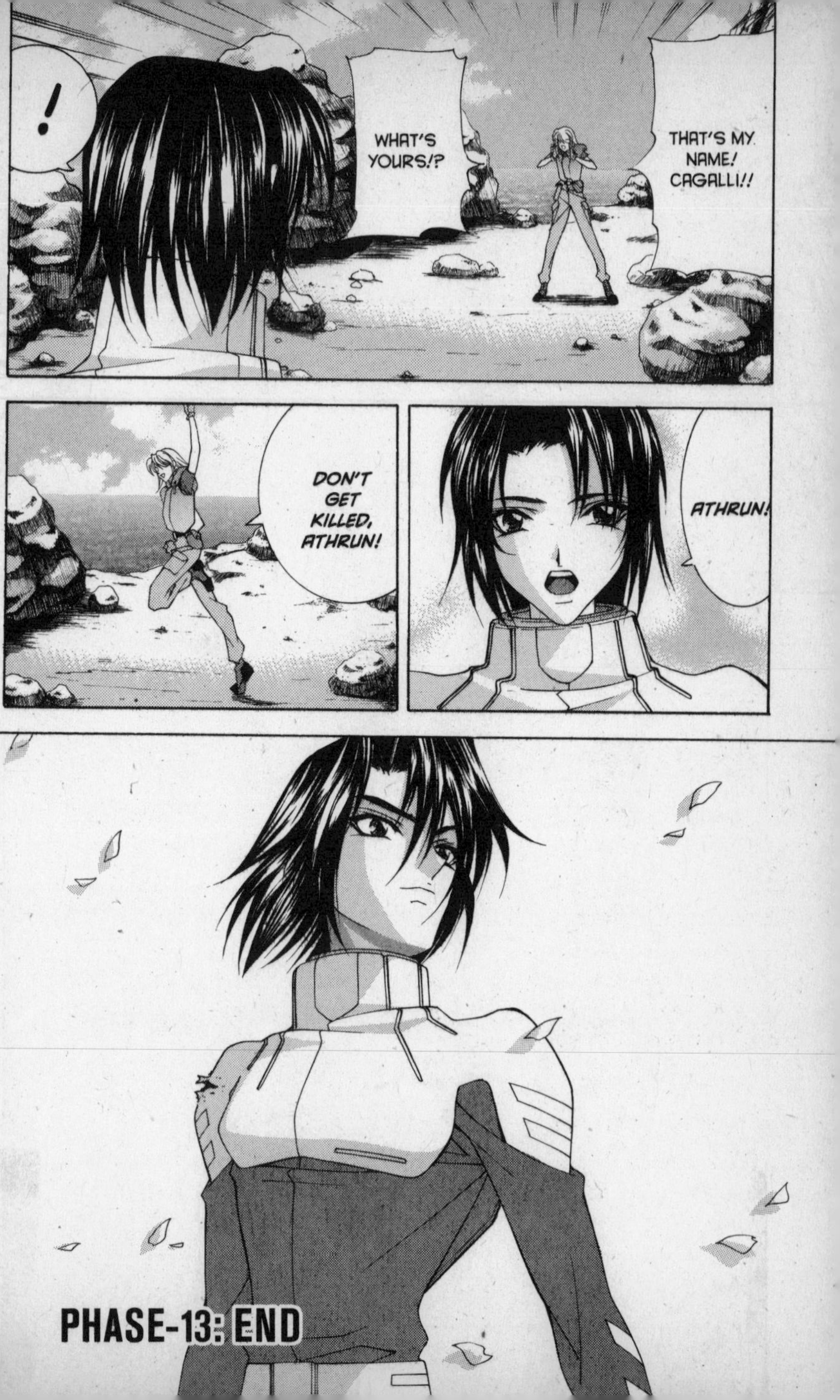
THAT'S MY NAME! CAGALLI!!
WHAT'S YOURS!?
!
ATHRUN!
DON'T GET KILLED, ATHRUN!
PHASE-13: END

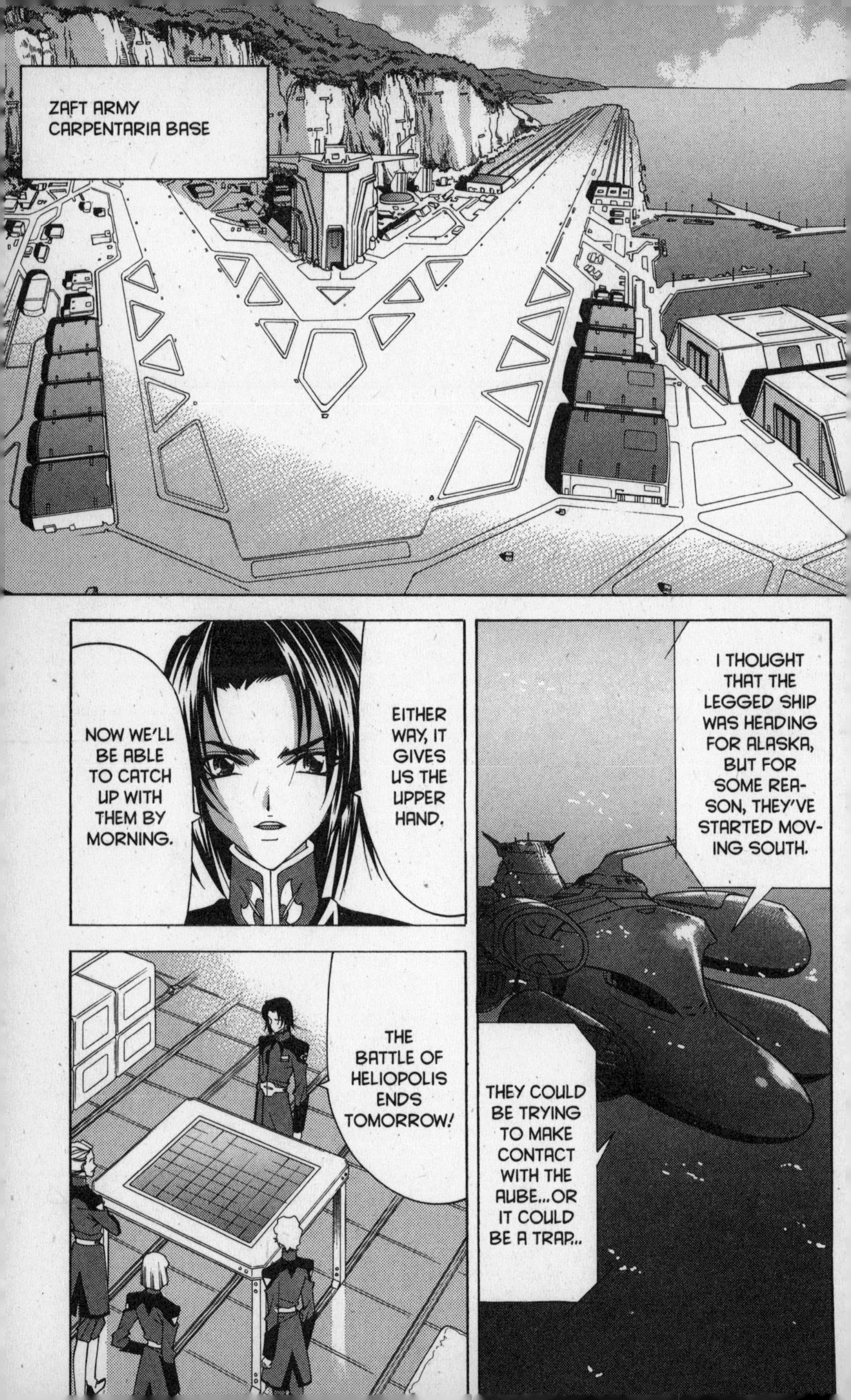
ZAFT ARMY CARPENTARIA BASE
I THOUGHT THAT THE LEGGED SHIP WAS HEADING FOR ALASKA, BUT FOR SOME REA-SON, THEY'VE STARTED MOV-ING SOUTH.
THEY COULD BE TRYING TO MAKE CONTACT WITH THE AUBE...OR IT COULD BE A TRAP...
EITHER WAY, IT GIVES US THE UPPER HAND.
NOW WE'LL BE ABLE TO CATCH UP WITH THEM BY MORNING.
THE BATTLE OF HELIOPOLIS ENDS TOMORROW!

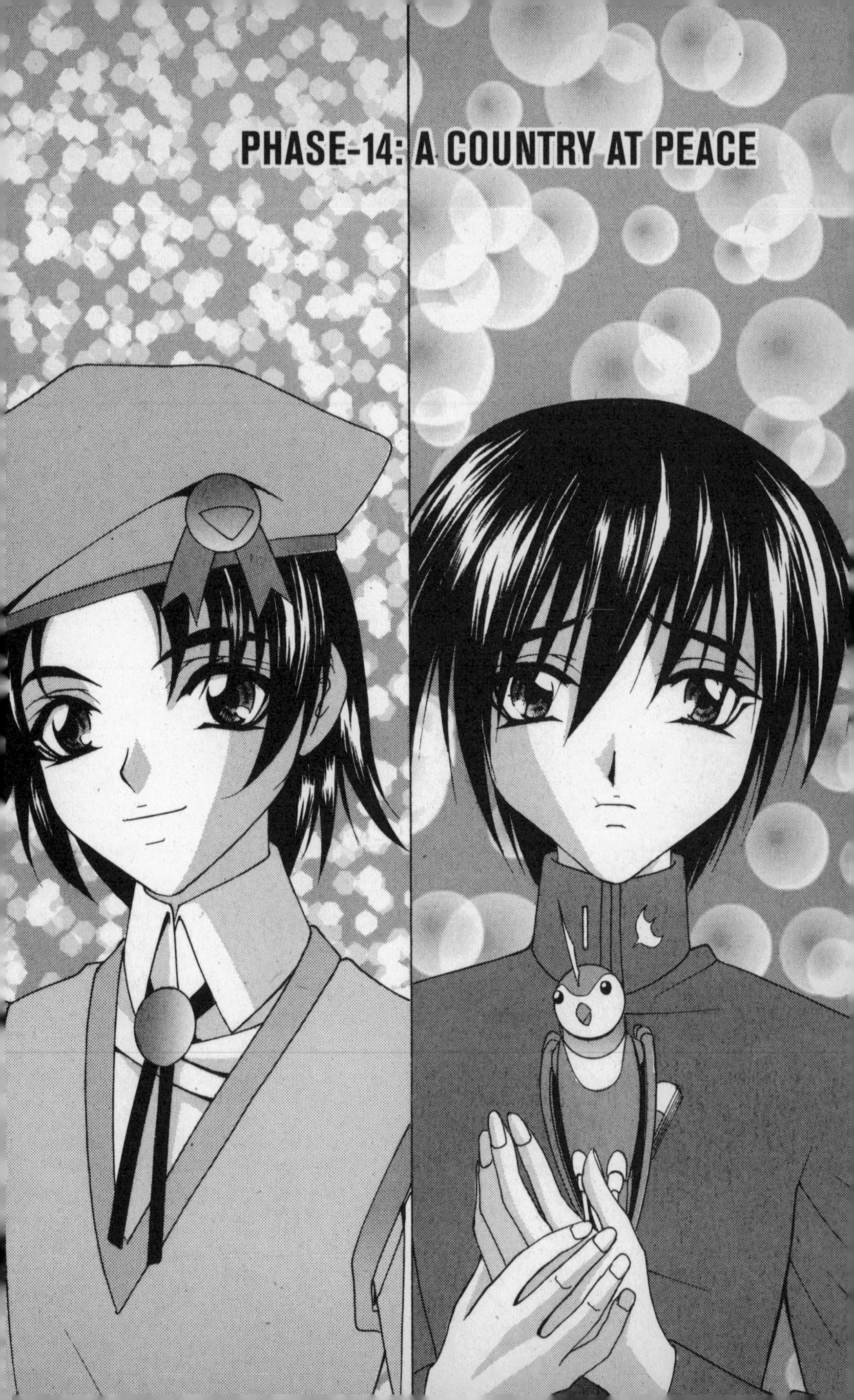
PHASE-14: A COUNTRY AT PEACE

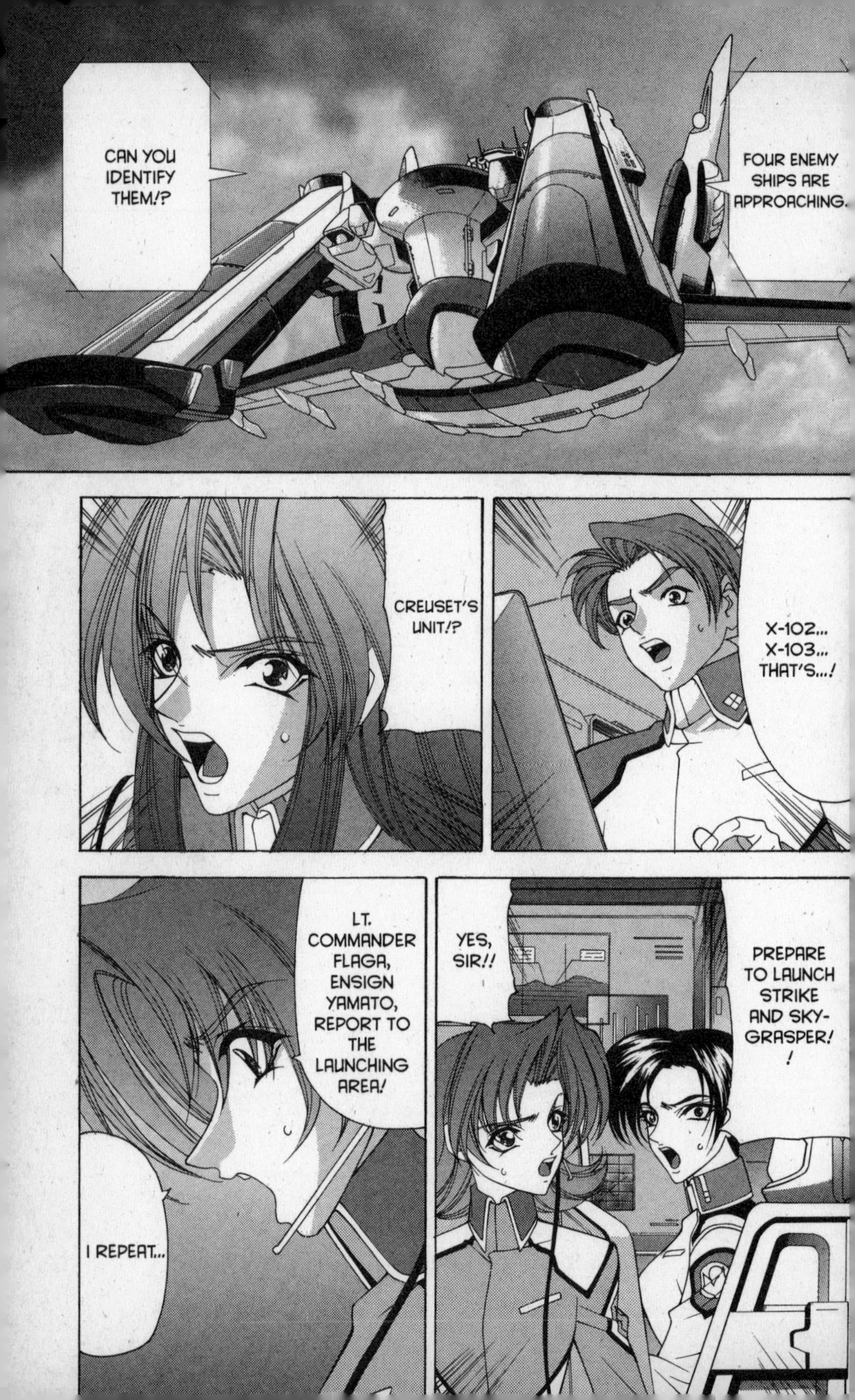
FOUR ENEMY SHIPS ARE APPROACHING.
CAN YOU IDENTIFY THEM!?
X-102... X-103... THAT'S...!
CREUSET'S UNIT!?
PREPARE TO LAUNCH STRIKE AND SKY-GRASPER!
YES, SIR!!
LT. COMMANDER FLAGA, ENSIGN YAMATO, REPORT TO THE LAUNCHING AREA!
I REPEAT...

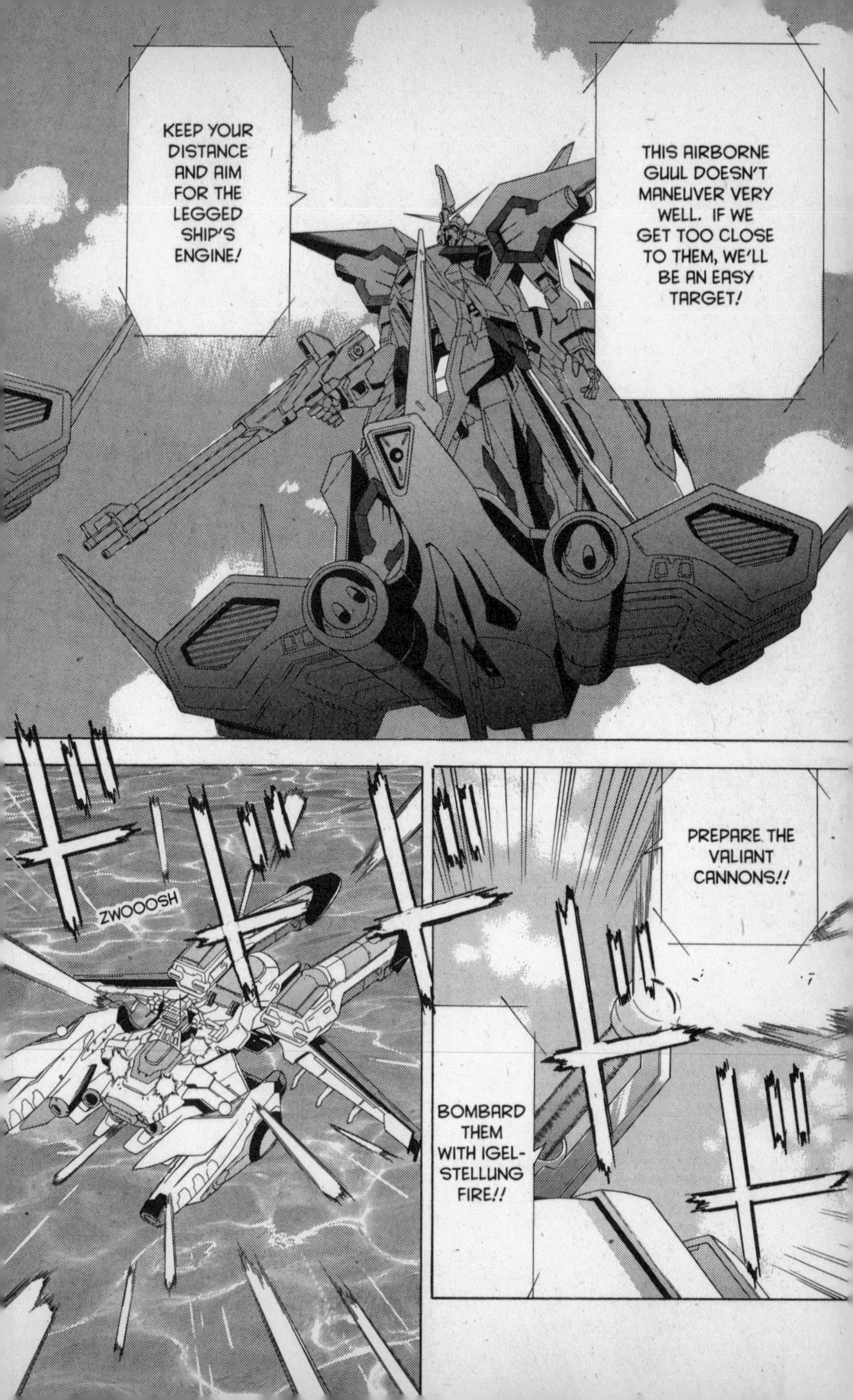
THIS AIRBORNE GUUL DOESN'T MANEUVER VERY WELL. IF WE GET TOO CLOSE TO THEM, WE'LL BE AN EASY TARGET!
KEEP YOUR DISTANCE AND AIM FOR THE LEGGED SHIP'S ENGINE!
PREPARE THE VALIANT CANNONS!!
BOMBARD THEM WITH IGEL-STELLUNG FIRE!!
ZWOOOSH

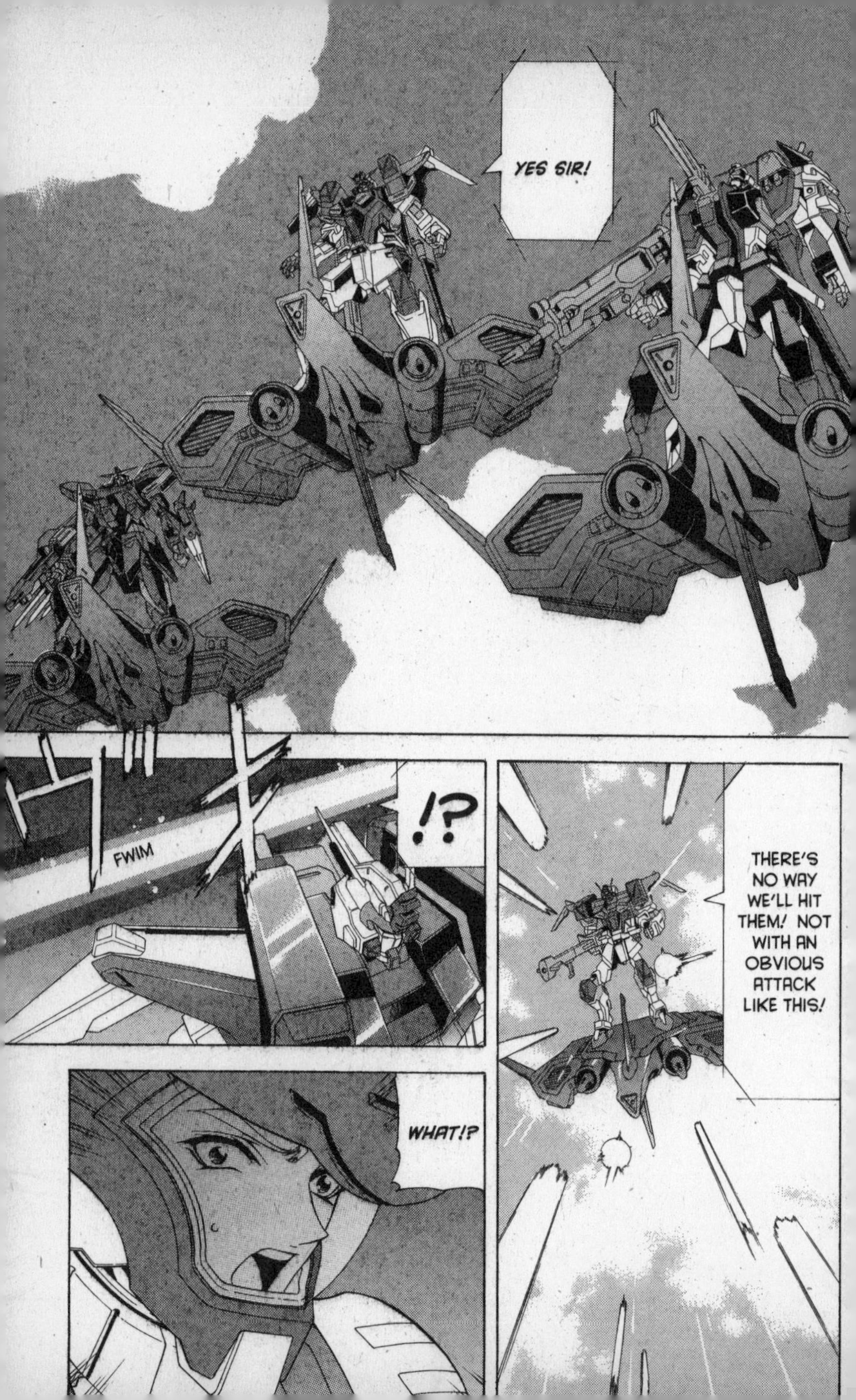
YES SIR!
THERE'S NO WAY WE'LL HIT THEM! NOT WITH AN OBVIOUS ATTACK LIKE THIS!
!?
FWIM
WHAT!?

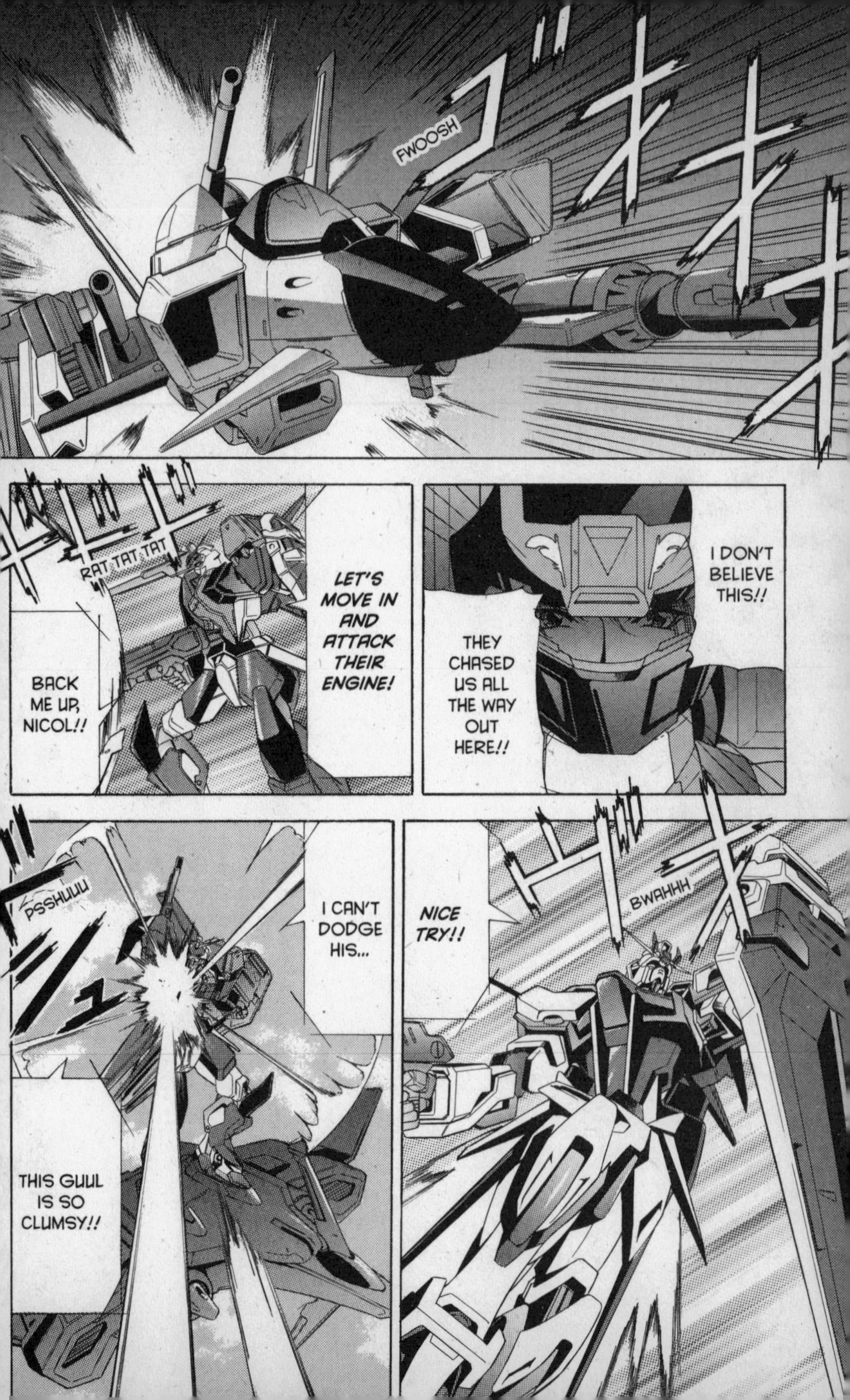
FWOOSH
I DON'T BELIEVE THIS!!
THEY CHASED US ALL THE WAY OUT HERE!!
LET'S MOVE IN AND ATTACK THEIR ENGINE!
RAT TAT TAT
BACK ME UP, NICOL!!
BWAHHH
NICE TRY!!
I CAN'T DODGE HIS...
PSSHUUU
THIS GUUL IS SO CLUMSY!!

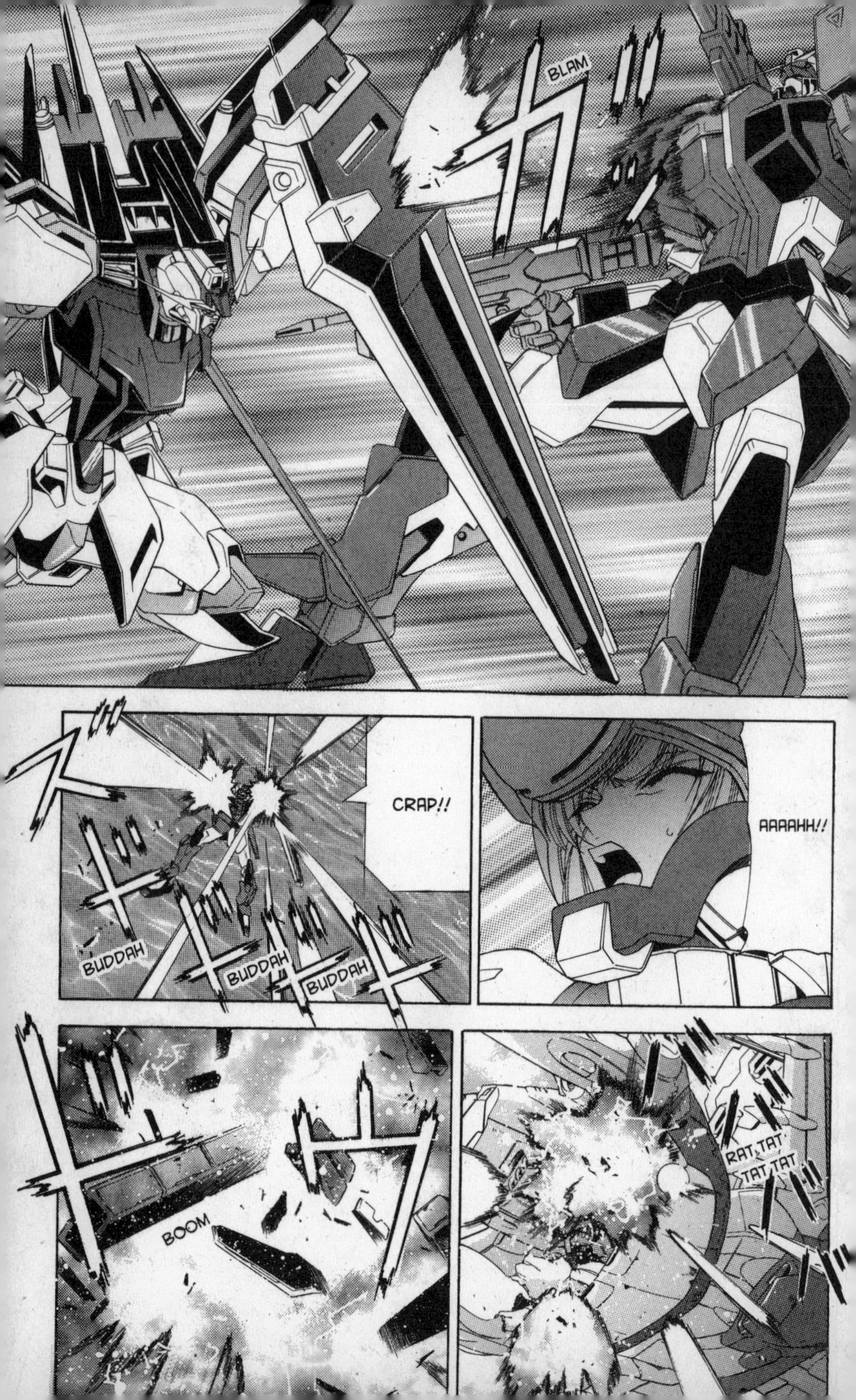
BLAM
AAAAHH!!
CRAP!!
BUDDAH
BUDDAH
BUDDAH
RAT TAT
TAT TAT
BOOM

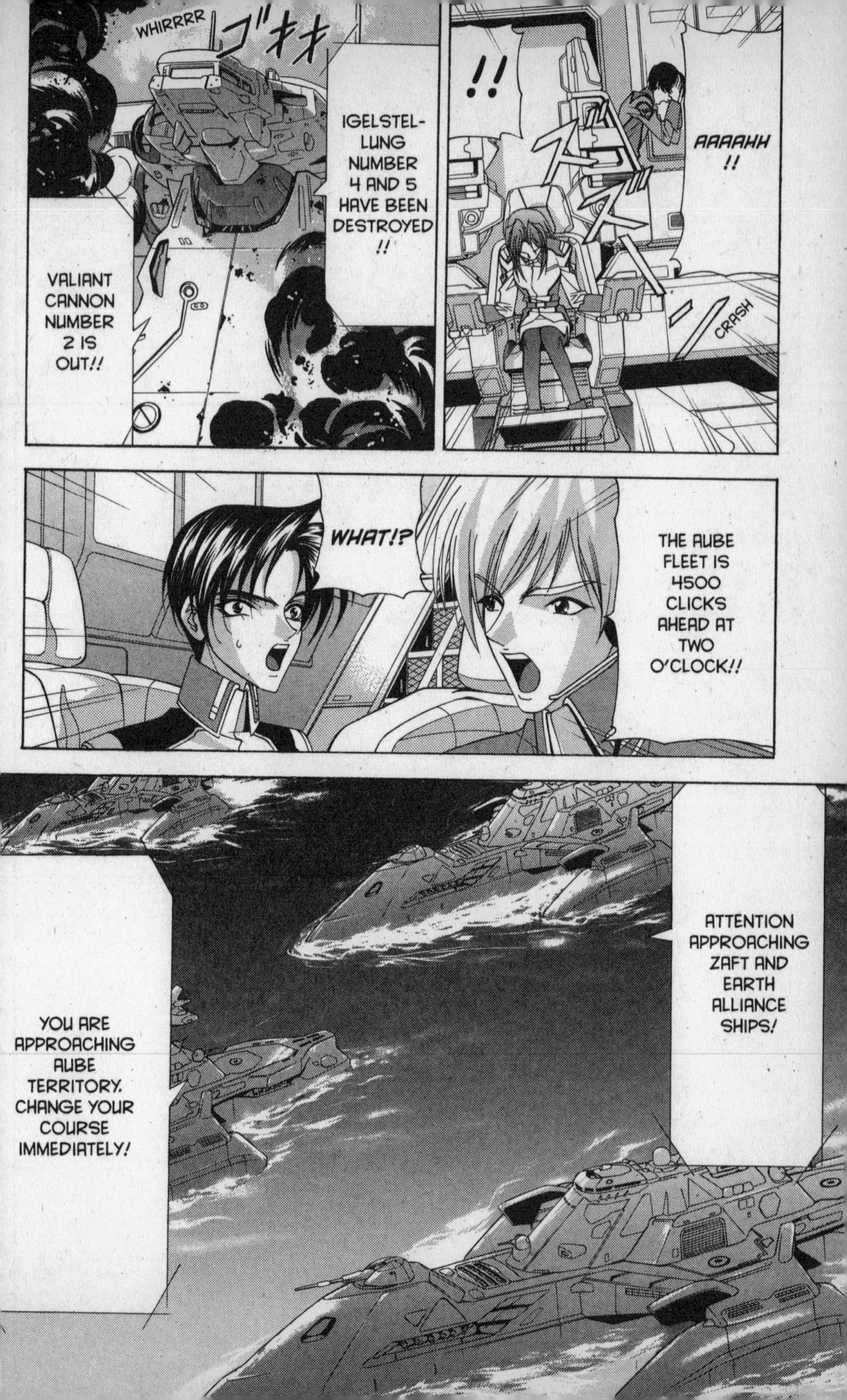
AAAAHH !!
!!
CRASH
WHIRRR
ゴオオ
IGELSTEL-LUNG NUMBER 4 AND 5 HAVE BEEN DESTROYED !!
VALIANT CANNON NUMBER 2 IS OUT!!
THE AUBE FLEET IS 4500 CLICKS AHEAD AT TWO O'CLOCK!!
WHAT!?
ATTENTION APPROACHING ZAFT AND EARTH ALLIANCE SHIPS!
YOU ARE APPROACHING AUBE TERRITORY. CHANGE YOUR COURSE IMMEDIATELY!

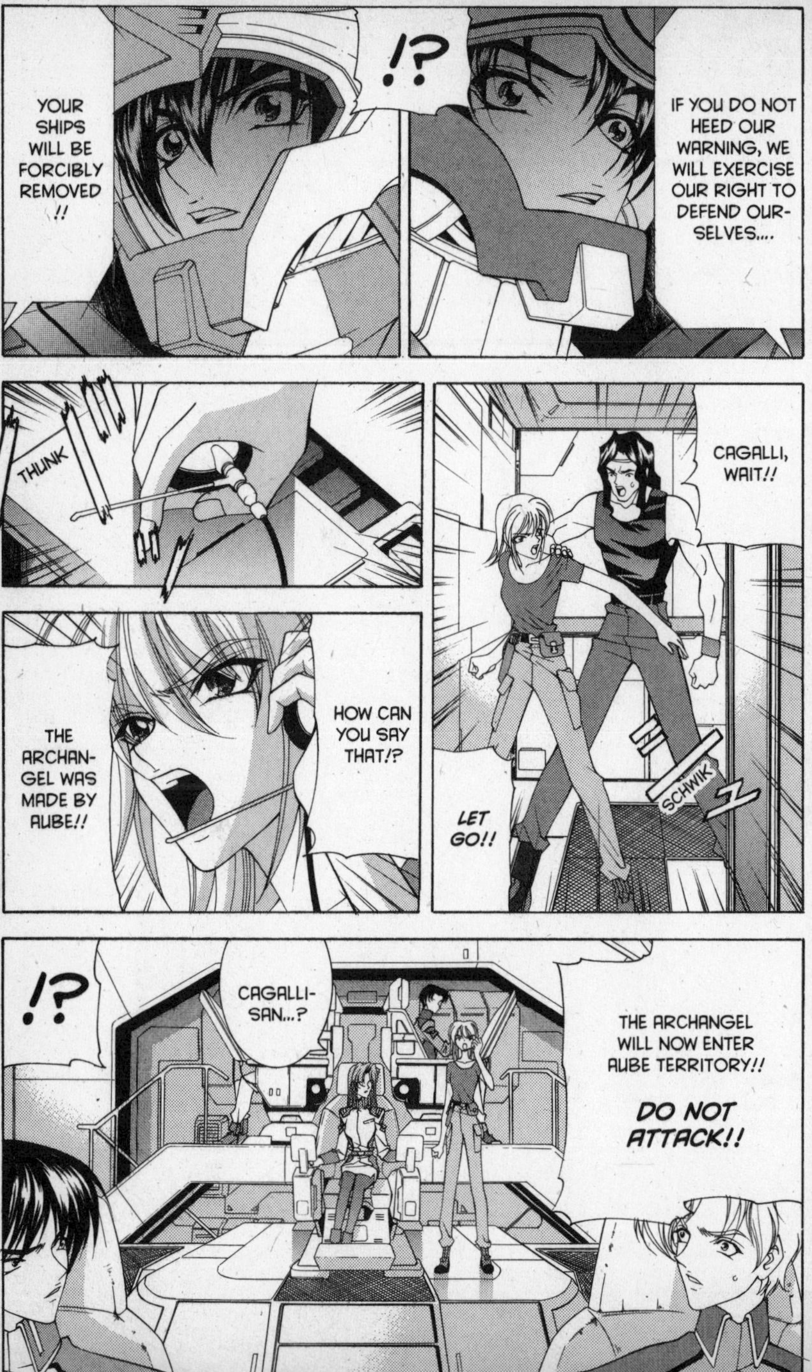
IF YOU DO NOT HEED OUR WARNING, WE WILL EXERCISE OUR RIGHT TO DEFEND OUR-SELVES....
!?
YOUR SHIPS WILL BE FORCIBLY REMOVED !!
CAGALLI, WAIT!!
SCHWIK
LET GO!!
THUNK
HOW CAN YOU SAY THAT!?
THE ARCHAN-GEL WAS MADE BY AUBE!!
THE ARCHANGEL WILL NOW ENTER AUBE TERRITORY!!
DO NOT ATTACK!!
CAGALLI-SAN...?
!?

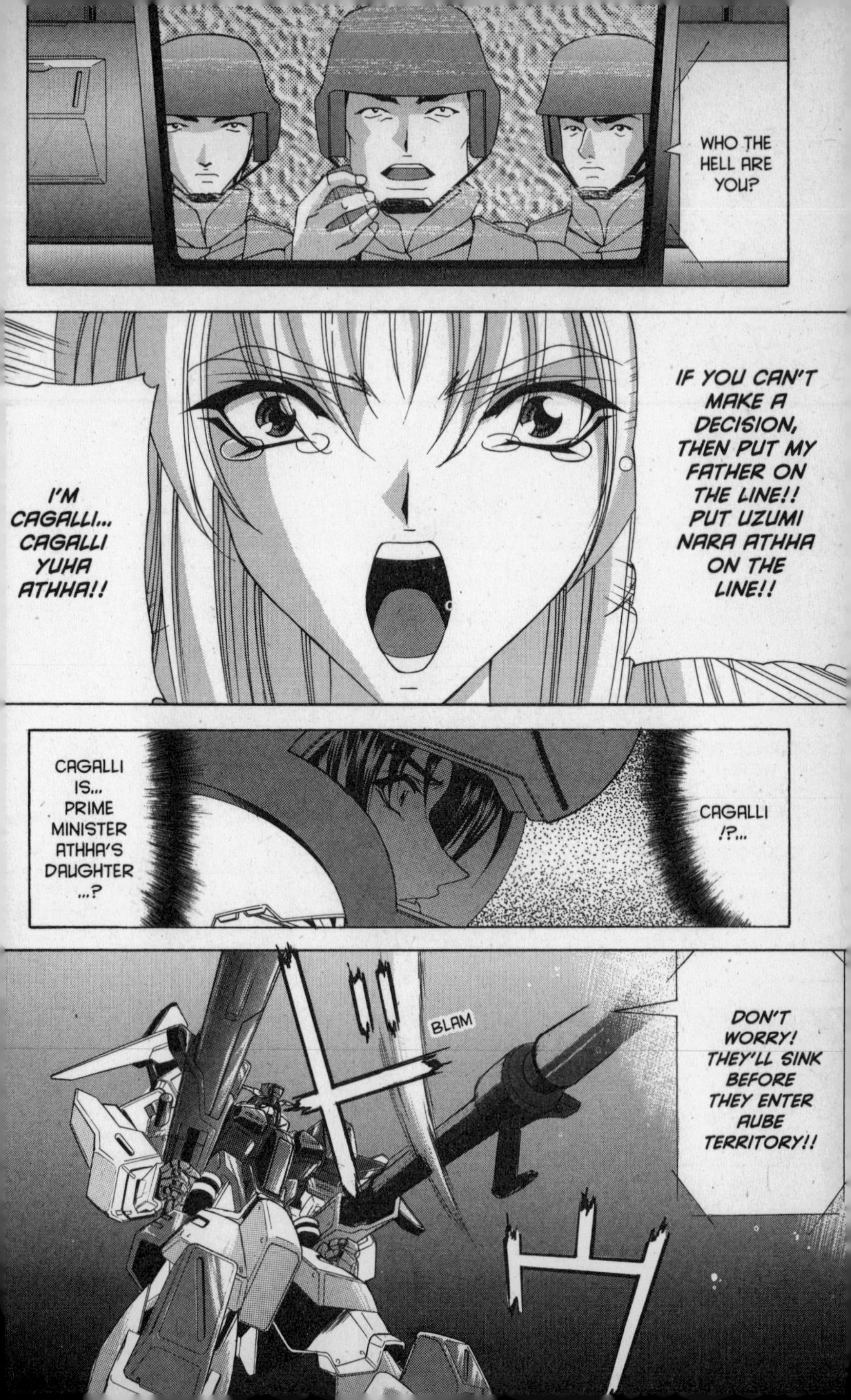
WHO THE HELL ARE YOU?
IF YOU CAN'T MAKE A DECISION, THEN PUT MY FATHER ON THE LINE!! PUT UZUMI NARA ATHHA ON THE LINE!!
I'M CAGALLI... CAGALLI YUHA ATHHA!!
CAGALLI !?...
CAGALLI IS... PRIME MINISTER ATHHA'S DAUGHTER ...?
DON'T WORRY! THEY'LL SINK BEFORE THEY ENTER AUBE TERRITORY!!
BLAM

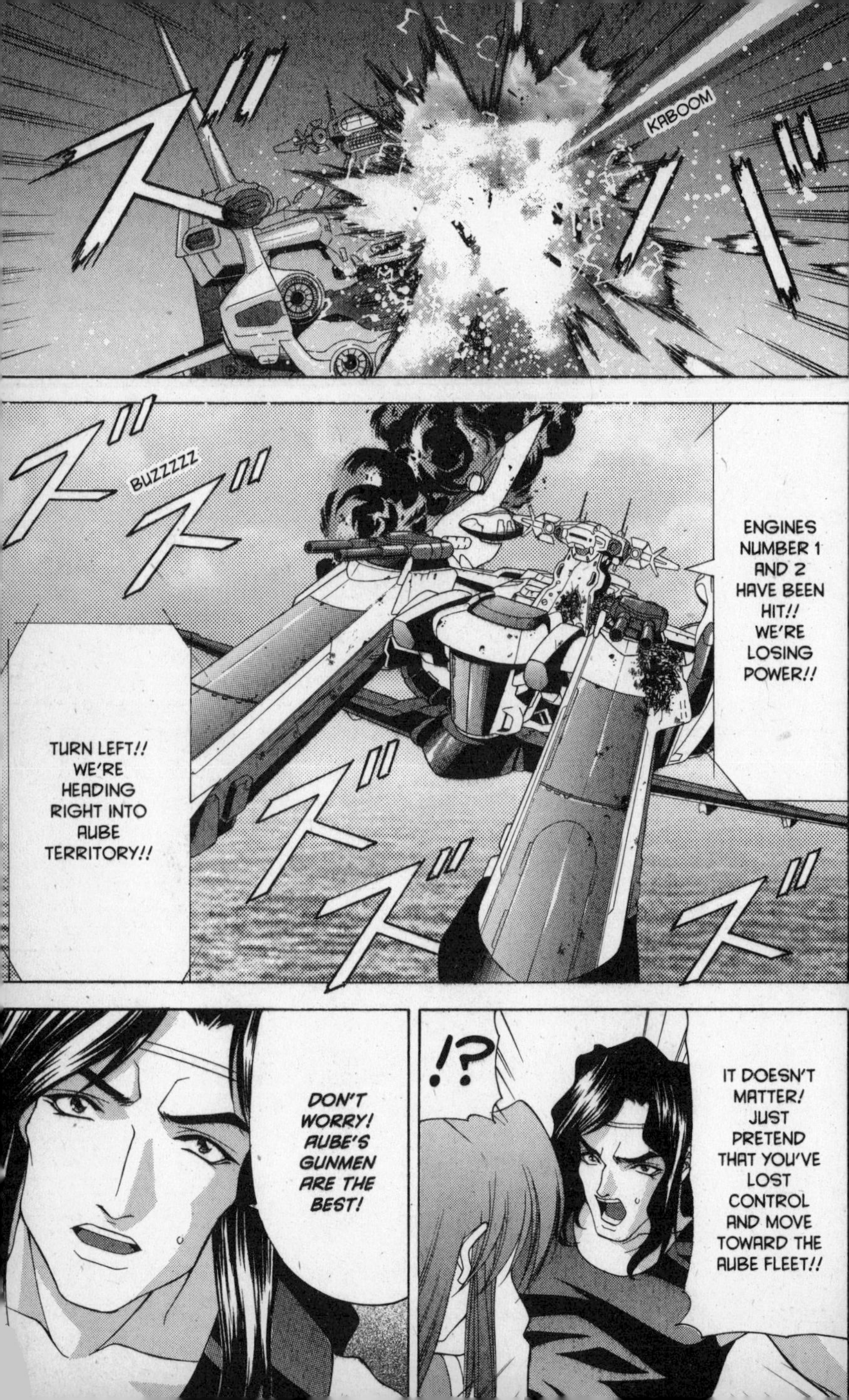
KABOOM
ENGINES NUMBER 1 AND 2 HAVE BEEN HIT!! WE'RE LOSING POWER!!
BUZZZZZ
TURN LEFT!! WE'RE HEADING RIGHT INTO AUBE TERRITORY!!
!?
IT DOESN'T MATTER! JUST PRETEND THAT YOU'VE LOST CONTROL AND MOVE TOWARD THE AUBE FLEET!!
DON'T WORRY! AUBE'S GUNMEN ARE THE BEST!

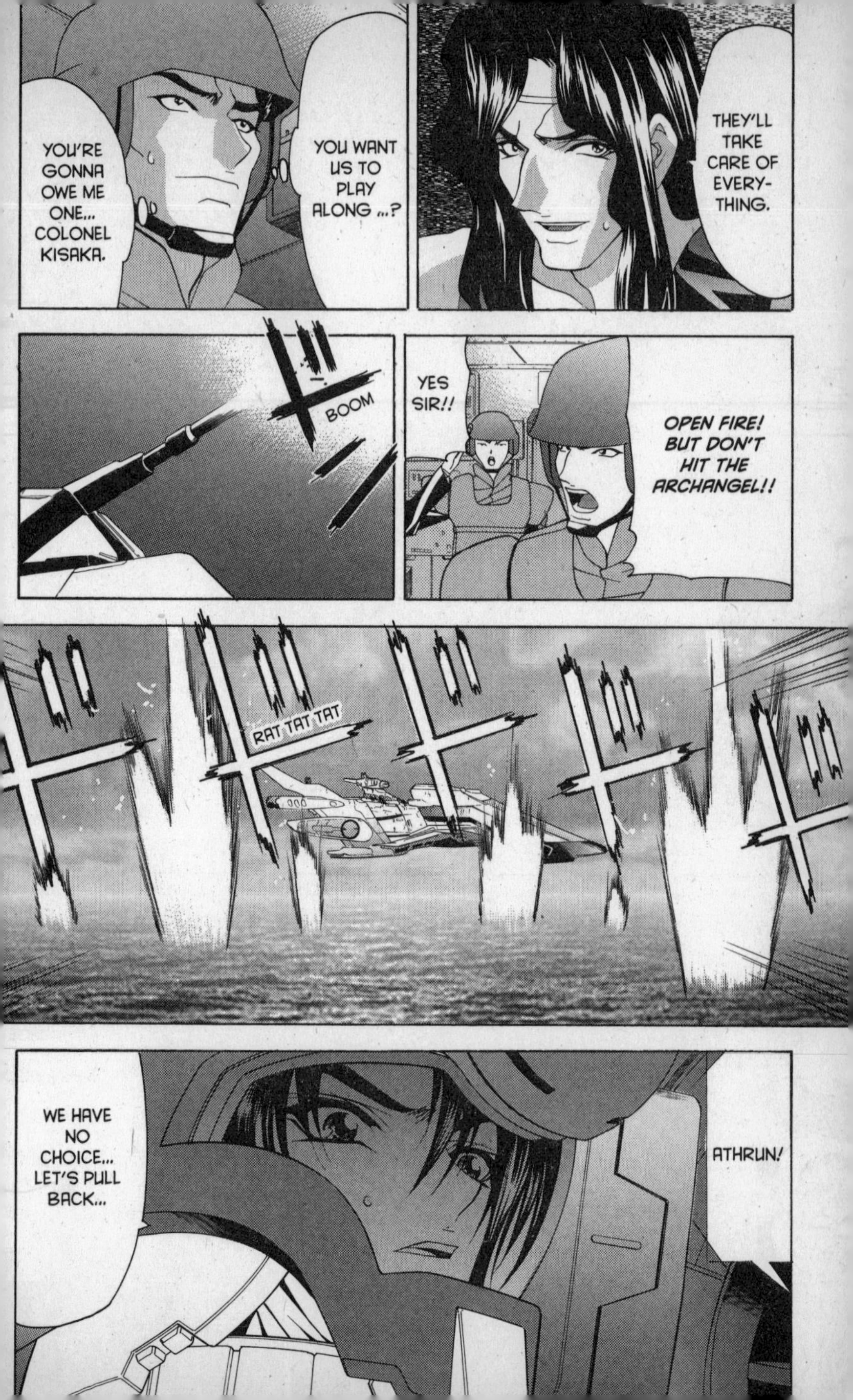
THEY'LL TAKE CARE OF EVERY-THING.
YOU WANT US TO PLAY ALONG ...?
YOU'RE GONNA OWE ME ONE... COLONEL KISAKA.
OPEN FIRE! BUT DON'T HIT THE ARCHANGEL!!
YES SIR!!
BOOM
RAT TAT TAT
ATHRUN!
WE HAVE NO CHOICE... LET'S PULL BACK...

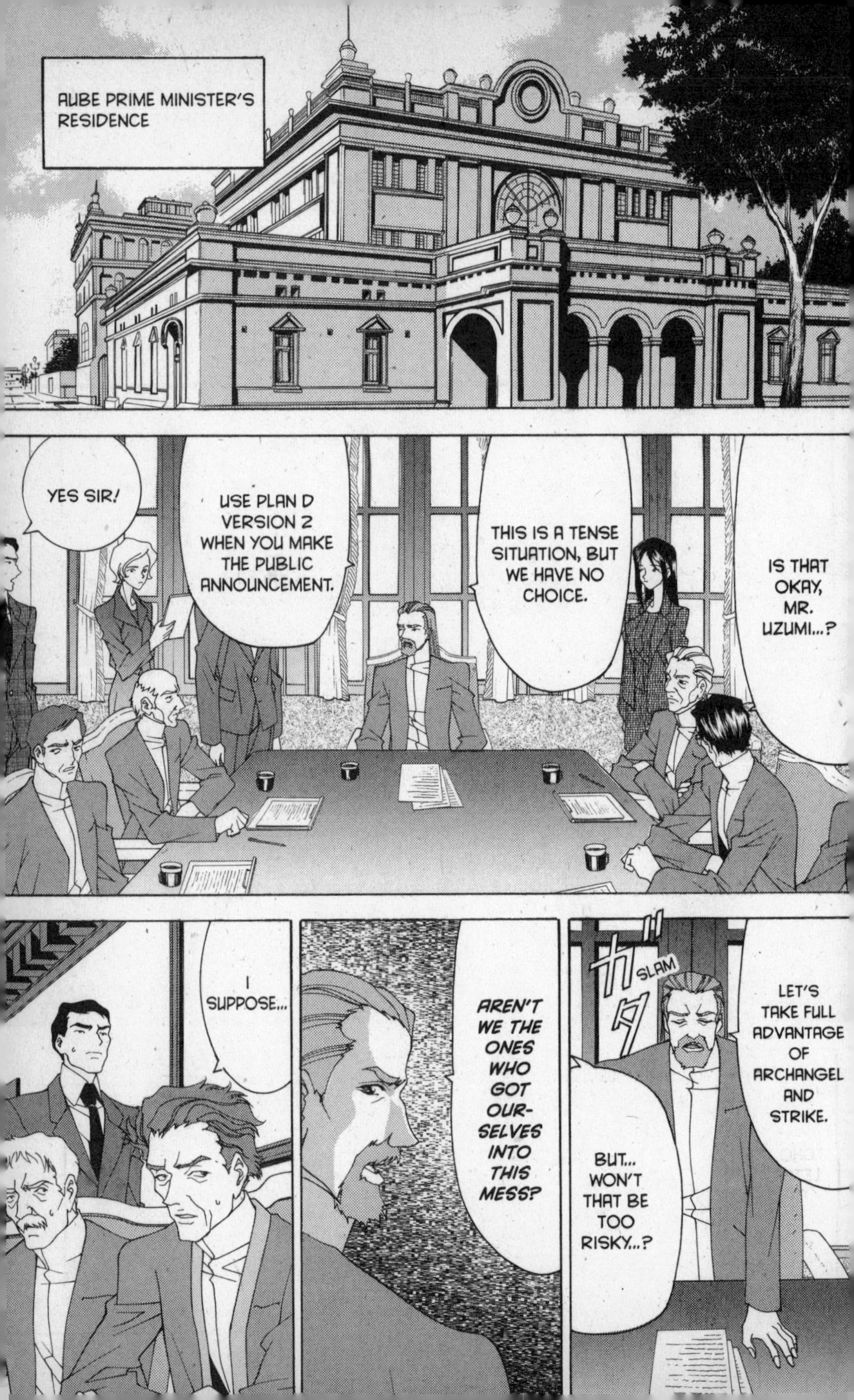
AUBE PRIME MINISTER'S RESIDENCE
IS THAT OKAY, MR. UZUMI...?
THIS IS A TENSE SITUATION, BUT WE HAVE NO CHOICE.
USE PLAN D VERSION 2 WHEN YOU MAKE THE PUBLIC ANNOUNCEMENT.
YES SIR!
LET'S TAKE FULL ADVANTAGE OF ARCHANGEL AND STRIKE.
ガタ SLAM
BUT... WON'T THAT BE TOO RISKY...?
AREN'T WE THE ONES WHO GOT OUR-SELVES INTO THIS MESS?
I SUPPOSE...

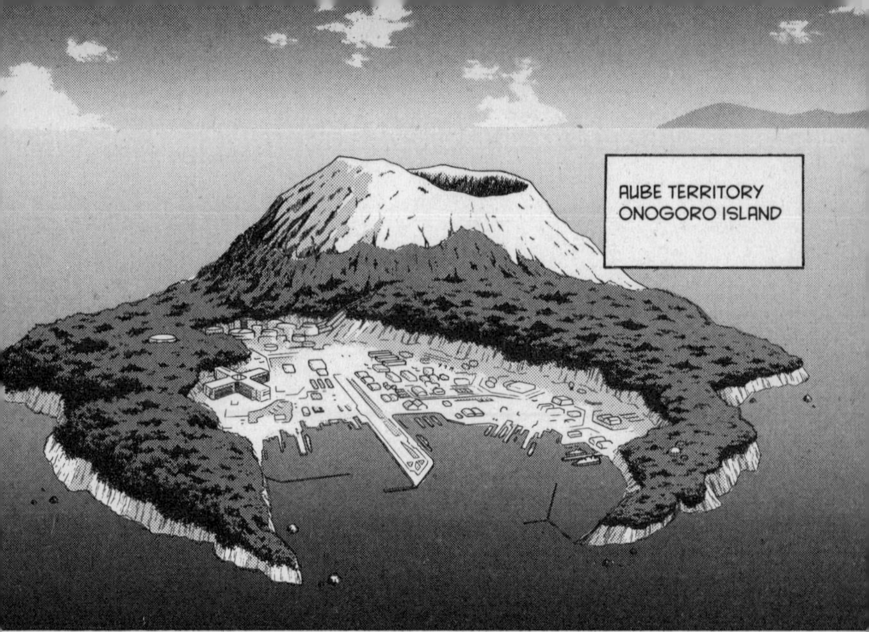
AUBE TERRITORY
ONOGORO ISLAND

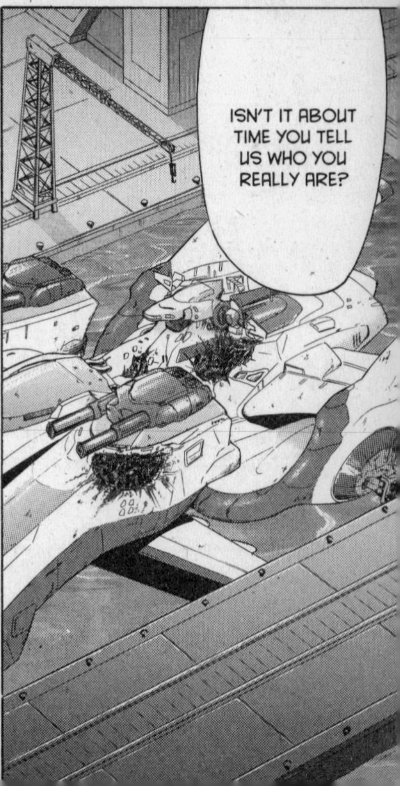
ISN'T IT ABOUT TIME YOU TELL US WHO YOU REALLY ARE?

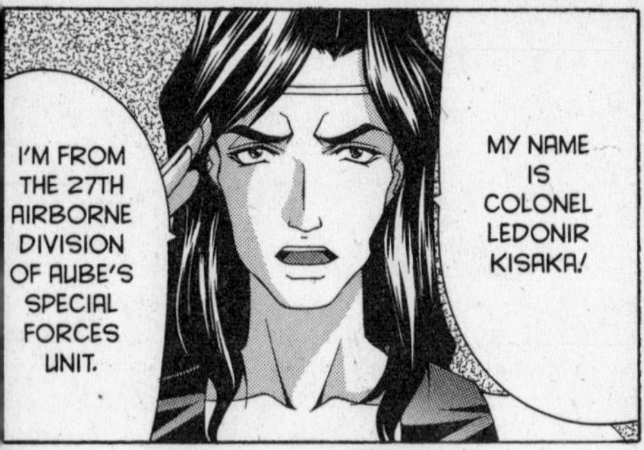
MY NAME IS COLONEL LEDONIR KISAKA!
I'M FROM THE 27TH AIRBORNE DIVISION OF AUBE'S SPECIAL FORCES UNIT.

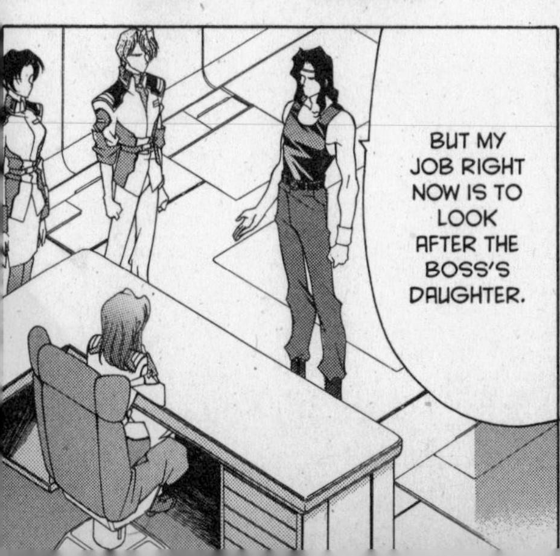
BUT MY JOB RIGHT NOW IS TO LOOK AFTER THE BOSS'S DAUGHTER.

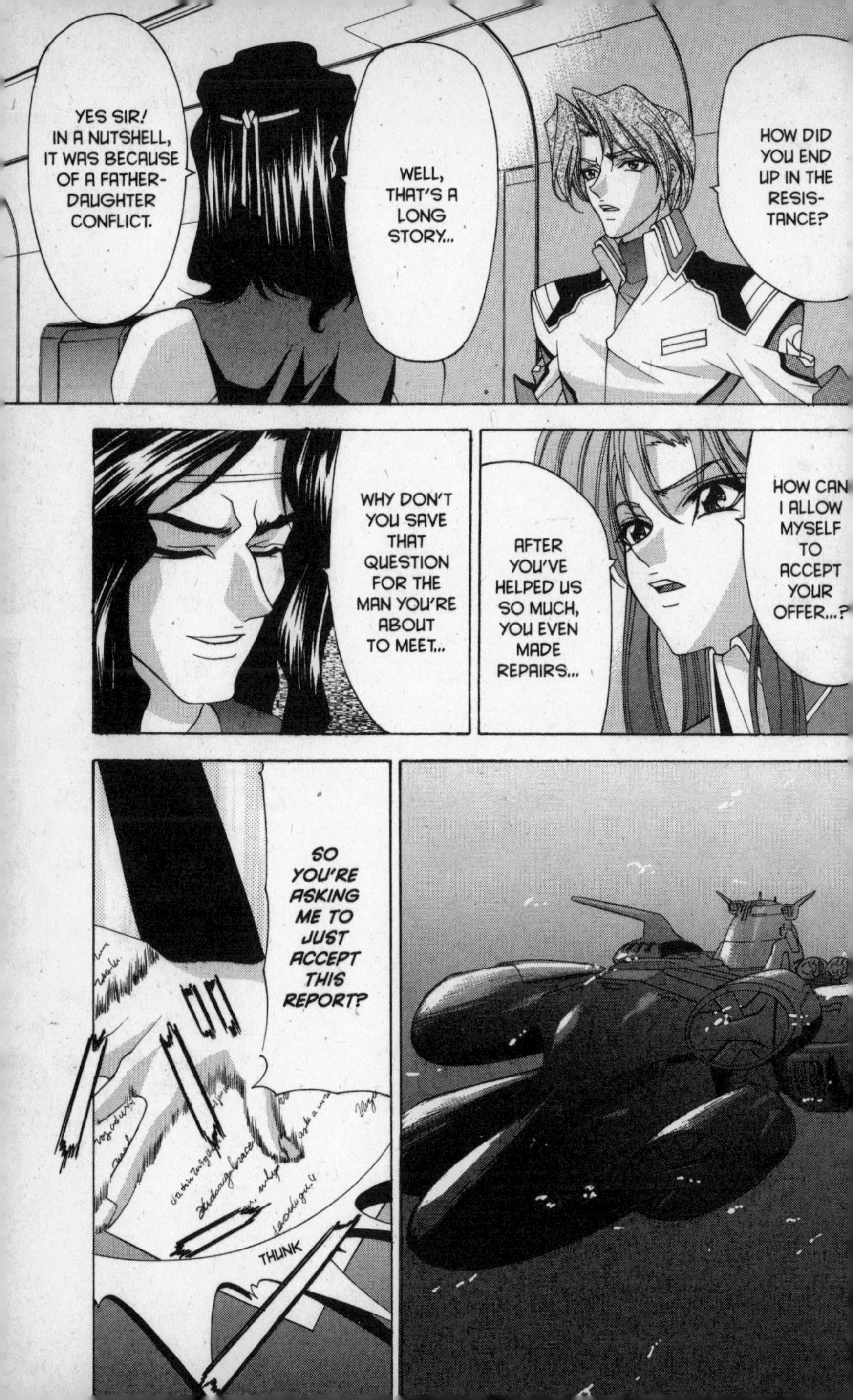
HOW DID YOU END UP IN THE RESIS-TANCE?
WELL, THAT'S A LONG STORY...
YES SIR! IN A NUTSHELL, IT WAS BECAUSE OF A FATHER-DAUGHTER CONFLICT.
HOW CAN I ALLOW MYSELF TO ACCEPT YOUR OFFER...?
AFTER YOU'VE HELPED US SO MUCH, YOU EVEN MADE REPAIRS...
WHY DON'T YOU SAVE THAT QUESTION FOR THE MAN YOU'RE ABOUT TO MEET...
SO YOU'RE ASKING ME TO JUST ACCEPT THIS REPORT?
THUNK

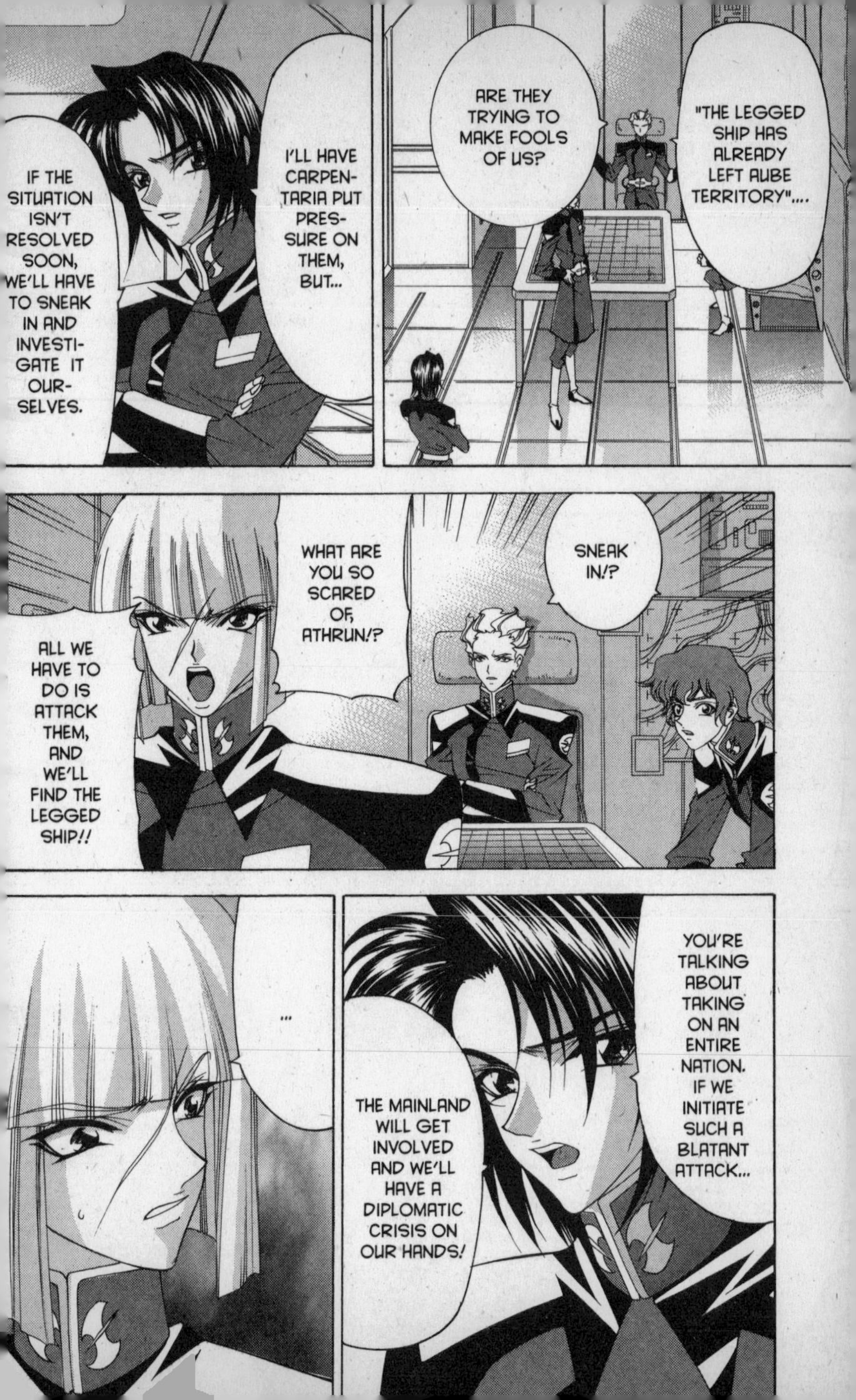
"THE LEGGED SHIP HAS ALREADY LEFT AUBE TERRITORY"....
ARE THEY TRYING TO MAKE FOOLS OF US?
I'LL HAVE CARPENTARIA PUT PRESSURE ON THEM, BUT...
IF THE SITUATION ISN'T RESOLVED SOON, WE'LL HAVE TO SNEAK IN AND INVESTIGATE IT OURSELVES.
SNEAK IN!?
WHAT ARE YOU SO SCARED OF, ATHRUN!?
ALL WE HAVE TO DO IS ATTACK THEM, AND WE'LL FIND THE LEGGED SHIP!!
YOU'RE TALKING ABOUT TAKING ON AN ENTIRE NATION. IF WE INITIATE SUCH A BLATANT ATTACK...
THE MAINLAND WILL GET INVOLVED AND WE'LL HAVE A DIPLOMATIC CRISIS ON OUR HANDS!
...

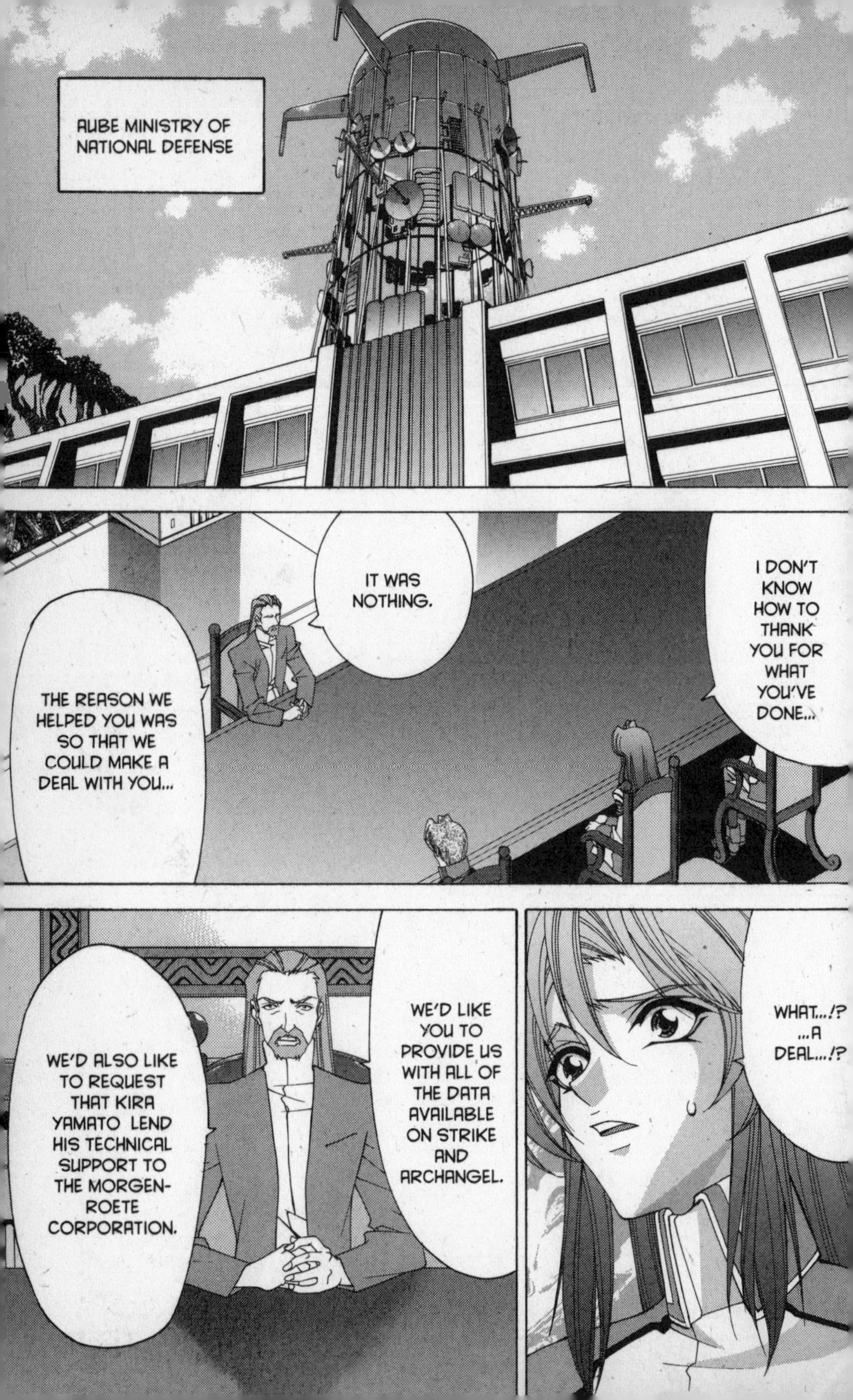
AUBE MINISTRY OF NATIONAL DEFENSE
I DON'T KNOW HOW TO THANK YOU FOR WHAT YOU'VE DONE...
IT WAS NOTHING.
THE REASON WE HELPED YOU WAS SO THAT WE COULD MAKE A DEAL WITH YOU...
WHAT...!? ...A DEAL...!?
WE'D LIKE YOU TO PROVIDE US WITH ALL OF THE DATA AVAILABLE ON STRIKE AND ARCHANGEL.
WE'D ALSO LIKE TO REQUEST THAT KIRA YAMATO LEND HIS TECHNICAL SUPPORT TO THE MORGEN-ROETE CORPORATION.

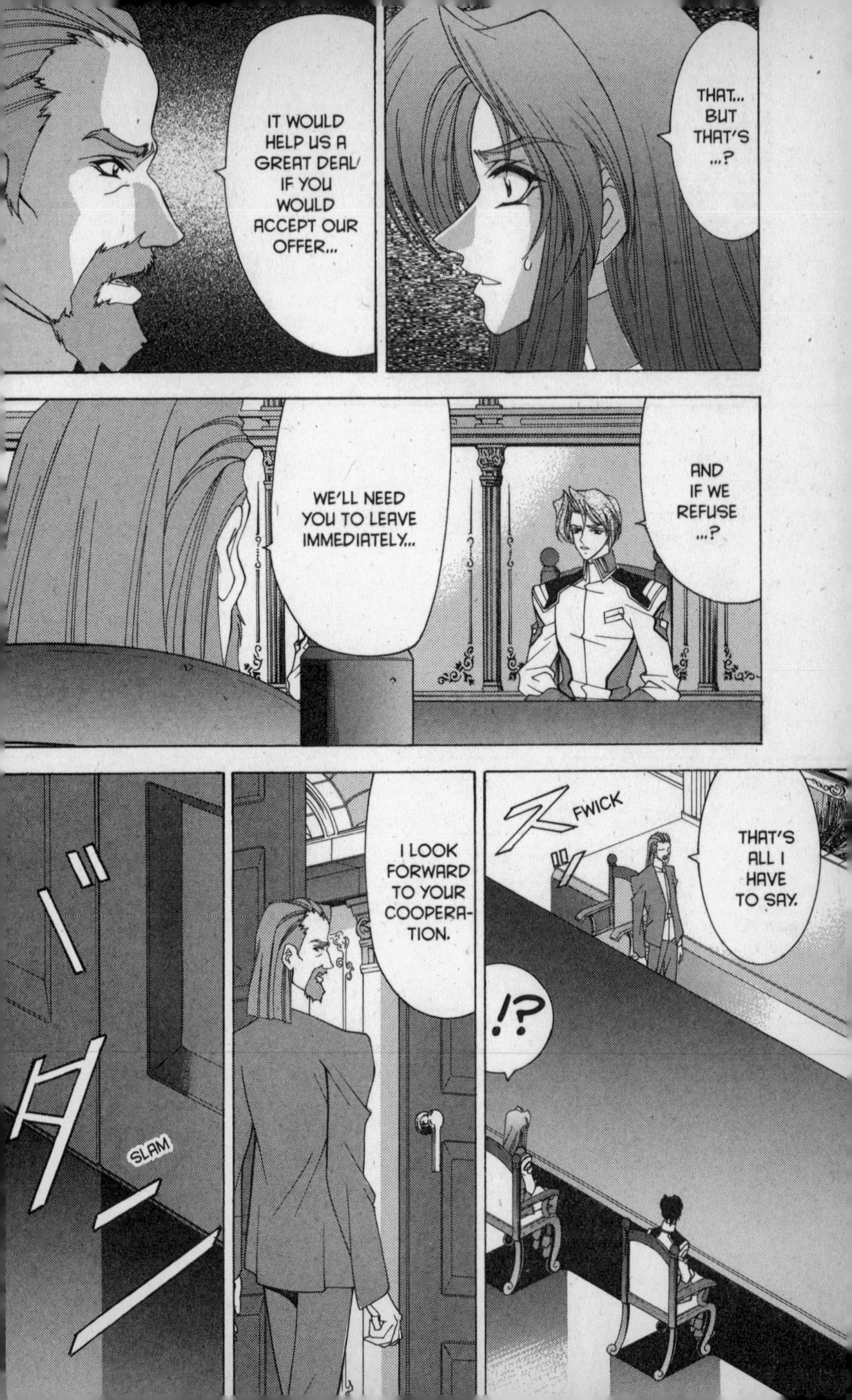
THAT... BUT THAT'S ...?
IT WOULD HELP US A GREAT DEAL IF YOU WOULD ACCEPT OUR OFFER...
AND IF WE REFUSE ...?
WE'LL NEED YOU TO LEAVE IMMEDIATELY...
THAT'S ALL I HAVE TO SAY.
FWICK
!?
I LOOK FORWARD TO YOUR COOPERA-TION.
SLAM

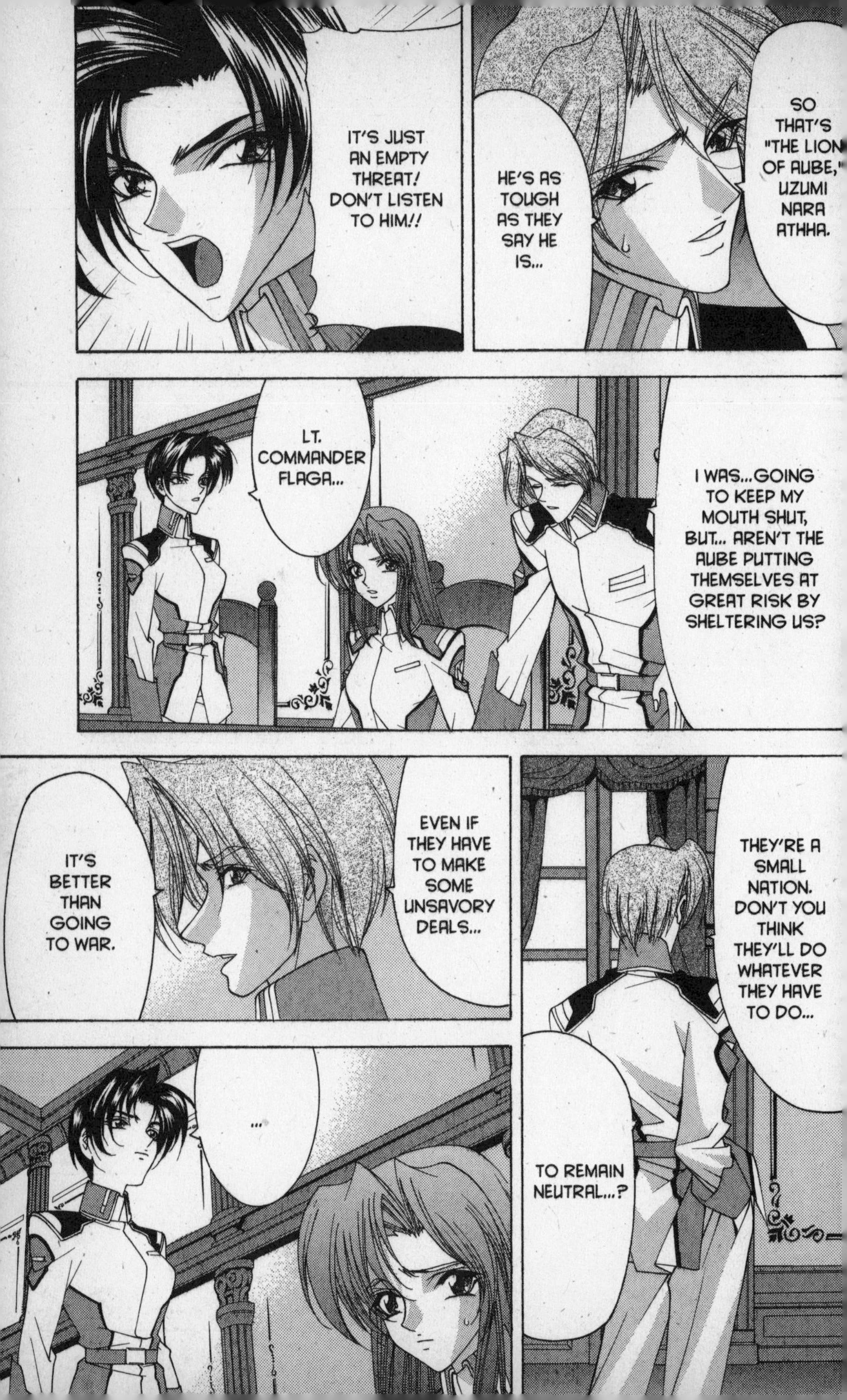
SO THAT'S "THE LION OF AUBE," UZUMI NARA ATHHA.
HE'S AS TOUGH AS THEY SAY HE IS...
IT'S JUST AN EMPTY THREAT! DON'T LISTEN TO HIM!!
I WAS...GOING TO KEEP MY MOUTH SHUT, BUT... AREN'T THE AUBE PUTTING THEMSELVES AT GREAT RISK BY SHELTERING US?
LT. COMMANDER FLAGA...
THEY'RE A SMALL NATION. DON'T YOU THINK THEY'LL DO WHATEVER THEY HAVE TO DO...
TO REMAIN NEUTRAL...?
EVEN IF THEY HAVE TO MAKE SOME UNSAVORY DEALS...
IT'S BETTER THAN GOING TO WAR.
...

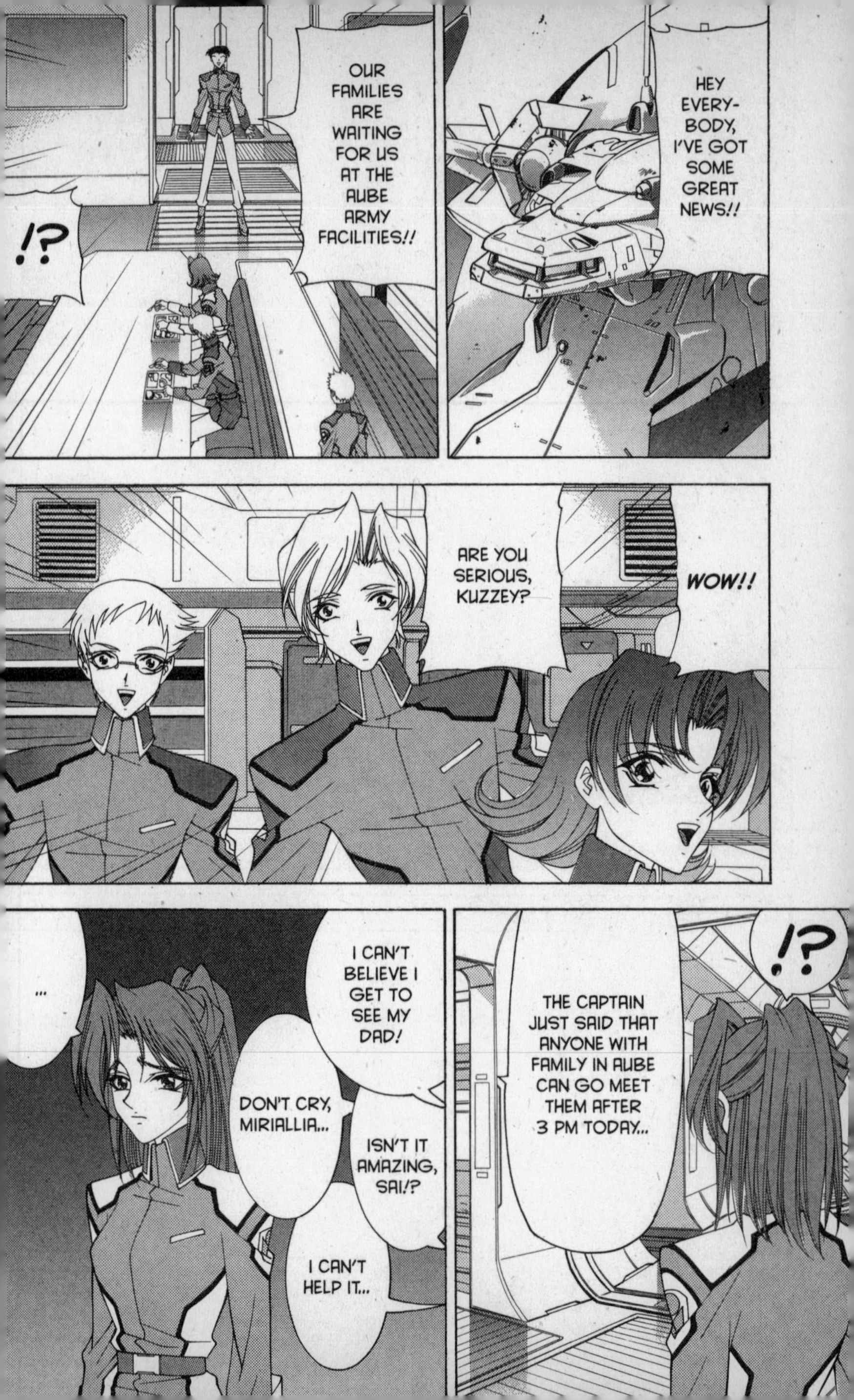
HEY EVERY-BODY, I'VE GOT SOME GREAT NEWS!!
OUR FAMILIES ARE WAITING FOR US AT THE AUBE ARMY FACILITIES!!
!?
WOW!!
ARE YOU SERIOUS, KUZZEY?
!?
THE CAPTAIN JUST SAID THAT ANYONE WITH FAMILY IN AUBE CAN GO MEET THEM AFTER 3 PM TODAY...
I CAN'T BELIEVE I GET TO SEE MY DAD!
ISN'T IT AMAZING, SAI!?
DON'T CRY, MIRIALLIA...
I CAN'T HELP IT...
...

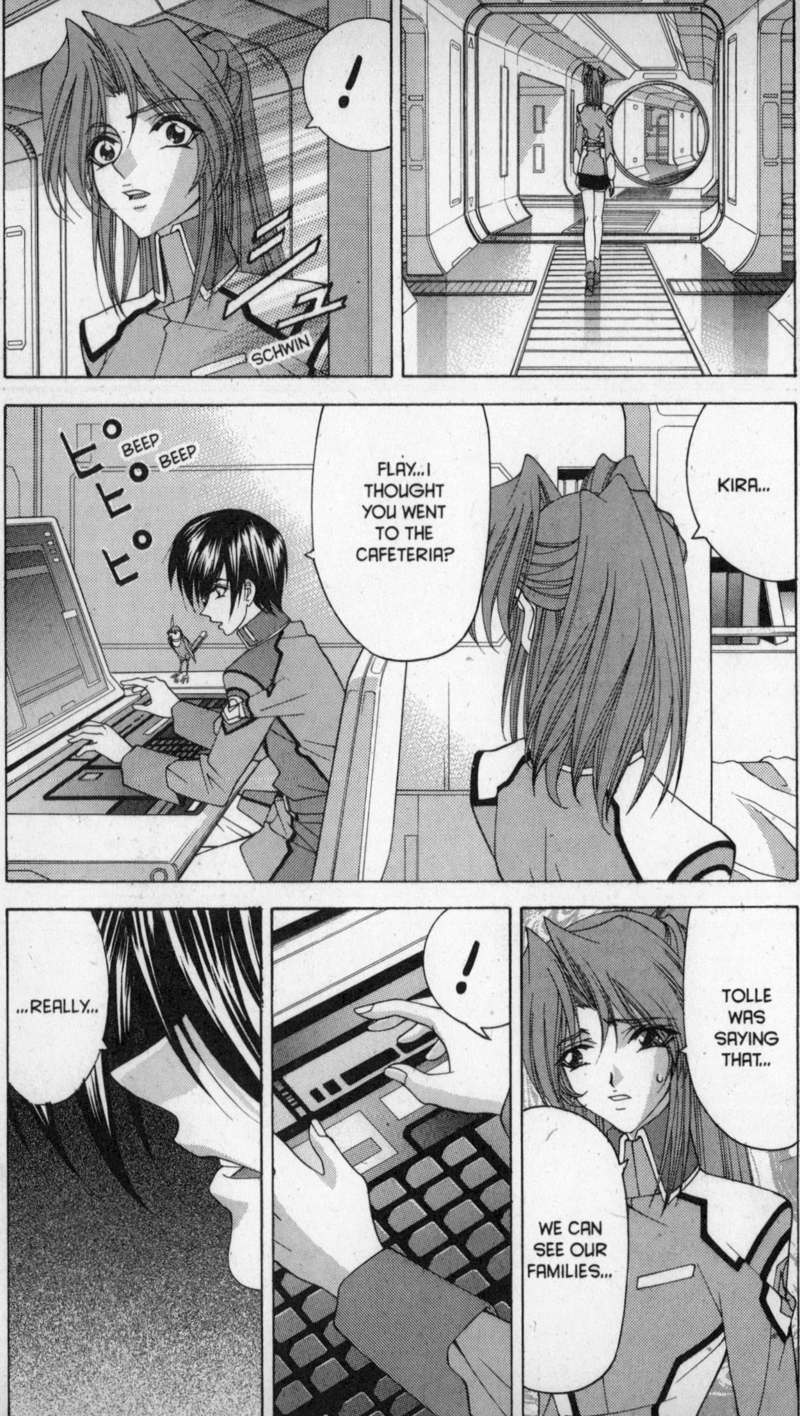
!
SCHWIN
KIRA...
BEEP BEEP
FLAY...I THOUGHT YOU WENT TO THE CAFETERIA?
TOLLE WAS SAYING THAT...
WE CAN SEE OUR FAMILIES...
!
...REALLY...

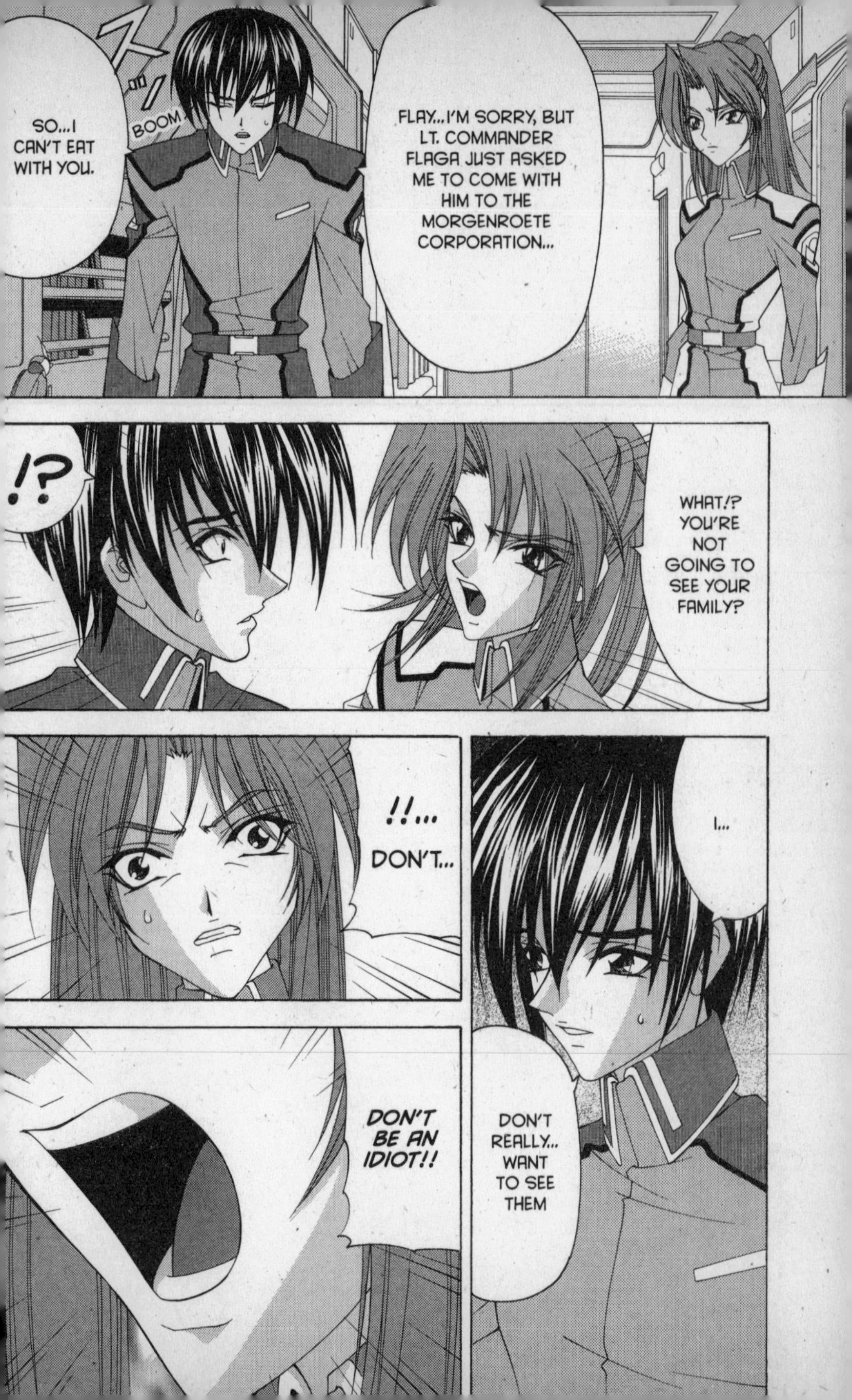
FLAY...I'M SORRY, BUT LT. COMMANDER FLAGA JUST ASKED ME TO COME WITH HIM TO THE MORGENROETE CORPORATION...
BOOM
SO...I CAN'T EAT WITH YOU.
WHAT!? YOU'RE NOT GOING TO SEE YOUR FAMILY?
!?
I...
!!...
DON'T...
DON'T REALLY... WANT TO SEE THEM
DON'T BE AN IDIOT!!

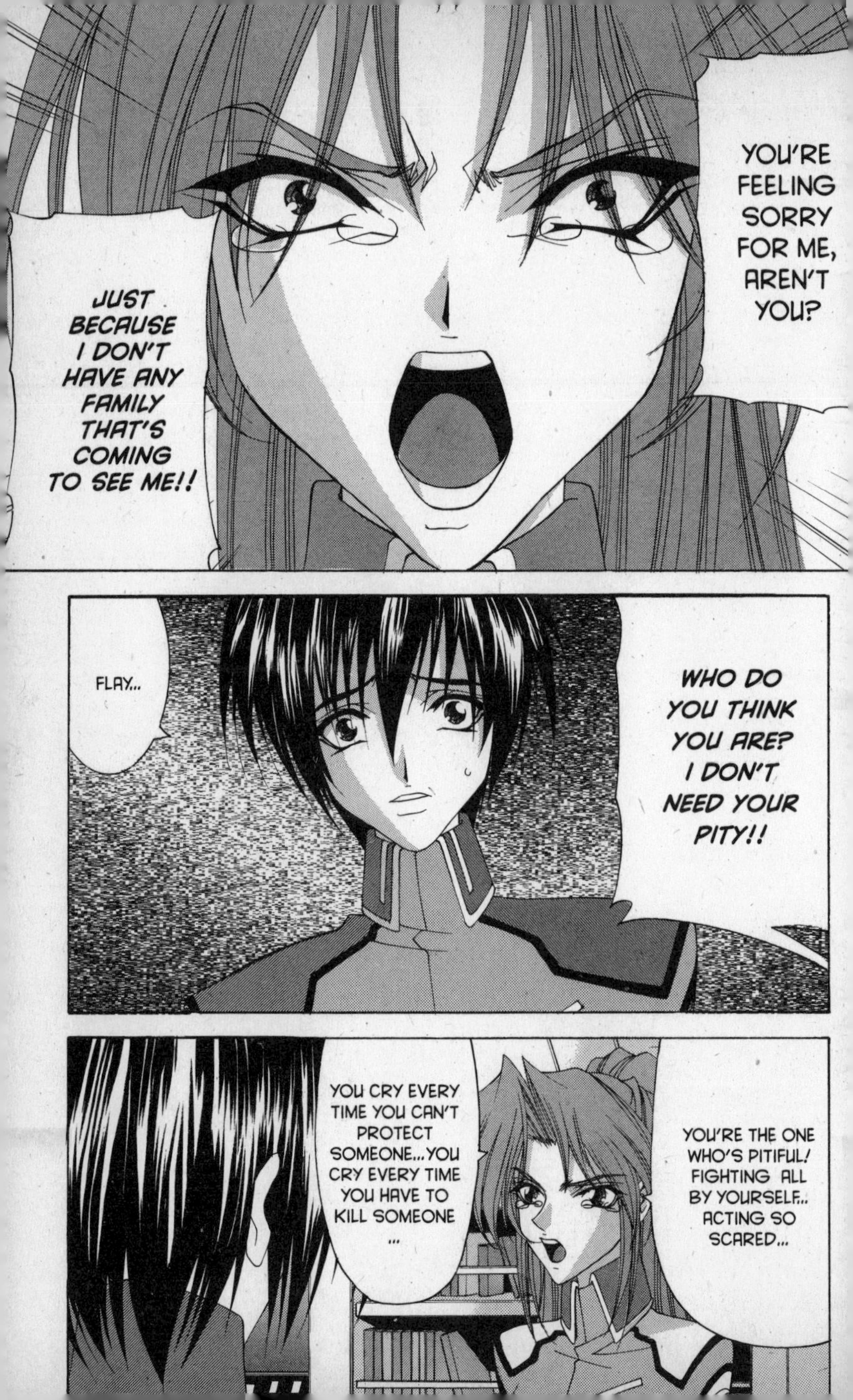
YOU'RE FEELING SORRY FOR ME, AREN'T YOU?
JUST BECAUSE I DON'T HAVE ANY FAMILY THAT'S COMING TO SEE ME!!
WHO DO YOU THINK YOU ARE? I DON'T NEED YOUR PITY!!
FLAY...
YOU'RE THE ONE WHO'S PITIFUL! FIGHTING ALL BY YOURSELF... ACTING SO SCARED...
YOU CRY EVERY TIME YOU CAN'T PROTECT SOMEONE...YOU CRY EVERY TIME YOU HAVE TO KILL SOMEONE ...

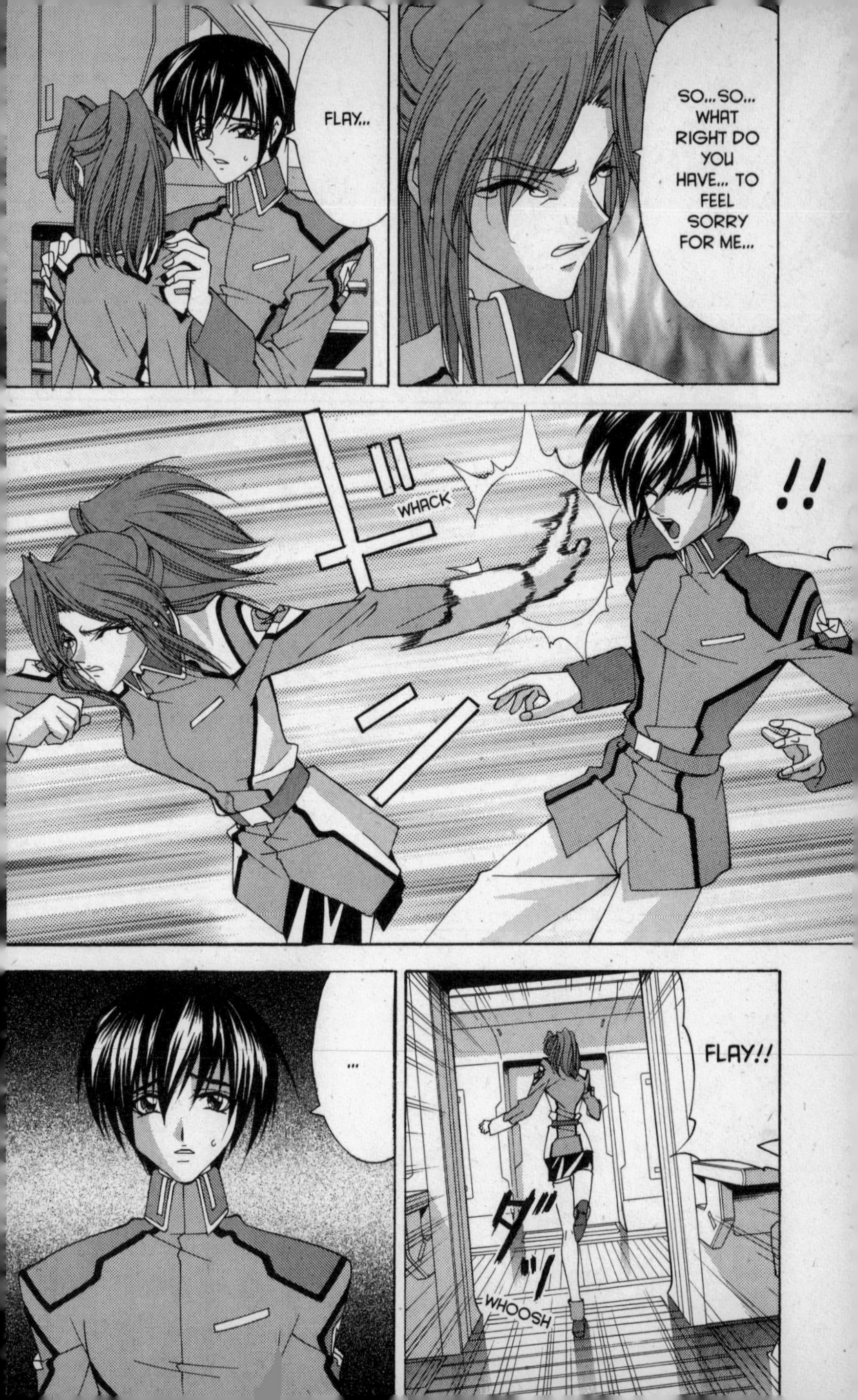
SO...SO... WHAT RIGHT DO YOU HAVE... TO FEEL SORRY FOR ME...
FLAY...
!!
WHACK
FLAY!!
WHOOSH
...

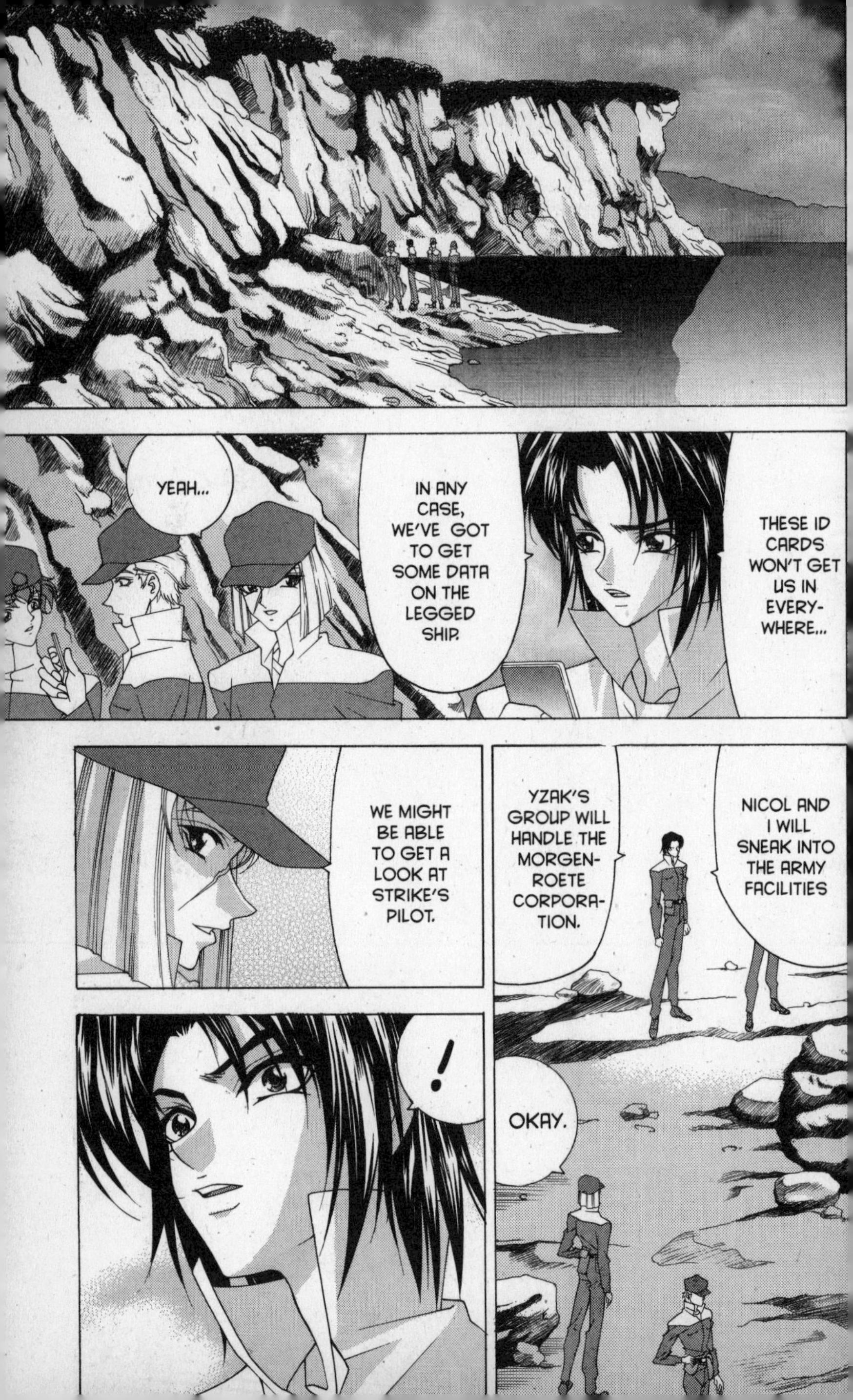
THESE ID CARDS WON'T GET US IN EVERY-WHERE...
IN ANY CASE, WE'VE GOT TO GET SOME DATA ON THE LEGGED SHIP.
YEAH...
NICOL AND I WILL SNEAK INTO THE ARMY FACILITIES
YZAK'S GROUP WILL HANDLE THE MORGEN-ROETE CORPORA-TION.
OKAY.
WE MIGHT BE ABLE TO GET A LOOK AT STRIKE'S PILOT.
!

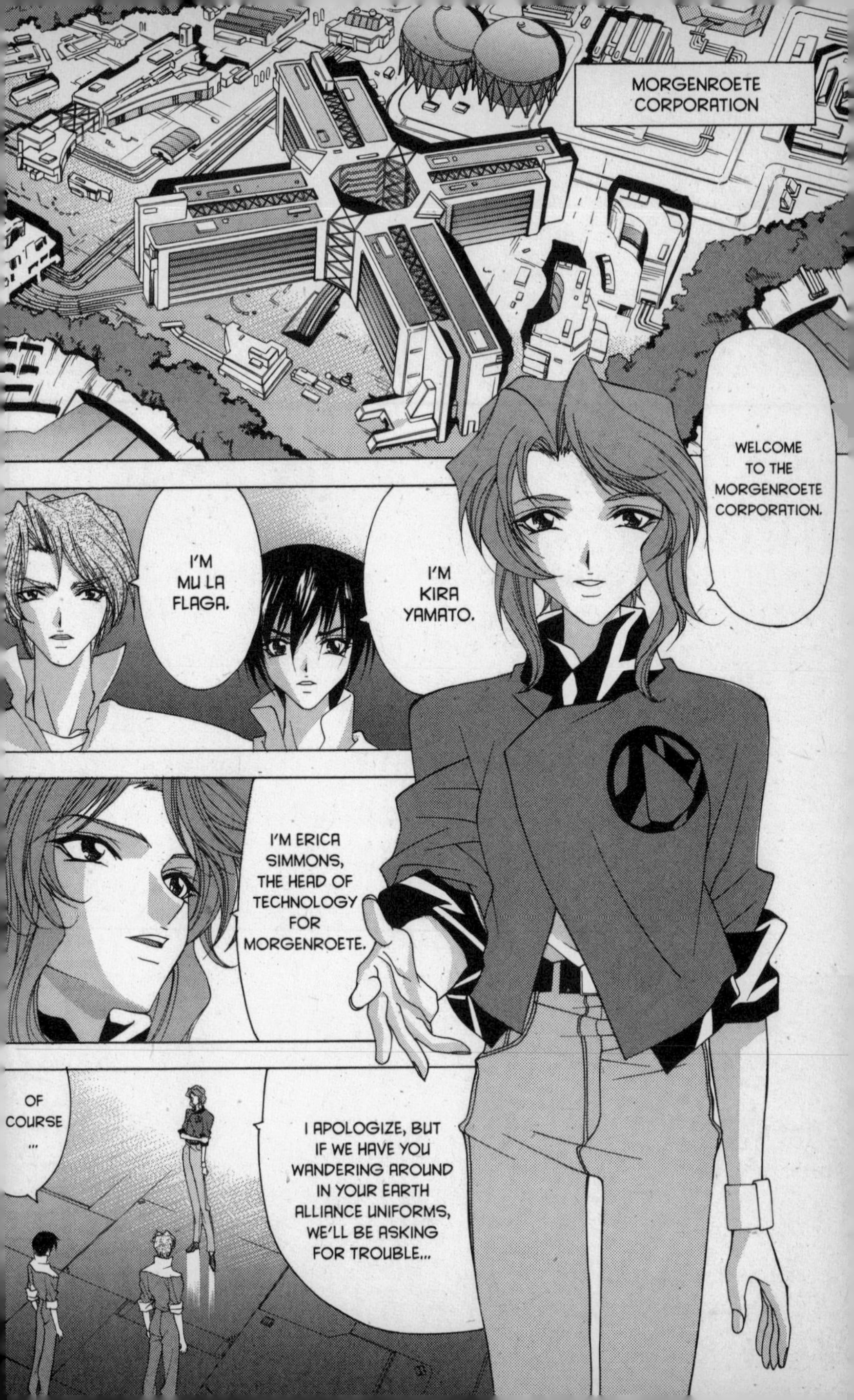
MORGENROETE CORPORATION
WELCOME TO THE MORGENROETE CORPORATION.
I'M KIRA YAMATO.
I'M MU LA FLAGA.
I'M ERICA SIMMONS, THE HEAD OF TECHNOLOGY FOR MORGENROETE.
I APOLOGIZE, BUT IF WE HAVE YOU WANDERING AROUND IN YOUR EARTH ALLIANCE UNIFORMS, WE'LL BE ASKING FOR TROUBLE...
OF COURSE ...

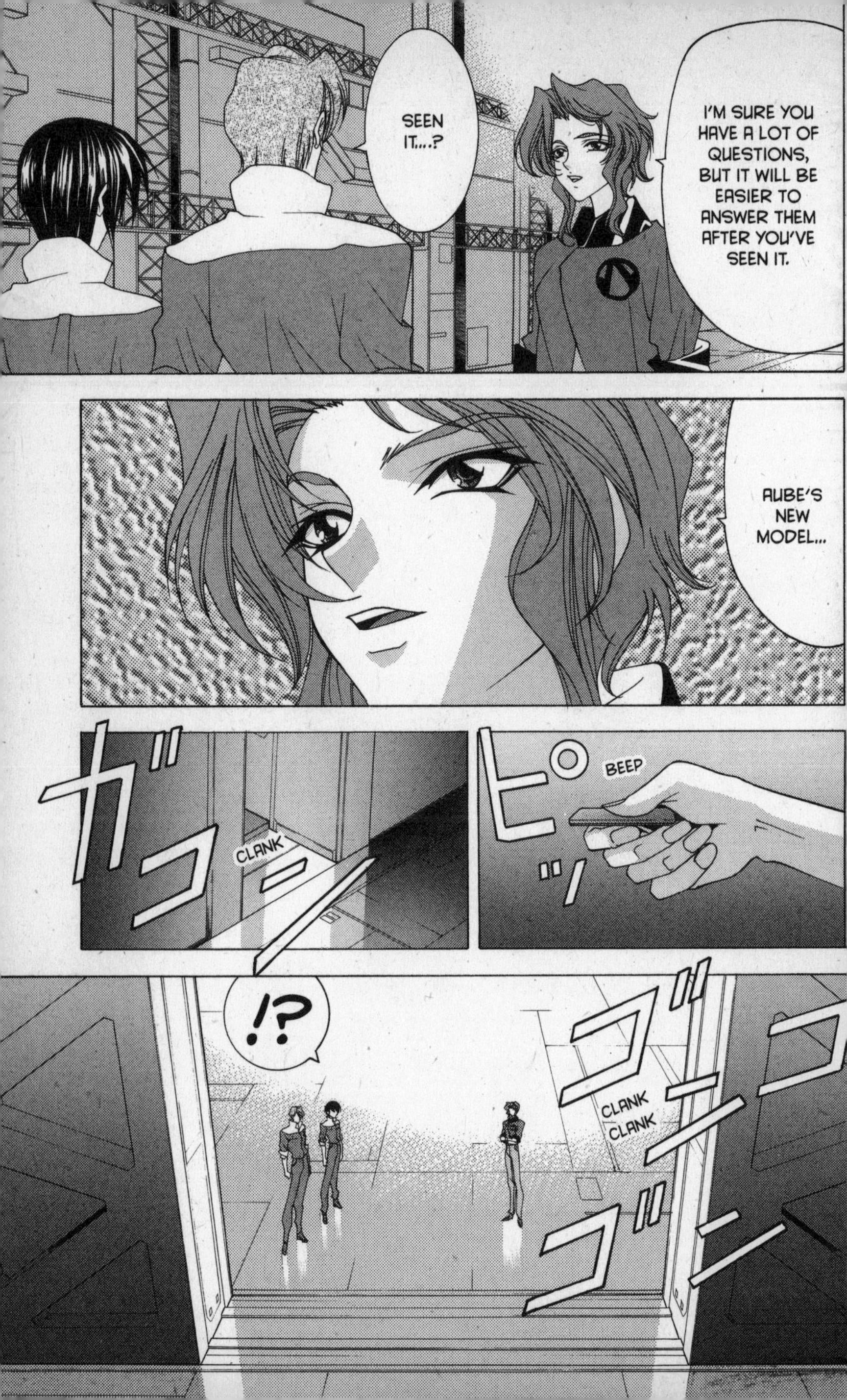
I'M SURE YOU HAVE A LOT OF QUESTIONS, BUT IT WILL BE EASIER TO ANSWER THEM AFTER YOU'VE SEEN IT.
SEEN IT....?
AUBE'S NEW MODEL...
ピッ
BEEP
ガコーン
CLANK
!?
ゴゴゴ
CLANK CLANK

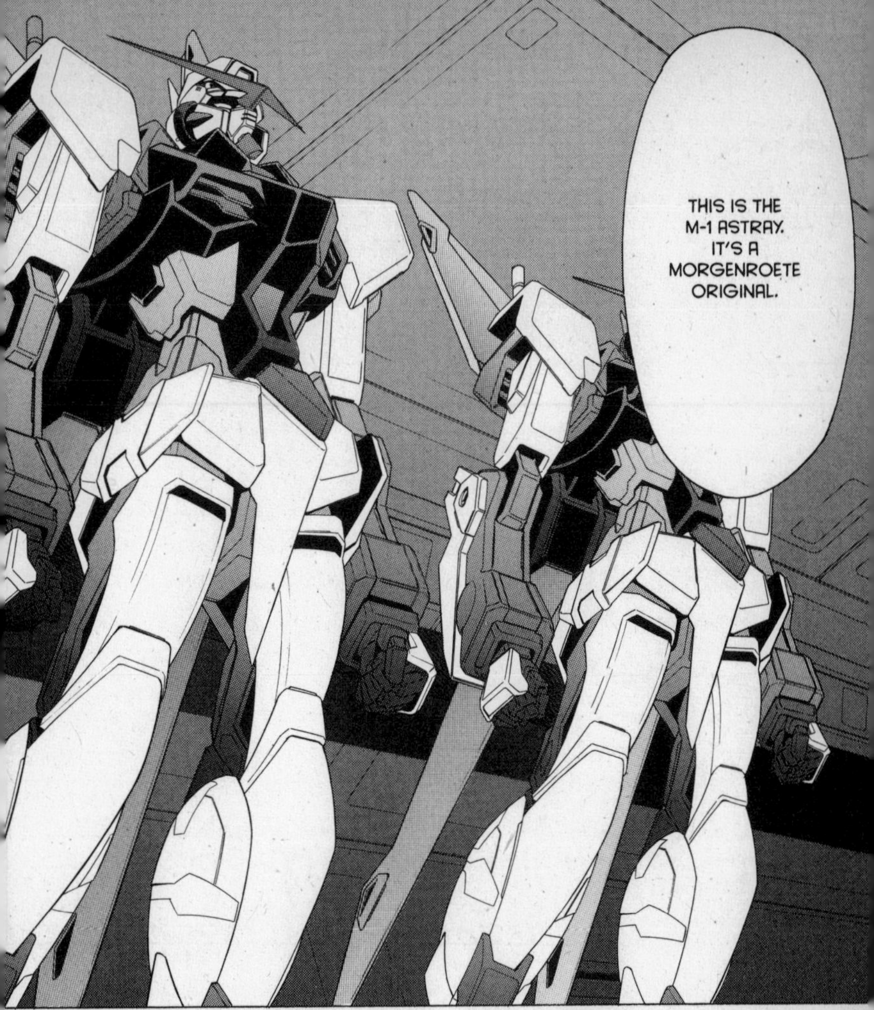
THIS IS THE M-1 ASTRAY. IT'S A MORGENROETE ORIGINAL.

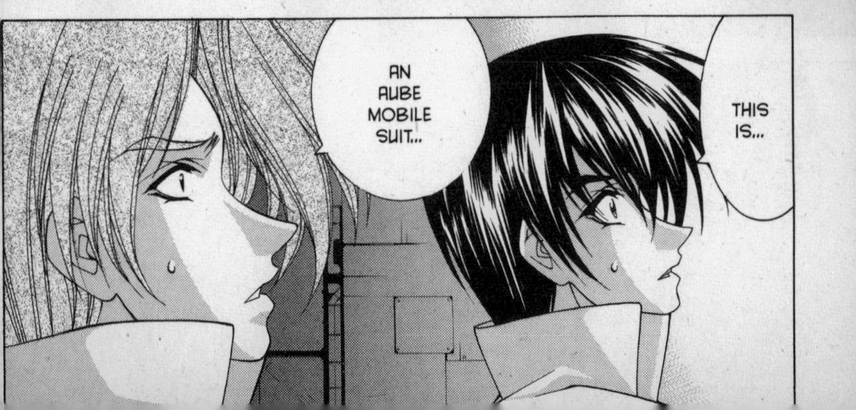
THIS IS...
AN AUBE MOBILE SUIT...

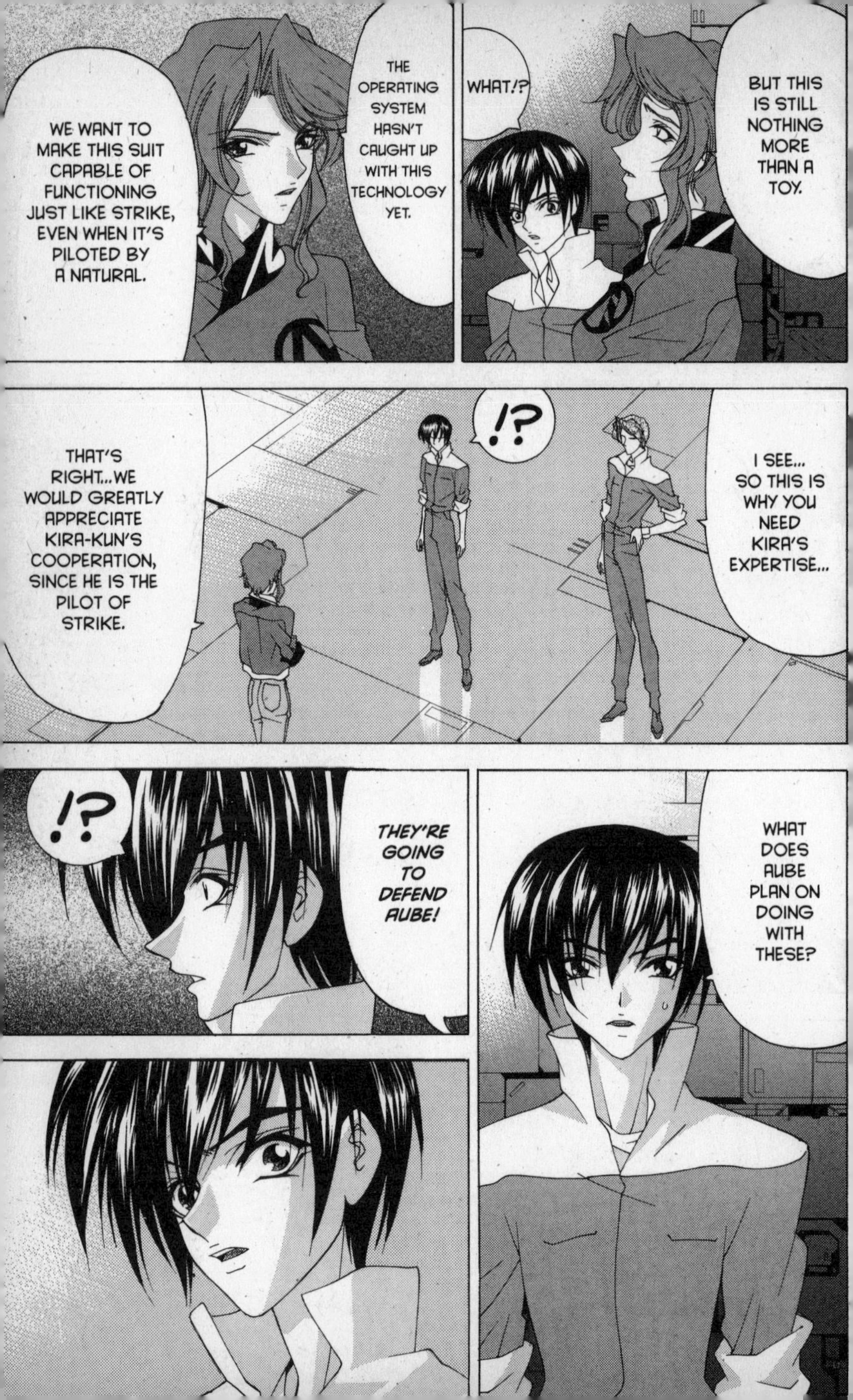
BUT THIS IS STILL NOTHING MORE THAN A TOY.
WHAT!?
THE OPERATING SYSTEM HASN'T CAUGHT UP WITH THIS TECHNOLOGY YET.
WE WANT TO MAKE THIS SUIT CAPABLE OF FUNCTIONING JUST LIKE STRIKE, EVEN WHEN IT'S PILOTED BY A NATURAL.
I SEE... SO THIS IS WHY YOU NEED KIRA'S EXPERTISE...
!?
THAT'S RIGHT...WE WOULD GREATLY APPRECIATE KIRA-KUN'S COOPERATION, SINCE HE IS THE PILOT OF STRIKE.
WHAT DOES AUBE PLAN ON DOING WITH THESE?
THEY'RE GOING TO DEFEND AUBE!
!?

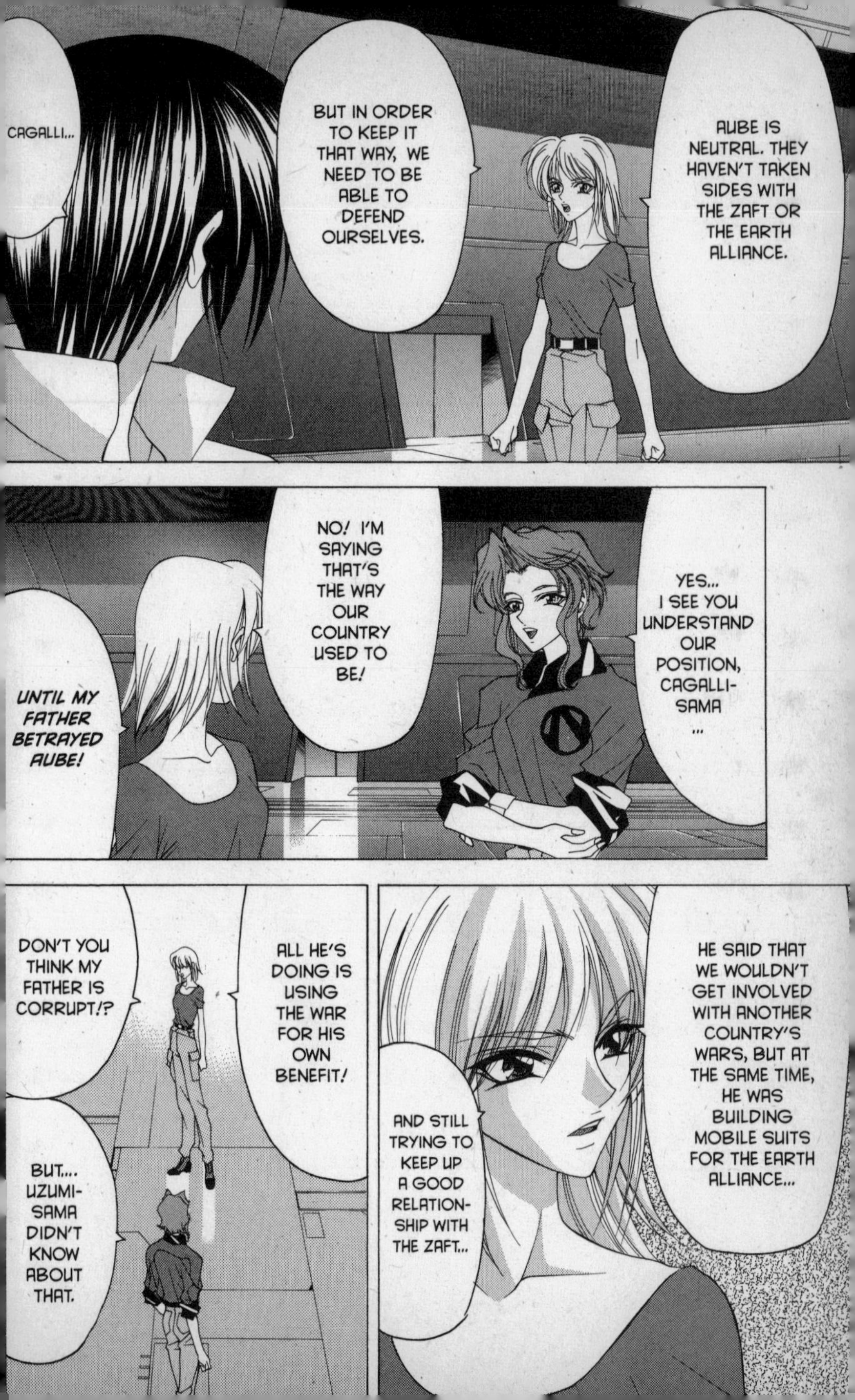
AUBE IS NEUTRAL. THEY HAVEN'T TAKEN SIDES WITH THE ZAFT OR THE EARTH ALLIANCE.
BUT IN ORDER TO KEEP IT THAT WAY, WE NEED TO BE ABLE TO DEFEND OURSELVES.
CAGALLI...
YES... I SEE YOU UNDERSTAND OUR POSITION, CAGALLI-SAMA ...
NO! I'M SAYING THAT'S THE WAY OUR COUNTRY USED TO BE!
UNTIL MY FATHER BETRAYED AUBE!
HE SAID THAT WE WOULDN'T GET INVOLVED WITH ANOTHER COUNTRY'S WARS, BUT AT THE SAME TIME, HE WAS BUILDING MOBILE SUITS FOR THE EARTH ALLIANCE...
AND STILL TRYING TO KEEP UP A GOOD RELATION-SHIP WITH THE ZAFT...
ALL HE'S DOING IS USING THE WAR FOR HIS OWN BENEFIT!
DON'T YOU THINK MY FATHER IS CORRUPT!?
BUT.... UZUMI-SAMA DIDN'T KNOW ABOUT THAT.

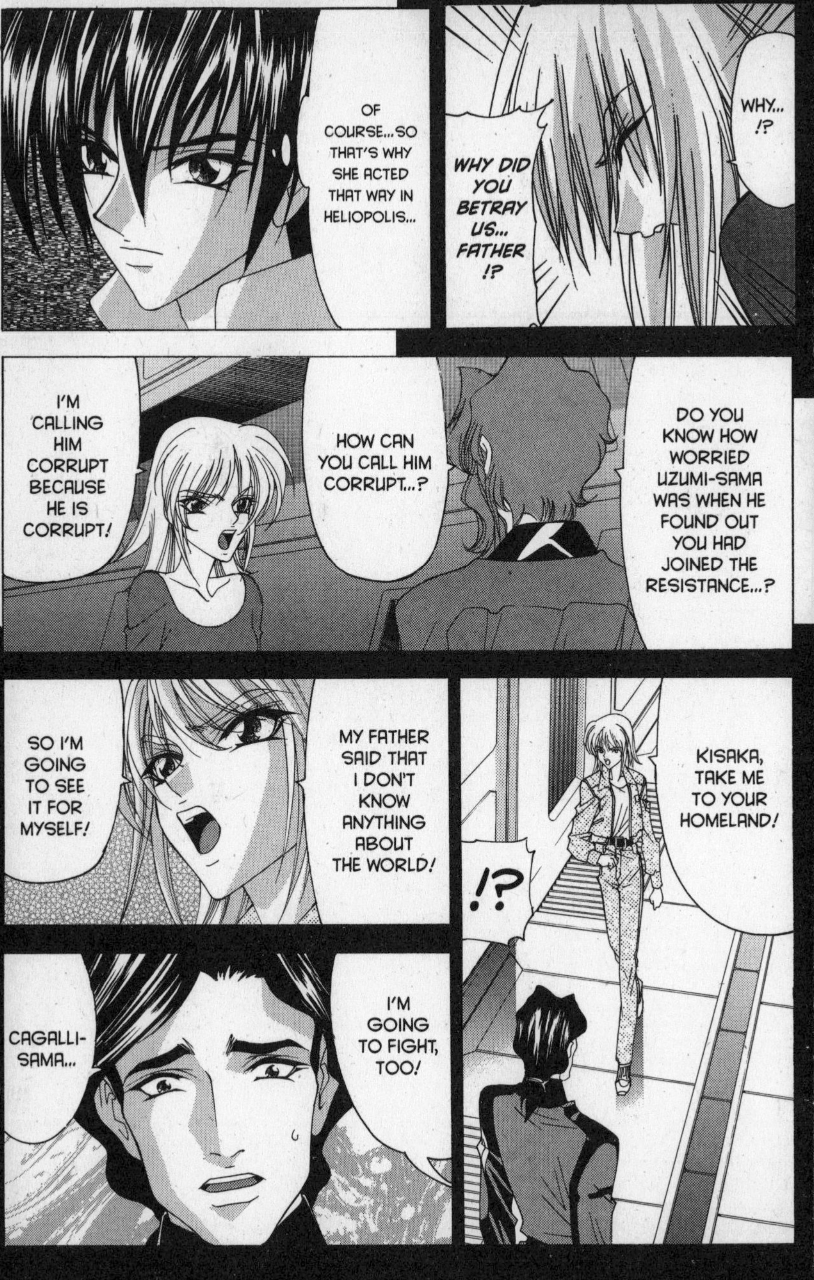
WHY... !?
WHY DID YOU BETRAY US... FATHER !?
OF COURSE...SO THAT'S WHY SHE ACTED THAT WAY IN HELIOPOLIS...
DO YOU KNOW HOW WORRIED UZUMI-SAMA WAS WHEN HE FOUND OUT YOU HAD JOINED THE RESISTANCE...?
HOW CAN YOU CALL HIM CORRUPT...?
I'M CALLING HIM CORRUPT BECAUSE HE IS CORRUPT!
KISAKA, TAKE ME TO YOUR HOMELAND!
!?
MY FATHER SAID THAT I DON'T KNOW ANYTHING ABOUT THE WORLD!
SO I'M GOING TO SEE IT FOR MYSELF!
I'M GOING TO FIGHT, TOO!
CAGALLI-SAMA...

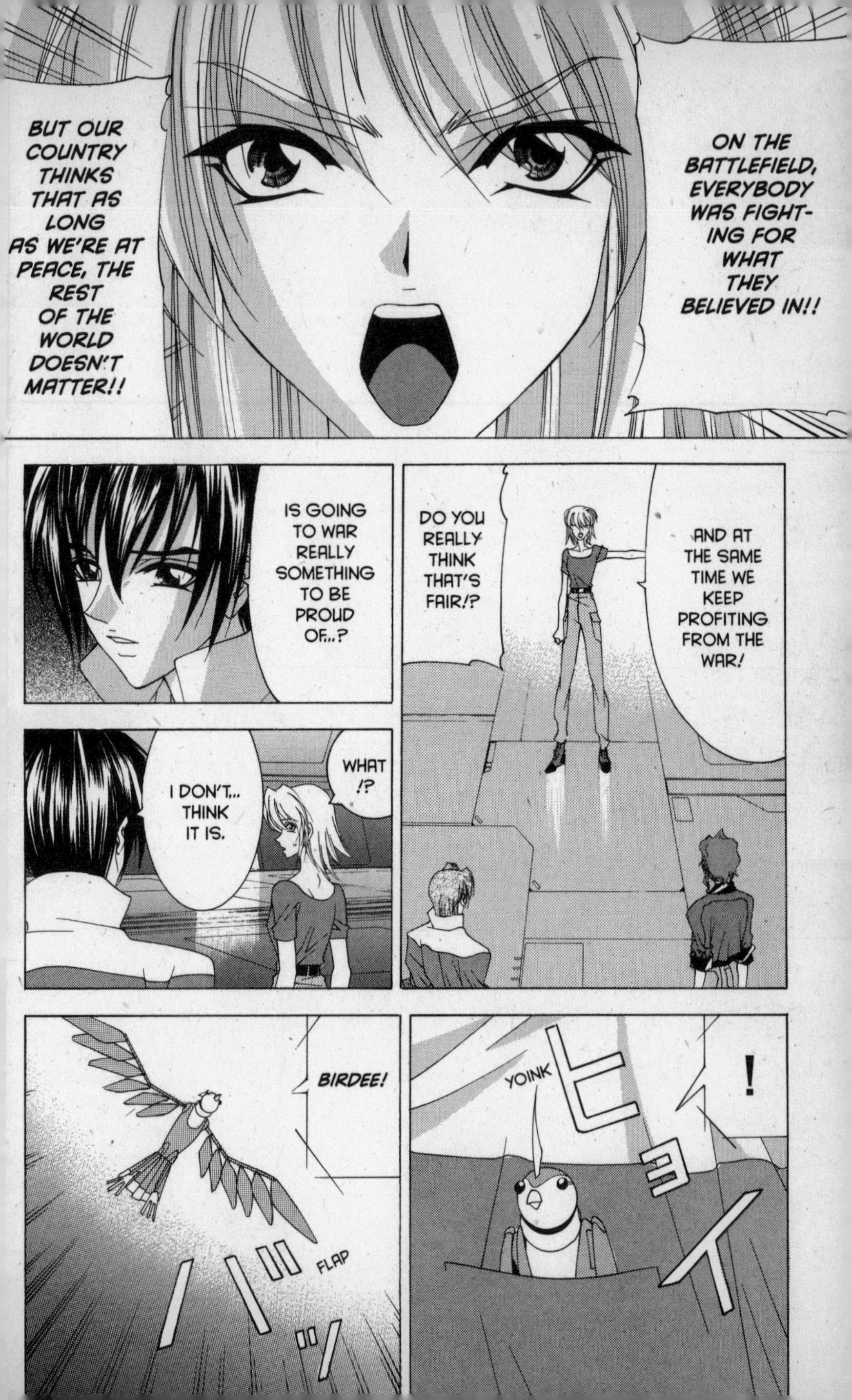
ON THE BATTLEFIELD, EVERYBODY WAS FIGHTING FOR WHAT THEY BELIEVED IN!!
BUT OUR COUNTRY THINKS THAT AS LONG AS WE'RE AT PEACE, THE REST OF THE WORLD DOESN'T MATTER!!
AND AT THE SAME TIME WE KEEP PROFITING FROM THE WAR!
DO YOU REALLY THINK THAT'S FAIR!?
IS GOING TO WAR REALLY SOMETHING TO BE PROUD OF...?
WHAT !?
I DON'T... THINK IT IS.
!
YOINK
BIRDEE!
FLAP

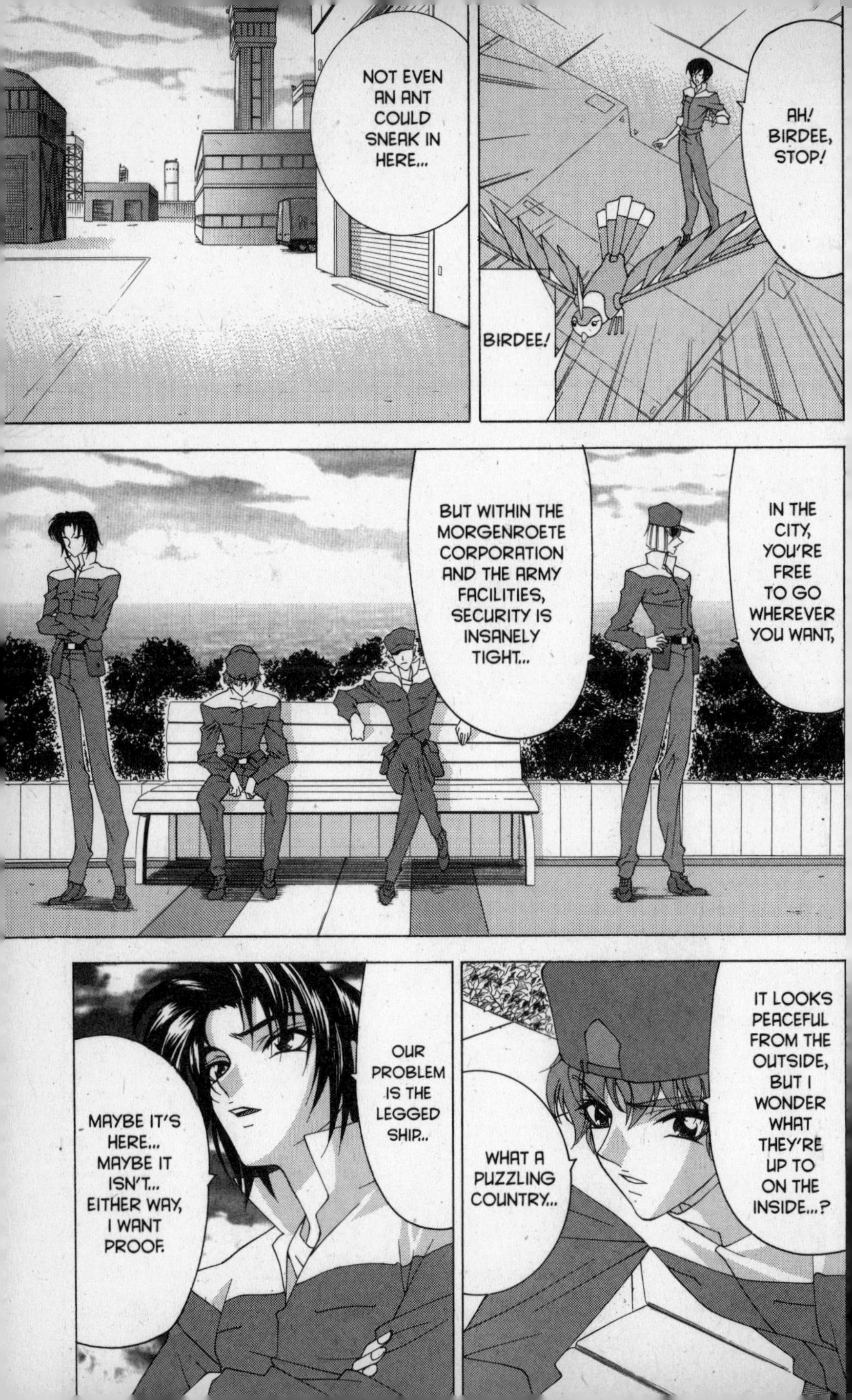
AH! BIRDEE, STOP!
BIRDEE!
NOT EVEN AN ANT COULD SNEAK IN HERE...
IN THE CITY, YOU'RE FREE TO GO WHEREVER YOU WANT,
BUT WITHIN THE MORGENROETE CORPORATION AND THE ARMY FACILITIES, SECURITY IS INSANELY TIGHT...
IT LOOKS PEACEFUL FROM THE OUTSIDE, BUT I WONDER WHAT THEY'RE UP TO ON THE INSIDE...?
WHAT A PUZZLING COUNTRY...
OUR PROBLEM IS THE LEGGED SHIP...
MAYBE IT'S HERE... MAYBE IT ISN'T... EITHER WAY, I WANT PROOF.

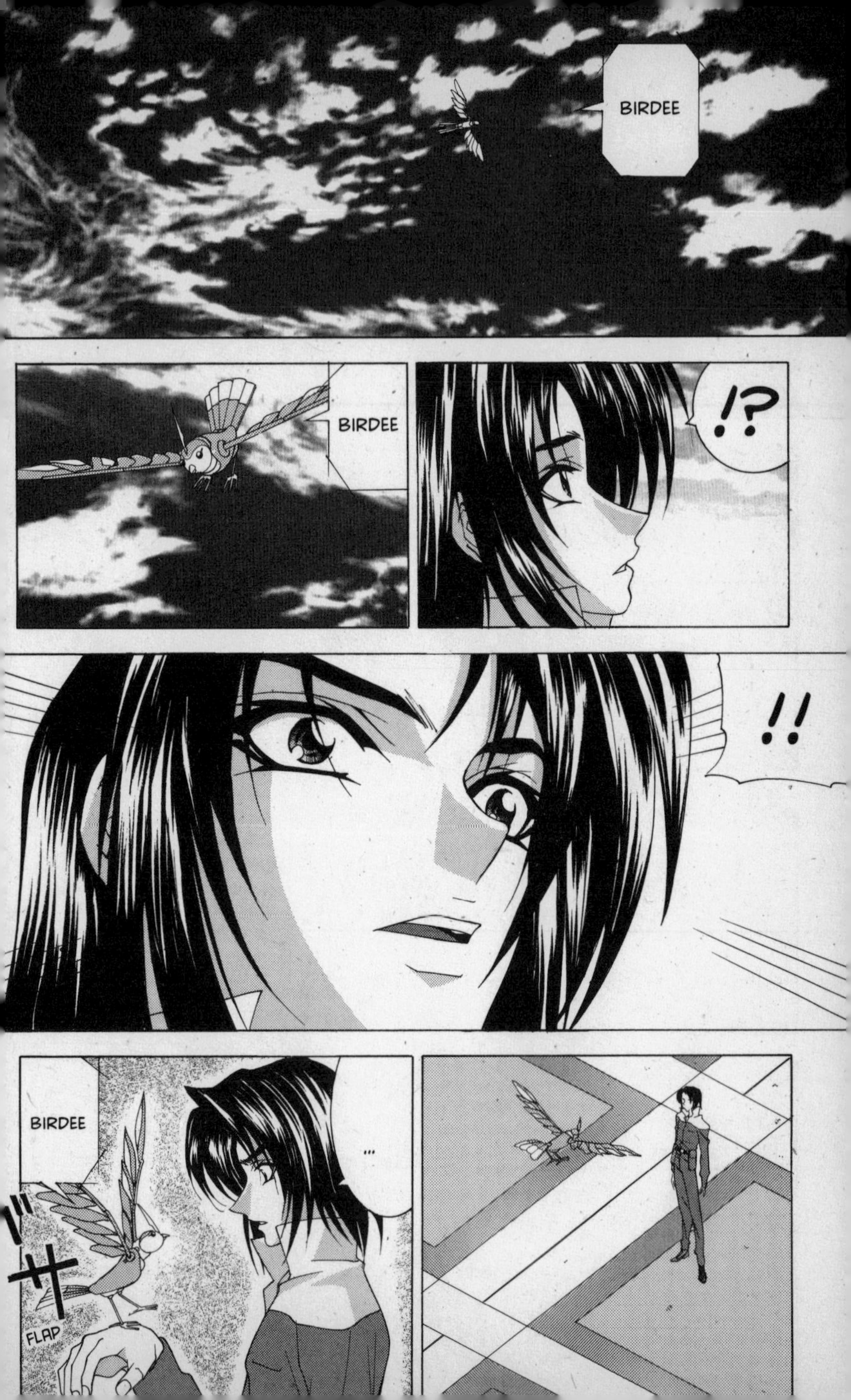
BIRDEE
!?
BIRDEE
!!
...
BIRDEE
FLAP

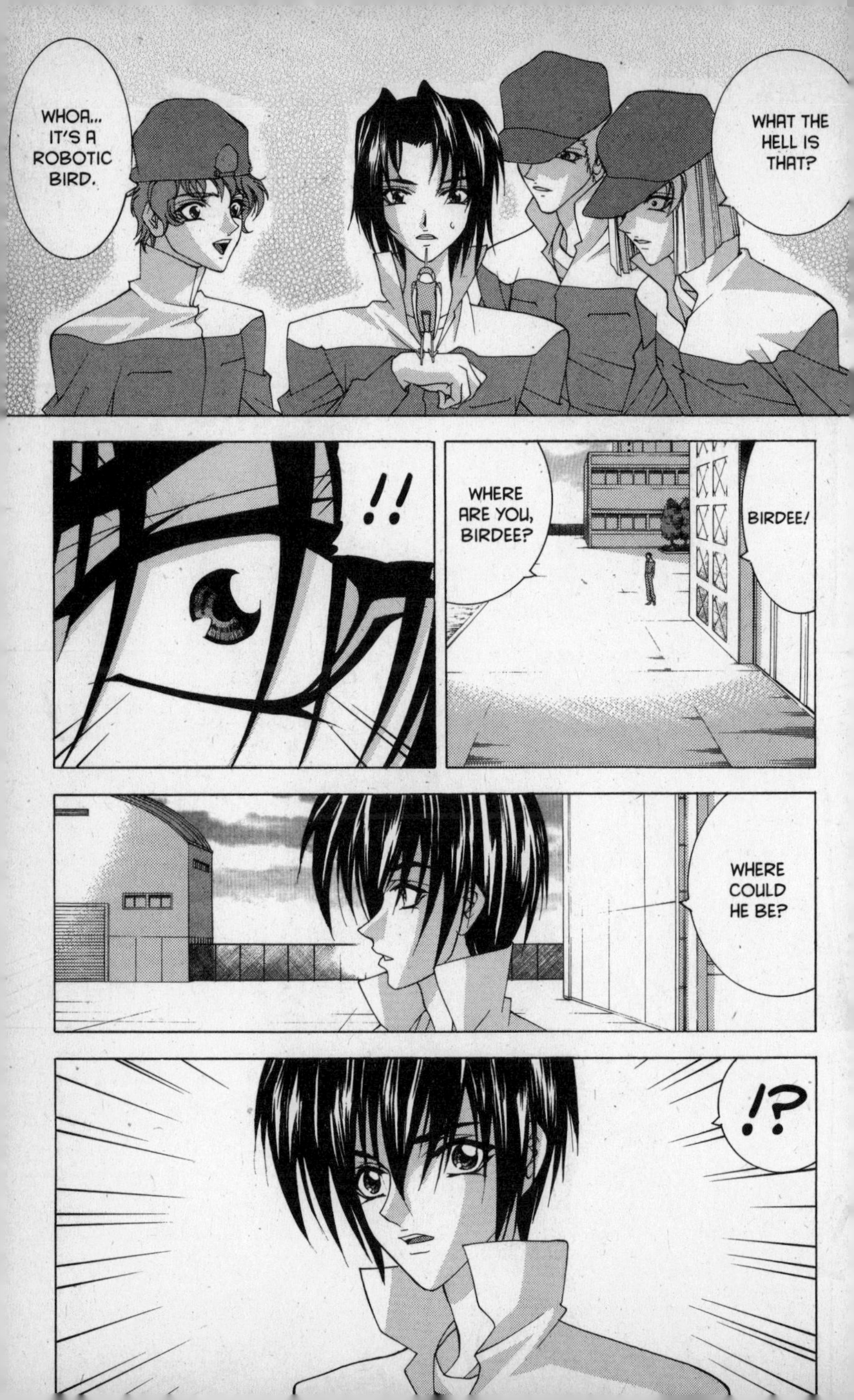
WHAT THE HELL IS THAT?
WHOA... IT'S A ROBOTIC BIRD.
BIRDEE!
WHERE ARE YOU, BIRDEE?
!!
WHERE COULD HE BE?
!?

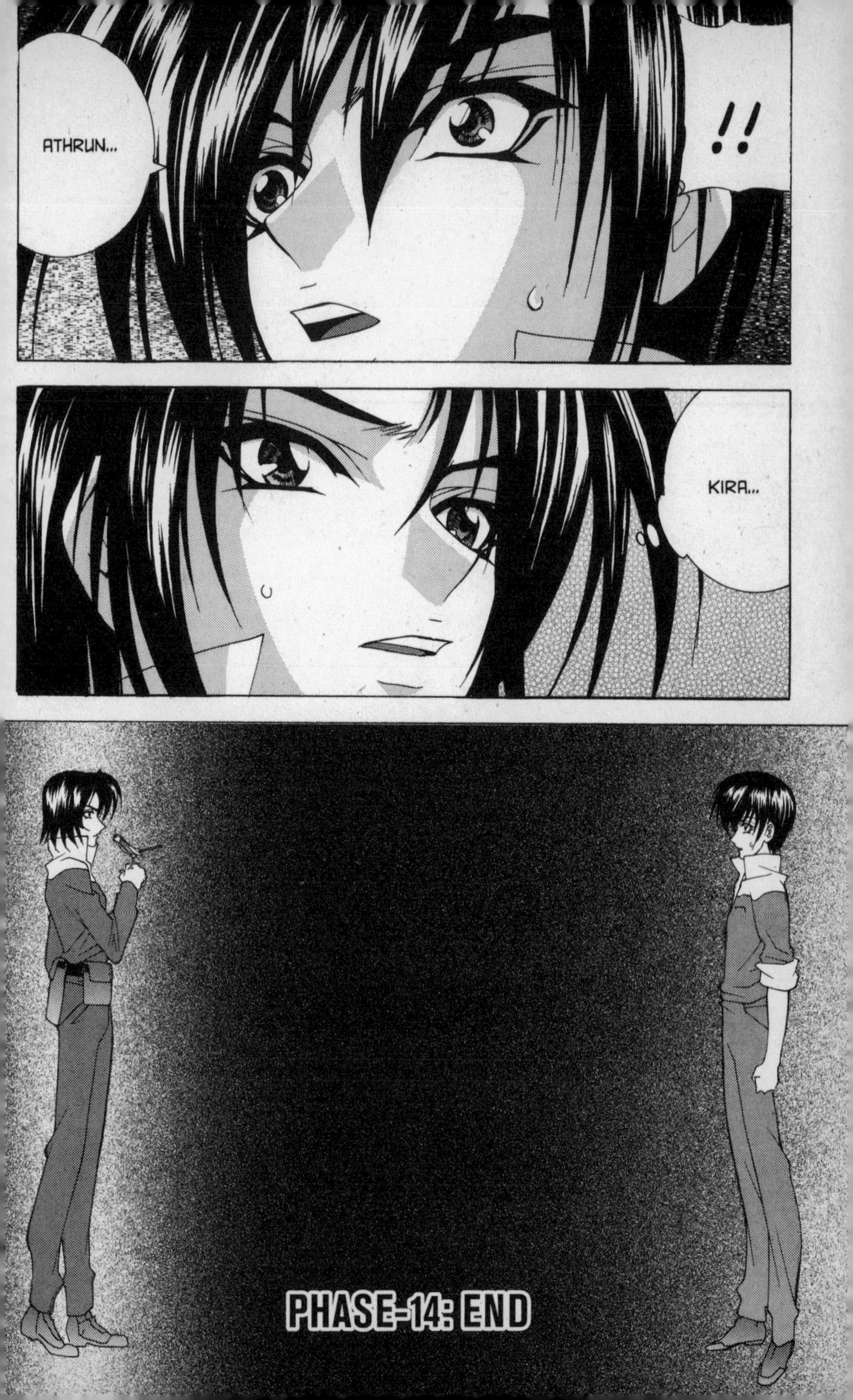
!!
ATHRUN...
KIRA...
PHASE-14: END

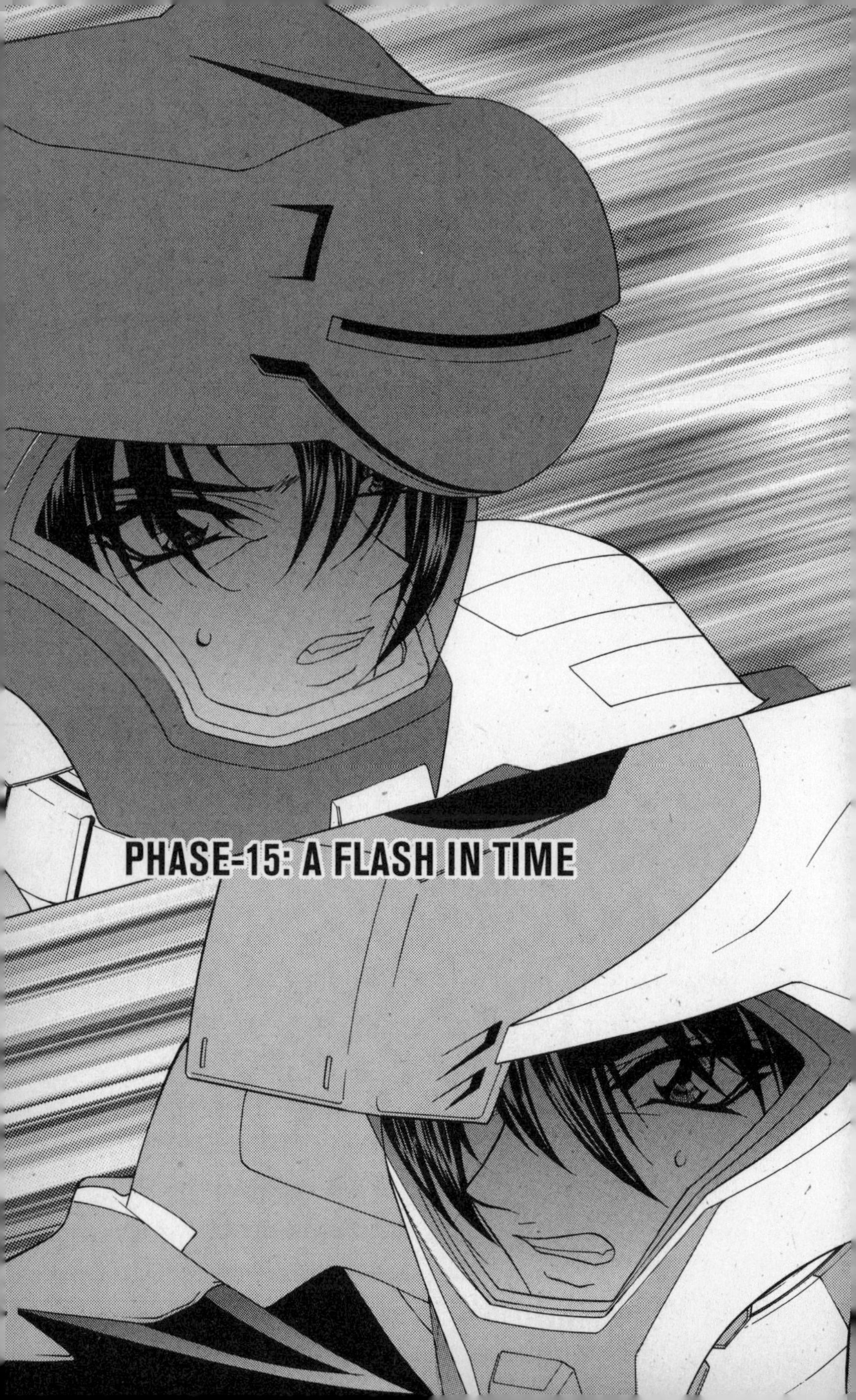
PHASE-15: A FLASH IN TIME

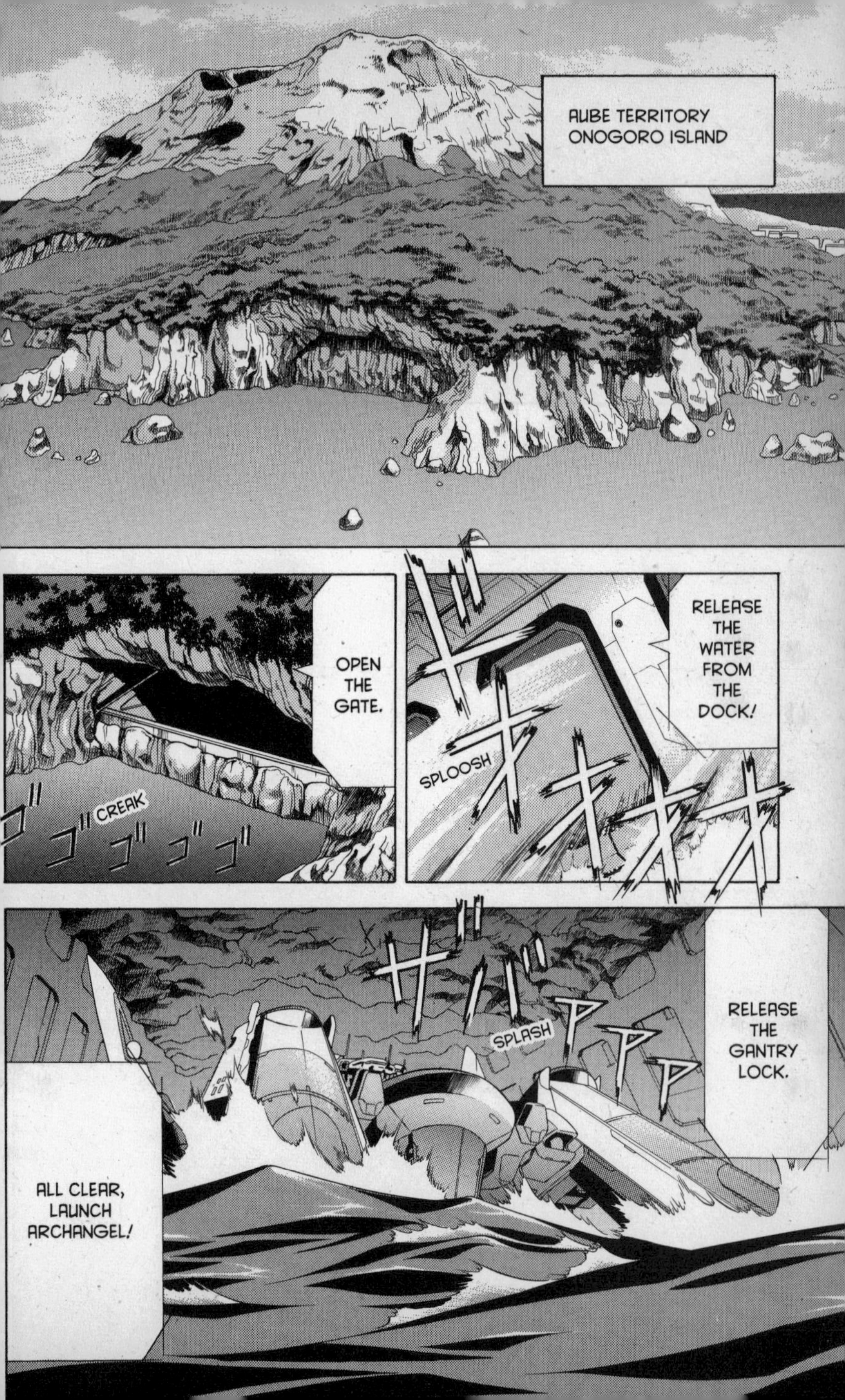
AUBE TERRITORY
ONOGORO ISLAND
RELEASE THE WATER FROM THE DOCK!
SPLOOSH
OPEN THE GATE.
CREAK
RELEASE THE GANTRY LOCK.
SPLASH
ALL CLEAR, LAUNCH ARCHANGEL!

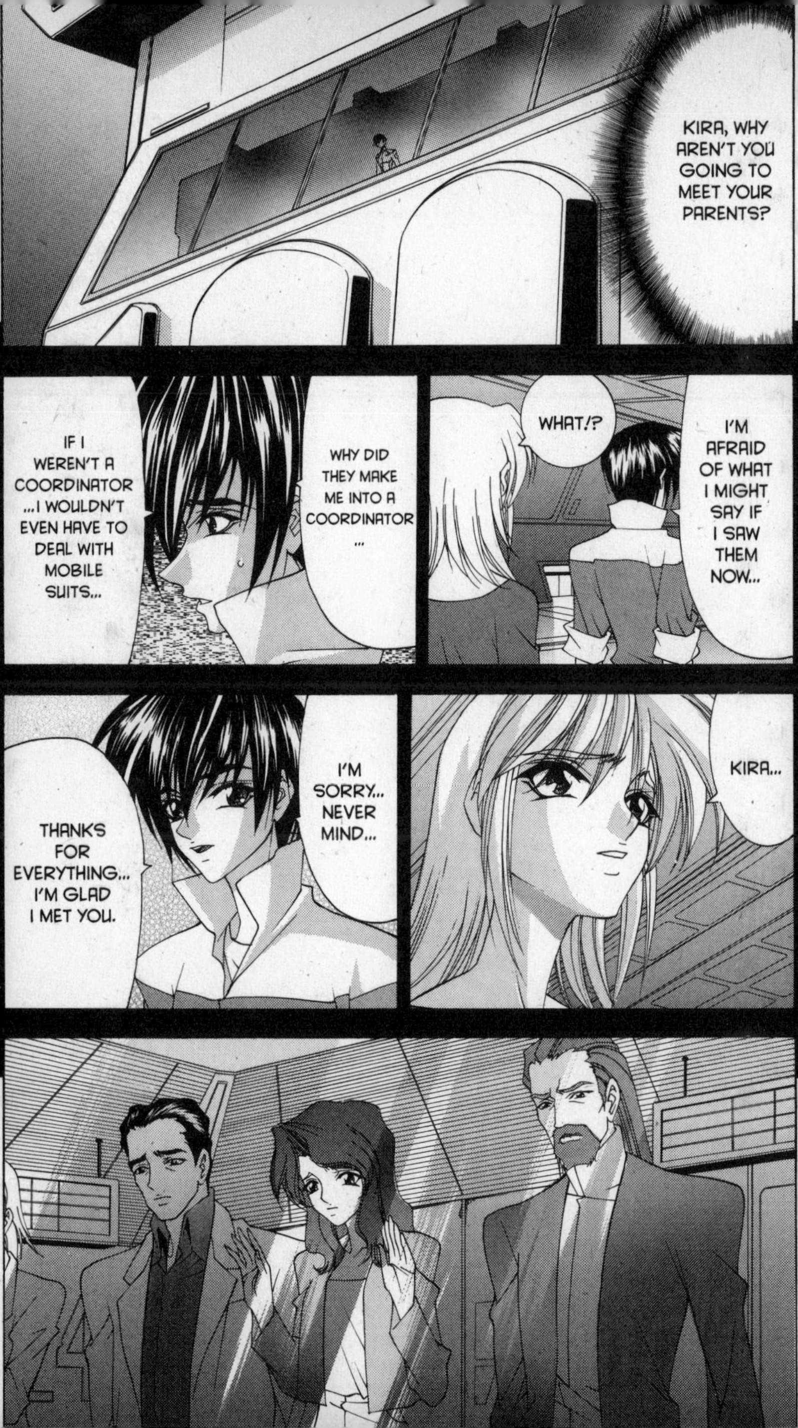
KIRA, WHY AREN'T YOU GOING TO MEET YOUR PARENTS?
WHAT!?
I'M AFRAID OF WHAT I MIGHT SAY IF I SAW THEM NOW...
WHY DID THEY MAKE ME INTO A COORDINATOR ...
IF I WEREN'T A COORDINATOR ...I WOULDN'T EVEN HAVE TO DEAL WITH MOBILE SUITS...
KIRA...
I'M SORRY... NEVER MIND...
THANKS FOR EVERYTHING... I'M GLAD I MET YOU.

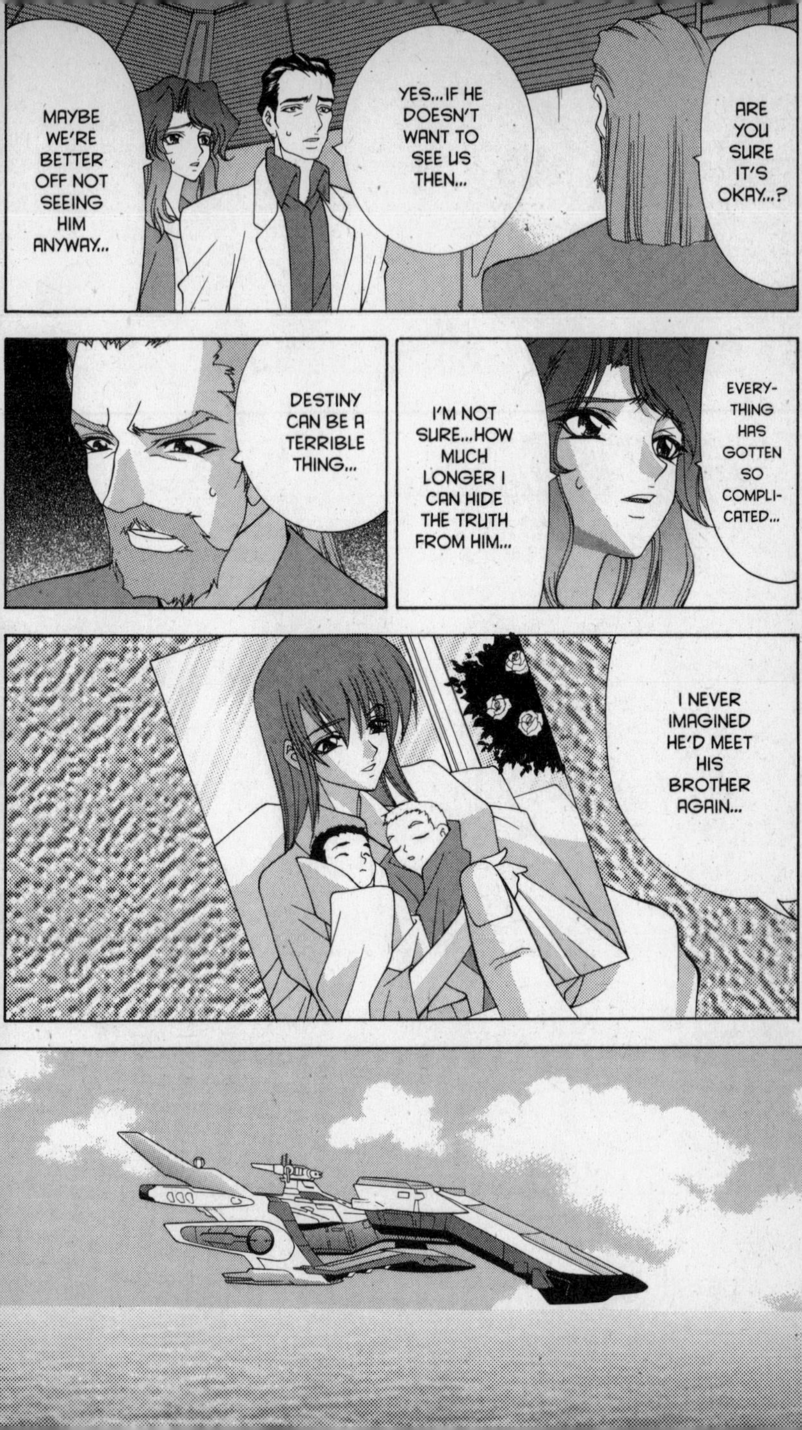
ARE YOU SURE IT'S OKAY...?
YES...IF HE DOESN'T WANT TO SEE US THEN...
MAYBE WE'RE BETTER OFF NOT SEEING HIM ANYWAY...
EVERY-THING HAS GOTTEN SO COMPLI-CATED...
I'M NOT SURE...HOW MUCH LONGER I CAN HIDE THE TRUTH FROM HIM...
DESTINY CAN BE A TERRIBLE THING...
I NEVER IMAGINED HE'D MEET HIS BROTHER AGAIN...

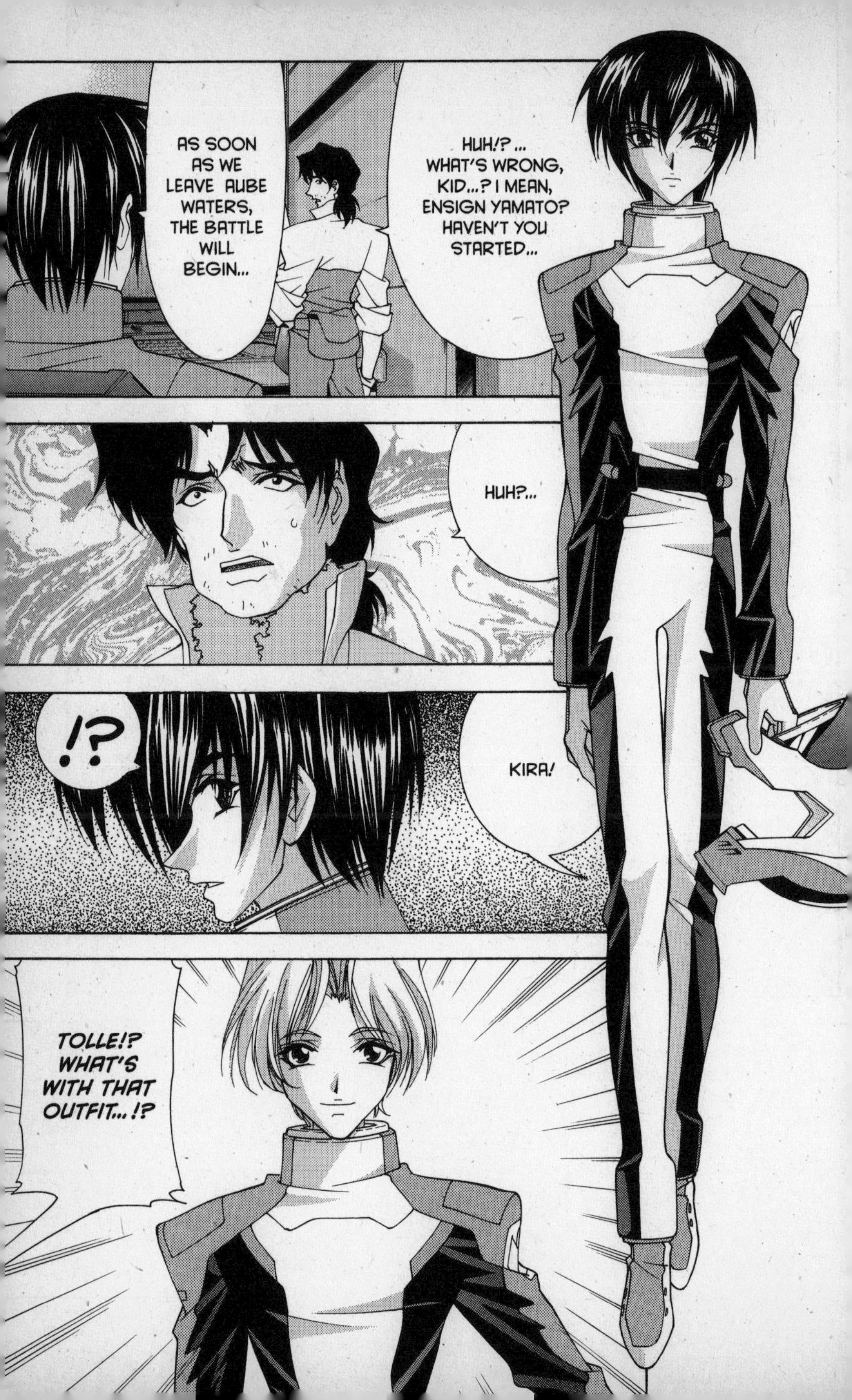
HUH!? ... WHAT'S WRONG, KID...? I MEAN, ENSIGN YAMATO? HAVEN'T YOU STARTED...
AS SOON AS WE LEAVE AUBE WATERS, THE BATTLE WILL BEGIN...
HUH?...
KIRA!
!?
TOLLE!? WHAT'S WITH THAT OUTFIT...!?

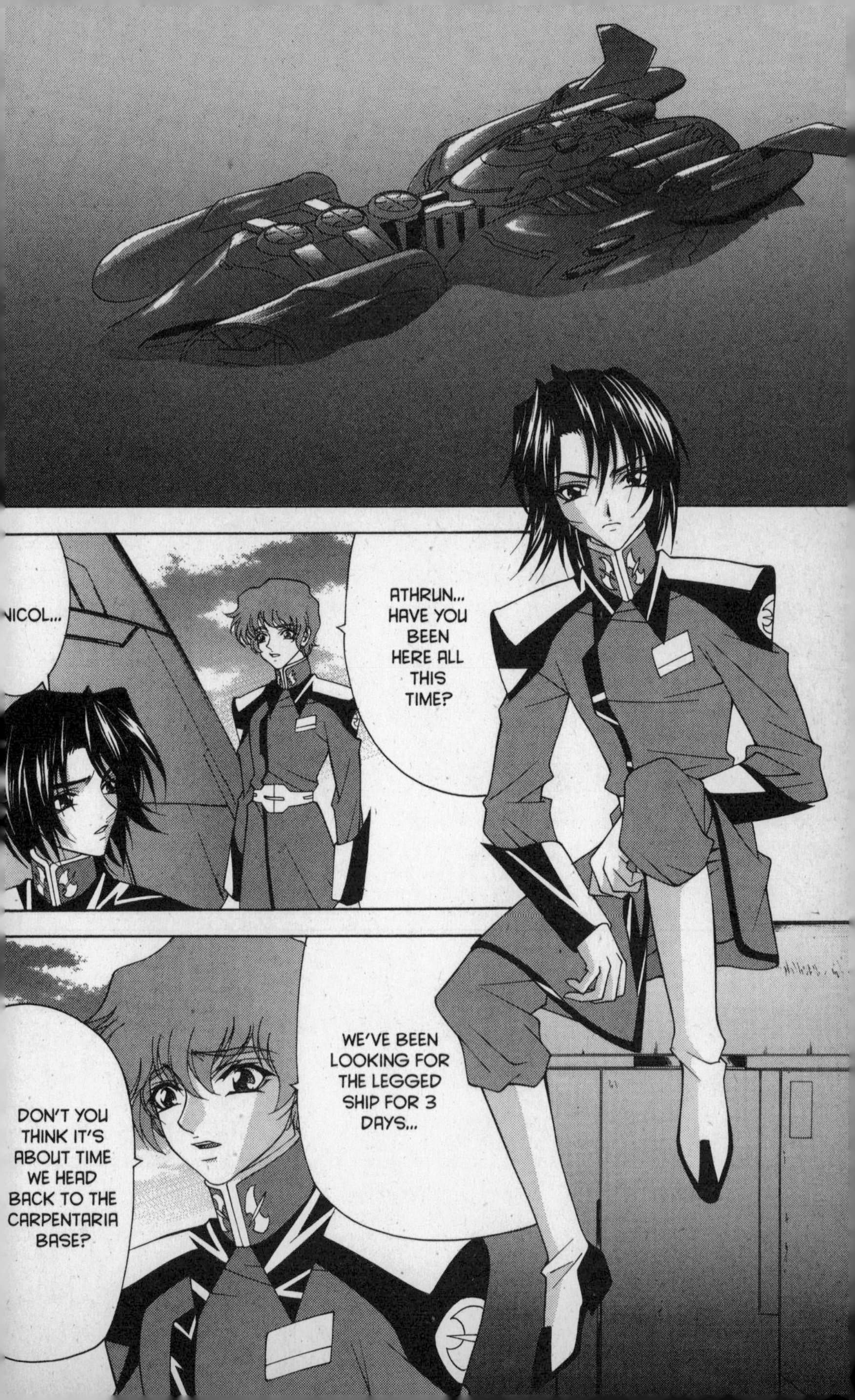
ATHRUN... HAVE YOU BEEN HERE ALL THIS TIME?
NICOL...
WE'VE BEEN LOOKING FOR THE LEGGED SHIP FOR 3 DAYS...
DON'T YOU THINK IT'S ABOUT TIME WE HEAD BACK TO THE CARPENTARIA BASE?

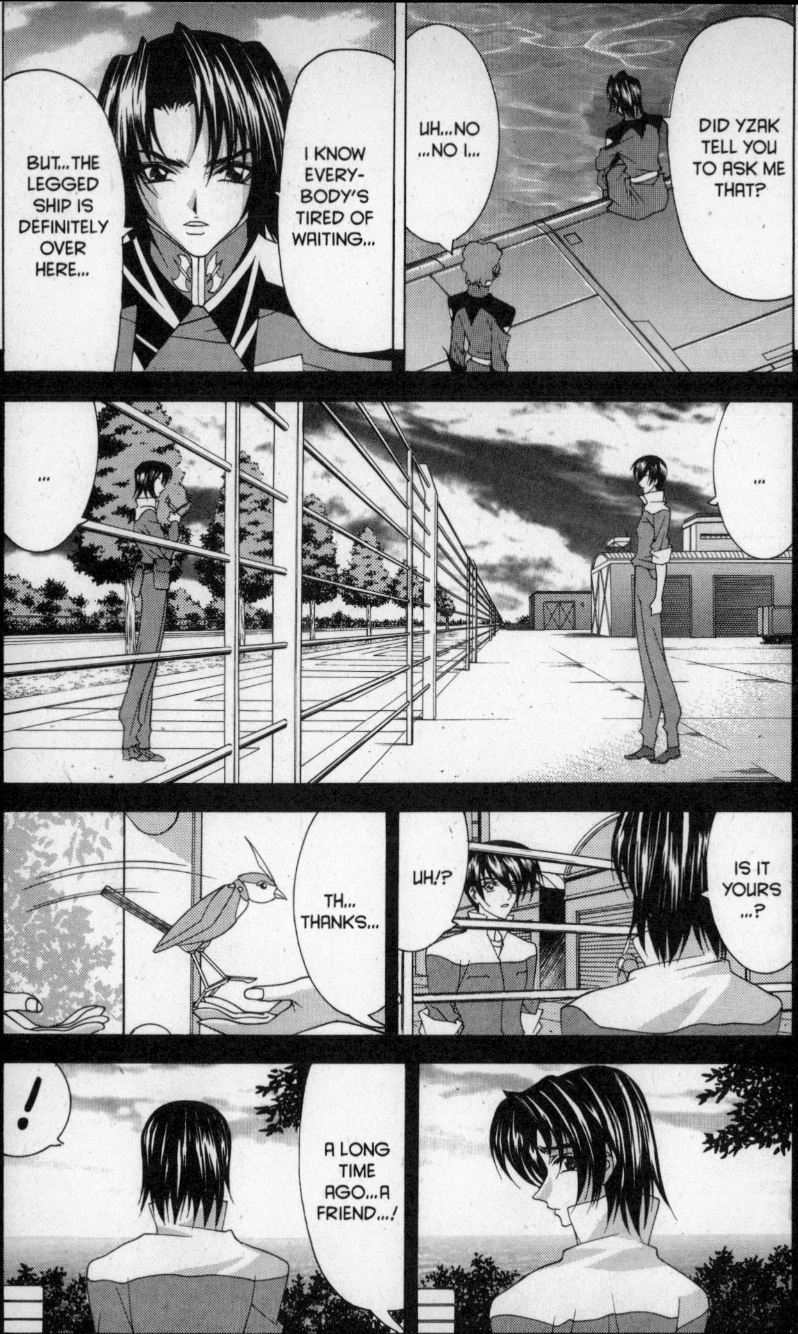
DID YZAK TELL YOU TO ASK ME THAT?
UH...NO ...NO I...
I KNOW EVERY-BODY'S TIRED OF WAITING...
BUT...THE LEGGED SHIP IS DEFINITELY OVER HERE...
...
...
IS IT YOURS ...?
UH!?
TH... THANKS...
A LONG TIME AGO...A FRIEND...!
!

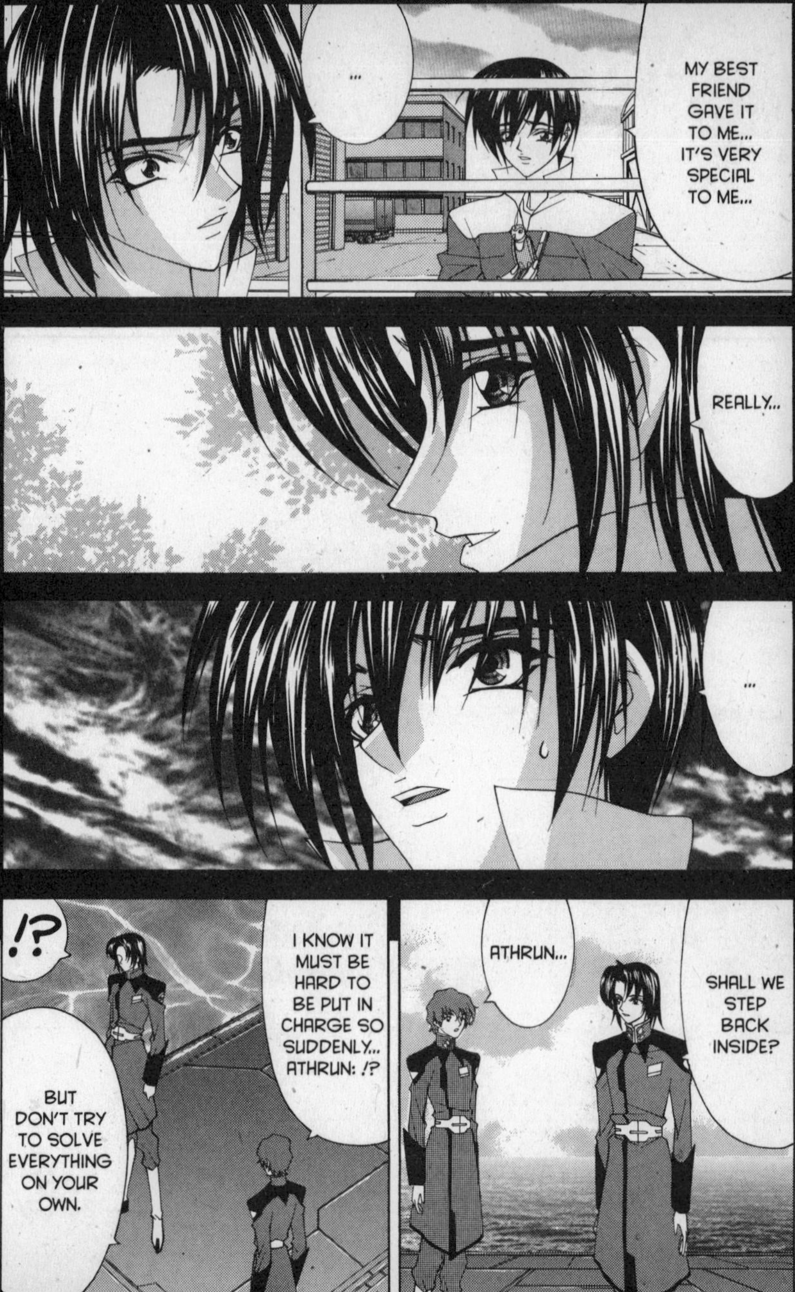
MY BEST FRIEND GAVE IT TO ME... IT'S VERY SPECIAL TO ME...
...
REALLY...
...
SHALL WE STEP BACK INSIDE?
ATHRUN...
I KNOW IT MUST BE HARD TO BE PUT IN CHARGE SO SUDDENLY... ATHRUN: !?
!?
BUT DON'T TRY TO SOLVE EVERYTHING ON YOUR OWN.

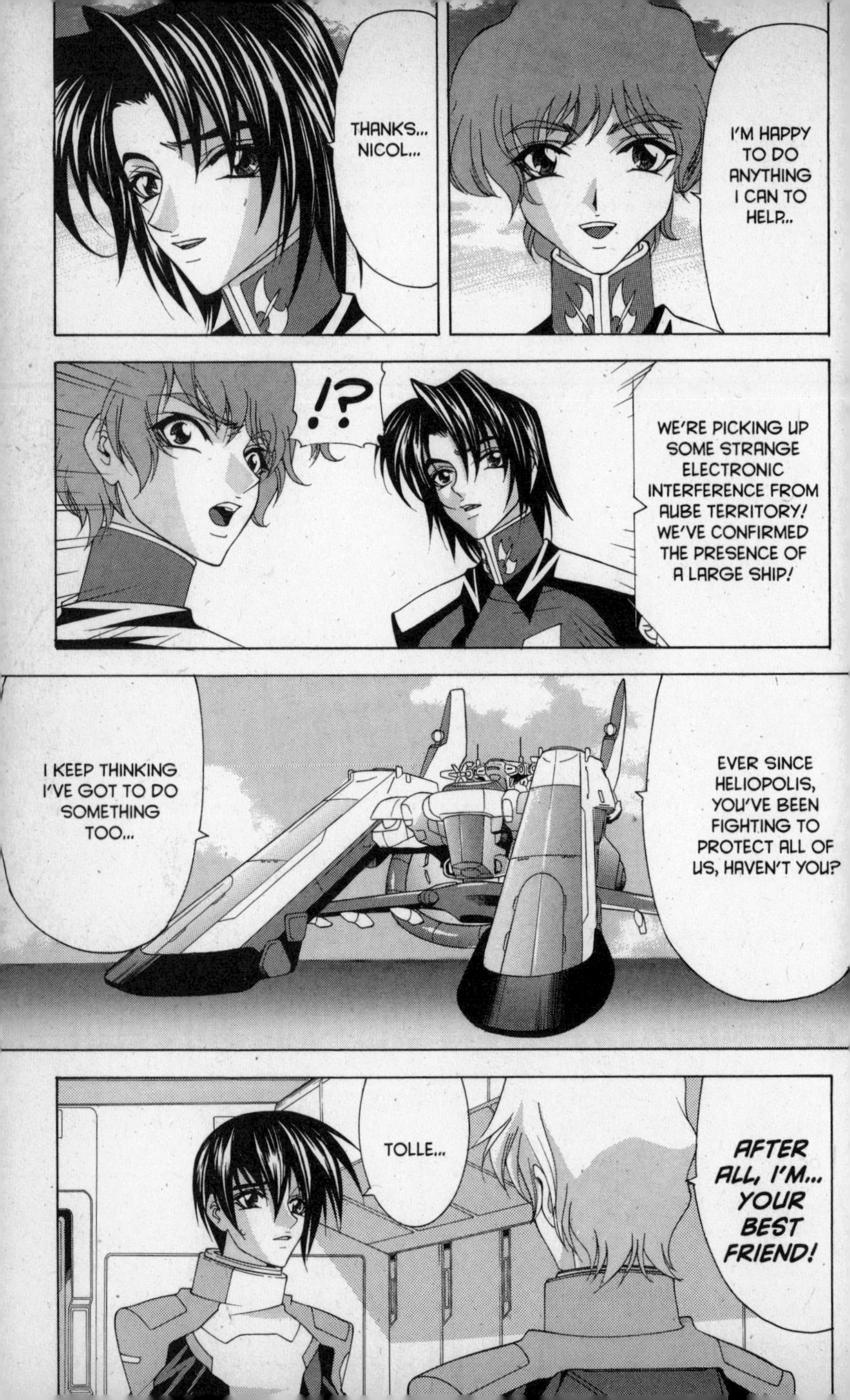
I'M HAPPY TO DO ANYTHING I CAN TO HELP...
THANKS... NICOL...
WE'RE PICKING UP SOME STRANGE ELECTRONIC INTERFERENCE FROM AUBE TERRITORY! WE'VE CONFIRMED THE PRESENCE OF A LARGE SHIP!
!?
EVER SINCE HELIOPOLIS, YOU'VE BEEN FIGHTING TO PROTECT ALL OF US, HAVEN'T YOU?
I KEEP THINKING I'VE GOT TO DO SOMETHING TOO...
AFTER ALL, I'M... YOUR BEST FRIEND!
TOLLE...

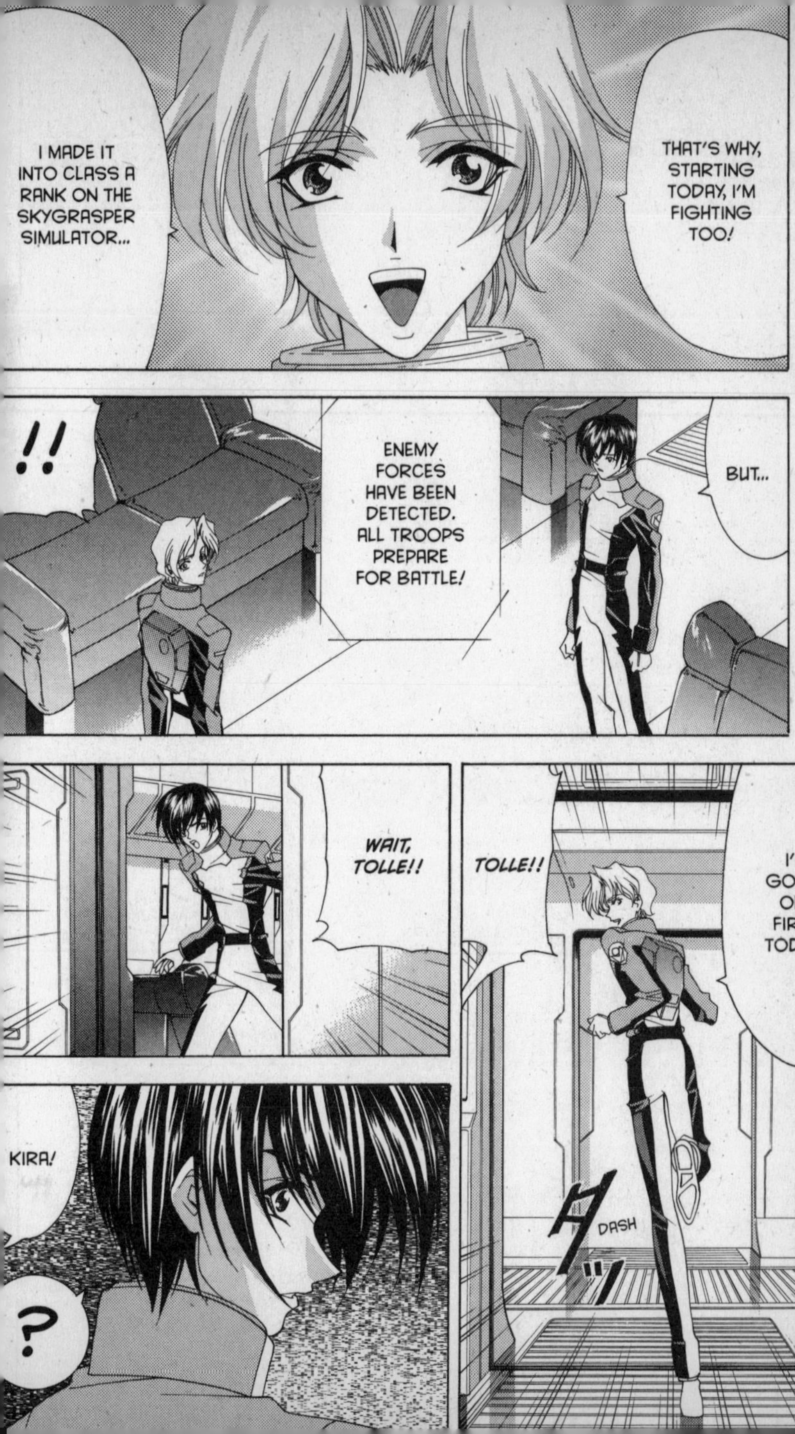
I MADE IT INTO CLASS A RANK ON THE SKYGRASPER SIMULATOR...
THAT'S WHY, STARTING TODAY, I'M FIGHTING TOO!
BUT...
ENEMY FORCES HAVE BEEN DETECTED. ALL TROOPS PREPARE FOR BATTLE!
!!
I'M GOING OUT FIRST TODAY!
TOLLE!!
DASH
WAIT, TOLLE!!
KIRA!
?

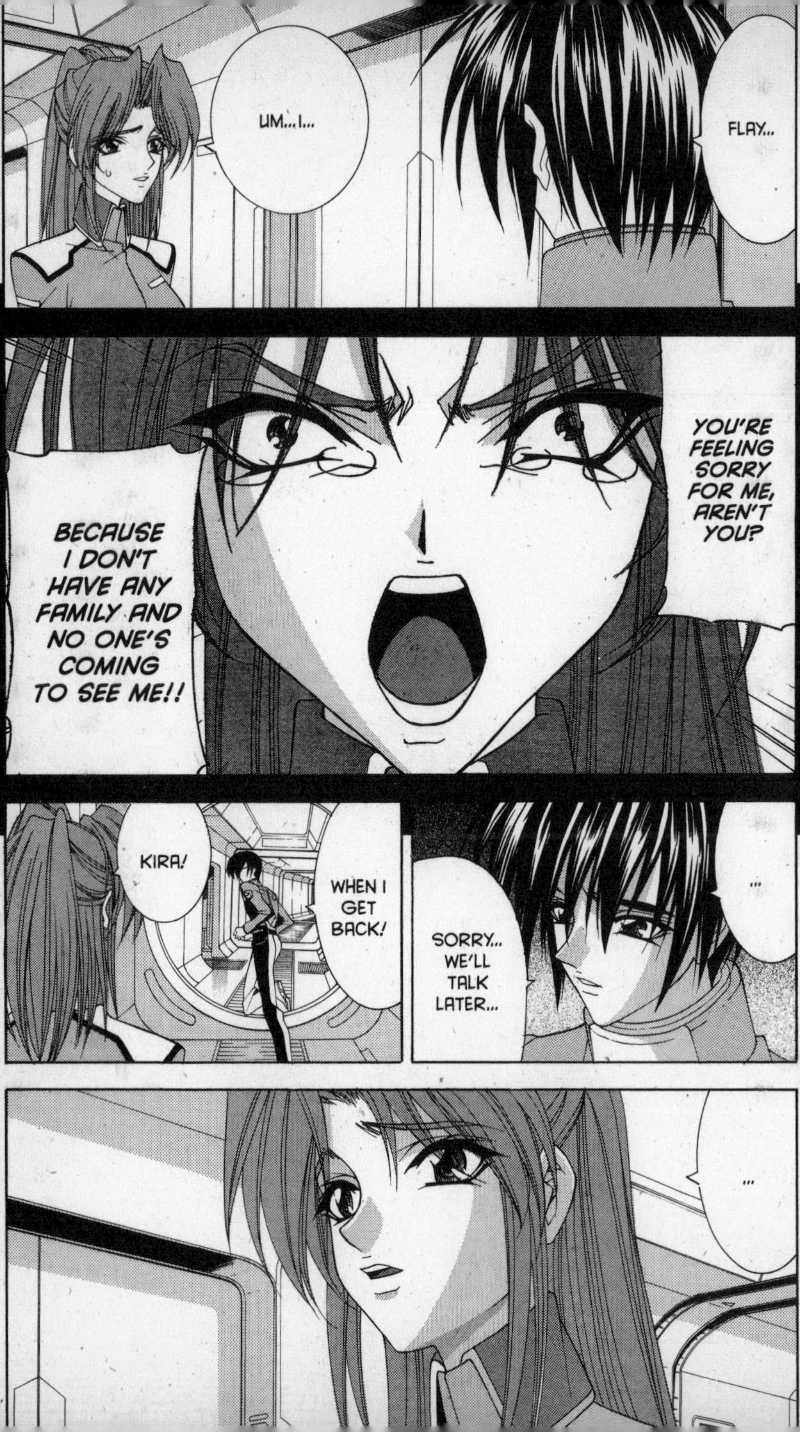
FLAY...
UM...I...
YOU'RE FEELING SORRY FOR ME, AREN'T YOU?
BECAUSE I DON'T HAVE ANY FAMILY AND NO ONE'S COMING TO SEE ME!!
...
SORRY... WE'LL TALK LATER...
WHEN I GET BACK!
KIRA!
...

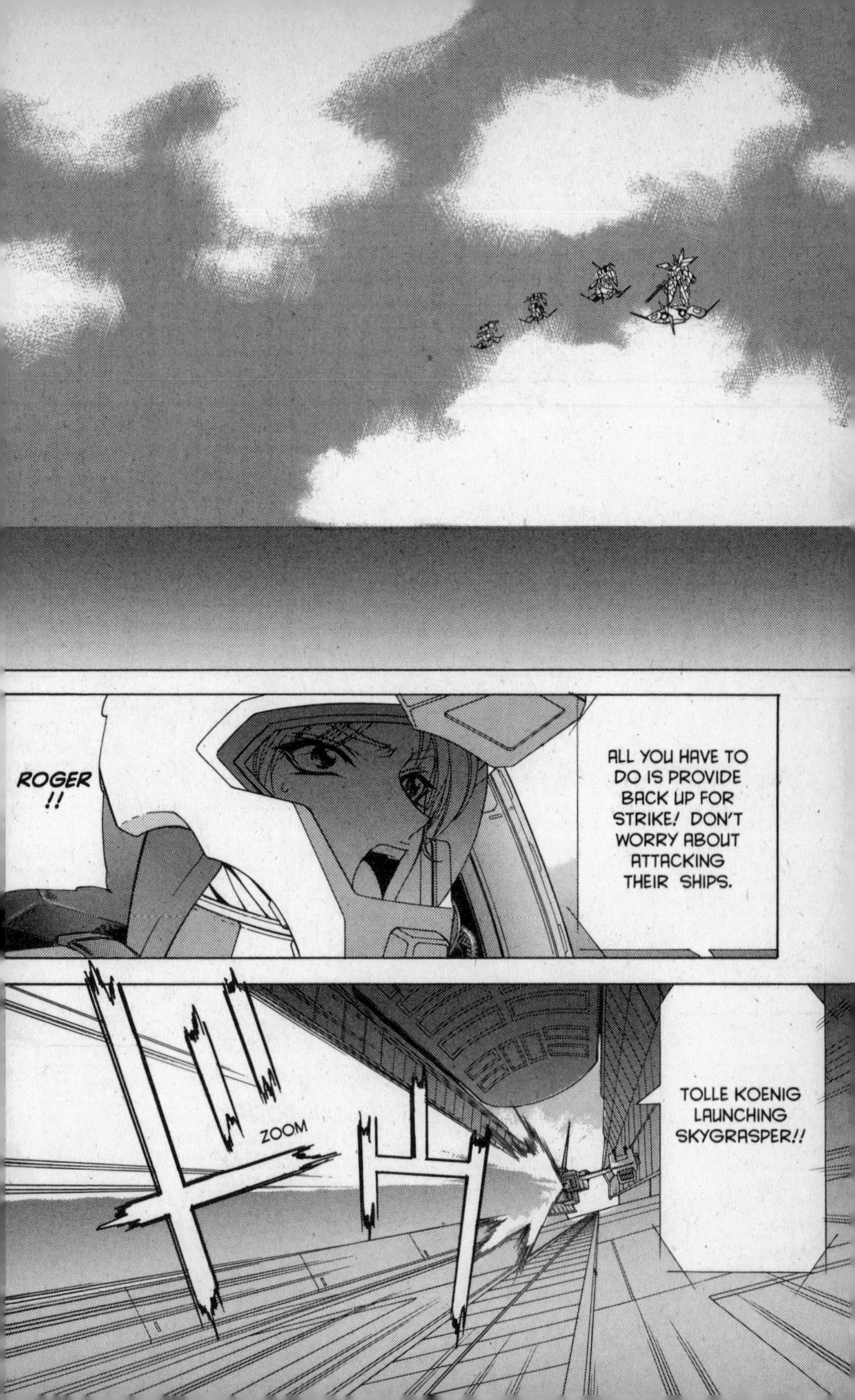
ALL YOU HAVE TO DO IS PROVIDE BACK UP FOR STRIKE! DON'T WORRY ABOUT ATTACKING THEIR SHIPS.
ROGER !!
TOLLE KOENIG LAUNCHING SKYGRASPER!!
ZOOM

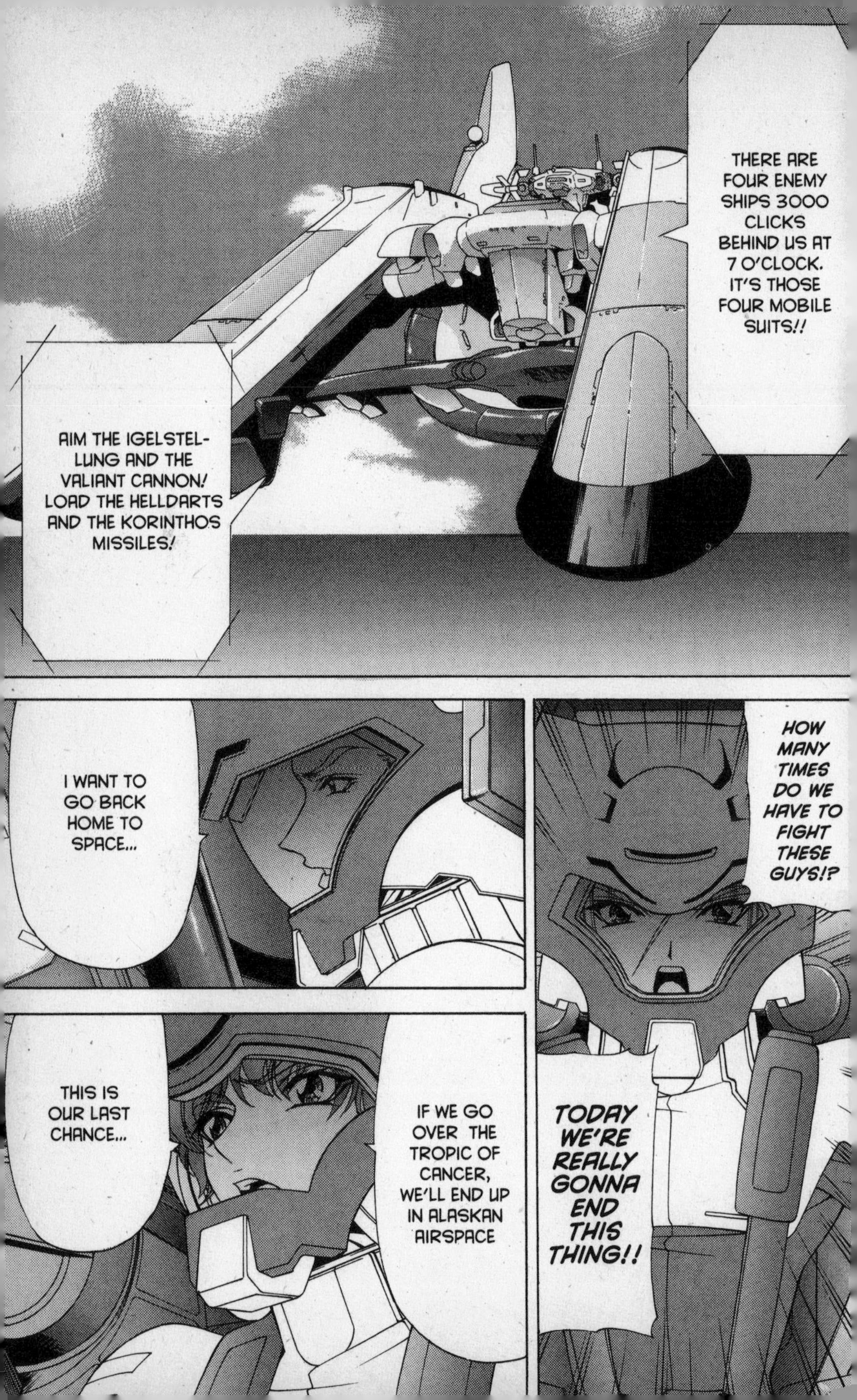
THERE ARE FOUR ENEMY SHIPS 3000 CLICKS BEHIND US AT 7 O'CLOCK. IT'S THOSE FOUR MOBILE SUITS!!
AIM THE IGELSTEL-LUNG AND THE VALIANT CANNON! LOAD THE HELLDARTS AND THE KORINTHOS MISSILES!
HOW MANY TIMES DO WE HAVE TO FIGHT THESE GUYS!?
TODAY WE'RE REALLY GONNA END THIS THING!!
I WANT TO GO BACK HOME TO SPACE...
IF WE GO OVER THE TROPIC OF CANCER, WE'LL END UP IN ALASKAN AIRSPACE
THIS IS OUR LAST CHANCE...

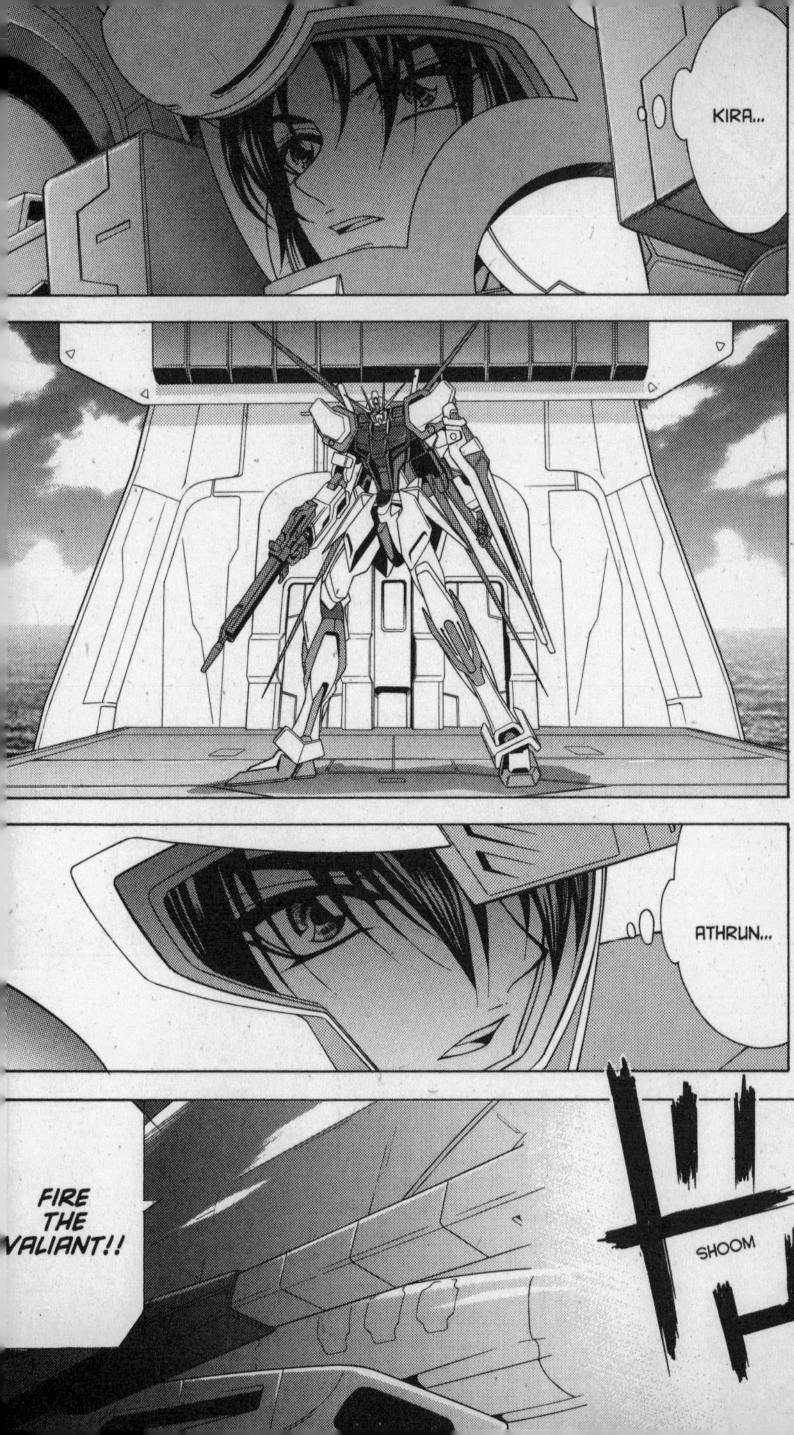
KIRA...
ATHRUN...
SHOOM
FIRE THE VALIANT!!

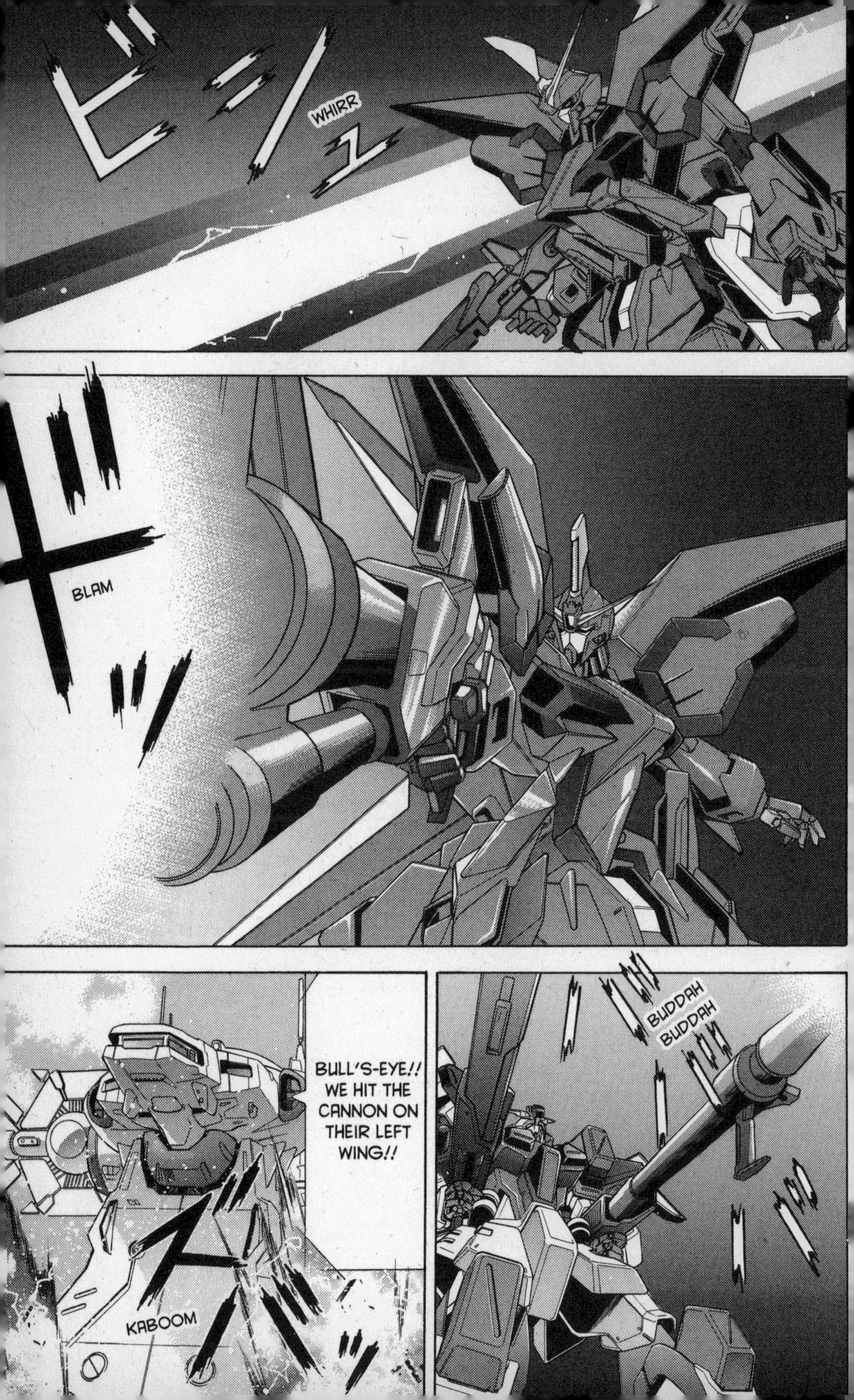
WHIRR
BLAM
BUDDAH BUDDAH
BULL'S-EYE!! WE HIT THE CANNON ON THEIR LEFT WING!!
KABOOM

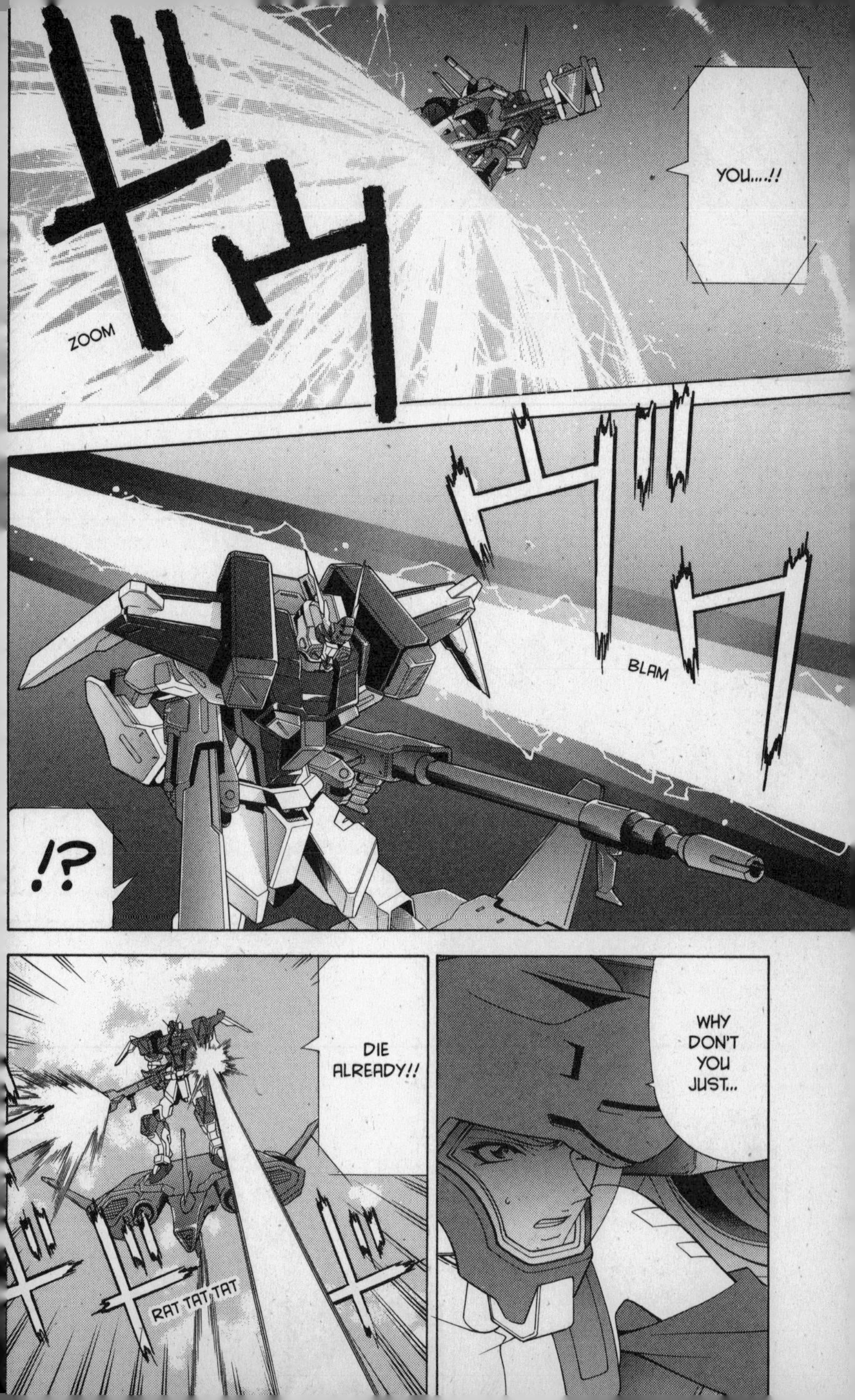
YOU....!!
ZOOM
BLAM
!?
WHY DON'T YOU JUST...
DIE ALREADY!!
RAT TAT TAT

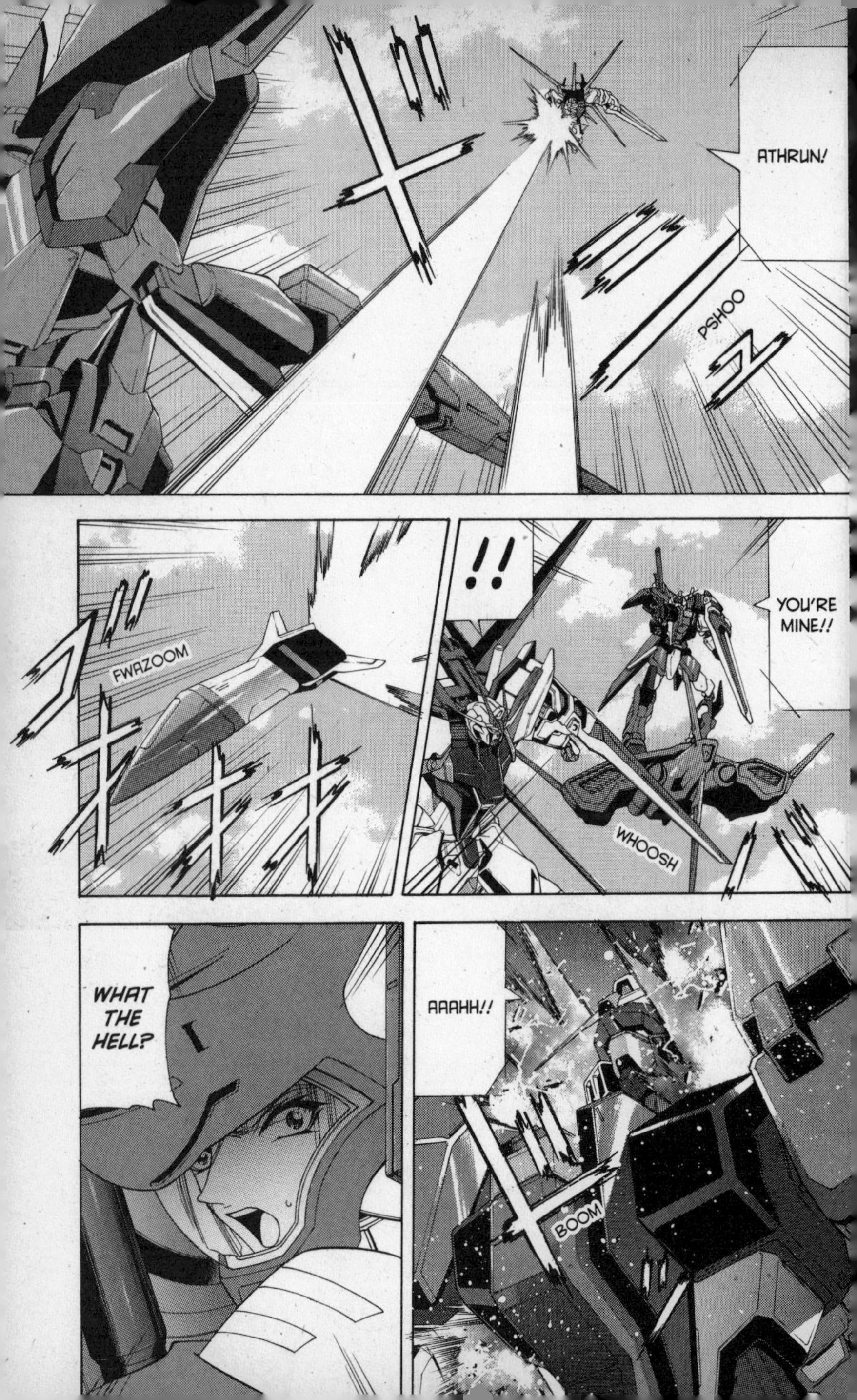
ATHRUN!
PSHOO
YOU'RE MINE!!
WHOOSH
!!
FWAZOOM
AAAHH!!
BOOM
WHAT THE HELL?

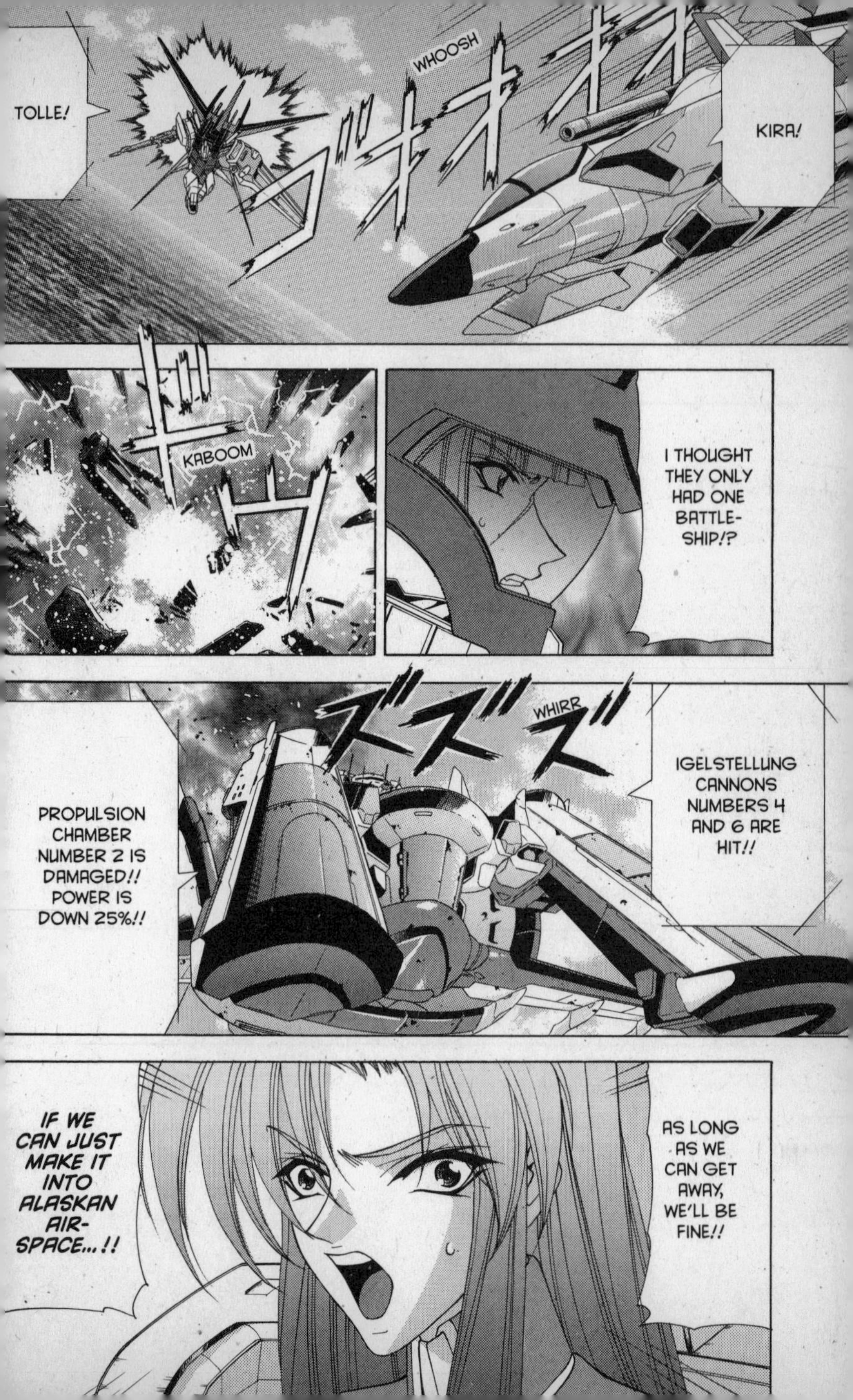
KIRA!
WHOOSH
TOLLE!
I THOUGHT THEY ONLY HAD ONE BATTLE-SHIP!?
KABOOM
IGELSTELLUNG CANNONS NUMBERS 4 AND 6 ARE HIT!!
WHIRR
PROPULSION CHAMBER NUMBER 2 IS DAMAGED!! POWER IS DOWN 25%!!
AS LONG AS WE CAN GET AWAY, WE'LL BE FINE!!
IF WE CAN JUST MAKE IT INTO ALASKAN AIR-SPACE...!!

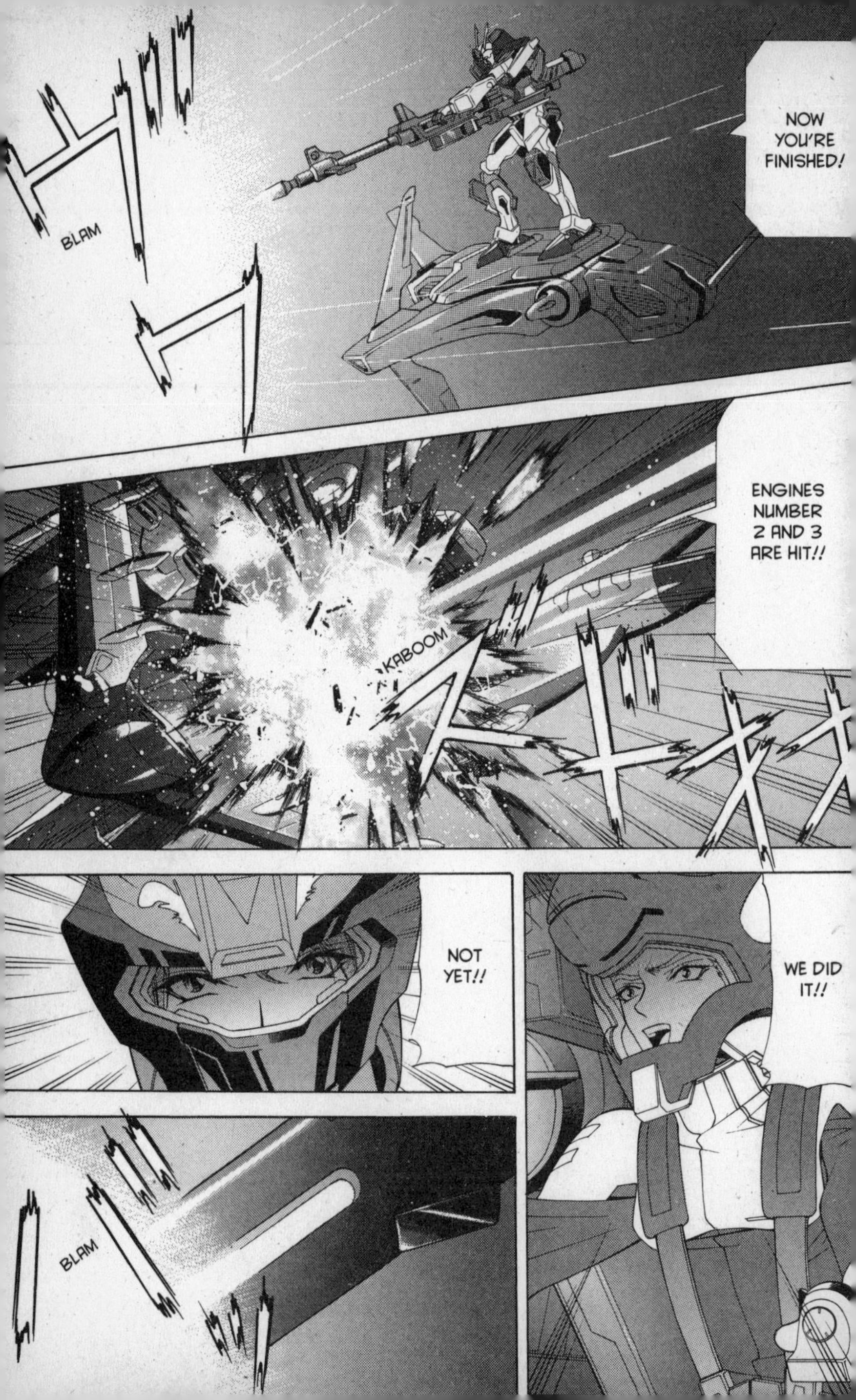
NOW YOU'RE FINISHED!
BLAM
ENGINES NUMBER 2 AND 3 ARE HIT!!
KABOOM
WE DID IT!!
NOT YET!!
BLAM

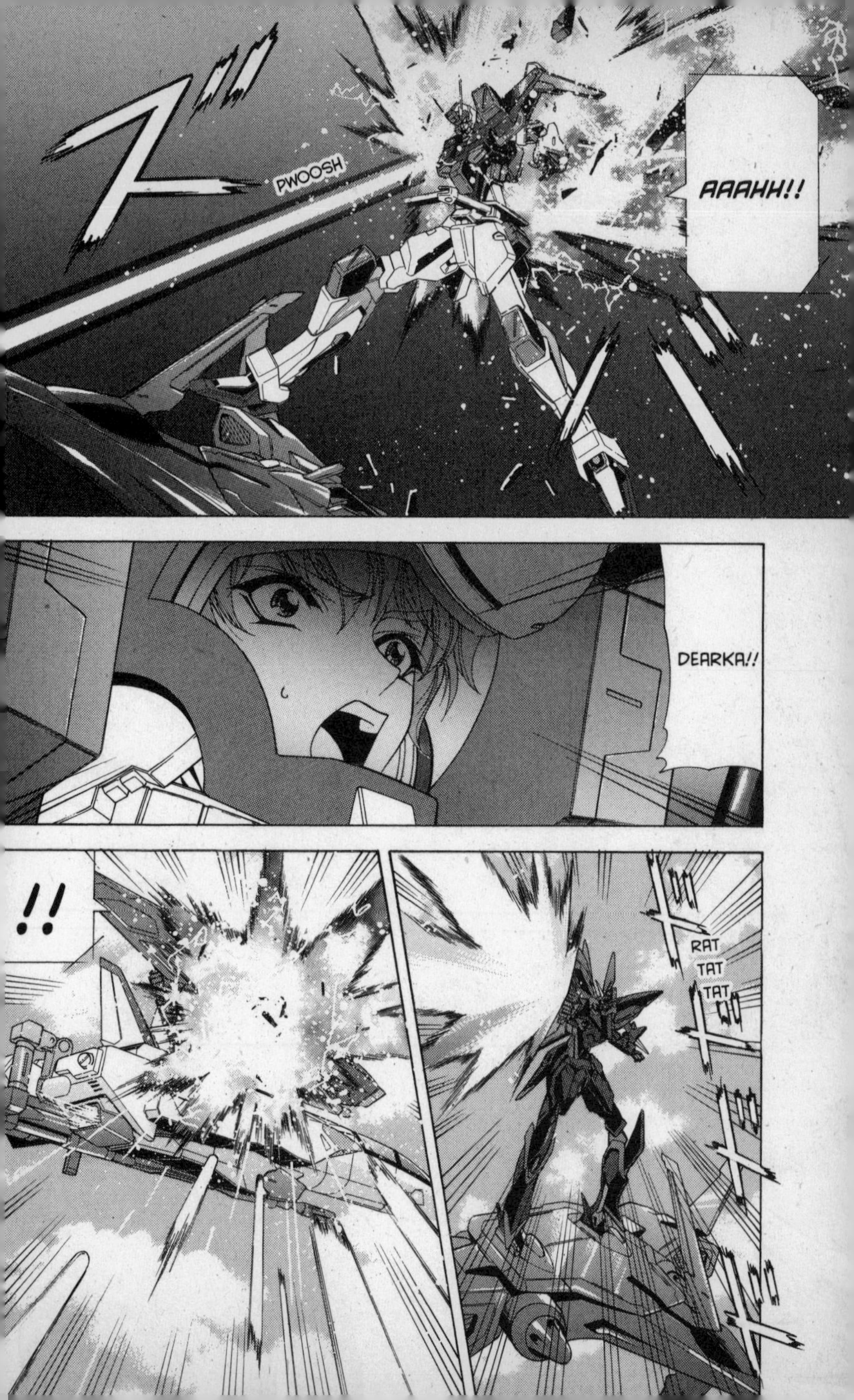
AAAHH!!
PWOOSH
DEARKA!!
RAT
TAT
TAT
!!

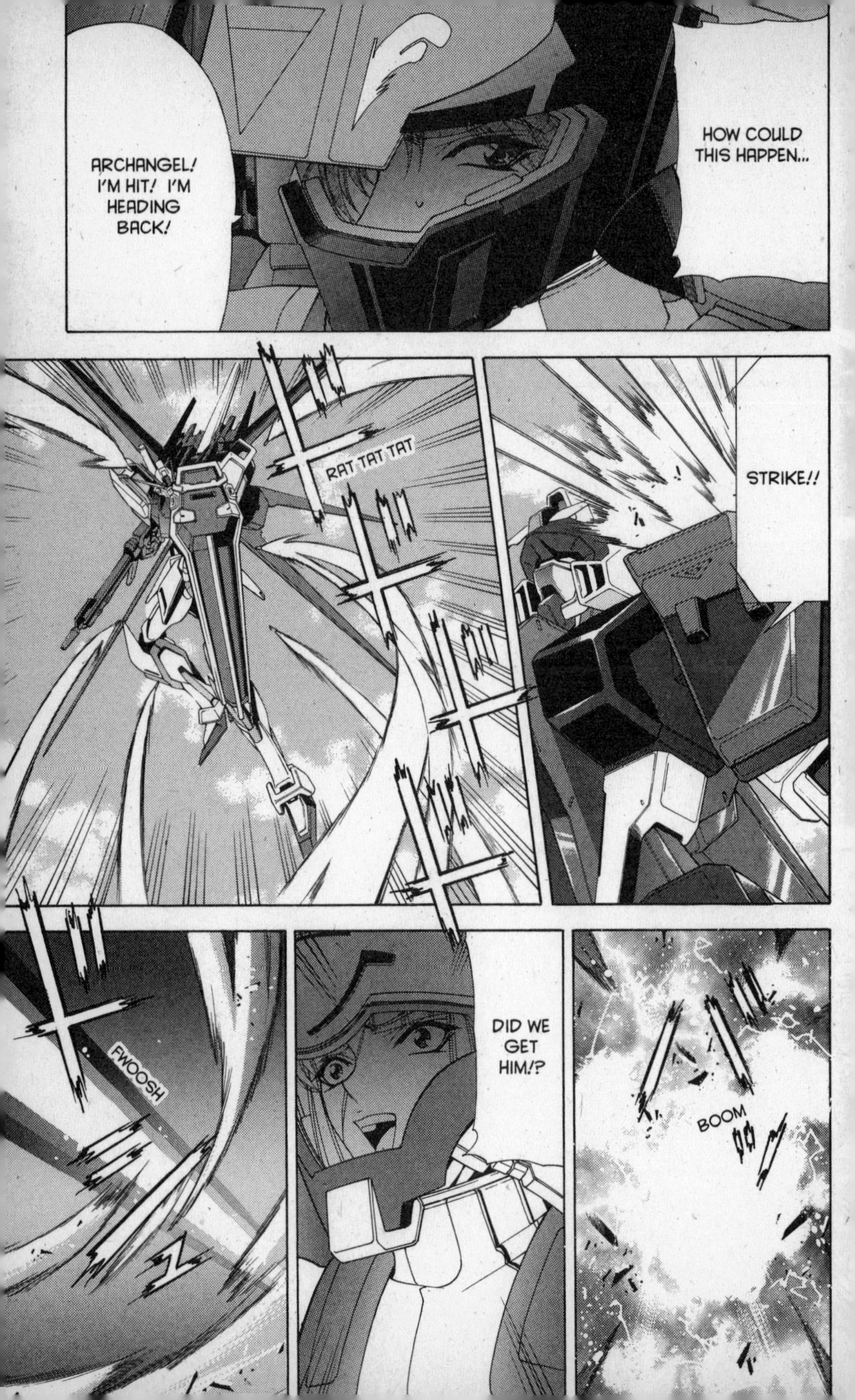
HOW COULD THIS HAPPEN...
ARCHANGEL! I'M HIT! I'M HEADING BACK!
STRIKE!!
RAT TAT TAT
BOOM
DID WE GET HIM!?
FWOOSH

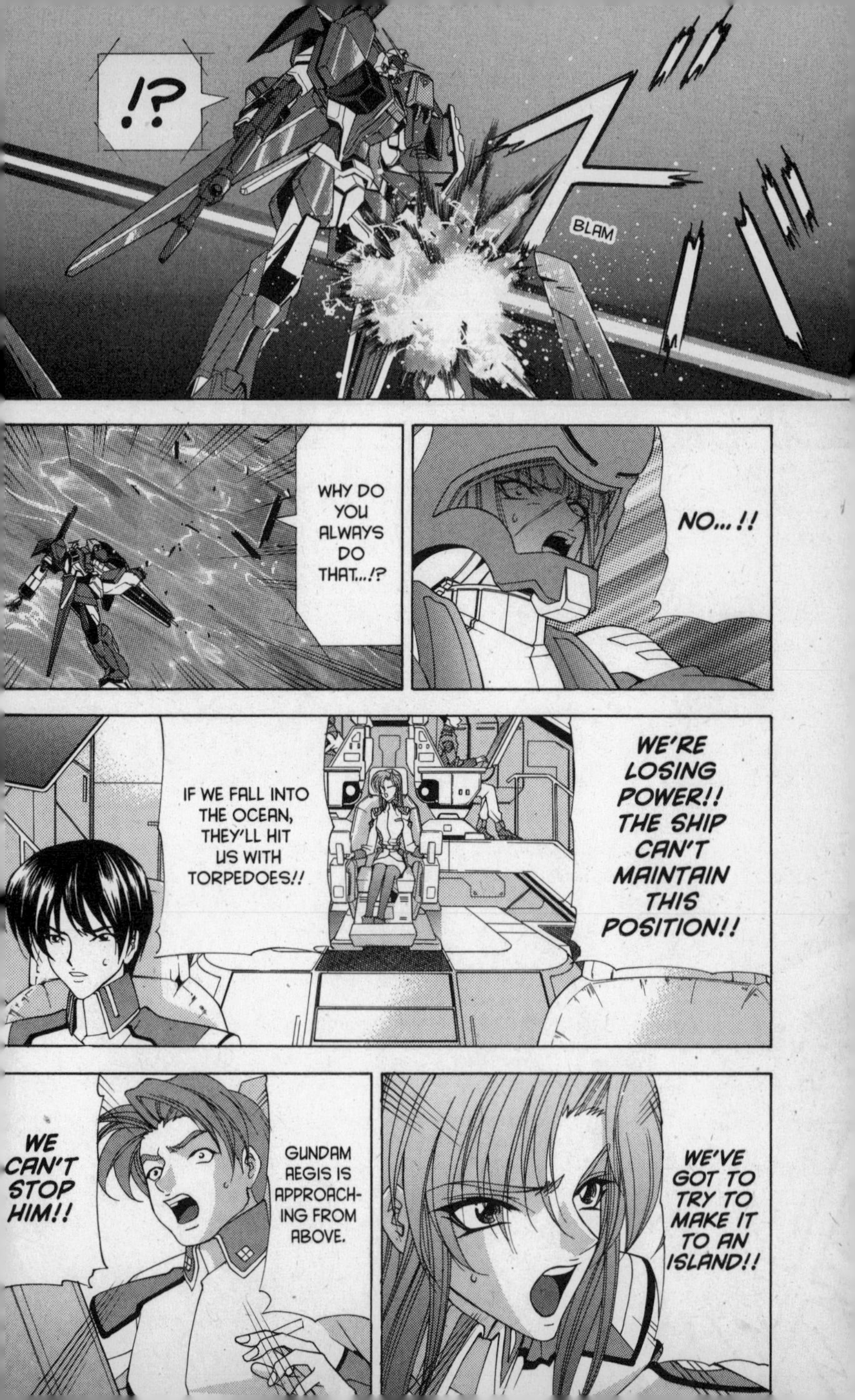
!?
BLAM
NO...!!
WHY DO YOU ALWAYS DO THAT...!?
WE'RE LOSING POWER!! THE SHIP CAN'T MAINTAIN THIS POSITION!!
IF WE FALL INTO THE OCEAN, THEY'LL HIT US WITH TORPEDOES!!
WE'VE GOT TO TRY TO MAKE IT TO AN ISLAND!!
GUNDAM AEGIS IS APPROACHING FROM ABOVE.
WE CAN'T STOP HIM!!

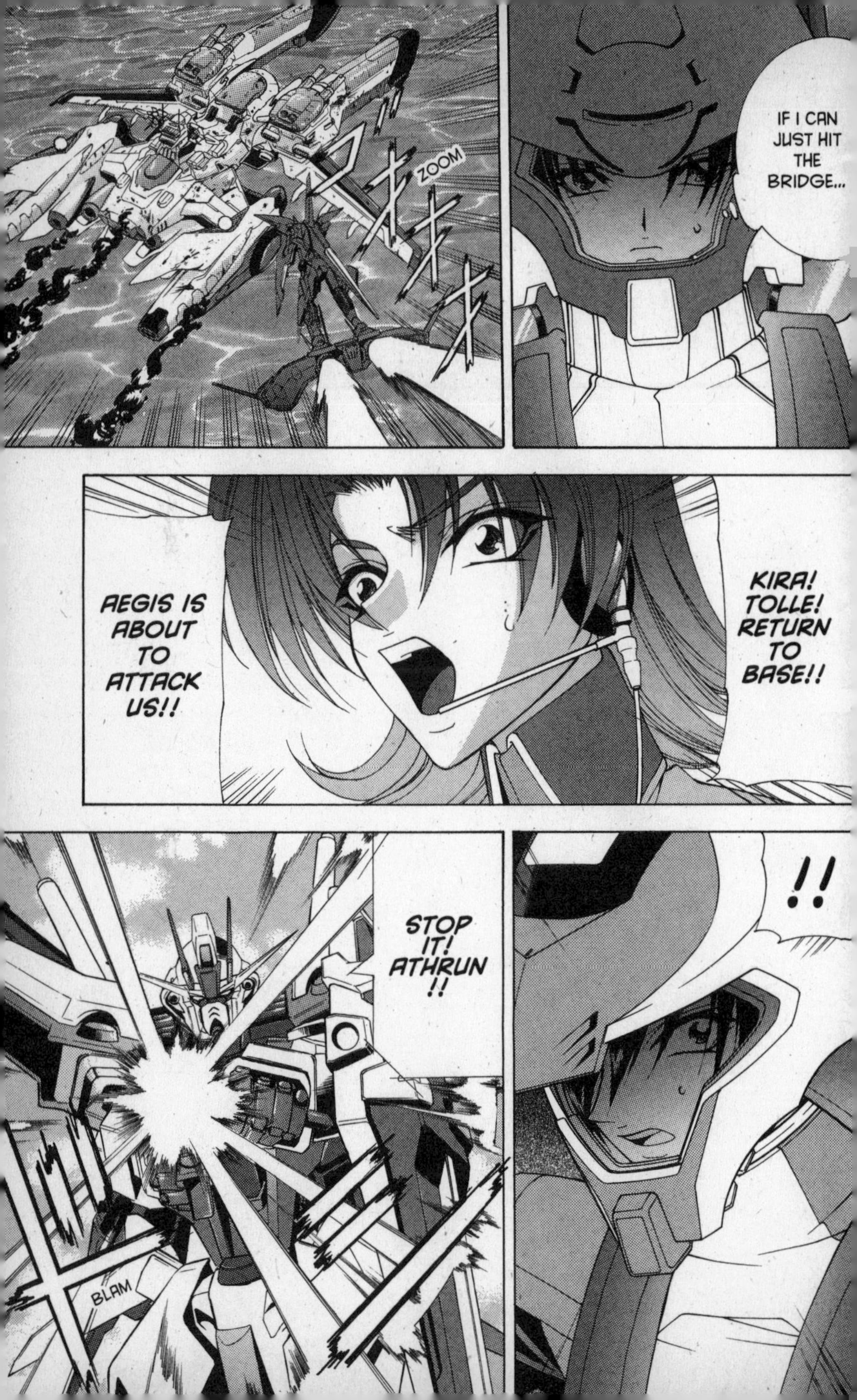
IF I CAN JUST HIT THE BRIDGE...
ZOOM
KIRA! TOLLE! RETURN TO BASE!!
AEGIS IS ABOUT TO ATTACK US!!
!!
STOP IT! ATHRUN !!
BLAM

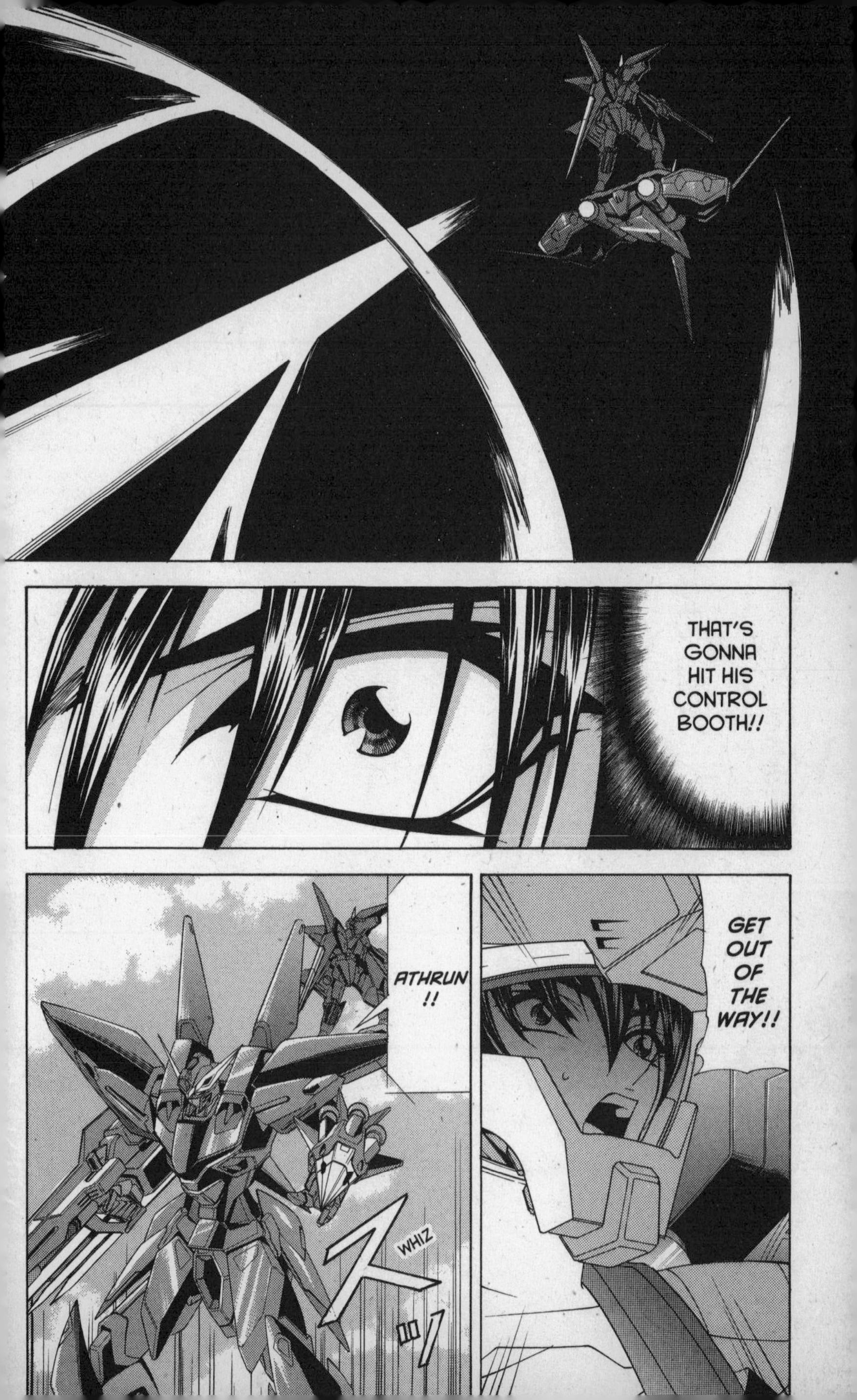
THAT'S GONNA HIT HIS CONTROL BOOTH!!
GET OUT OF THE WAY!!
ATHRUN !!
WHIZ

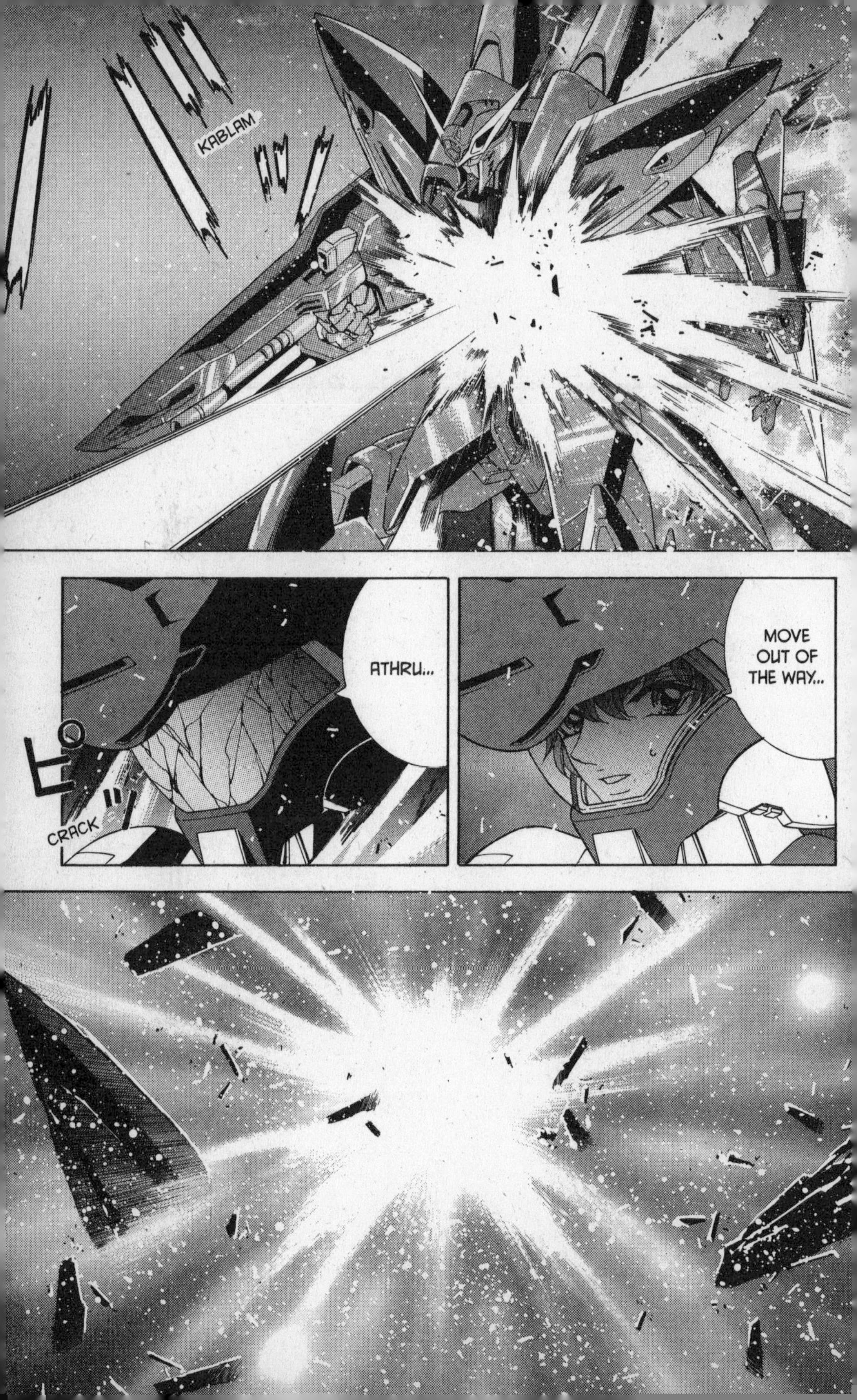
KABLAM
MOVE OUT OF THE WAY...
ATHRU...
CRACK

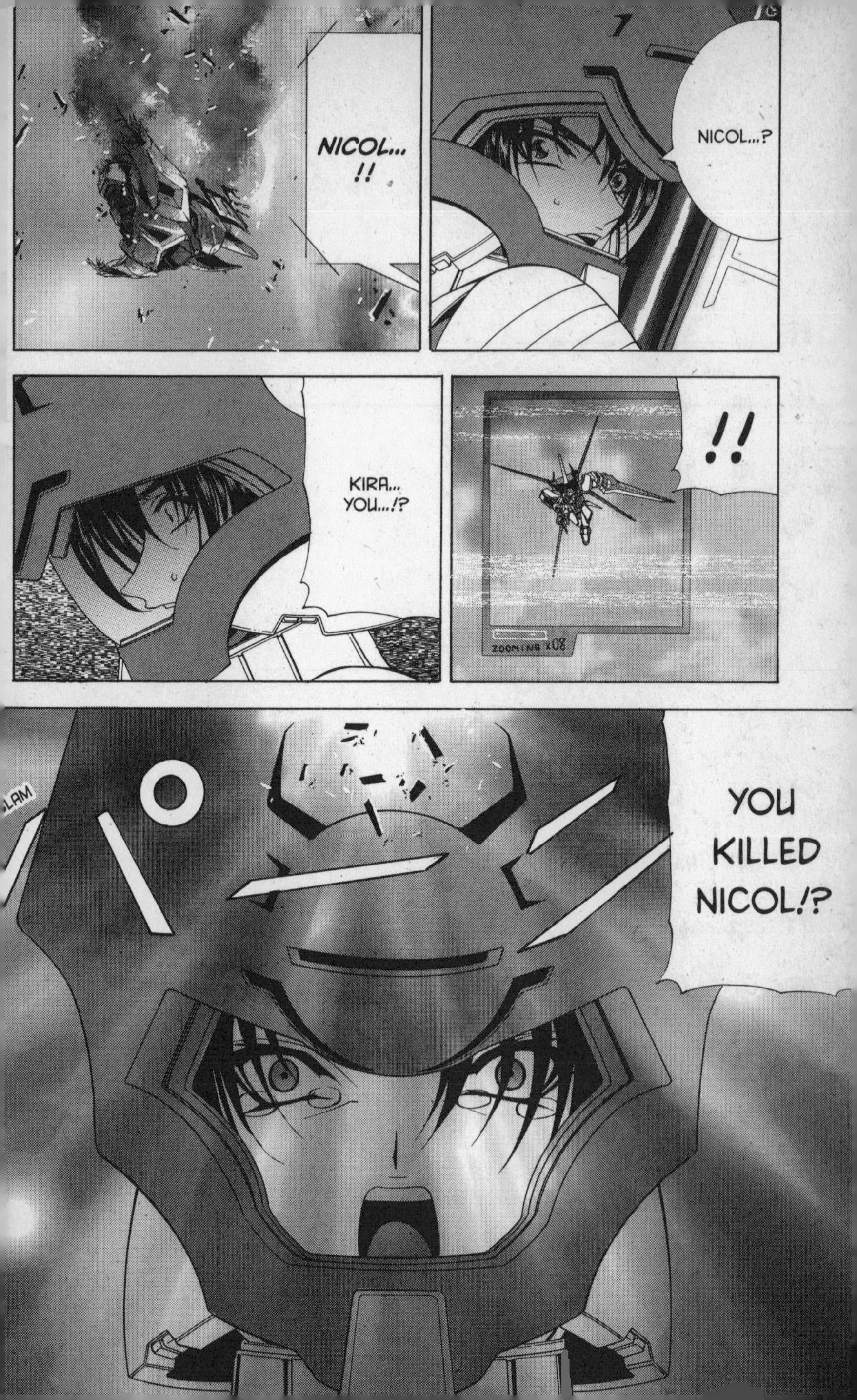
NICOL...?
NICOL...
!!
!!
ZOOMING x08
KIRA...
YOU...!?
YOU
KILLED
NICOL!?
SLAM

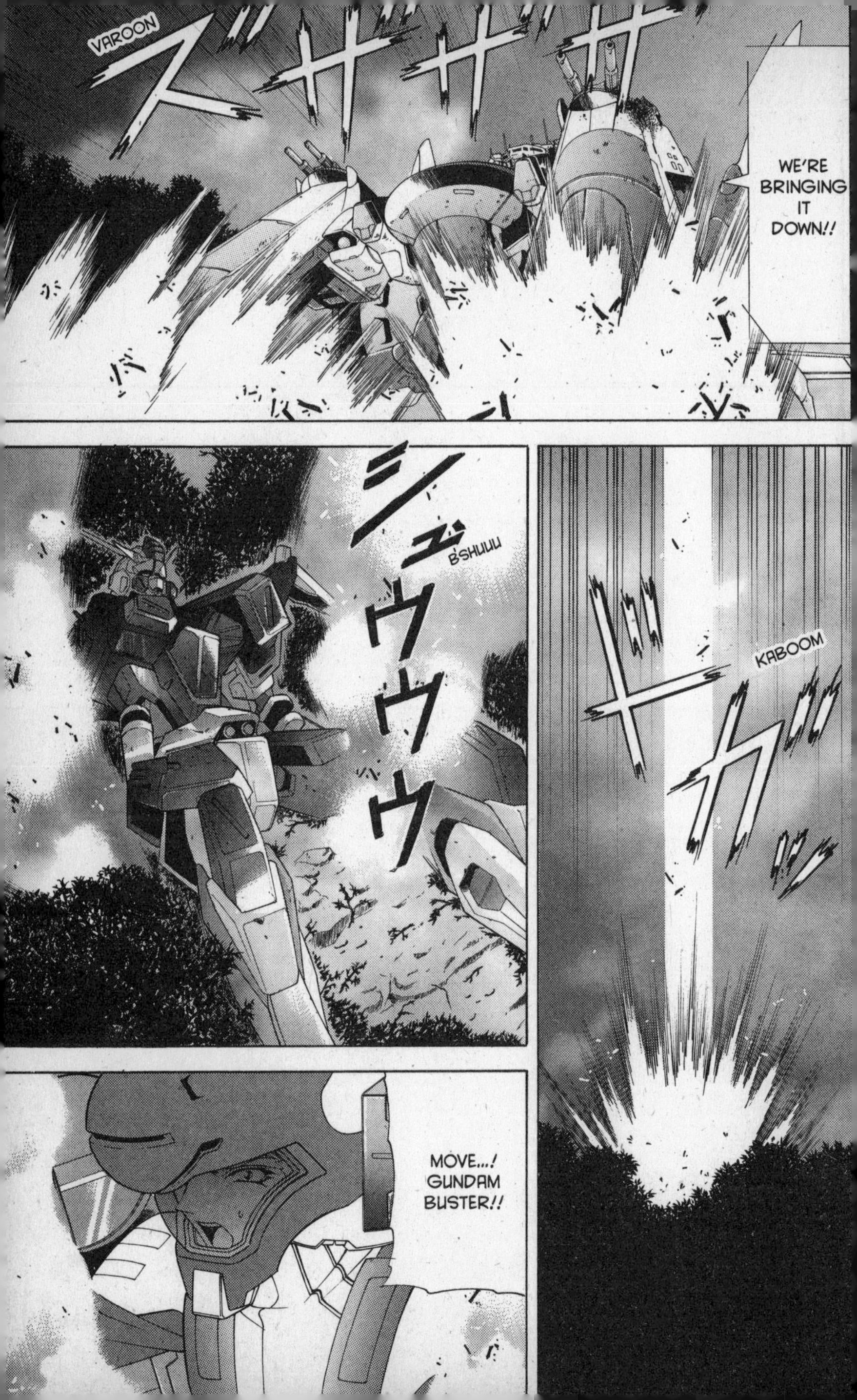
VAROON
WE'RE BRINGING IT DOWN!!
KABOOM
B'SHUUU
MOVE...! GUNDAM BUSTER!!

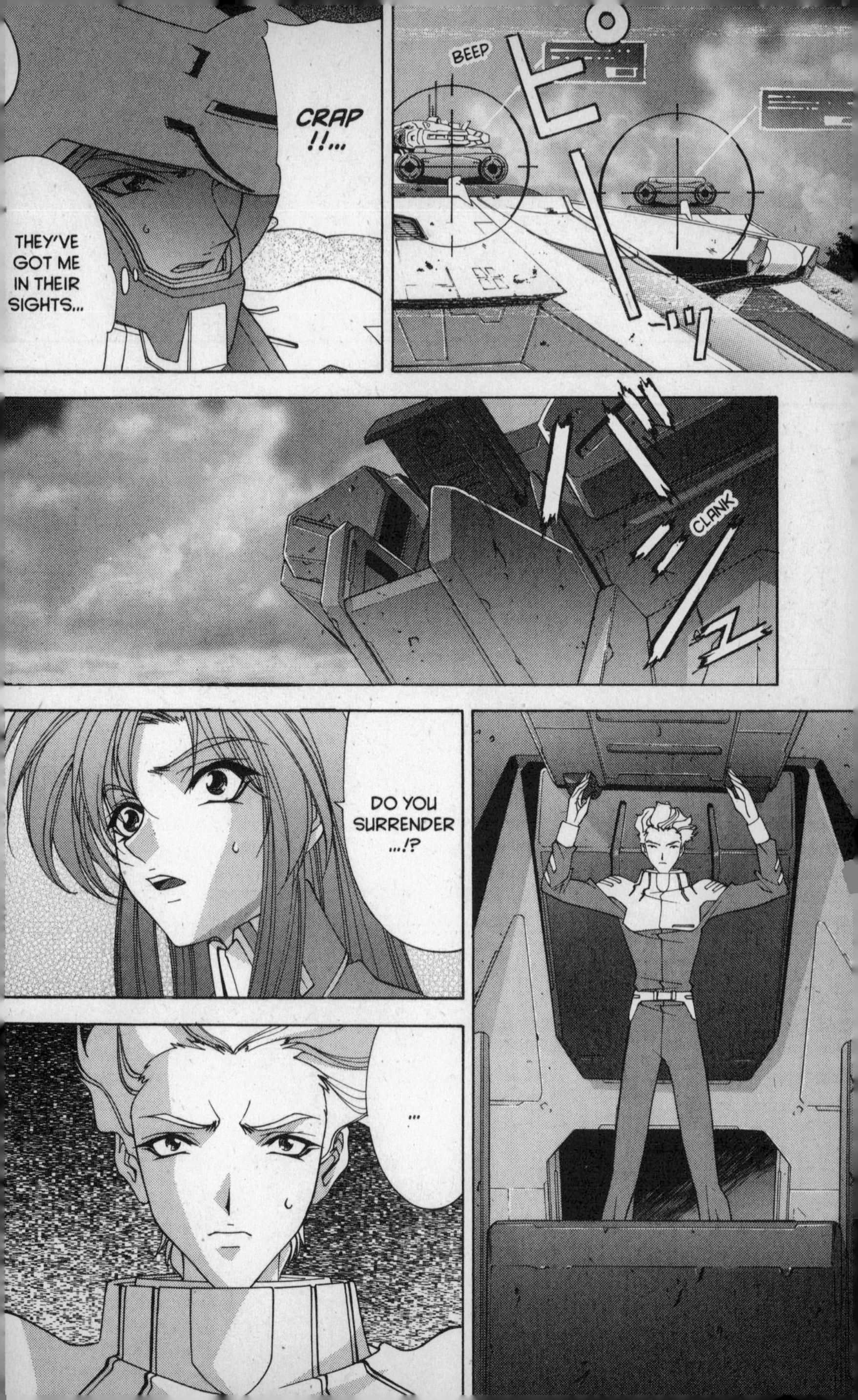
BEEP
CRAP !!...
THEY'VE GOT ME IN THEIR SIGHTS...
CLANK
DO YOU SURRENDER ...!?
...

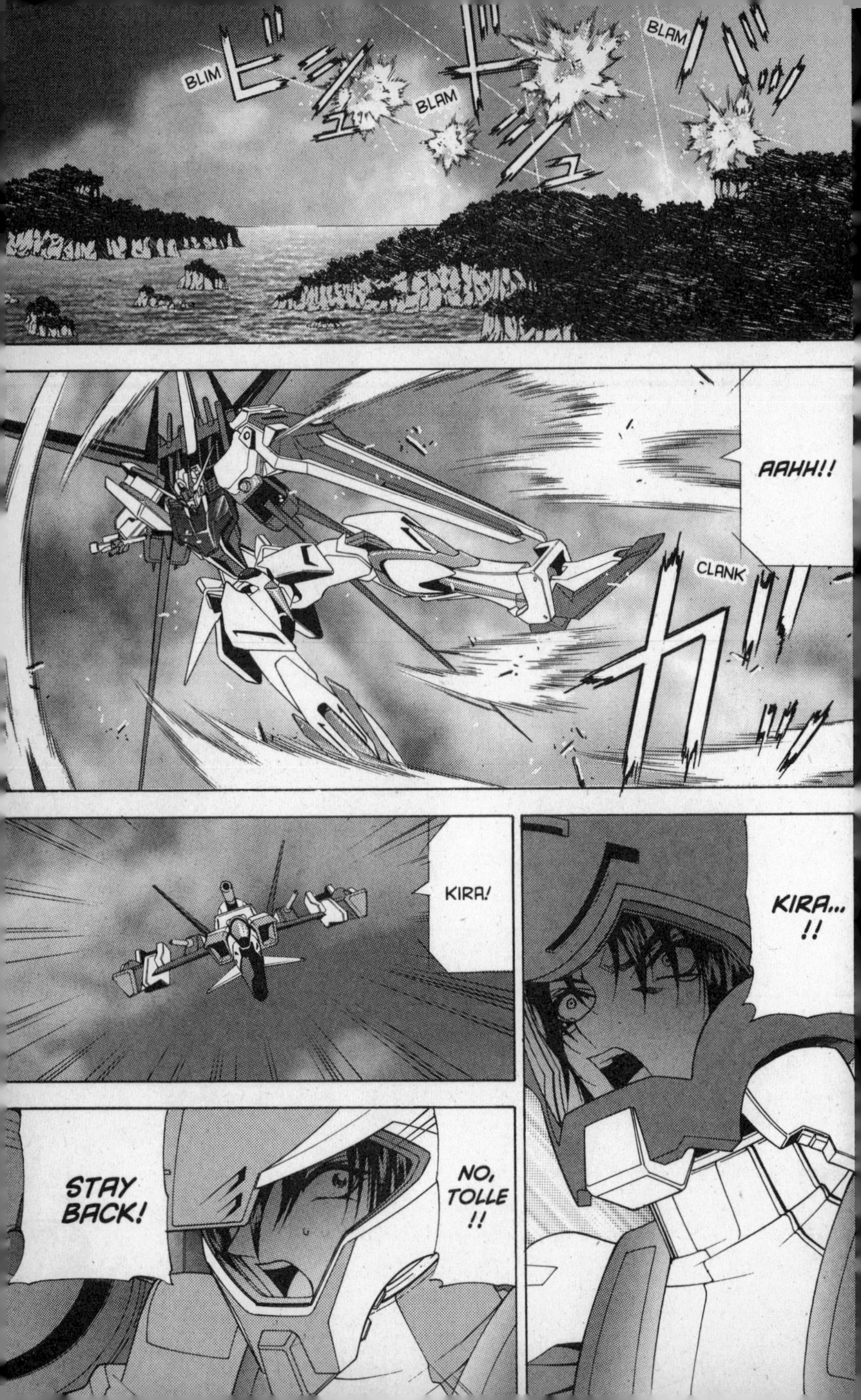
BLAM
BLAM
BLIM
AAHH!!
CLANK
KIRA... !!
KIRA!
NO, TOLLE !!
STAY BACK!

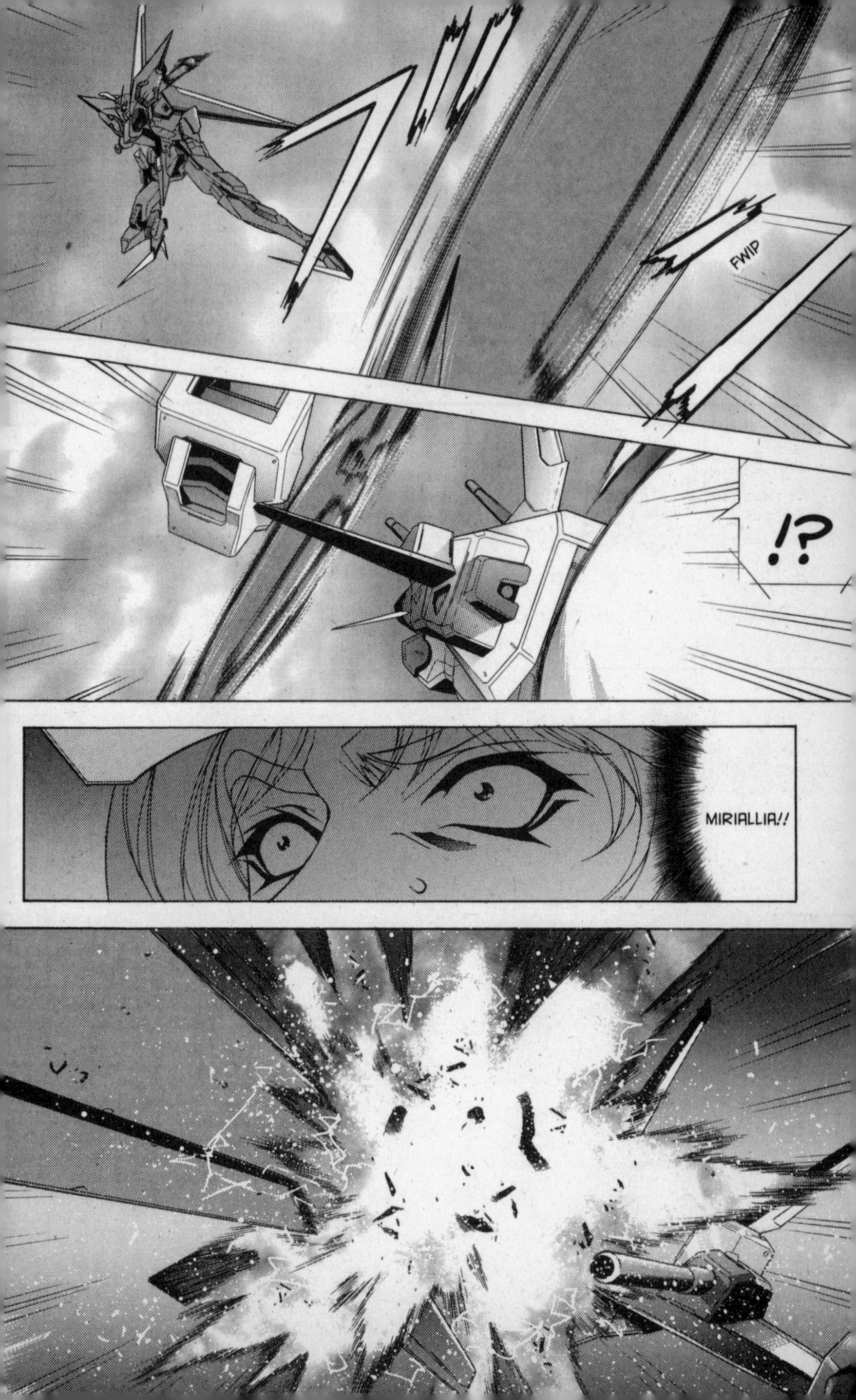
FWIP
!?
MIRIALLIA!!

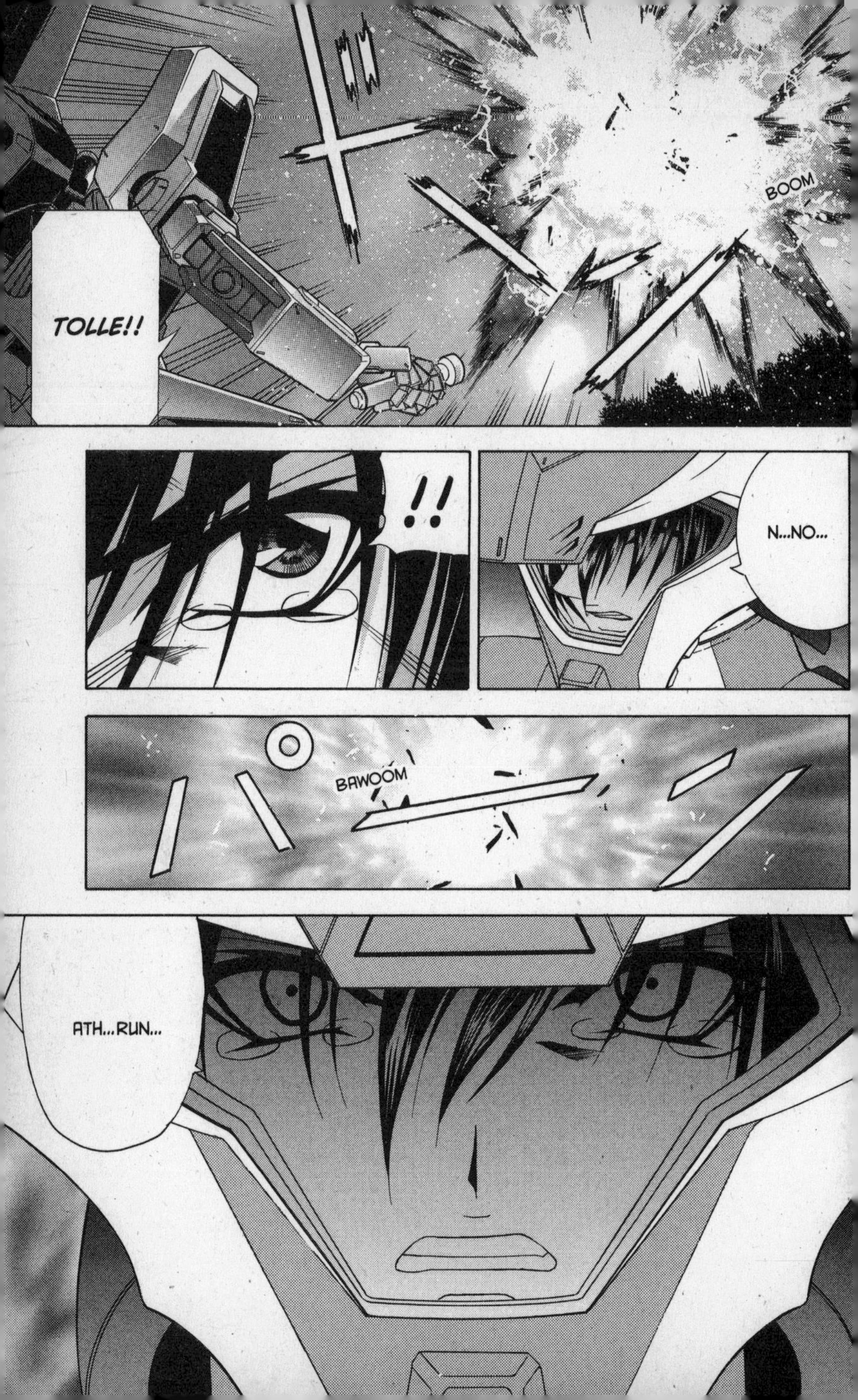
BOOM
TOLLE!!
N...NO...
!!
BAWOOM
ATH...RUN...

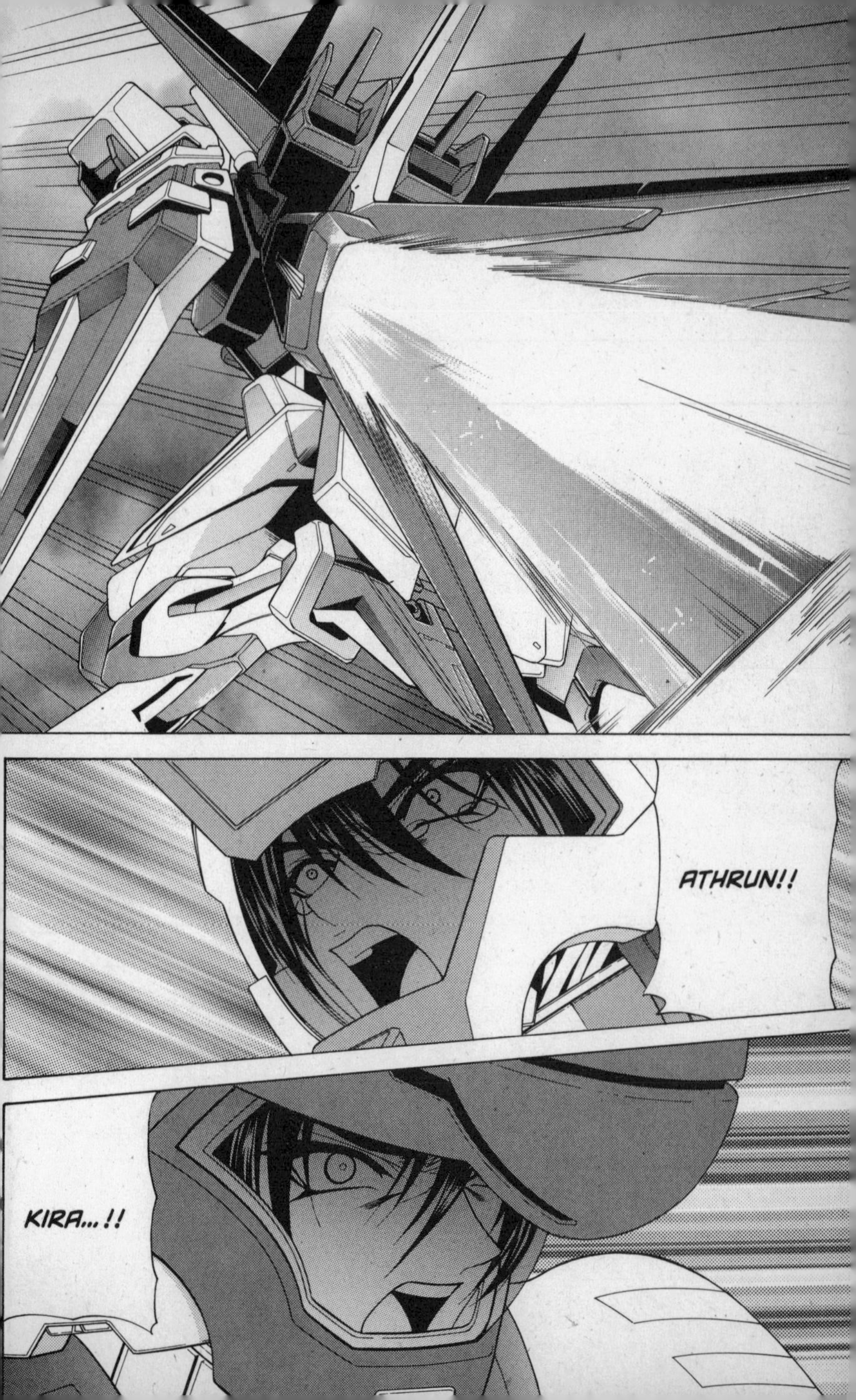
ATHRUN!!
KIRA...!!

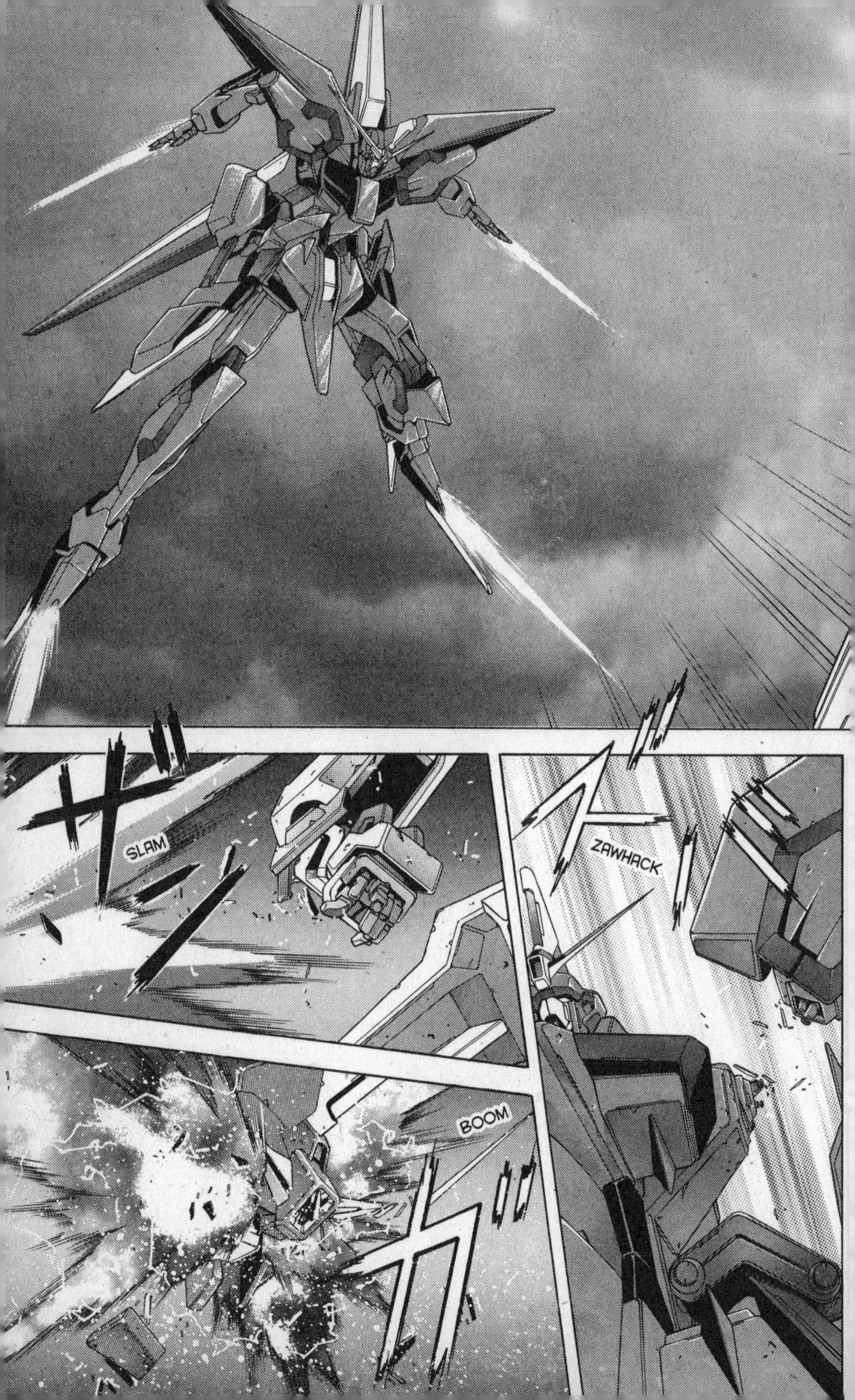
ZAWHACK
SLAM
BOOM

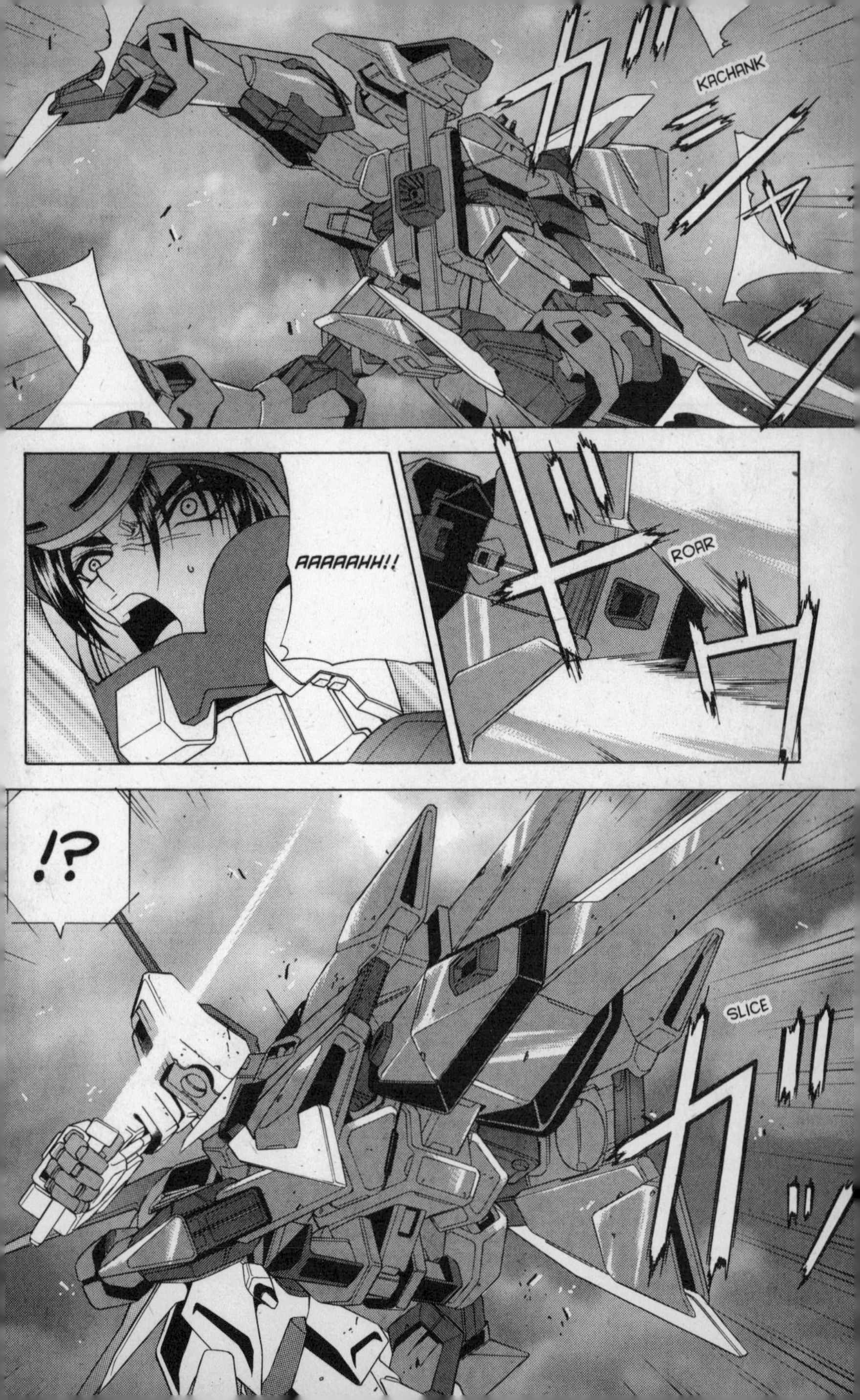
KACHANK
ROAR
AAAAAHH!!
SLICE
!?

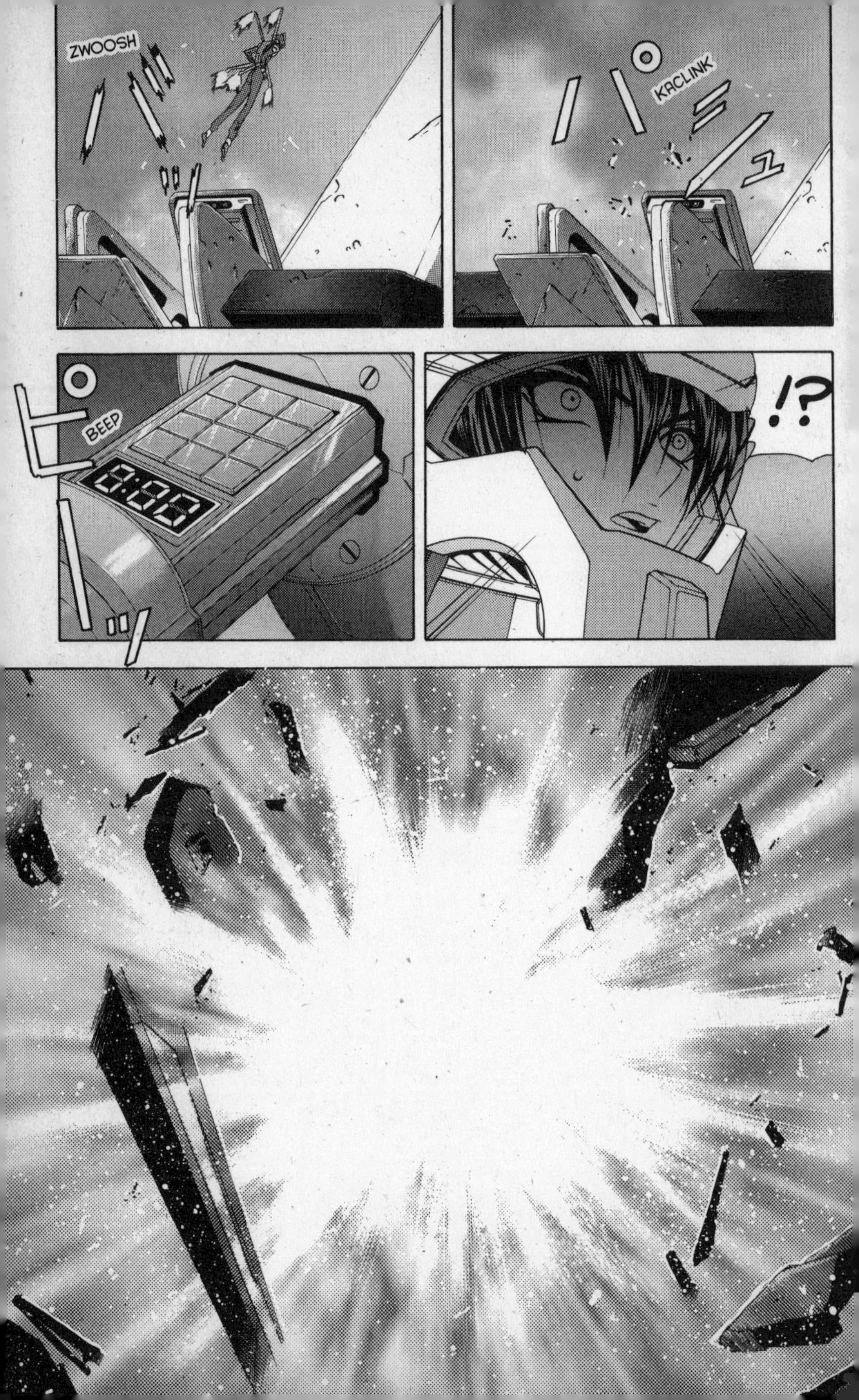
KRCLINK
ZWOOSH
!?
BEEP

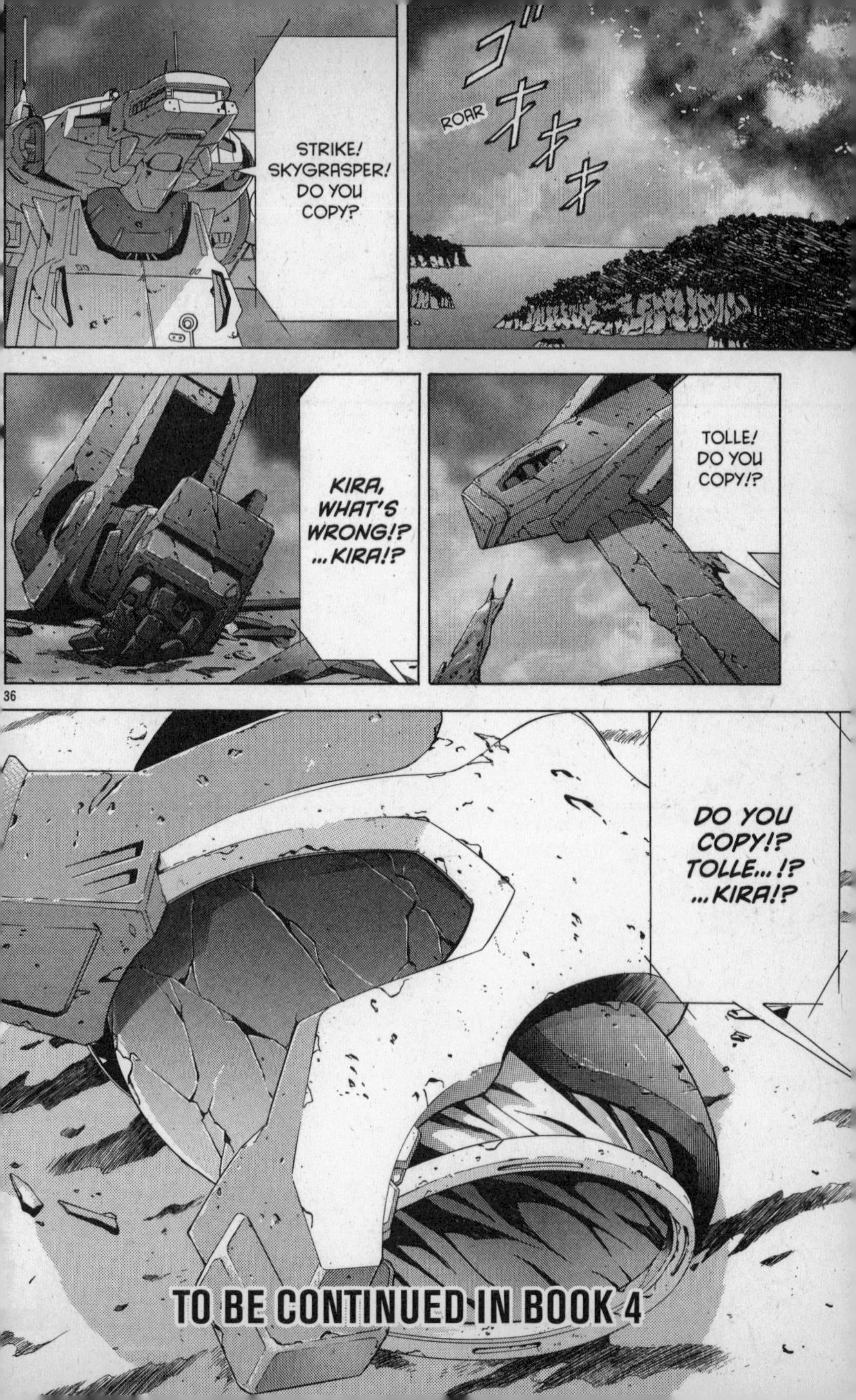
ROAR
STRIKE! SKYGRASPER! DO YOU COPY?
TOLLE! DO YOU COPY!?
KIRA, WHAT'S WRONG!? ...KIRA!?
DO YOU COPY!? TOLLE...!? ...KIRA!?
TO BE CONTINUED IN BOOK 4

[BONUS SECTION]

C.E.71 ARCHANGEL TIMELINE

AFTER HELIOPOLIS IS DESTROYED THE ARCHANGEL CONTINUES ITS BITTER VOYAGE. THIS TIMELINE CHRONICLES THE ARCHANGEL'S VOYAGE THROUGH BOOK THREE AND PROVIDES THE DATES OF ALL IMPORTANT EVENTS.

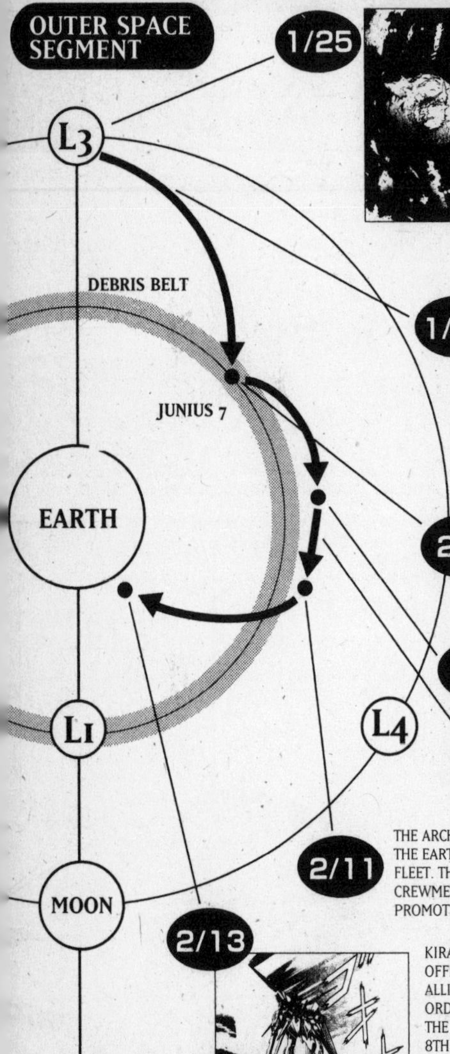
OUTER SPACE SEGMENT
L3
DEBRIS BELT
JUNIUS 7
EARTH
L1
L4
MOON
L2

1/25

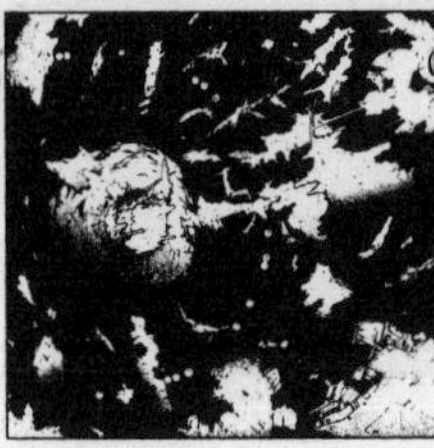

HELIOPOLIS IS INVADED BY THE CREUSET UNIT. APPROXIMATELY 6 HOURS LATER, HELIOPOLIS IS DESTROYED. AN ARCHANGEL DECOY AIDS THEIR ESCAPE FROM L3.

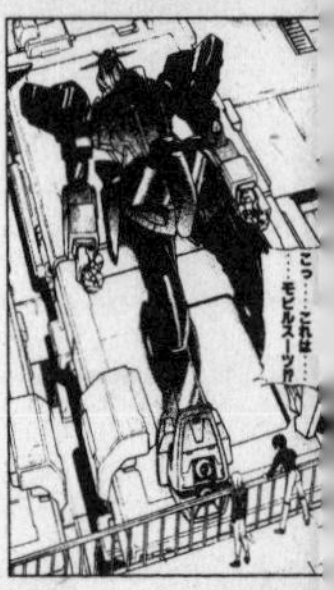
こっ……これは……モビルスーツ!?

1/26

THE CREUSET UNIT CHASES THE ARCHANGEL. KIRA AND MU LA FLAGA DRIVE BACK THE ENEMY FORCES, BUT ENGINE TROUBLE OCCURS AND THE ARCHANGEL IS PULLED INTO THE DEBRIS BELT.

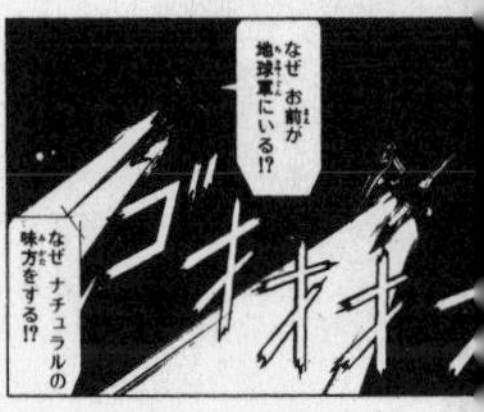
なぜ お前が 地球軍にいる!?
なぜ ナチュラルの 味方をする!?

2/3

IN THE DEBRIS BELT THE CREW FINDS THE RUINS OF JUNIUS SEVEN, AND KIRA SAVES LACUS.

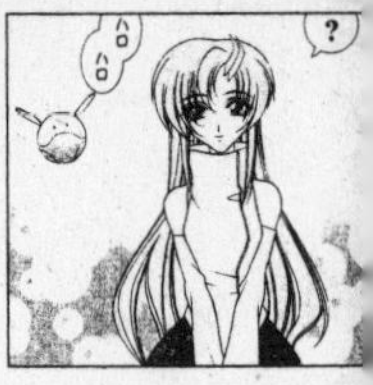
ハロ ハロ
?

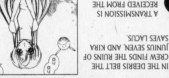

2/6

A TRANSMISSION IS RECEIVED FROM THE EARTH ALLIANCE FORCES 8TH FLEET.

2/7

THEY MOVE IN FOR A RESCUE BUT THE REMAINING TROOPS ARE OBLITERATED. KIRA HANDS LACUS OVE TO ATHRUN.

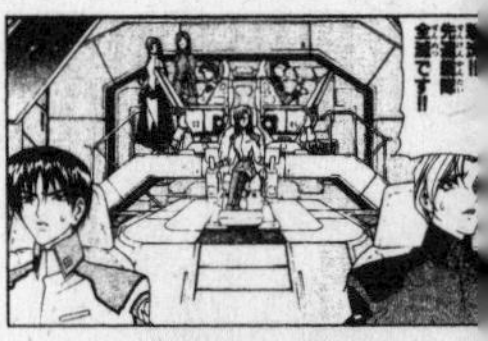

2/11

THE ARCHANGEL IS UNITED WITH THE EARTH ALLIANCE FORCES 8TH FLEET. THE ARCHANGEL'S CREWMEMBERS ARE EACH PROMOTED TO A HIGHER RANK.

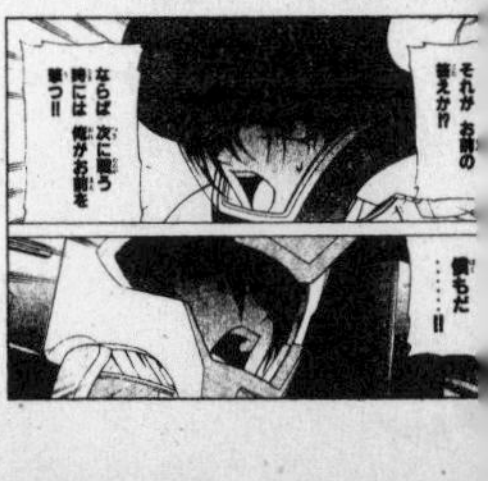
それが お前の 答えか!?
ならば 次に戦う 時には 俺がお前を 撃つ!!
僕もだ……!!

2/13

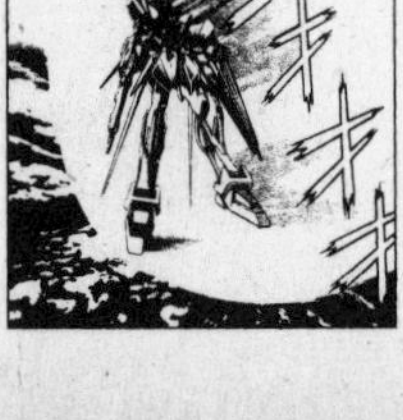

KIRA AND HIS FRIENDS OFFICIALLY JOIN THE EARTH ALLIANCE FORCES AND ARE ORDERED TO LAND IN ALASKA. THE EARTH ALLIANCE FORCES 8TH FLEET IS COMPLETELY WIPED OUT BY CREUSET'S UNIT. KIRA AND STRIKE ARE PULLED INTO THE EARTH'S ATMOSPHERE.

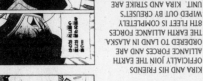

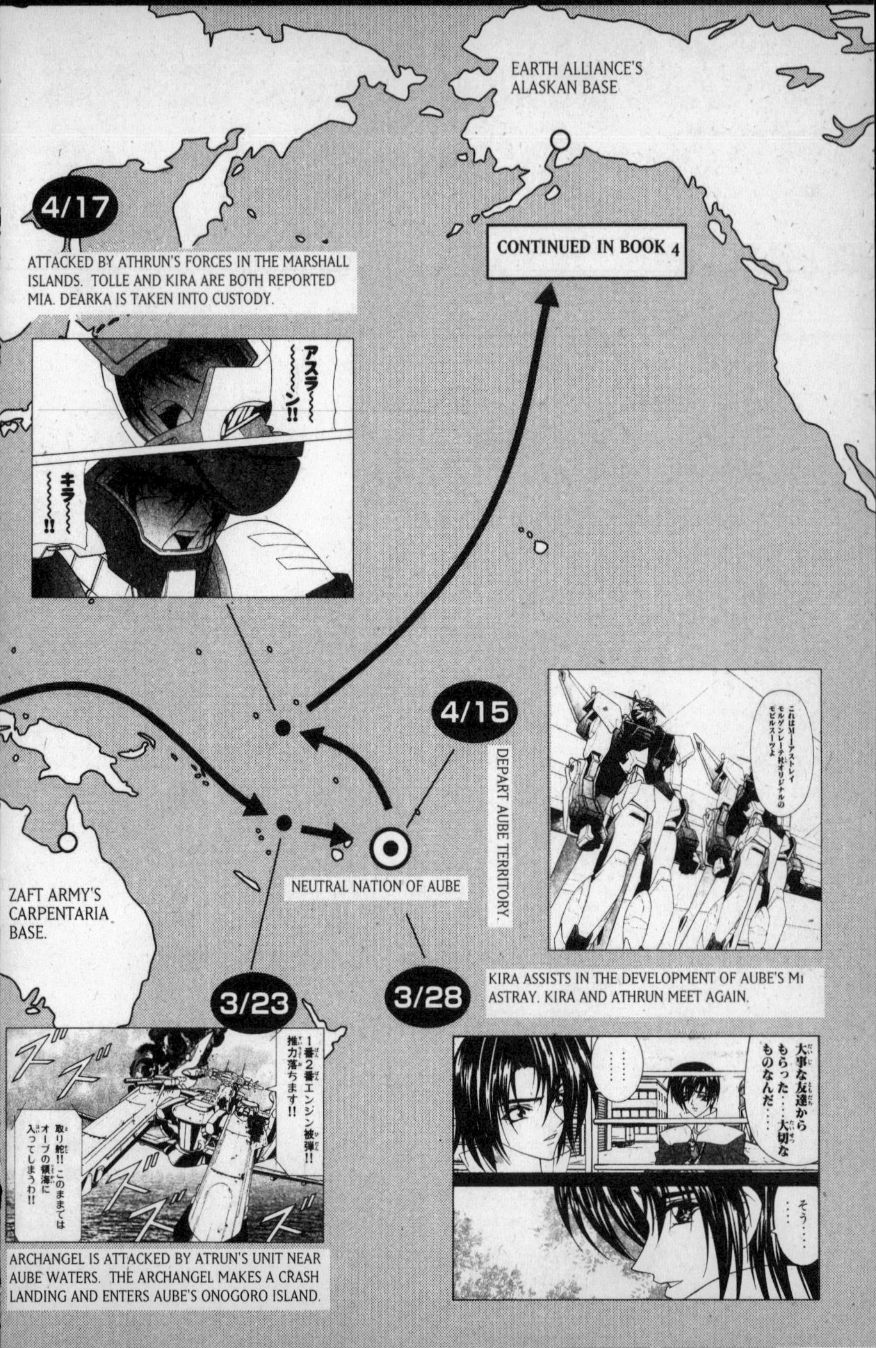
EARTH ALLIANCE'S
ALASKAN BASE
CONTINUED IN BOOK 4
4/17
ATTACKED BY ATHRUN'S FORCES IN THE MARSHALL ISLANDS. TOLLE AND KIRA ARE BOTH REPORTED MIA. DEARKA IS TAKEN INTO CUSTODY.
アスラ〜〜〜ン!!
キラ〜〜〜〜!!
4/15
DEPART AUBE TERRITORY.
これはM1アストレイ モルゲンレーテ社オリジナルの モビルスーツよ
NEUTRAL NATION OF AUBE
ZAFT ARMY'S
CARPENTARIA
BASE.
3/23
1番2番エンジン被弾!! 推力落ちます!!
取り舵!! このままでは オーブの領海に 入ってしまうわ!!
ARCHANGEL IS ATTACKED BY ATRUN'S UNIT NEAR AUBE WATERS. THE ARCHANGEL MAKES A CRASH LANDING AND ENTERS AUBE'S ONOGORO ISLAND.
3/28
KIRA ASSISTS IN THE DEVELOPMENT OF AUBE'S M1 ASTRAY. KIRA AND ATHRUN MEET AGAIN.
大事な友達から もらった……大切な ものなんだ……
……
そう……

C.E.71 ARCHANGEL TIMELINE

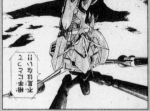

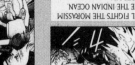

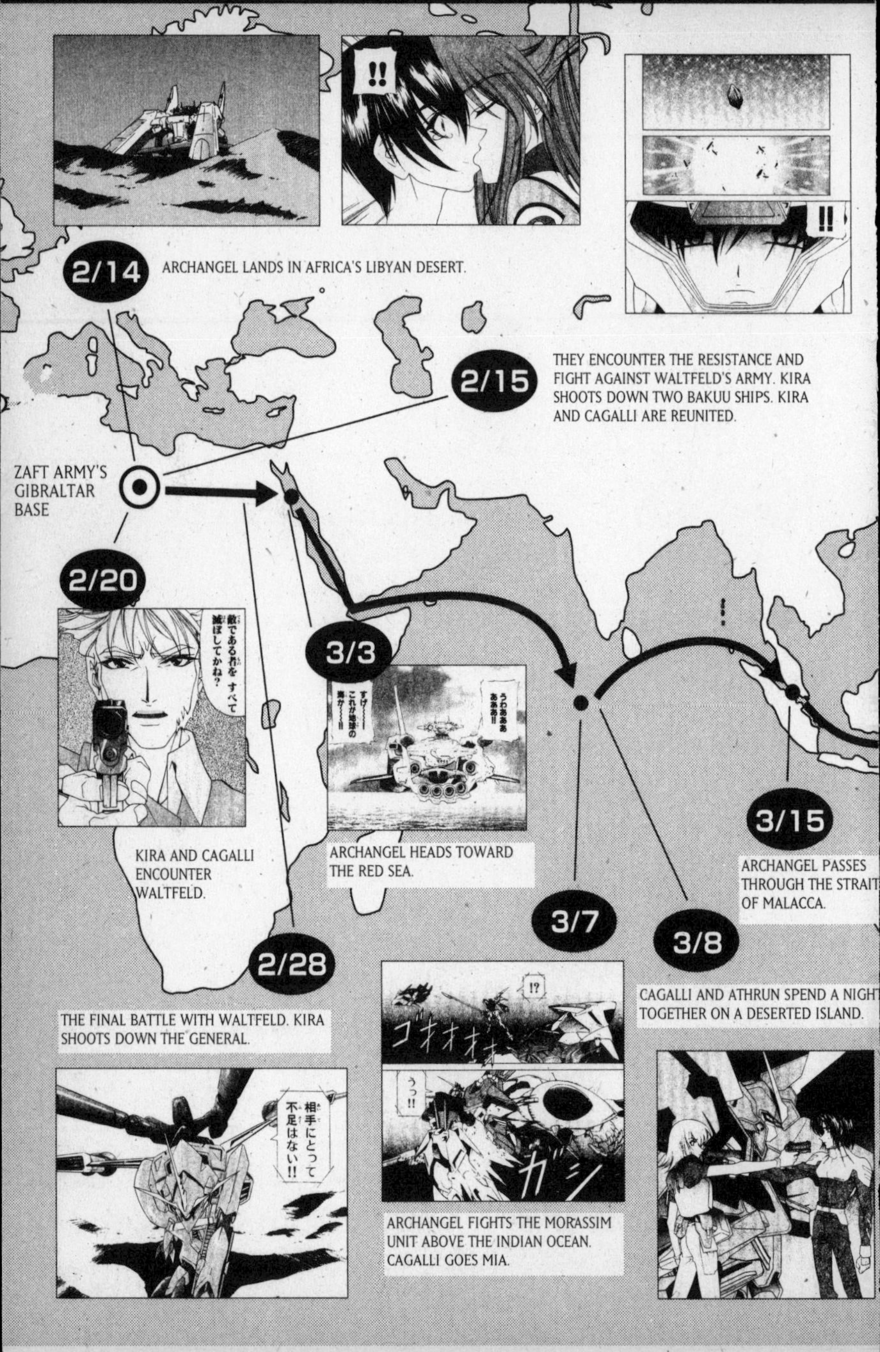

2/14
ARCHANGEL LANDS IN AFRICA'S LIBYAN DESERT.
!!
!!
2/15
THEY ENCOUNTER THE RESISTANCE AND FIGHT AGAINST WALTFELD'S ARMY. KIRA SHOOTS DOWN TWO BAKUU SHIPS. KIRA AND CAGALLI ARE REUNITED.
ZAFT ARMY'S GIBRALTAR BASE
2/20
敵である者を すべて滅ぼしてかね?
KIRA AND CAGALLI ENCOUNTER WALTFELD.
3/3
うわあああああ!!
すげ~~~これが地球の海か~~~!!
ARCHANGEL HEADS TOWARD THE RED SEA.
2/28
THE FINAL BATTLE WITH WALTFELD. KIRA SHOOTS DOWN THE GENERAL.
相手にとって不足はない!!
3/7
!?
ゴオオオオ
うっ!!
ガシ
ARCHANGEL FIGHTS THE MORASSIM UNIT ABOVE THE INDIAN OCEAN. CAGALLI GOES MIA.
3/8
CAGALLI AND ATHRUN SPEND A NIGHT TOGETHER ON A DESERTED ISLAND.
3/15
ARCHANGEL PASSES THROUGH THE STRAIT OF MALACCA.

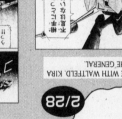

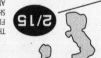

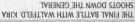

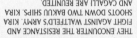

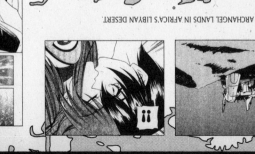

A Brief History of Gundam
Part 3: Building a World
By Mark Simmons

One of the hallmarks of the *Mobile Suit Gundam* saga is the
creation of complex, fully realized future worlds populated by equally
complicated characters, and *Gundam SEED* is no exception. Inspired
by the example of earlier *Gundam* series, the creators have planned
out a detailed historical and technological background for the
adventures of the Archangel crew. Many of the key characters have
mysteries and secrets of their own, only some of which are revealed
in the the animated story and in Masatsugu Iwase's manga
adaptation. And building on this framework, the creators have been
able to spin off new characters and adventures—a process which
continues as of this writing, eight months after the conclusion of
the animated series.

Behind the Scenes

In classic *Gundam* fashion, the creators of *Gundam SEED* have
produced reams of documentation on the futuristic world of the
Cosmic Era. Maps of Earth and space, technological explanations,
historical information, and detailed timelines all served to flesh out
the story setting. The creative staff even includes a world-building
specialist—Shigeru Morita of Studio Nue, the studio which created
the famous *Macross* series—to help keep track of the show's complex
background and technical terminology.

The individual characters haven't been neglected, either. A series
of five "Suit CD" albums released in Japan includes brief audio dramas
depicting past encounters between Kira Yamato, Athrun Zala, Lacus
Clyne, and the quarrelsome members of the elite Le Creuset team; manga
adaptations of these tales have also appeared in the monthly anthology
Gundam Ace. Meanwhile, new animation footage produced for DVD
releases and compilation videos provides more glimpses of the characters'
adventures during and after the animated series. If you're wondering
how Athrun fared when he first joined the Le Creuset team, or what
our heroes will do after the end of the final episode, then you can rest
assured the answers are out there somewhere.

Gundam Seed Astray

The world of *Gundam Seed* was designed to support other tales of adventure besides those of the Archangel crew. In fact, an official spinoff story—what's known in Japan as a *gaiden*, or "side story"—titled *Mobile Suit Gundam Seed Astray* was launched simultaneously with the animated series. This ongoing multimedia project encompasses two different manga serials, an ongoing novelization, and an illustrated photo-story in the model magazine *Dengeki Hobby*, plus the obligatory selection of toys and model kits. *Gundam Seed Astray* focuses on two new protagonists, junk dealer Lowe Guele and mercenary soldier Gai Murakumo, who have managed to get their hands on a pair of prototype mobile suits developed by the neutral nation Aube. As they travel to and fro, taking on assignments and waging their own battles, Lowe and Gai cross paths not only with each other but also with the characters on the main *Gundam SEED* storyline.

Aces and Variations

The latest addition to the *Gundam SEED* cosmos is the "Seed Mobile Suit Variation" series, or "Seed MSV" for short. Like the MSV series created in the early 1980s as a continuation of the original *Mobile Suit Gundam*, the Seed MSV franchise consists of a menagerie of new robots—prototypes, specialized variants, and personal customizations—to help populate the *Gundam SEED* toy and model-kit lineups.

And where there are new mobile suits, there must of course be new pilots. The Seed MSV project introduces a roster of hitherto unknown ace pilots whose exploits are comparable to those of Mu La Flaga and Rau Le Creuset. By documenting the adventures of the ZAFT and Earth Alliance aces, and their off-camera encounters with *Gundam SEED* regulars like Yzak Joule and Andy Waltfeld, the Seed MSV series further expands the world of the Cosmic Era. Thus, even after the end of the animated series, the story of *Gundam SEED* continues to unfold...

Continued in Volume 4!

Nasake o kakeru

This is similar to the example noted on page 31. here Cag humiliated and dishonored that Athrun doesn't perceive serious threat. Cagalli uses the term "nasake o kakeru," to "show mercy."

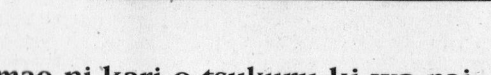

HE WENT EASY ON ME BECAUSE I'M A GIRL!

Omae ni kari o tsukuru ki wa nai

This literally means " I don't want to be in your debt." Ca to make up for having shot Athrun.

LET ME MAKE IT UP TO YOU!!

About the Creators

Yoshiyuki Tomino

Gundam was created by Yoshiyuki Tomino. Prior to Gundam, Tomino had worked on the original *Astro Boy* anime, as well as *Princess Knight* and *Brave Raideen*, among others. In 1979, he created and directed *Mobile Suit Gundam*, the very first in a long line of Gundam series. The show was not immediately popular and was forced to cut its number of episodes before going off the air, but as with the American show *Star Trek*, the fans still had something to say on the matter. By 1981, the demand for Gundam was so high that Tomino oversaw the re-release of the animation as three theatrical movies (a practice still common in Japan, and rarely if ever seen in the U.S.). It was now official: Gundam was a blockbuster.

Tomino would go on to direct many Gundam series, including *Gundam ZZ*, *Char's Counterattack*, *Gundam F91* and *Victory Gundam*, all of which contributed to the rich history of the vast Gundam universe. In addition to Gundam, Tomino created *Xabungle*, *L.Gaim*, *Dunbine*, and *Garzey's Wing*. His most recent anime is *Brain Powered*, which was released by Geneon in the United States.

Masatsugu Iwase

Masatsugu Iwase writes and draws the manga adaptation of *Gundam SEED*. It is his first work published in the U.S. The manga creator is better known in Japan, however, for his work on *Calm Breaker*, a hilarious parody of anime, manga, and Japanese pop culture.

st westerners, and translation
our edification and reading
the places where we could have
ranslation of the work, or where
d.

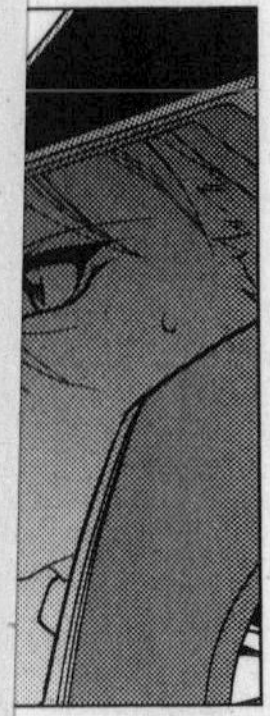

When Andy says, "He acts like I'm not even a real threat," he uses the phrase "namerareru." This is a Japanese idea that is difficult to translate. This concept means to be underestimated and thereby made a fool
a doesn't seem to feel threatened.

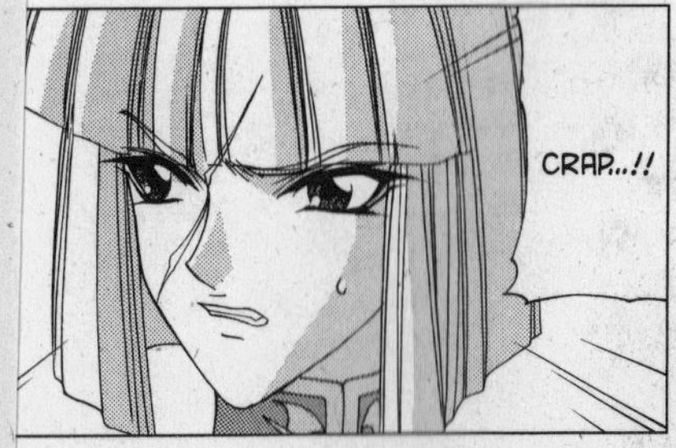
CRAP...!!

lli feels
ıer as a
hich means

alli is trying

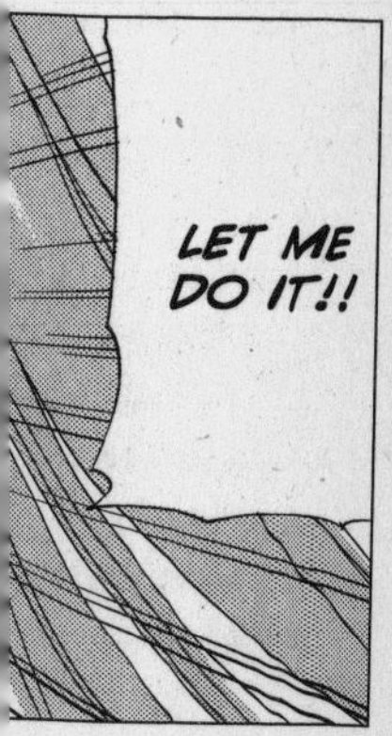
LET ME DO IT!!

...

You may notice that it's common in this, and other manga, for characters to state each others' names followed by "..." when reacting to important dialogue. This usually indicates that the speaker is shocked, surprised, questioning or emotionally moved. In this case Kira seems to be expressing doubt or surprise. This technique of dialogue is also frequently seen in Japanese dramas.

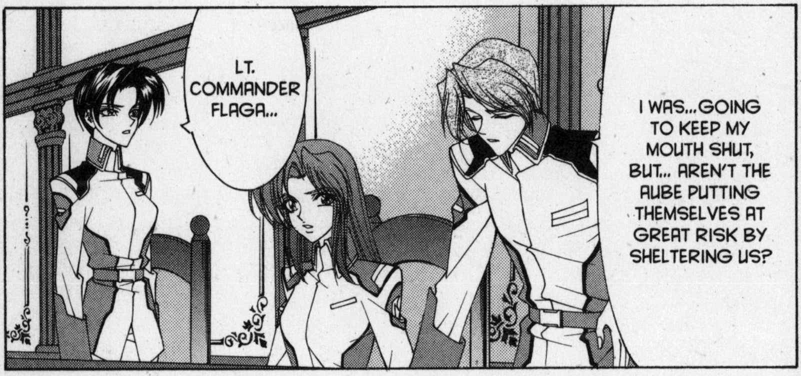
I WAS...GOING TO KEEP MY MOUTH SHUT, BUT... AREN'T THE AUBE PUTTING THEMSELVES AT GREAT RISK BY SHELTERING US?
LT. COMMANDER FLAGA...

Preview of Volume Four

Because we're running about one year behind the release of the Japanese *Gundam SEED* manga, we have the opportunity to present to you a preview from Volume Four. This volume will be available in English in March 2005, but for now you'll have to make do with Japanese!

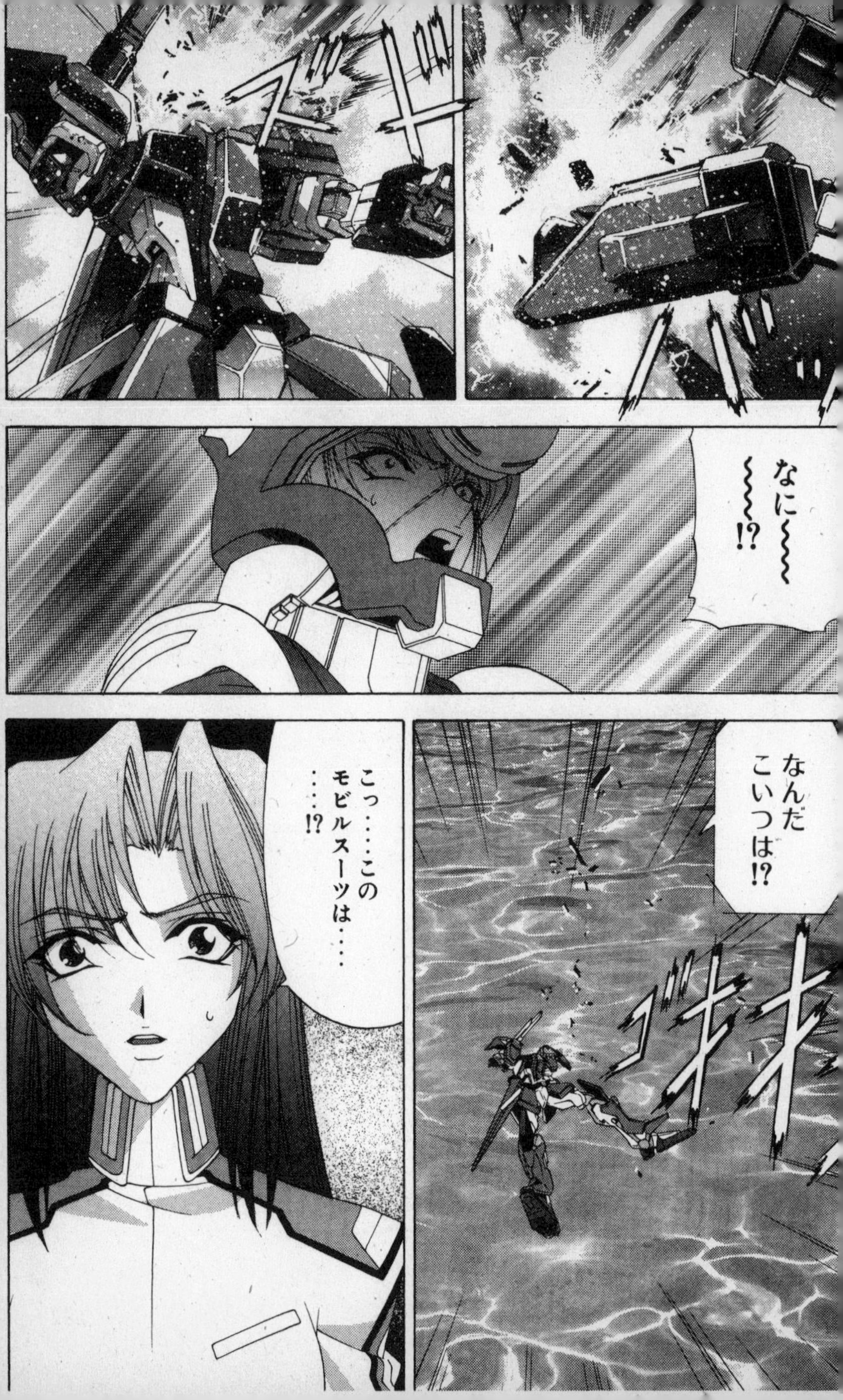
なに〜〜〜〜!?
なんだこいつは!?
こっ……このモビルスーツは……!?

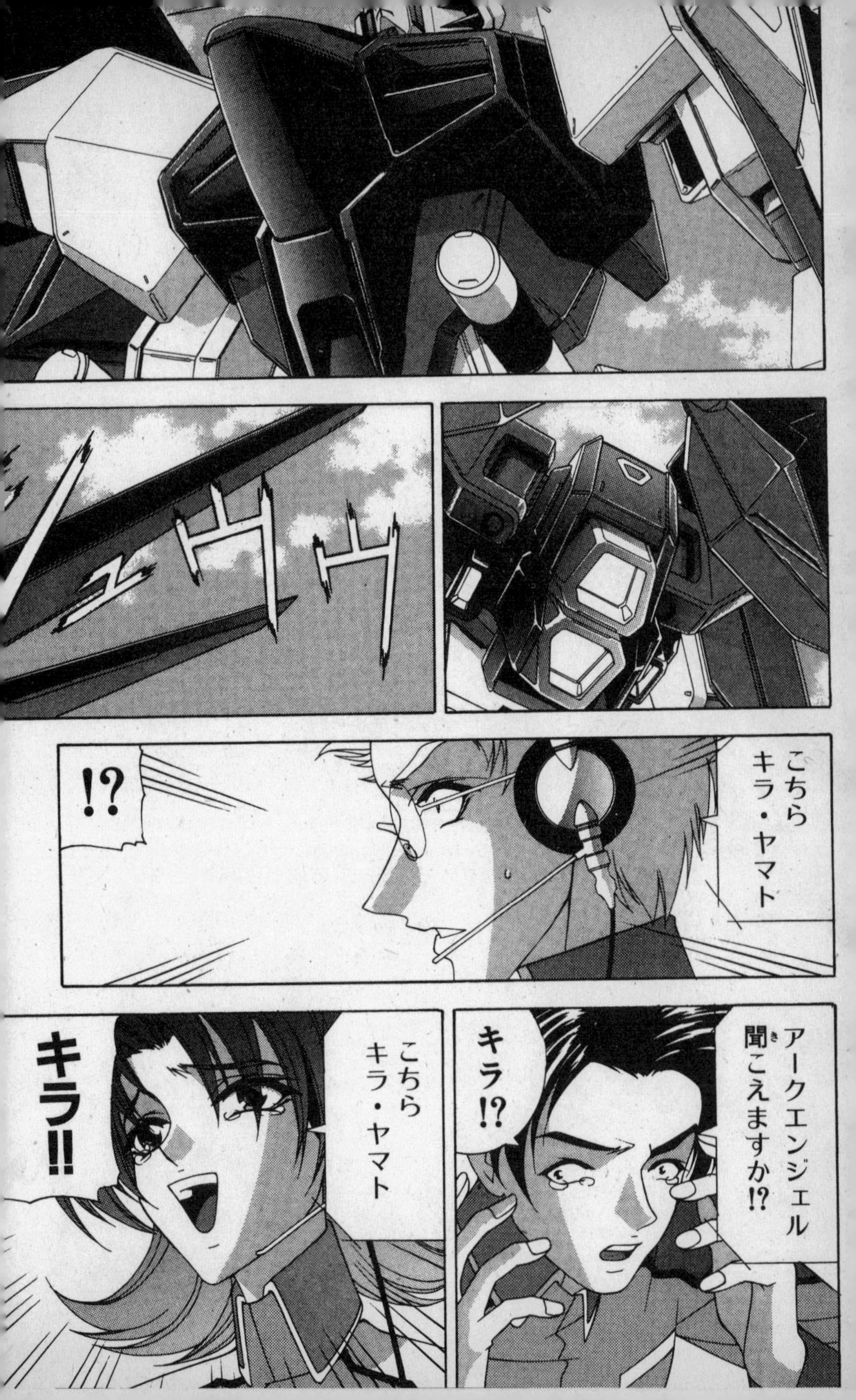
こちらキラ・ヤマト
!?
アークエンジェル聞こえますか!?
キラ!?
こちらキラ・ヤマト
キラ!!

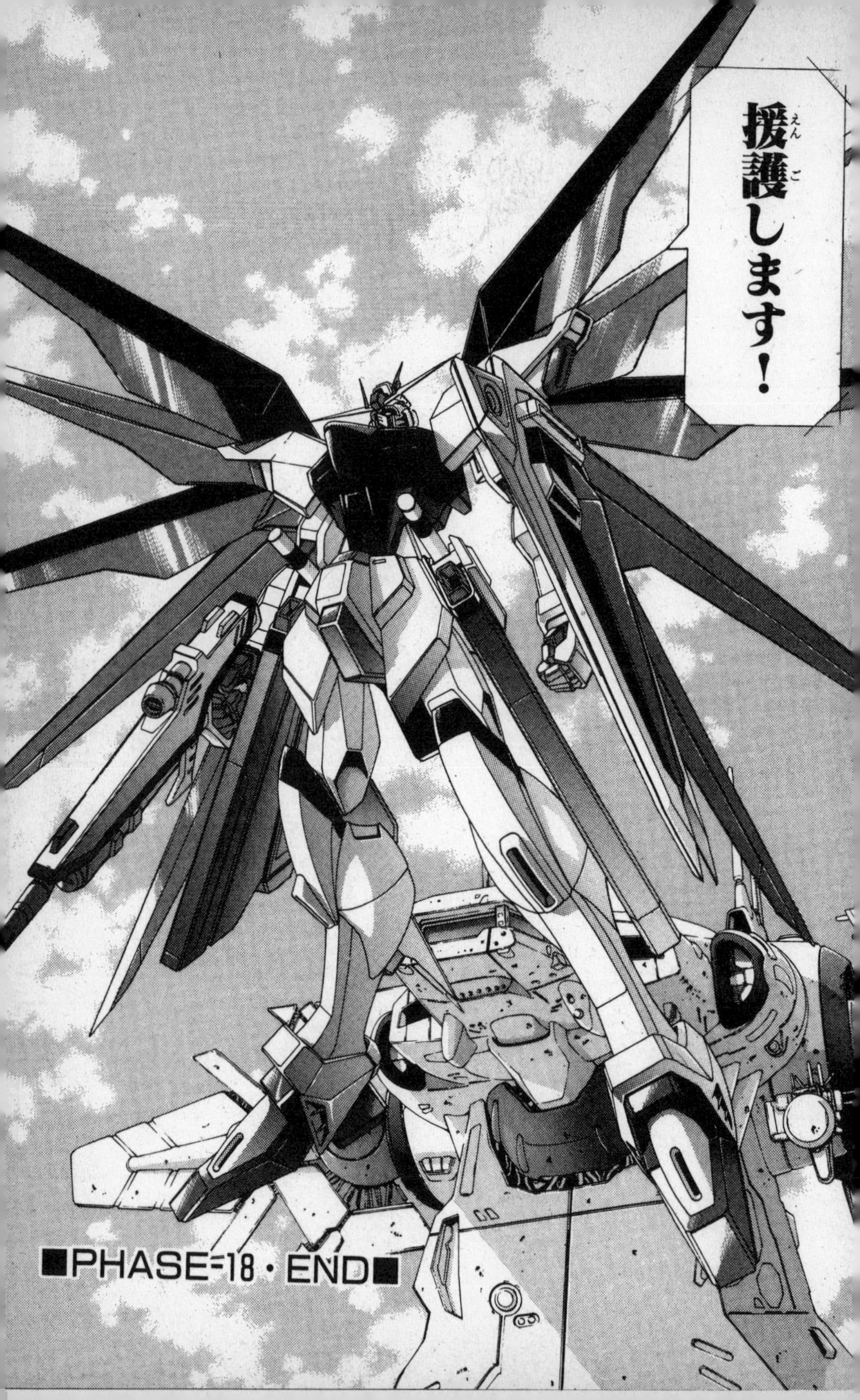
援護(えんご)します!
■PHASE=18・END■

TOMARE!

[STOP!]

You're going the wrong way!

Manga is a completely different type of reading experience.

To start at the *beginning*, go to the *end*!

That's right! Authentic manga is read the traditional Japanese way—from right to left. Exactly the *opposite* of how American books are read. It's easy to follow: Just go to the other end of the book, and read each page—and each panel—from right side to left side, starting at the top right. Now you're experiencing manga as it was meant to be.